NOTE: *We realize that this issue is not in full color, is not a hardback, and its cover does not fold out to become some kind of shroud. We struggled with exactly how to follow up Issue No. 13, and we decided that the best thing to do was publish some of the best fiction we possibly could, and also a long piece of journalism about giant Chinese gerbils. The writing assembled below features some brilliant new voices, and might very well be our favorite group of stories we have yet put together. To help you know which stories to read first, we have indicated with either a * or a † those that deserve special consideration from you, the reader. If you see either a * or a †, do not miss that story.*

MCSWEENEY'S *welcomes your correspondence, and will happily send at least two pieces of official McSwys letterhead to anyone who encloses a self-addressed stamped envelope. Our address is 826 Valencia, San Francisco, CA 94110.*

In our continuing quest to serve as a transparent conduit, the following letters are, for the most part, neither to nor from McSwys, and were actually sent in the actual mail, by people who are real. The first, for example, is from Timothy McSweeney, and is addressed to you.

DEAR READER,

Yes, my friends, unlike Santa Claus, I do exist. Maybe I am not Dave's long lost uncle but I think it likely that I am a second or third cousin once removed. I am certainly not aware of having had a sister called Adelaide Mary (Dave's mom's name) and, even though I was one of a large brood, I think that I know all of my siblings. It is not true that my father, when asked how many of us there were, admitted he did not know because "'Tis herself counts them". He knew full well that there were nine of us, even though the amount of time he spent at home was limited due to the attractions of the local pubs, of which there were seventy-five in the small town called Listowel in County Kerry in the southwest of Ireland, where I was born and grew up. How do I know that? Well, one of our favorite pastimes in bed at night in the boys' room—there were five of us—was counting the various types of shops in the town, when we were not listening to the soundtracks from the Plaza Cinema just across the road.

I came fourth in the family and shared a birthday with my eldest brother who was six years older than me. The odd thing is that as adults we were and are very much alike. He lived in England and we saw very little of him for many years but when he turned up for my father's eightieth birthday party we were both wearing the same brown sweater over a white shirt and carried the exact same half glass reading glasses suspended from a string around our necks. The family theory was that we were really twins and that I had skulked around in my mother's womb for six years, reluctant to come out. I don't believe that because neither of the other two who passed through in the intervening period remembers seeing me there. What is true though is that my mother always swore that she carried me for eleven months but that when I came I came in a rush. She was the librarian in the local Carnegie Library and was at work when the contractions started. She made a dash for our house which was about one hundred and fifty yards away and apparently had got one leg into the bed when I slipped out onto the floor.

That was the first knock I got on the head but it was as nothing compared to the one I got at the age of four. My dad was a carpenter and was working replacing the upstairs floor at the local fire station. I ran in the door with a message and dived through the floor that was not there, landing on my head on the concrete floor fourteen feet below. I am now sixty-six years old but I can still remember my Dad running down the stairs shouting "Is he dead, is he dead?", wrapping me up in his arms and running like a wild man up the street to the doctor's house.

I survived, but I still have the mark on my forehead. From then on I was regarded as the pisawn, or weakling, of the family and was my mother's favorite, or so my siblings say. For some reason I decided for myself that I would not live beyond twenty-seven. I do not know why twenty-seven, because thirty-three would have been more appropriate for the son of a carpenter with an inflated opinion of himself. You see, I was one of those unfortunate children who right up to Leaving Certificate at age seventeen found school too easy and had to make a painful adjustment as an adult when most of the others caught up with me and passed me by. Sidney Carton was not the only one of whom it could be said "Nothing in Life became him like his Leaving."

I was a very innocent child, even if I was a bit precocious. For instance, there was the time at six years of age that I shocked my teacher when she asked for an example of a sentence with the word *slap* in it. I said "I will go up and take down your knickers and give you a slap on the bottom." I could not understand the fuss that was made over it because as far as I was concerned I had just done what she asked. A year later I caused uproar at the end-of-year school concert by, in all innocence, repeating a salacious double-meaning riddle I had picked up from some adult. This innocence continued on into my young adult life. I remember being very puzzled in University when a friend of mine called Tom Bates was regularly referred to in a jeering fashion as Master Bates. I simply did not know the meaning of the word, even though I was three years older than the rest, having worked for three years before going back to college.

Who knows, maybe even today

I am still a bit naïve. I am certainly much too open for my own good and I have none of the cuteness for which Kerrymen are famous in Ireland. The apocryphal story about Kerrymen is of the visitor who asked "Is it true that all Kerrymen answer one question with another?" The reply was "Who told you that?"

In any case, I will leave my adult life for another day. Suffice it to say that I am married to a marvelous woman called Maura, who is the real writer in the family. Maybe she and our two adult children, Mairin and Donal, will tell their own stories another day.
Sincerely,
TIMOTHY MCSWEENEY
DUBLIN, IRELAND

[*An urgent message from the author of "Why Not a Spider Monkey Jesus?" (Issue No. 11).*]

July 11, 2003
DEAR JULIE,
"Tomb Food Could Be A Fresh-Killed Duck, A Picture or Hieroglyph of A Duck, A Container Shaped Like A Duck, Or A Mummified Duck."
—From "Egypt's Crowning Glory" by Doug Stewart, *Smithsonian*, July 2003 (p.54) [Capitalization Mine]:
Your friend,
A.G. PASQUELLA
TORONTO, ONTARIO

[*Writer and talker Sarah Vowell to a friend, concerning important research.*]

March 18, 8:17 a.m.
BENNETT,
Walking down to the financial district this evening to look at the old customs building at William & Wall. Basically, it's the building that got Garfield shot.

Also where Liza Minelli had her wedding reception. And was renovated into a bank at the turn of the last century, including bizarre racist allegorical sculptures of the continents by Daniel Chester French (Lincoln Memorial sculptor)—the one of America has us sitting on an Aztec god and Africa is basically taking a nap. Anyway, you're invited to come with if you'd like. I can't imagine it would be more boring than anything else I've dragged you to. (She said enticingly.)

SARAH

NEW YORK, NEW YORK

[*A proposition, decades old, awaiting a brave industrialist unfettered by fear and convention.*]

January, 1973

DEAR DAN, AMITY, JEFF, AND SUSAN,
I have the most incredible news. We're all going to be rich rich rich. I have a great idea. All we have to do is patent it and sell it and start counting, as they say. There's no name yet, but I'll describe it to you.

Its purpose is to do away with dishes and thus having to wash them. It seemed to me that the problem with washing dishes was that they were three-dimensional. It also seemed that dogs eat off the floor. I mean, we throw food onto the floor and they eat it up and nothing ever happens to them in the line of getting sick. So it seemed that since dogs are not any stronger than us, and since we are not trying to poison them, we could eat off the "floor" also. (Note the quotation marks.)

So. What we have is a table with plates and everything built into them already. Similar to a formica top, only some miracle plastic that is better. This doesn't replace silverware. It is also not

to be viewed as a replacement for dishes. Just as an everyday convenience for, perhaps, families where there are a lot of children and the dishes after each meal are a major hassle. The plates are built in and of course all glasses are built in in the shape of a soup bowl. Slight adjustment there. Straws would be the main way that people drink. So, when the meal is over, the silverware is cleared off, as are all the leftovers, and someone takes a sponge and just wipes off the table and pushes everything over to a corner where there is a trap door that leads to the garbage

The variations on this are endless. For instance, the top can swivel around for different size plates or some other reason. There can be an extra one-inch wall or gully going around the table to catch anything that spills. More expensive models could have a dome-shaped attachment that when placed on top of something would keep the heat in, or perhaps the dome plugs in and is a heater. The advance model could even have a large see-through dome which forms the top of a table washer. Just put the water-tight dome on (made watertight by screwing it on), press a button, and the whole thing is like a dishwasher. You could even hang the silverware onto something. When the cycle is finished everything goes down an attached garbage disposal.

The table could have any number of designs on it. The deluxe model could really be fancy. Get that, the deluxe model. Deluxe.

The potential of the thing as I see it is its everyday use as opposed to for a formal dinner. Wiping up the dishes in the same way one wipes up the table is an incredible time saver. There is the possibility of buying ones with different number of place-settings, or perhaps different ones for different meals, etc. The basic idea is that the plates are built into the table and are easier to wash because of that reason.

That's basically the idea. In a sentence, it's what I have just underlined.

I'm really excited about this. I remember when I was excited over making pipes out of apples, and that was nothing in comparison. There doesn't seem to be the same feeling coming from the folks around here. Doreen likes it, Carole hasn't said much, and Lincoln regards it as a folly. He said something about eating his hat if it worked. But I think that I have the emotional momentum to carry it through. I hope that you people understand the whole thing. I'd be interested in what you (second person plural) have to say. In any event write to me airmail at the American Express in San Diego. I should be passing through in about 10 days. Probably stay for a day or two. Depending on what you say, we could be rich.

Otherwise, what else could possibly be exciting? I mean, the rainy season has started and we're about to leave. So, take care.

CHARLIE
SAN FRANCISCO, CALIFORNIA

[*Brent Hoff, author of Issue No. 3's "Spider Silk Is a Neat Material the World Wants. Can We Make This in Goats?", stands athwart the path of progress.*]

February 12, 2004
DEAR DR. THRESHER OF THE HOBART MARINE RESEARCH LABORATORY
Dr. Thresher! Congratulations on having successfully bred a genetically modified carp incapable of producing female offspring! May this "Terminator Fish" wipe out all the world's European carp as planned. When I read about the T-fish, I remembered a hilarious story I wanted to share with you.

A few years ago I was doing a piece on a company that had just created a genetically modified spider-goat (using the genes of a black widow spider and, you guessed it, a goat.) While interviewing the head geneticist on the project I asked him, "What will you do if one of your freaky spider-goats contracts scrapie?" You know what he said? You'll never guess. He said "What's scrapie?" Isn't that crazy?! The head geneticist on a U.S. military-funded project responsible for creating genetically modified ungulates not knowing one of the most common diseases to infect ungulates? I mean, scrapie is the habitually-mutating prion disease responsible for Mad Cow, for crying out loud! When scrapie comes into contact with a new creature you never know what's gonna happen. I imagine mutant spider-goat scrapie could mutate into some airborne strain of real sci-fi nastiness. Here I had been expecting a long tirade about "Don't worry kid, we've taken every possible precaution to isolate our research animals and blah blah blah" and instead I had to explain to him how prion diseases cross species easily, rapidly mutating into more virulent forms, and he was like "Yeah I'm sure they wouldn't get that, we keep them isolated from other goats." I'm not making this up! He hadn't even heard how foot and mouth disease was able to spread across herds continents apart on the soles of researchers' shoes. As we talked on the phone, I could almost see him suspiciously examining the soles of his Timbs.

Anyway later I went and read Jose Gassett's chapter in *The Revolt of The Masses* titled "The Barbarism of Specialization." For a Spanish philosopher, Gassett makes a convincing argument when he says modern scientists have become so specialized in their hyper-complex fields they end up becoming dangerously isolated from the kind of general information necessary to keep them from creating bigger problems than the problems their work seeks to fix. Dude was sooo right. Anyway, let me know how your massive ecological experiment turns out.

Your friend in science,
BRENT HOFF
NEW YORK, NEW YORK

[*The fickle Bennett expresses reservations, but Ms. Vowell presses her case.*]

March 18, 8:24 a.m.
BENNETT,
Good point about the weather. I'll let you know if I put it off until Saturday, when it's supposed to be in the 40s and not snow.

Melville was a customs inspector for the entire time I care about the New York Custom House imbroglio. He worked mainly on the Gansevoort docks though. But Chester Arthur was his boss. And it is interesting that Melville stayed on for almost twenty years, under the radar. Because—this was the problem that got Garfield shot—most of the customs jobs went to political muckety-mucks. Melville never got a raise the whole time, twenty years. I pass his dock almost every day on my walk and always think of him, having to keep track of shipping cargos when he'd rather be home writing.

SARAH
NEW YORK, NEW YORK

[*Having exhausted Annandale's amusements, someone named Simon decides to leave.*]

July 12, 2000
DEAR ELI,
James and I are taking off for Charlottesville. We will continue our charade as a pair of freelance reporters working for a gay Internet magazine titled *Notions*. Have begun reading *Well Done!: The Common Guy's Guide to Everyday Success,* by Dave Thomas. Apparently, Dave Thomas and the Colonel used to have drinking matches that often ended in fistfights. Also, Colonel Sanders once met Ray Kroc at a tiki bar in the Keys, exchanged words with him, and then "plugged a chicken leg between his buns" while saying nyuck, nyuck, nyuck.

SIMON
ANNANDALE, VIRGINIA

[*We briefly abandon our conceit and include a letter written to us, because it concerns the Gorilla Girl affair last addressed in Issue No. 12. We received many responses: the overwhelming majority was indignantly against Mr. Ryan Bradley's claim of authorship, while a handful took a more nuanced position. The following letter is from the second camp, the camp that fit in our hand. To recap: GG arrived anonymously at McSwys; we asked that the author step forth; Mr. RB either did so or posed as the author doing so.*]

December 24, 2004
HELLO TO YOU.
I have some answers to your questions regarding the Gorilla Girl debate.

1. Yes, I think he wrote the christing story. 2. No. I don't think it is at all plausible to write in some state, forget, blah blah 3. He wrote it. 4. If bradleyryanbradley has anything to do

with it, our generation is a poncey baby cat made up entirely of horseshit who will never survive any generational battles with other cats of any make or model.

Let me start off by saying: I am drunk. Also, my name is Laura. I live in Portland, Oregon. I am now in a suburb of Illinois for stupidstupid Christmas. As I said, I am drunk. I drank many drinks in bars, and then I drank out of necessity at family functions. It is an experiment—I am trying to work myself into the same fugue as ryan and write up a bunch of words. We'll see. Begin!

I think, as mentioned, he wrote the story, but I don't want to read it. Between you and me, I don't want to read it because I think that Ryan is a big sucky fucking baby. Maybe every writer is, maybe everyone is, but I don't read their published email exchanges; but since I read Ryan's, I don't like him, and I don't want the story, gorillacum or not. Generally, I think this is some Merry Prankster "look at me! look at me in the quad!" shit. I don't accept the state he thinks and wants me to think he gets into when he writes: I CALL BULLSHIT. However, maybe these states are better than his whiny meow meow car broken meow meow states.

Any damn way, I also call bullshit on the computer story, and how he tells you about his BBBBOOOOOOring relationship details with the vegan or feminist or drunk girl, but he forgets to tell you, for two weeks, that his computer, which he shipped off somehow somewhere, is forever broken. I was really creeped out about "the bio," and I felt protective about him threatening you with the mommydaddy lawyer.

Again, I don't like his "meow meow my life is a soap opera" bit.

Finally, what most bothered me is his defense of his, my, our generation as being tagged as lazy and goalless. My god man, he can't: generally maintain a computer or back up computer files, make copies of materials he wishes he could publish, remember anyfuckingthing about anything, sustain a relationship, have a job, or achieve an acceptable living arrangement. Also, he associates with other zombies. I mean, I hope that biochemistry does not demand the attention that the ever-confusing worlds of the postal service and basic written communication seems to for Jeffy. I am not saying I am any better, and since I am not, I am not also calling out for some kind of a battle between generations of cats.

This exact kind of shit that Ryan has pulled would have made my father (rest his driven, working, working, working, working soul) stare at me in horror. "What do you MEAN you lost your ONLY COPY?" He would then begin his lecture on my being distracted by meaningless "grabass" and "having another think coming" before becoming visibly disgusted with me, this, my generation, and walking off to do some more work. He was a member of the Battle Cats, focused, attentive, achieving, working. Ryan/this generation seems to be born under the star of the Boring Sucky Fucking Adult-Baby Cats. However, if there is to be a rumble, I hope it is televised and hosted by a sexy sexy woman and a strong man.

I am going to shut up now.

Merry Christmas!

Your loving wife,
LAURA JENSEN
CHICAGO, ILLINOIS

[*From Nick Hornby,* Believer *columnist, to the coach of Arsenal, which we believe to be a sports team of some kind.*]

April 13, 2004

DEAR ARSENE,

At the time of writing, it would appear that only an unthinkable and unprecedented collapse can prevent Arsenal from becoming English champions for the second time in three years. After last year, some of the more negative amongst us thought that another second place was the best we could possibly hope for this season. Instead, we're seven points clear at the top, and currently undefeated. There is every chance, in fact, that we're going to go through the entire league season undefeated, which no team has ever done before. No team has ever done as well as we've done already.

The problem last year was, in the opinion of many, the central defence, and the size of our squad. Martin Keown wasn't and indeed still isn't getting any younger, Sol was suspended for those last crucial few games, and Cygan looked like an inadequate replacement for either of them. There was a lot of grumbling about the untimely sale of Matthew Upson, too. (I agree that he hasn't quite got it, but why flog him mid-season?) No one believed that we could do any better this year without signing at least one, maybe two centre-backs.

And you signed none. What you did instead was convert Kolo Toure, a young, inexperienced and apparently wayward utility player, into one of the quickest, strongest and most disciplined defenders in the Premiership. It's true that Henry and Vieira have been unbelievable this year, but without Toure's emergence, Thierry could

have scored a hat-trick a week and it wouldn't have made much difference. How did you know?

None of the fans could see it. We remembered his disastrous half-hour at left-back against PSV Eindhoven last season: he only lasted half an hour because he got a red card for two hopeless fouls on their right winger, who was beating him for fun, as Ron Atkinson would say. And we remembered his tragi-comic own goal against Aston Villa away, when he lashed a clearance into the roof of our net. If you'd told me a year ago that you were going to play Kolo in the middle of the defence for a whole season, I would have burst into tears and begged you to think again. I might have poured petrol on myself and set myself on fire.

And I would have been dead wrong (and dead, thus missing the whole thing). We have conceded fewer goals than anyone in the division. He's been outstanding. He and Sol have formed a formidable partnership. Did you know it was going to work? And what was Plan B if it didn't? Cygan? Bloody hell.

I wanted to write this letter to congratulate you, to marvel out how a great coach's eyes are different from anyone else's. But now I've put it down on paper, I'm wondering whether you just got lucky. If it hadn't worked, we would have had a long season of misery and frustration. You might have been able to buy someone in the December transfer window, but we wouldn't have been able to catch United and Chelsea. And Tel, Paddy and Bob would have got pissed off and gone to Real Madrid, and we'd be in a state of turmoil.

So don't do it again, okay? You already know that Cygan will never make a left-sided midfield player. (And what was that about, in the Man U home game?) Bentley isn't a fullback. Wiltord can't replace PV4. Unless you think they can, in which case…

Oh, I don't know.

Thank you, thank you, thank you for all the pleasure you have given all of us this year, and the last eight years.

Warmest best wishes, and (eek) well done,
NICK HORNBY
LONDON, ENGLAND

[*From Jonathan Ames to his son, who was five years old at the time.*]

December 20, 1991

DEAR FUTURE NATHANIEL,
Some sad jazz is playing on the radio, just simple lonely piano, and that's how I feel sitting here in my taxi.

It's night, a full moon in the somewhat hazy black sky. I just called you and you didn't sound happy to hear from me. We were together eight straight days, morning, noon, and night, and who knows how many times I zipped your coat, and towards the end I was losing patience… please forgive me, we were cooped up in my room. You already put yourself down and then I give you a hard time, and you want, want, want, and even if I had money I couldn't give you all that you fleetingly "want…"

So we parted today on a sour note. You had trouble sleeping last night, I read you extra stories, and sang to you again and again and then you woke up coughing for hours and I lay awake, unable to sleep, you slept and coughed, I prayed to God for patience, for love, for you to stop coughing. A lot of times I can't wait for you to be a man so that I can explain to you that I hadn't meant to be a dad, and that I'm still

all confused and broken up inside… I'm running out of space, I have to go, my first job of the night—I'm back, two jobs, no tips… but $14.50 for me in one hour. Nathaniel, when you saw me in the airport you came running, bursting with a smile, you leapt into my arms… you are beautiful… I do love you. I'm doing the best I can. God please help me. The end.

{*Then scrawled along the edge:*}
P.S. You liked Waldo books, you started learning how to fence, we went to NY… lots of things. No more room.
JONATHAN
PRINCETON, NEW JERSEY

[*Vowell cannot be denied. James Garfield makes an appearance. Pity poor Bennett.*]

March 18, 4:25 p.m.

BENNETT,
Herman spent half his time on the docks poking into boatloads and the other half of his workday at the Custom House filing his red tape.

I figured something out: looking at the corruption of the custom house under Arthur et al.—you cannot believe the sleaze that was going on there, the NY customs collector being the most lucrative position in the whole federal government because of all the graft—I've come to appreciate Melville's two decades of misery as a government bean counter. He was honest, maybe the only honest man in the whole sorry place. Literature's loss to his nine-to-five prison was maybe the citizenry's gain. If every civil servant had been as conscientious and decent as Herman Melville, civil service would never have had to be reformed and Garfield might never have gotten shot.
SARAH
NEW YORK, NEW YORK

A CHILD'S BOOK OF SICKNESS AND DEATH

by CHRIS ADRIAN

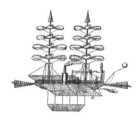

MY ROOM, 616, is always waiting for me when I get back, unless it is the dead of winter, rotavirus season, when the floor is crowded with gray-faced toddlers rocketing down the halls on fantails of liquid shit. They are only transiently ill, and not distinguished. You earn something in a lifetime of hospitalizations that the rotavirus babies, the RSV wheezers, the accidental ingestions, the rare tonsillectomy, that these sub-sub-sickees could never touch or have. The least of it is the sign that the nurses have hung on my door, silver glitter on yellow poster board: *Chez Cindy*.

My father settles me in before he leaves. He likes to turn down the bed, to tear off the paper strap from across the toilet, and to unpack my clothes and put them in the little dresser. "You only brought halter tops and hot pants," he tells me.

"And pajamas," I say. "Halter tops make for good access. To my veins." He says he'll bring me a robe when he comes back, though he'll likely not be back. If you are the sort of child who only comes into the hospital once every ten years, then the whole world comes to visit, and your room is filled with flowers and chocolates and aluminum balloons. After the tenth or fifteenth admission the people and the flowers stop coming. Now I get flowers only if I'm septic, but my Uncle Ned makes a donation to the Short Gut

Foundation of America every time I come in.

"Sorry I can't stay for the H and P," my father says. He would usually stay to answer all the questions the intern du jour will ask, but during this admission we are moving. The new house is only two miles from the old house, but is bigger, and has views. I don't care much for views. This side of the hospital looks out over the park and beyond that to the Golden Gate. On the nights my father stays he'll sit for an hour watching the bridge lights blinking while I watch television. Now he opens the curtains and puts his face to the glass, taking a single deep look before turning away, kissing me goodbye, and walking out.

After he's gone, I change into a lime-green top and bright white pants, then head down the hall. I like to peep into the other rooms as I walk. Most of the doors are open, but I see no one I know. There are some orthopedic-looking kids in traction; a couple wheezers smoking their albuterol bongs; a tall thin blonde girl sitting up very straight in bed and reading one of those fucking Narnia books. She has CF written all over her. She notices me looking and says hello. I walk on, past two big-headed syndromes and a nasty rash. Then I'm at the nurse's station, and the welcoming cry goes up, "Cindy! Cindy! Cindy!" Welcome back, they say, and where have you *been*, and Nancy, who always took care of me when I was little, makes a booby-squeezing motion at me and says, "My little baby is becoming a woman!"

"Hi everybody," I say.

See the cat? The cat has feline leukemic indecisiveness. He is losing his fur, and his cheeks are hurting him terribly, and he bleeds from out of his nose and his ears. His eyes are bad. He can hardly see you. He has put his face in his litter box because sometimes that makes his cheeks feel better, but now his paws are hurting and his bladder is getting nervous and there is the feeling at the tip of his tail that comes every day at noon. It's like someone's put it in their mouth and they're chewing and chewing.

Suffer, cat, suffer!

I am a former twenty-six-week miracle preemie. These days you have to be a twenty-four-weeker to be a miracle preemie, but when I was born you were still pretty much dead if you emerged at twenty-six weeks. I did well except for a belly infection that took about a foot of my gut—nothing a big person would miss but it was a lot to one-kilo me. So I've got difficult bowels. I don't absorb well, and get this hideous pain, and barf like mad, and need tube feeds, and beyond that sometimes have to go on the sauce, TPN—total parenteral nutrition, where they skip my wimpy little gut and feed me through my veins. And I've never gotten a pony despite asking for one every birthday for the last eight years.

I am waiting for my PICC—you must have central access to go back on the sauce—when a Child Life person comes rapping at my door. You can always tell when it's them because they knock so politely, and because they call out so politely, "May I come in?" I am watching the meditation channel (twenty-four hours a day of string ensembles and trippy footage of waving flowers or shaking leaves, except late, late at night, when between two and three a.m. they show a bright field of stars and play a howling theremin) when she simpers into the room. Her name is Margaret. When I was much younger I thought the Child Life people were great because they brought me toys and took me to the playroom to sniff Play-Doh, but time has sapped their glamour and their fun. Now they are mostly annoying, but I am never cruel to them, because I know that being mean to a Child Life specialist is like kicking a puppy.

"We are collaborating with the children," she says, "in a collaboration of color, and shapes, and words! A collaboration of poetry and prose!" I want to say, people like you wear me out, honey. If you don't go away soon I know my heart will stop beating from weariness, but I let her go on. When she asks if I will make a submission to their hospital literary magazine I say, "Sure!" I won't, though. I am working on my own project, a child's book of sickness and death, and cannot spare thoughts or words for Margaret.

Ava, the IV nurse, comes while Margaret is paraphrasing a submission— the story of a talking IV pump written by a seven-year-old with only half a brain—and bringing herself nearly to tears at the recollection of it.

"And if he can do that with half a brain," I say, "imagine what I could do with my whole one!"

"Sweetie, you can do anything you want," she says, so kind and so encouraging. She offers to stay while I get my PICC but it would be more comforting to have my three-hundred-pound Aunt Mary sit on my face during the procedure than to have this lady at my side, so I say no thank you, and she finally leaves. "I will return for your submission," she says. It sounds much darker than she means it.

The PICC is the smoothest sailing. I get my morphine and a little Versed, and I float through the fields of the meditation channel while Ava threads the catheter into the crook of my arm. I am in the flowers but also riding the tip of the catheter, à la fantastic voyage, as it sneaks up into my heart. I don't like views, but I like looking down through the cataract of blood into the first chamber. The great valve opens. I fall through and land in daisies.

I am still happy-groggy from Ava's sedatives when I think I hear the cat, moaning and suffering, calling out my name. But it's the intern calling me. I wake in a darkening room with a tickle in my arm and look at Ava's handiwork before I look at him. A slim PICC disappears into me just below the antecubital fossa, and my whole lower arm is wrapped in a white mesh glove that looks almost like lace, and would have been cool back in 1983, when I was negative two.

"Sorry to wake you," he says. "Do you have a moment to talk?" He is a tired-looking fellow. At first I think he must be fifty, but when he steps closer to the bed I can see he's just an ill-preserved younger man. He is thin, with strange hair that is not so much wild as just wrong somehow, beady eyes and big ears, and a little beard, the sort you scrawl on a face, along with devil horns, for purposes of denigration.

"Well, I'm late for cotillion," I say. He blinks at me and rubs at his throat.

"I'm Dr. Chandra," he says. I peer at his name tag: Sirius Chandra, MD.

"You don't look like a Chandra," I say, because he is as white as me.

"I'm adopted," he says simply.

"Me too," I say, lying. I sit up and pat the bed next to me, but he leans against the wall and takes out a notepad and pen from his pocket. He proceeds to flip the pen in the air with one hand, launching it off the tips of his fingers and catching it again with finger and thumb, but he never writes down a single thing that I say.

See the pony? She has dreadful hoof dismay. She gets a terrible pain every time she tries to walk, and yet she is very restless, and can hardly stand to sit still. Late at night her hooves whisper to her, asking, "Please, please, just make us into glue," or they strike at her as cruelly as anyone who ever hated her. She hardly knows how she feels about them anymore, her hooves, because they hurt her so much, yet they are still so very pretty—her best feature, everyone says—and biting them very hard is the only thing that makes her feel any better at all. There she is, walking over the hill, on her way to the horse fair, where she'll not get to ride on the Prairie Wind, or play in the Haunted Barn, or eat hot buttered morsels of cowboy from a stand, because wise carnival horses know better than to let in somebody with highly contagious dismay.

She stands at the gate watching the fun, and she looks like she is dancing but she is not dancing.

Suffer, pony, suffer!

"What do you know about Dr. Chandra?" I ask Nancy, who is curling my hair at the nursing station. She has tremendous sausage curls and a variety of distinctive eyewear that she doesn't really need. I am wearing her rhinestone-encrusted granny glasses and can see Ella Thims, another short-gut girl, in all her glorious, gruesome detail where she sits in her little red wagon by the clerk's desk. Ella had some trouble finishing up her nether parts, and so was born without an anus, or vagina, or a colon, or most of her small intestine, and her kidneys are shaped like spirals. She's only two, but she is on the sauce, also. I've known her all her life.

"He hasn't rotated here much. He's pretty quiet. And pretty nice. I've never had a problem with him."

"Have you ever thought someone was interesting? Someone you barely knew, just interesting, in a way?"

"Do you like him? You like him, don't you?"

"Just interesting. Like a homeless person with really great shoes. Or a dog without a collar appearing in the middle of a graveyard."

"Sweetie, you're not his type. I know that much about him." She puts her hand out, flexing it swiftly at the wrist. I look blankly at her, so she does it again, and sort of sashays in place for a moment.

"Oh."

"Welcome to San Francisco." She sighs. "Anyway, you can do better than that. He's funny-looking, and he needs to pull his pants up. Somebody should tell him that. His mother should tell him that."

"Write this down under 'chief complaint,'" I had told him. "I am *sick* of love." He'd flipped his pen and looked at the floor. When we came to the social history I said my birth mother was a nun who committed indiscretions with the parish deaf-mute. And I told him about my book—the cat and the bunny and the peacock and the pony, each delightful creature afflicted with a uniquely horrible disease.

"Do you think anyone would buy that?" he asked.

"There's a book that's just about shit," I said. "Why not one that's just about sickness and death? Everybody poops. Everybody suffers. Everybody dies." I even read the pony page for him, and showed him the picture.

"It sounds a little scary," he said, after a long moment of pen-tossing and silence. "And you've drawn the intestines on the outside of the body."

"Clowns are scary," I told him. "And everybody loves them. And hoof dismay isn't pretty. I'm just telling it how it is."

"There," Nancy says, "you are *curled!*" She says it like, you are *healed.* Ella Thims has a mirror on her playset. I look at my hair and press the big purple button underneath the mirror. The playset honks, and Ella claps her hands. "Good luck," Nancy adds, as I scoot off on my IV pole, because I've got a date tonight.

One of the bad things about not absorbing very well and being chronically malnourished your whole life long is that you turn out to be four and a half feet tall when your father is six-four, your mother is five-ten, and your sister is six feet even. But one of the good things about being four and a half feet tall is that you are light enough to ride your own IV pole, and this is a blessing when you are chained to the sauce.

When I was five I could only ride in a straight line, and only at the pokiest speeds. Over the years I mastered the trick of steering with my feet, of turning and stopping, of moderating my speed by dragging a foot, and of spinning in tight spirals or wide loops. I take only short trips during the day, but at night I cruise as far as the research building that's attached to, but not part of, the hospital. At three a.m. even the eggiest heads are at home asleep, and I can fly down the long halls with no one to see me or stop me except the occasional security guard, always too fat and too slow to catch me, even if they understand what I am.

My date is with a CFer named Wayne. He is the best-fed CF kid I have ever laid eyes on. Usually they are blond, and thin, and pale, and look like they might cough blood on you as soon as smile at you. Wayne is tan, with dark brown hair and blue eyes, and big, with a high wide chest, and arms I could not wrap my two hands around. He is pretty hairy for sixteen. I caught a glimpse of his big hairy belly as I scooted past his room. On my fourth pass (I slowed each time and looked back over my shoulder at him) he called me in. We played a karate video game. I kicked his ass, then I showed him the meditation channel.

He is here for a tune up—every so often the cystic fibrosis kids will get more tired than usual, or cough more, or cough differently, or a routine test of their lung function will be precipitously sucky, and they will come in for two weeks of IV antibiotics and aggressive chest physiotherapy. He is halfway through his course of tobramycin, and bored to death. We go down to the cafeteria and I watch him eat three stale donuts. I have some water and a sip of his tea. I'm never hungry when I'm on the sauce, and I am absorbing so poorly now that if I ate a steak tonight a whole cow would come leaping from my ass in the morning.

I do a little history on him, not certain why I am asking the questions, and less afraid as we talk that he'll catch on that I'm playing intern. He doesn't notice, and fesses up the particulars without protest or reservation as we review his systems.

"My snot is green," he says. "Green like that." He points to my green toenails. He tells me that he has twin cousins who also have CF, and when they are together at family gatherings he is required to wear a mask so as not to pass on his highly resistant mucoid strain of Pseudomonas. "That's why there's no camp for CF," he says. "Camps for diabetes, for HIV, for kidney failure, for liver failure, but no CF camp. Because we'd infect each other." He wiggles his eyebrows then, perhaps not intentionally. "Is there a camp for people like you?" he asks.

"Probably," I say, though I know that there is, and would have gone this past summer if I had not been banned the year before for organizing a game where we rolled a couple of syndromic kids down a hill into a soccer goal. Almost everybody loved it, and nobody got hurt.

Over Wayne's shoulder I see Dr. Chandra sit down two tables away. At the same time that Wayne lifts his last donut to his mouth, Dr. Chandra lifts a slice of pizza to his, but where Wayne nibbles like an invalid at his food, Dr. Chandra stuffs. He just pushes and pushes the pizza into his mouth. In less than a minute he's finished it. Then he gets up and shuffles past us, sucking on a bottle of water, with bits of cheese in his beard. He doesn't even notice me.

When Wayne has finished his donut I take him upstairs, past the sixth floor to the seventh. "I've never been up here," he says.

"Heme-Onc," I say.

"Are we going to visit someone?"

"I know a place." It's a call room. A couple of years back an intern left his code cards in my room, and there was a list of useful door combinations on one of them. Combinations change slowly in hospitals. "The intern's never here," I tell him as I open the door. "Heme-Onc kids have a lot of problems at night."

Inside are a single bed, a telephone, and a poster of a kitten in distress coupled with an encouraging motto. I think of my dream cat, moaning and crying.

"I've never been in a call room before," Wayne says nervously.

"Relax," I say, pushing him toward the bed. There's barely room for both our IV poles, but after some doing we get arranged on the bed. He lies on his side at the head with his feet propped on the nightstand. I am curled up at the foot. There's dim light from a little lamp on the bed stand, enough to make out the curve of his big lips and to read the sign above the door to the hall: LASCIATE OGNE SPERANZA, VOI CH'INTRATE.

"Can you read that?" he asks.

"It says, 'I believe that children are our future.'"

"That's pretty. It'd be nice if we had some candles." He scoots a little closer toward me. I stretch and yawn. "Are you sleepy?"

"No."

He's quiet for a moment. He looks down at the floor, across the thin, torn bedspread. My IV starts to beep. I reprogram it. "Air in the line," I say.

"Oh." I have shifted a little closer to him in the bed while fixing the IVs. "Do you want to do something?" he asks, staring into his lap. "Maybe," I say. I walk my hand around the bed, like a five-legged spider, in a circle, over my own arm, across my thighs, up my belly, up to the top of my head to leap off back onto the blanket. He watches, smiling less and less as it walks up the bed, up his leg, and down his pants.

See the zebra? She has atrocious pancreas oh! Her belly hurts her terribly—sometimes it's like frogs are crawling in her belly, and sometimes it's like snakes are biting her inside just below her belly button, and sometimes it's like centipedes dancing with cleats on every one of their little feet, and sometimes it's a pain she can't even describe, even though all she can do, on those days, is sit around and try to think of ways to describe the pain. She must rub her belly on very particular sorts of trees to make it feel better, though it never feels very much better. Big round scabs are growing on her tongue, and every time she sneezes another big piece of her mane falls out. Her stripes have begun to go all the wrong way, and sometimes her own poop follows her, crawling on the ground or floating in the air, and calls her cruel names.

Suffer, zebra, suffer!

Asleep in my own bed, I'm dreaming of the cat when I hear the team; the cat's moan frays and splits, and the tones unravel from each other and become their voices. I am fully awake with my eyes closed. He lifts a mangy paw, saying goodbye.

"Dr. Chandra," says a voice. I know it must belong to Dr. Fell, the GI attending. "Tell me the three classic findings on X-ray in necrotizing enterocolitis." They are rounding outside my room, six or seven of them, the whole GI team: Dr. Fell and my intern and the fellow and the nurse practitioners and the poor little med students. Soon they'll all come in and want to poke on my belly. Dr. Fell will talk for five minutes about shit: mine, and other people's, and sometimes just the idea of shit, a Platonic ideal not extant on this earth. I know he dreams of gorgeous, perfect shit the way I dream of the cat.

Chandra speaks. He answers *free peritoneal air* and *pneumatosis* in a snap but then he is silent. I can see him perfectly with my eyes still closed: his hair all ahoo; his beady eyes staring intently at his shoes; his stethoscope twisted crooked around his neck, crushing his collar. His feet turn in, so his toes are almost touching. Upstairs with Wayne I thought of him.

Dr. Fell, too supreme a fussbudget to settle for two out of three, begins to castigate him: a doctor at your level of training should know these things; children's lives are in your two hands; you couldn't diagnose your way out of a wet paper bag; your ignorance is deadly, your ignorance can *kill.* I get out of bed, propelled by rage, angry at haughty Dr. Fell, and at hapless Dr. Chandra, and angry at myself for being this angry. Clutching my IV pole like a staff I kick open the door and scream, scaring every one of them: "Portal fucking air! Portal fucking air!" They are all silent, and some of them white-faced. I am panting, hanging now on my IV pole. I look over at Dr. Chandra. He is not panting, but his mouth has fallen open. Our eyes meet for three eternal seconds and then he looks away.

Later I take Ella Thims down to the playroom. The going is slow, because her sauce is running and my sauce is running, so it takes some coordination to push my pole and pull her wagon while keeping her own pole, which trails behind her wagon like a dinghy, from drifting too far left or right. She lies on her back with her legs in the air, grabbing and releasing her feet, and turning her head to say hello to every one she sees. In the hall we pass nurses and med students and visitors and every species of doctor, attendings and fellows and residents and interns, but not my intern. Everyone smiles and waves at Ella, or stoops or squats to pet her or smile closer to her face. They nod at me, and don't look at all at my face. I look back at her, knowing her fate. "Enjoy it while you have it, honey," I say to her, because I know how quickly one exhausts one's cuteness in a place like this. Our cuteness has to work very hard here. It must extend itself to cover horrors—ostomies and scars and flipper-hands and harelips and agenesis of the eyeballs—and it rises to every miserable occasion of the sick body. Ella's strange puffy face is covered, her yellow eyes are covered, her bald spot is covered, her extra fingers are covered, her ostomies are covered, and the bitter, nose-tickling odor of urine that rises from her always is covered by the tremendous faculty of cuteness generated from some organ deep within her. Watching faces I can see how it's working for her, and how it's stopped working for me. Your organ fails, at some point—it fails for everybody, but for people like us it fails faster, having more to cover than just the natural ugliness of body and soul. One day you are more repulsive than attractive, and the good will of strangers is lost forever.

It's a small loss. Still, I miss it sometimes, like now, walking down the hall and remembering riding down this same hall ten years ago on my Big Wheel. Strangers would stop me for speeding and cite me with a hug. I can remember their faces, earnest and open and unassuming, and I wonder now if I ever met someone like that where I could go with them, after such a blank beginning. Something in the way that Dr. Chandra looks at me has that. And the Child Life people look at you that way, too. But they have all been trained in graduate school not to notice the extra head, or the smell, or the missing nose, or to love these things, professionally.

In the playroom I turn Ella over to Margaret and go sit on the floor in a patch of sun near the door to the deck. The morning activity, for those of us old enough or coordinated enough to manage it, is the weaving of gods' eyes. At home I have a trunkful of gods' eyes and potholders and terra-cotta sculptures the size of your hand, such a collection of crafts that you might think I'd spent my whole life in camp. I wind and unwind the yarn, making and then unmaking, because I don't want to add anything new to the collection. I watch Ella playing at a water trough, dipping a little red bucket and pouring it over the paddles of a waterwheel. It's a new toy. There are always new toys, every time I come, and the room is kept pretty and inviting, repainted and recarpeted in less time than some people wait to get a haircut, because some new wealthy person has taken an interest in it. The whole floor is like that, except where there are pockets of plain beige hospital nastiness here and there, places that have escaped the attentions of the rich. The nicest rooms are those that once were occupied by a privileged child with a fatal syndrome.

I pass almost a whole hour like this. Boredom can be a problem for anybody here, but I am never bored watching my gaunt yellow peers splashing in water or stacking blocks or singing along with Miss Margaret. Two wholesome Down's syndrome twins—Dolores and Delilah Cutty, who both have leukemia and are often in for chemo at the same time I am in for the sauce—are having a somersault race across the carpet. A boy named Arthur who has Crouzon's syndrome—the bones of his skull have fused together too early—is playing Chutes and Ladders with a girl afflicted with Panda syndrome. Every time he gets to make a move, he cackles wildly. It makes his eyes bulge out of his head. Sometimes they pop out—then you're supposed to catch them with a piece of sterile gauze and push them back in.

Margaret comes over, after three or four glances in my direction, noticing that my hands have been idle. Child Life specialists abhor idle hands, though there was one here a few years ago, named Eldora, who encouraged meditation and tried to teach us Yoga poses. She did not last long. Margaret crouches down—they are great crouchers, having learned that children like to be addressed at eye level—and, seeing my gods' eye half-finished and my yarn tangled and trailing, asks if I have any questions about the process.

In fact I do. How do your guts turn against you, and your insides become your enemy? How can Arthur have such a big head and not be a super-genius? How can he laugh so loud when tomorrow he'll go back to surgery again to have his face artfully broken by the clever hands of well-intentioned sadists? How can someone so unattractive, so unavailable, so shlumpy, so low-panted, so pitiable, keep rising up, a giant in my thoughts? All these questions and others run through my head, so it takes me a while to answer, but she is patient. Finally a question comes that seems safe to ask. "How do you make someone not gay?"

See the peacock? He has crispy lung surprise. He has got an aching in his chest, and every time he tries to say something nice to someone, he only coughs. His breath stinks so much it makes everyone run away, and he tries to run away from it himself, but of course no matter where he goes, he can still smell it. Sometimes he holds his breath, just to escape it, until he passes out, but he always wakes up, even when he would rather not, and there it is, like rotten chicken, or old, old crab, or hippopotamus butt. He only feels ashamed now when he spreads out his feathers, and the only thing that gives him any relief is licking a moving tire—a very difficult thing to do.

Suffer, peacock, suffer!

It's not safe to confide in people here. Even when they aren't prying—and they do pry—it's better to be silent or to lie than to confide. They'll ask when you had your first period, or your first sex, if you are happy at home, what drugs you've done, if you wish you were thinner and prettier, or that your hair was shiny. And you may tell them about your terrible cramps, or your distressing habit of having compulsive sex with homeless men and women in Golden Gate Park, or how you can't help but sniff a little bleach every morning when you wake up, or complain that you are fat and your hair always looks as if it had just been rinsed with drool. And they'll say, I'll help you with that bleach habit that has debilitated you separately but equally from your physical illness, that dreadful habit that's keeping you from becoming more perfectly who you are. Or they may offer to teach you how the homeless are to be shunned and not fellated, or promise to wash your hair with the very shampoo of the gods. But they come and go, these interns and residents and attendings, nurses and Child Life specialists and social workers and itinerant tamale-ladies—only you and the hospital and the illness are constant. The interns change every month, and if you gave yourself to each of them they'd use you up as surely as an entire high-school football team would use up their dreamiest cheerleading slut, and you'd be left like her, compelled by your history to lie down under the next moron to come along.

Accidental confidences, or accidentally fabricated secrets, are no safer. Margaret misunderstands; she thinks I am fishing for validation. She is a professional validator, with skills honed by a thousand hours of role playing—she has been both the querulous young lesbian and the supportive adult. "But there's no reason to change," she tells me. "You don't have to be ashamed of who you are."

This is a lesson I learned long ago, from my mother, who really was a lesbian, after she was a nun but before she was a wife. "I did not give it up because it was inferior to anything," she told me seriously, the same morning she found me in the arms of Shelley Woo, my neighbor and one of the few girls I was ever able to lure into a sleepover. We had not, like my mother assumed, spent the night practicing tender, heated frottage. We were hugging as innocently as two stuffed animals. "But it's all *right*," she kept saying against my protests. So I know not to argue with Margaret's assumption, either.

It makes me pensive, having become a perceived lesbian. I wander the ward thinking, "Hello, nurse!" at every one of them I see. I sit at the station, watching them come and go, spinning the big lazy Susan of misfortune that holds all the charts. I can imagine sliding my hands under their stylish scrubs—not toothpaste-green like Dr. Chandra's scrubs, but hot pink or canary yellow or deep-sea blue, printed with daisies or sun faces or clouds or even embroidered with dancing hula girls—and pressing my fingers in the hollows of their ribs. I can imagine taking off Nancy's rhinestone granny-glasses with my teeth, or biting so gently on the ridge of her collarbone. The charge nurse—a woman from the Philippines named Jory—sees me opening and closing my mouth silently, and asks if there is something wrong with my jaw. I shake my head. There's nothing wrong. It's only that I am trying to open wide enough for an imaginary mouthful of her soft brown boob.

If it's this easy for me to do, to imagine the new thing, then is he somewhere wondering what it would feel like to press a cheek against my scarred belly, or to gather my hair in his fists? When I was little my pediatrician, Dr. Sawyer, used to look in my pants every year and say, "Just checking to make sure everything is *normal*." I imagine an exam, and imagine him imagining it with me. He listens with his ear on my chest and back, and when it is time to look in my pants he stares long and long and says, "It's not just *normal*, it's *extraordinary!*"

A glowing radiance has just burst from between my legs, and is bathing him in converting rays of glory, when he comes hurrying out of the doctor's room across from the station. He drops his clipboard and apologizes to no one in particular, and glances at me as he straightens up. I want him to smile and look away, to duck his head in an aw-shucks gesture, but he just nods stiffly then walks away. I watch him pass around the corner, then give the lazy Susan a hard spin. If my own chart comes to rest before my eyes, it will mean that he loves me.

See the monkey? He has chronic kidney doom. His kidneys are always yearning toward things—other monkeys and trees and people and different varieties of fruit. He feels them stirring in him and pressing against his flank whenever he gets near to something that he likes. When he tells a girl monkey or a boy monkey that his kidneys want to hug them, they slap him or punch him or kick him in the eye. At night his kidneys ache wildly. He is always swollen and moist-looking. He smells like a toilet because he can only pee when he doesn't want to, and every night he asks himself, how many pairs of crisp white slacks can one monkey ruin?

Suffer, monkey, suffer!

Every fourth night he is on call. He stays in the hospital from six in the morning until six the following evening, awake all night on account of various intern-sized crises. I see him walking in and out of rooms, or peering at the two-foot-long flow sheets that lean on giant clipboards on the walls by every door, or looking solemnly at the nurses as they castigate him for slights against their patients or their honor—an unsigned order, an incorrectly dosed medication, the improper washing of his hands. I catch him in the corridor in what I think is a posture of despair, sunk down outside Wayne's door with his face in his knees, and I think that he has heard about me and Wayne, and it's broken his heart. But I have already dismissed Wayne days ago. We were like two IV poles passing in the night, I told him.

Dr. Chandra is sleeping, not despairing, not snoring but breathing loud through his mouth. I step a little closer to him, close enough to smell him—coffee and hair gel and something like pickles. A flow sheet lies discarded beside him, so from where I stand I can see how much Wayne has peed in the last twelve hours. I stoop next to him and consider sitting down and falling asleep myself, because I know it would constitute a sort of intimacy to mimic his posture and let my shoulder touch his shoulder, to close my eyes and maybe share a dream with him. But before I can sit Nancy comes creeping down the hall in her socks, a barf basin half full of warm water in her hands. A phalanx of nurses appears in the hall behind her, each of them holding a finger to her lips as Nancy kneels next to Dr. Chandra, puts the bucket on the floor, and takes his hand away from his leg so gently I think she is going to kiss it before she puts it in the water. I just stand there, afraid that he'll wake up as I'm walking away, and think I'm responsible for the joke. Nancy and the nurses all disappear around the corner to the station, so it's just me and him again in the hall. I drum my fingers against my head, trying to think of a way to get us both out of this, and realize it's just a step or two to the dietary cart. I take a straw and kneel down next to him. It's a lot of volume, and I imagine, as I drink, that it's flavored by his hand. When I throw it up later it seems like the best barf I've ever done, because it is for him, and as Nancy holds my hair back for me and asks me what possessed me to drink so much water at once I think at him, it was for you, baby, and feel both pathetic and exalted.

I follow him around for a couple call nights, not saving him again from any more mean-spirited jokes, but catching him scratching or picking when he thinks no one is looking, and wanting, like a fool, to be the hand that scratches or the finger that picks, because it would be so interesting and gratifying to touch him like that, or touch him in any way, and I wonder and wonder what I'm doing as I creep around with increasingly practiced nonchalance, looking bored while I sit across from him, listening to him cajole the radiologist on the phone at one in the morning, when I could be sleeping, or riding my pole, when he is strange-looking, and cannot like me, and talks funny, and is rumored to be an intern of small brains. But I see him stand in the hall for five minutes staring at an abandoned tricycle, and he puts his palm against a window and bows his head at the blinking lights on the bridge in a way that makes me want very much to know what he is thinking, and I see him, from a hiding place behind a bin full of dirty sheets, hopping up and down in a hall he thinks is empty save for him, and I am sure he is trying to fly away.

Hiding on his fourth call night in the dirty utility room while he putters with a flow sheet at the door to the room across the hall, I realize that it could be easier than this, and so when he's moved on, I go back to my room and watch the meditation channel for a little while, then practice a few moans, sounding at first too distressed, then not distressed enough, then finally getting it just right before I push the button for the nurse. Nancy is off tonight. It's Jory who comes, and finds me moaning and clutching at my belly. I get Tylenol and a touch of morphine, but am careful to moan only a little less, so Jory calls Dr. Chandra to come evaluate me.

It's romantic, in its way. The lights are low, and he puts his warm, freshly washed hands on my belly to push in every quadrant, a round of light palpation, a round of deep. He speaks very softly, asking me if it hurts more here, or here, or here. "I'm going to press in on your stomach and hold my hand there for a second, and I want you to tell me if it makes it feel better or worse when I let go." He listens to my belly, then takes me by the ankle, extending and flexing my hip.

"I don't know," I say, when he asks me if that made the pain better or worse. "Do it again."

See the bunny? She has high colonic ruin, a very fancy disease. Only bunnies from the very best families get it, but when she cries bloody tears and the terrible spiders come crawling out of her bottom, she would rather be poor, and not even her fancy robot bed can comfort her, or even distract her. When her electric pillow feeds her dreams of happy bunnies playing in the snow, she only feels jealous and sad, and she bites her tongue while she sleeps, and bleeds all night while the bed dabs at her lips with cotton balls on long steel fingers. In the morning a servant drives her to the Potty Club, where she sits with other wealthy bunny girls on a row of crystal toilets. They are supposed to be her friends, but she doesn't like them at all.

Suffer, bunny, suffer!

* * *

When he visits I straighten up, carefully hiding the books that Margaret brought me, biographies of Sappho and Billie Jean King and HD. She entered quietly into my room, closed the door, and drew the blinds before producing them from out of her pants and repeating that my secret was safe with her, though there was no need for it to be secret, and nothing to be ashamed of, and she would support me as fully in proclaiming my homosexuality as she did in the hiding of it. She has already conceived of a banner to put over my bed, a rainbow hung with stars, on the day that I put away all shame and dark feelings. I hide the books because I know all would really be lost if he saw them and assumed the assumption. I do not want to be just his young lesbian friend. I lay out refreshments, spare cookies and juices and puddings from the meal trays that come, though I get all the food I can stand from the sauce.

I don't have many dates, on the outside. Rumors of my scarred belly or my gastrostomy tube drive most boys away before anything can develop, and the only boys that pay persistent attention to me are the creepy ones looking for a freak. I have better luck in here, with boys like Wayne, but those dates are still outside the usual progressions, the talking more and more until you are convinced they actually know you, and the touching more and more until you are pregnant and wondering if this guy ever even liked you. There is nothing normal about my midnight trysts with Dr. Chandra, but there's an order about them, and a progression. I summon him and he puts his hands on me, and he orders an intervention, and he comes back to see if it worked or didn't. For three nights he stands there, watching me for a few moments, leaning on one foot and then the other, before he asks me if I need anything else. All the things I need flash through my mind, but I say no, and he leaves, promising to come back and check on me later, but never doing it. Then, on the fourth night, he does his little dance and asks, "What do you want to do when you grow up. I mean, when you're bigger. When you're out of school, and all that."

"Medicine," I say. "Pediatrics. What else?"

"Aren't you sick of it?" he asks. He is backing toward the door, but I have this feeling like he's stepping closer to the bed.

"Maybe. But I have to do it."

"You could do anything you want," he says, not sounding like he means it.

"What else could Tarzan become, except lord of the jungle?"

"He could have been a dancer, if he wanted. Or an ice-cream man. Whatever he wanted."

"Did you ever want to do anything else, besides this?"

"Never. Not ever."

"How about now?"

"Oh," he says. "Oh, no. I don't think so. No, I don't think so." He startles when his pager vibrates. He looks down at it. "I've got to go. Just tell Jory if the pain comes back again."

"Come over here for a second," I say. "I've got to tell you something."

"Later," he says.

"No, now. It'll just take a second." I expect him to leave, but he walks over and stands near the bed.

"What?"

"Would you like some juice?" I ask him, though what I really meant to do was to accuse him, ever so sweetly, of being the same as me, of knowing the same indescribable thing about this place and about the world. "Or a cookie?"

"No thanks," he says. As he passes through the door I call out for him to wait, and to come back. "What?" he says again, and I think I am just about to know how to say it when the code bell begins to chime. It sounds like an ice-cream truck, but it means someone on the floor is trying to die. He jumps in the air like he's been goosed, then takes a step one way in the hall, stops, starts the other way, then goes back, so it looks like he's trying to decide whether to run toward the emergency or away from it.

I get up and follow him down the hall, just in time to see him run into Ella Thims's room. From the back of the crowd at the door I can see him standing at the head of the bed, looking depressed and indecisive, a bag mask held up in his hand. He asks someone to page the senior resident, then puts the mask over Ella's face. She's bleeding from her nose and mouth, and from her ostomy sites. The blood shoots around inside the mask when he squeezes the bag, and he can't seem to get a tight seal over Ella's chin. The mask keeps slipping while the nurses ask him what he wants to do.

"Well," he says. "Um. How about some oxygen?" Nancy finishes getting Ella hooked up to the monitor and points out that she's in a bad rhythm. "Let's get her some fluid," he says. Nancy asks if he wouldn't like to shock her, instead. "Well," he says. "Maybe!" Then I get pushed aside by the PICU team, called from the other side of the hospital by the chiming of the ice-cream bell. The attending asks Dr. Chandra what's going on, and he turns even redder, and says something I can't hear, because I am being pushed farther and farther from the door as more people squeeze past me to cluster around the bed, ring after ring of saviors and spectators. Pushed back to the nursing station, I am standing in front of Jory, who is sitting by the telephone reading a magazine.

"Hey, honey," she says, not looking at me. "Are you doing okay?"

See the cat? He has died. Feline leukemic indecisiveness is always terminal. Now he just lies there. You can pick him up. Go ahead. Bring him home and put him under your pillow and pray to your parents or your stuffed plush Jesus to bring him back, and say to him, "Come back, come back." He will be smellier in the morning, but no more alive. Maybe he is in a better place, maybe his illness could not follow him where he went, or maybe everything is the same, the same pain in a different place. Maybe there is nothing all, where he is. I don't know, and neither do you.

Goodbye, cat, goodbye!

Ella Thims died in the PICU, killed, it was discovered, by too much potassium in her sauce. It put her heart in that bad rhythm they couldn't get her out of, though they worked over her till dawn. She'd been in it for at least a while before she was discovered, so it was already too late when they put her on the bypass machine. It made her dead alive—her blood was moving in her, but by midmorning of the next day she was rotting inside. Dr. Chandra, it was determined, was the chief architect of the fuck-up, assisted by a newly graduated nurse who meticulously verified the poisonous contents of the solution and delivered them without protest. Was there any deadlier combination, people asked each other all morning, than an idiot intern and a clueless nurse?

I spend the morning on my IV pole, riding the big circle around the ward. It's strange, to be out here in the daylight, and in the busy morning crowd—less busy today, and a little hushed because of the death. I go slower than usual, riding like my grandma would, stepping and pushing leisurely with my left foot, and stopping often to let a team go by. They pass like a family of ducks, the attending followed by the fellow, resident, and students, all in a row, with the lollygagging nutritionist bringing up the rear. Pulmonary, Renal, Neurosurgery, even the Hypoglycemia team are about in the halls, but I don't see the GI team anywhere.

The rest of the night I lay awake in bed, waiting for them to come round on me. I could see it already: everybody getting a turn to kick Dr. Chandra outside my door, or Dr. Fell standing casually with his foot on Dr. Chandra's neck as the team discussed my latest ins and outs. Or maybe he wouldn't even be there. Maybe they send you home early when you kill somebody. Or maybe he would just run and hide somewhere. Not sleeping, I still dreamed about him, huddled in a linen closet, sucking on the corner of a blanket, or sprawled on the bathroom floor, knocking his head softly against the toilet, or kneeling naked in the medication room, shooting up with Benadryl and morphine. I went to him in every place, and put my hands on him with great tenderness, never saying a thing, just nodding at him, like I knew how horrible everything was. A couple rumors float around in the late morning—he's jumped from the bridge; he's thrown himself under a trolley; Ella's parents, finally come to visit, have killed him; he's retired back home to Virginia in disgrace. I add and subtract details—he took off his clothes and folded them neatly on the sidewalk before he jumped; the trolley was full of German choir boys; Ella's father choked while her mother stabbed; his feet hang over the end of his childhood bed.

I don't stop even to get my meds—Nancy trots beside me and pushes them on the fly. Just after that, around one o'clock, I understand that I am following after something, and that I had better speed up if I am going to catch it. It seems to me, who should really know better, that all the late, new sadness of the past twenty-four hours ought to count for something, ought to do something, ought to change something, inside of me, or outside in the world. But I don't know what it is that might change, and I expect that nothing will change—children have died here before, and hapless idiots have come and gone, and always the next day the sick still come to languish and be poked, and they will lie in bed hoping, not for healing, a thing which the wise have all long given up on, but for something to make them feel better, just for a little while, and sometimes they get this thing, and often they don't. I think of my animals and hear them all, not just the cat but the whole bloated menagerie, crying and crying, *make it stop.*

Faster and faster and faster—not even a grieving short-gut girl can be forgiven for speed like this. People are thinking, *she loved that little girl* but I am thinking, *I will never see him again.* Still, I almost forget I am chasing something and not just flying along for the exhilaration it brings. Nurses and students and even the proudest attendings try to leap out of the way but only arrange themselves into a slalom course. It's my skill, not theirs, that keeps them from being struck. Nancy tries to stand in my way, to stop me, but she wimps away to the side long before I get anywhere near her. Doctors and visiting parents and a few other kids, and finally a couple security guards, one almost fat enough to block the entire hall, try to arrest me, but they all fail, and I can hardly even hear what they are shouting. I am concentrating on the window. It's off the course of the circle, at the end of a hundred-foot hall that runs past the playroom and the PICU. It's a portrait frame of the near tower of the bridge, which looks very orange today against the bright blue sky. It is part of the answer when I understand that I am running the circle to rev up for a run down to the window that right now seems like the only way out of this place. The fat guard and Nancy and a parent have made themselves into a roadblock just beyond the turn into the hall. They are stretched like a Red-Rover line from one wall to the other, and two of them close their eyes, but don't break, as I come near them. I make the fastest turn of my life and head away down the hall.

It's Miss Margaret who stops me. She steps out of the playroom with a crate of blocks in her arms, sees me, looks down the hall toward the window, and shrieks "Motherfucker!" I withstand the uncharacteristic obscenity, though it makes me stumble, but the blocks she casts in my path form an obstacle I cannot pass. There are twenty of them or more. As I try to avoid them I am reading the letters, thinking they'll spell out the name of the thing I am chasing, but I am too slow to read any of them except the farthest one, an R, and the red Q that catches under my wheel. I fall off the pole as it goes flying forward, skidding toward the window after I come to a stop on my belly outside the PICU, my central line coming out in a pull as swift and clean as a tooth pulled out with a string and a door. The end of the catheter sails in an arc through the air, scattering drops of blood against the ceiling, and I think how neat it would look if my heart had come out, still attached to the tip, and what a distinct, once-in-a-lifetime noise it would have made when it hit the floor.

HADRIAN'S WALL

by JIM SHEPARD

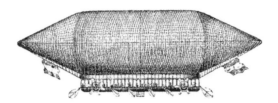

WHO HASN'T HEARD by now of that long chain of events, from the invasion by the Emperor Claudius to the revolt of Boudica and the Iceni in the reign of Nero to the seven campaigning seasons of Agricola, which moved our presence ever northward to where it stands today? From the beginning, information has never ceased being gathered from all parts of the province, so it's not hard to see how historians and scribes of the generation before me have extended the subject's horizons.

In my father's day, before my morning lessons began I would recite for my tutor the story of the way the son of all deified emperors, the Emperor Caesar Trajan Hadrian Augustus, after the necessity of keeping the empire within its limits had been laid on him by divine command, and once the Britons had been scattered and the province of Brittania recovered, added a frontier between either shore of Ocean for eighty miles. The army of the province built the wall under the direction of Aulus Platorius Nepos, Propraetorian Legate of Augustus.

I would finish our lesson by reminding the tutor that my father had worked on that wall. He would remind me that I had already reminded him.

The line chosen for the wall lay a little to the north of an existing line of forts along the northernmost road across the province. The wall was composed of three separate defensive features: a ditch to the north, a wide, stone curtain-wall with turrets, milecastles and forts strung along it, and a large earthwork to the south. Its construction took three legions five years.

I have memories of playing in material from the bottom of the ditch, after it had been freshly dug. I found worms.

The ditch is V-shaped, with a scarp and counterscarp and a square-cut ankle-breaker channel at the bottom. Material from the ditch was thrown to the north of it during construction to form a mound to further expose the attacking enemy. As for the wall, the turrets, milecastles, and forts were built with that fortification as their north faces. Double-portal gates front and rear at the milecastles and forts are the only ways through. The country-side where we're stationed is naked and windswept. The grass on the long ridges is thin and sere. Sparse rushes accentuate the hollows and give shelter to small gray birds.

The milecastles are placed at intervals of a mile; the turrets between them, each in sight of its neighbor, to ensure mutual protection and total surveillance. The forts are separated by the distance that can be marched in half a day.

This then is the net strength of the Twentieth Cohort of Tungrians whose commander is Julius Verecundus: 752 men, including 6 centurions, of which 46 have been detached for service as guards with the governor of the province, assigned to Ferox, legionary legate in command of the Ninth Legion. Of which 337 with 2 centurions have been detached for temporary service at Coria. Of which 45 with 1 centurion are in garrison in a milecastle six miles to the west. Of which 31 are unfit for service, comprising 15 sick, 6 wounded, and 10 suffering from inflammation of the eyes. Leaving 293 with 3 centurions present and fit for active service.

I am Felicius Victor, son of the centurion Annius Equester, on active ser-vice in the Twentieth Cohort and scribe for special services for the adminis-tration of the entire legion. All day, every day, I'm sad. Over the heather the wet wind blows continuously. The rain comes pattering out of the sky. My bowels fail me regularly and others come and go on the continuous bench of our latrine while I huddle there on the cold stone. In the days before his constant visits my father signed each of his letters *Now in whatever way you wish, fulfill what I expect of you.* My messmates torment me with pranks. Most recently they added four great boxes of papyrus and birch leaves for which I'm responsible to two wagonloads of hides bound for Isurium. I would have already gone to collect them except that I do not care to injure the animals while the roads are bad. My only friend is my own counsel, kept in this Account. I enter what I can at days' end, while the others play at Twelve Points, and Robber-Soldiers. I sit on my clerk's stool, scratching and scratching at numbers, while even over the wind the bone-click of dice in the hollow of the dice box clatters and plocks from the barracks. Winners shout their good fortune. Field mice peer in at me before continuing on their way.

Our unit was raised in Gallia Belgica according to the time-honored logic concerning auxiliaries that local loyalties are less dangerous when the unit's not allowed to serve in its native region. Since spring, sickness and nuisance raids have forced the brigading of different cohorts together to keep ourselves at fighting muster.

Scattered tribes from the north appear on the crests of the low hills opposite us and try to puzzle out our dispositions. The wind whips through what little clothing they wear. It looks like they have muddy flags between their legs. We call them *Brittunculi*, or "filthy little Britons."

They don't fully grasp, even with their spies, how many of the turrets and milegates go undermanned. Periodically our detachments stream swiftly through those gates and we misleadingly exhibit strength in numbers.

We've been characterized by the governor of our province as shepherds guarding the flock of empire. During our punitive raids all males capable of bearing arms are butchered. Women and children are caravanned to the rear as slaves. Those elderly who don't attempt to interfere are beaten and robbed. Occasionally their homes are torched.

Everyone in our cohort misses our homeland except me. I would have been a goat in a sheep pen there, and here I contribute so little to our martial spirit that my barracks nickname is Porridge. When I asked why, with some peevishness, I was dangled over a well until I agreed that Porridge was a superior name.

Every man is given a daily ration of barley. When things are going badly and there's nothing else about to eat and no time to bake flatbread, we grind it up to make a porridge.

I was a firebrand as a brat, a world-beater. I was rambunctious. I was always losing a tooth to someone's fist. My father was an auxiliary conscripted in his twenty-first year in Tungria, granted citizenship and the privilege of the tria nomina—forename, family name, and surname—after his twenty-five-year discharge. I was born in the settlement beside the cavalry fort at Cilurnum. My mother worked in a gambling establishment whose inscription above the door was DRINK, HAVE SEX, AND WASH. My father called Cilurnum a roaring, rioting, cock-fighting, wolf-baiting, horse-riding town, and admired the cavalry. My mother became his camp wife, and gave him three children: a sickly girl who died at birth, Chrauttius, and me. Chrauttius was older and stronger and beat me regularly and died of pinkeye before he came of age. Our father was on a punitive raid against the Caledonii when it happened. He returned with a great suppurating wound across his bicep and had a fever for three days. When my mother wasn't at work in the gambling establishment, she attended to him with an affectionate irritation. She dressed and bound his wound with particular vigor. Neighbors held him down and I was instructed to sit on his chest, and while she flushed the cut with alcohol his bellows filled our ears. When he was recovered he brooded about his elder son. "Look at him," he said to my mother, indicating me.

"Look at him yourself," she told him back.

He favored a particular way of being pleasured that required someone to hold his legs down while the woman sat astride him. Usually my mother's sister assisted but during his fever she feared for her own children so I was conscripted. I'd been on the earth for eight summers at that point. I was instructed to sit on his knees. I was frightened and first faced my mother but then she asked me to turn the other way. I held both ankles and pitched and bucked before my father kicked me off onto the floor.

At the start of my eighteenth summer I armed myself with a letter of introduction from him to one of his friends still serving with the Tungrian cohort. My father's command of the language was by no means perfect and since my mother had had the foresight to secure me a tutor for Latin and figures, I helped him with it. *Annius to Priscus, his old messmate, greetings. I recommend to you a worthy man…* and so on. I've since read thousands.

I then presented myself for my interview held on the authority of the governor. I had no citizenship but the exception was made for the son of a serving soldier and I was given the domicile *castris* and enrolled in the tribe of *Pollia*. Three different examiners were required to sign off on a provisional acceptance before I received my advance of pay and was posted to my unit. Attention was paid to my height, physical capacity, and mental alertness, and especially my skill in writing and experience with arithmetic. I was told that a number of offices in the legion required men of good education: that the details of duties, parade states, and pay were entered daily in the ledgers, with as much care as revenue records were by the civil authorities.

Thus I was posted to my century, and my name entered on the rolls. I trained for two summers in marching, physical training, swimming, weapons, and field-service so that when I was finished I might sit at my stool and generate mounds of papyrus and birch-bark beside me, like an insanely busy and ceaselessly twitching insect.

I have a cold in my nose.

We're so undermanned that during outbreaks of additional sickness, detachments from the Ninth Legion are dispatched for short periods to reinforce our windblown little tract. "Felicius Victor," I overheard a centurion scoff outside my window after having conducted some business with me. "Any rag-a-bend from any backwater announces he's now to be called Antonius Maximus."

There are other auxilaries manning the wall on both sides of us. Asturians, Batavians, and Sabines to our east, and Frisiavones, Dalmatians, and Nervii to the west.

My father's agitating to be put back on active duty. He's discovered the considerable difference in practice between the standard of living possible on a soldier's pay and on a veteran's retirement pension. He's tried to grow figs and sweet chestnuts on his little farm, with a spectacular lack of success. He claims he's as healthy as ever and beats his chest with his fist and forearm when he tells me. He's not. The recruiting officers laugh at him to his face. Old friends beg to be left alone. He's asked me to intercede for him, as he interceded for me. He believes I have special influence with the garrison commander. "Oh, let him join up and march around until he falls over," my mother tells me, exasperated.

He rides his little wagon four miles each way every day to stop by my clerk's stool and inquire about his marching orders. The last phrase is his little joke. It's not clear to me when he acquired his sense of humor. When the weather is inclement he presents himself with his same crooked smile nonetheless, soaked and shivering. His arms and chest have been diminished by age. "This is my son," he tells the other clerk each day: another joke. "Who? This man?" the other clerk answers, each time. There's never anyone else in our little chamber.

Sometimes I've gone to the latrine and he waits, silent, while the other clerk labors.

Upon hearing that I still haven't spoken to the garrison commander, he'll stand about while we continue our work, warming himself at our peat fire. Each time he refashions his irritation into patience. "I've brought you sandals," he might say after a while. Or, "Your mother sends regards."

"Your bowels never worked well," he'll commiserate, if I've been gone an especially long time.

On a particularly filthy spring day, dark with rain, he's in no hurry to head home. Streams of mud slurry past our door. The occasional messenger splashes by; otherwise, everyone but the wall sentries are under cover. The peat fire barely warms itself. The other clerk and I continually blow on our hands, and the papyrus cracks from the chill if one presses too hard. I work surreptitiously on a letter to the supplymaster in Isurium, asking for our boxes of letter material back. My father recounts for us bits of his experiences at work on the wall. The other clerk gazes at me in silent supplication.

"We're quite a bit behind here," I finally remind my father.

"You think *this* is work?" he says.

"Oh, god," the other clerk mutters. The rain hisses down in wavering sheets.

"I'm just waiting for it to let up," my father explains. He gazes shyly at some wet thatch. He smells faintly of potash. He re-knots a rope cincture at his waist. He seems to be developing the chilblains. He stands like someone who sees illness and hard use approaching.

"Were you really there from the very beginning?" I ask. The other clerk looks up at me from his work, his mouth open.

My father doesn't reply. He seems to be spying great sadness somewhere out there in the rain.

"Without that wall there'd be Britons on this very spot at this very moment," I point out.

The other clerk gazes around. Water's braiding in at two corners and puddling. Someone's bucket of moldy lentils sits on a shelf. "And they'd be welcome to it," he says.

It was begun in the spring of his second year in the service, my father tells us. Following yet another revolt the season before in which the Britons couldn't be kept under control. He reminds us that it was Domitius Corbulo's adage that the pick and the shovel were the weapons with which to beat the enemy.

"What a wise, wise man was he," the other clerk remarks wearily.

Nepos had come from a governorship of Germania Inferior. Three legions—the Second Augusta, the Sixth Victrix Pia Fidelis, and the Twentieth Valeria Victrix—had been summoned from their bases and organized into work parties. The complement of each had included surveyors, ditch diggers, architects, roof-tile makers, plumbers, stonecutters, lime burners, and woodcutters. My father had been assigned to the lime burners. Five years, with the working season from April to October, since frosts ruled out mortar work.

Three hundred men, my father tells us, working ten hours a day in good weather extended the wall a sixth of a mile. The other clerk sighs and my father looks around for the source of the sound. Everything was harvested locally except iron and lead for clamps and fittings. The lime came from limestone burnt at very high temperatures in kilns on the spot. The proportion of sand to lime in a good mortar mix was three to one for pit-sand and two to one for river sand.

"Now I've written *two to one*," the other clerk moans. He stands from his stool and crushes the square on which he was working.

"Water for the lime and mortar was actually one of the biggest problems," my father continues. "It was brought in continuously in barrels in gigantic oxcarts. Two entire cohorts were assigned just to the transport of water."

The other clerk and I scratch and scratch at our tablets.

As for the timber, if oak was unavailable, then alder, birch, elm, and hazel were acceptable.

While I work, a memory-vision revisits me from after my brother's death: my father standing on my mother's wrist, by way of encouraging her to explain something she'd said.

Locals had been conscripted for the heavy laboring and carting, he tells us. And everyone pitched in when a problem arose. He outlines the difficulties of ditch digging through boulder clay, centurions checking the work with ten-foot rods to insure that no one through laziness had dug less than his share, or gone off line.

The rain finally lets up a bit. Our room brightens. A little bit of freshness blows through the damp. My father rubs his forearms and thanks us for our hospitality. The other clerk and I nod at him, and he nods back. He wishes us good fortune for the day. And you as well, the other clerk answers. He acknowledges the response, flaps out his cloak, cinches it near his neck with a fist, and steps out into the rain. After he's gone a minute or two, it redoubles in force.

On my half-day of rest I make the journey on foot to their little farmstead. When I arrive I discover that my father's gone to visit me. He never keeps track of my rest days. A cold sun is out and my mother entertains me in their little garden. She sets out garlic paste and radishes, damsons and dill. My father's trained vines to grow on anything that will hold them. There's also a small shrine now erected to Viradecthis, set on an altar. It's a crude marble of Minerva that he's altered with a miniature Tungrian headdress.

I ask if he's now participating in the cult. My mother shrugs and says it could be worse. One of her neighbors' sons has come back from his travels a Christian. Worships a fish.

She asks after my health. She recommends goat cheese in porridge for my bowels. She asks after gossip. It always saddens her that I have so little. How did her fierce small wonderboy grow into such a pale little herring?

She smiles and lays a hand on my knee. "You have a good position," she reminds me proudly. And I do.

It would appear from my father's things that a campaign is about to begin. His scabbards are neatly arrayed next to his polishing tin. His kit is spread on a bench to dry in the sun. His marching sandals have been laid out to be reshod with iron studs. A horsefly negotiates one of the studs.

She tells me that he claims at intervals that he'll go back to Gallia Belgica, where the climate is more forgiving for both his figs and his aches. And having returned from service in Britain as a retired centurion, he'd be a large fish in that pond. But he knows no one there, and his family's dead, and there's ill feeling bound to be stirred up by the family of a previous wife who died of overwork and exposure.

Besides, there's much that the unit could do with an old hand, she complains he's always telling her. Sentry duty alone: some of the knot-heads taking turns on that wall would miss entire baggage-trains headed their way.

She asks conversationally about my daily duties. A soldier's daily duties include muster, training, parades, inspections, sentry duty, cleaning our centurions' kit, latrine and bathhouse duty, firewood and fodder collection. My skills exempt me from the latter four, I tell her.

She wants to know if my messmates still play their tricks on me. I tell her they don't, and that they haven't in a long while. I regret having told her in the first place.

When I leave she presents me with a wool tunic with woven decorations. I wear it on the walk back.

During training, those recruits who failed to reach an adequate standard with any particular weapon received their rations in barley instead of wheat, the wheat ration not restored until they'd demonstrated proficiency. And while I was quickly adequate with the sword, I was not with the pilum, and could hit nothing no matter how close I brought myself to the target. Even my father tried to take a hand in the training. My instructor called me the most hopeless sparrow he'd ever seen when it came to missile weapons. For three weeks I ate only barley, and had the shits forever afterward. On the one and only raid in which I took part, I threw my pilum immediately, to get it over with. It stuck in a cattle pen.

Night falls on the long trek back to the barracks. I strike out across the countryside, following the river instead of the road, the sparse grasses a light thrashing at my ankles. At a bend I stop to drink like a dog on all fours and hear the rattle-trap of my father's little wagon heading toward the bridge above me. When he crosses it his head bobs against the night sky. He's singing one of his old unit's songs. He's guiding himself by the light of the moon. It takes him a long while to disappear down the road.

By any standards, our army is one of the most economical institutions ever invented. The effective reduction and domination of vast tracts of frontier by what amounts in the end to no more than a few thousand men depends on an efficiency of communication which enables the strategic occupation of key points in networks of roads and forts. Without runners we have only watchfires, and without scribes we have no runners.

In my isolation and sadness I've continued my history of our time here. So that I might have posterity as a companion, as well.

More rain. Our feet have not been warm for two weeks. We are each and every one of us preoccupied with food. We trade bacon lard, hard biscuits, salt, sour wine, and wheat. The wheat is self-milled, made into bread, porridge, or pasta. We trade meat when it's available. Ox, sheep, pig, goat, roe deer, boar, hare, and fowl. We hoard and trade local fruit and vegetables. Barley, bean, dill, coriander, poppy, hazelnut, raspberry, bramble, strawberry, bilberry, celery. Apples, pears, cherries, grapes, elderberries, damsons and pomegranates, sweet chestnuts, walnuts and beechnuts. Cabbages, broad beans, horse beans, radishes, garlic, and lentils. Each group of messmates has their own shared salt, vinegar, honey, and fish sauces. Eight men to a table, with one taking on the cooking for all. On the days I cook, I'm spoken to. On the days I don't, I'm not. The other clerk runs a gambling pool and is therefore more accepted.

The muster reports worsen as the rain goes on. Eleven additional men are down with whipworm and roundworm. One of the granaries turns out to be contaminated with weevils.

For two nights one of the turrets between the milecastles—off on its own on a lonely outcropping here at the world's end, the wall running out into the blackness on each side—contains only one garrisoned sentry. No one else can be spared. He's instructed to light torches and knock about on both floors, to speak every so often as though carrying on a conversation.

It's on this basis that we might be able to answer the puzzling question, how is it that our occupation can be so successful with so few troops? The military presence is by such methods made to seem stronger and more pervasive than it actually is. We remind ourselves that our detachments can appear swiftly and cavalry forts are never far away.

This could also be seen to illuminate the relationship between the core of the empire and its periphery. Rome has conquered the world by turning brother against brother, father against son: understanding that the periphery of the empire could be controlled and organized with troops raised from areas which themselves had just been peripheral. Frontiers absorbed and then flinging themselves outward against other frontiers. They used Spaniards to conquer Gaul, Gauls to conquer Tungrians, Tungrians to conquer Britain. That's been their genius all along: turning brother against brother and father against son. Since what could have been easier than that?

Peace on a frontier, I've come to suspect, is always relative. For the past two years of my service there've been minor troubles, small punitive raids, our units spending much of their time preventing livestock-rustling and showing the flag. The last few days we've noted our scouts—lightly armed auxiliaries in fast-horsed little detachments—flying in and out of our sally ports at all hours. Rumors fly around the barracks. Having no friends, I hear none of them. When I ask at the evening meal, having cooked dinner, I'm told that the Britons are after our porridge.

My night-watch duty comes around. I watch it creep toward me on my own duty lists, the lists we update each morning to ensure that no one's unjustly burdened or given exemption. The night my turn arrives it's moonless. The three companions listed to serve with me are all laid low with whipworm.

At the appointed hour I return to the barracks to don my mail shirt and scabbard and find my helmet. As I'm heading out with it under my arm one of my messmates calls wearily from across the room, "That's mine." At the duty barracks I'm handed a lantern that barely lights my feet and a small fasces with which to start the warning fire. All of this goes in a sack I sling over my shoulder on a short pole and carry the mile and a half through the dark along the wall to the turret. Before I leave, the duty officer ties a rawhide lead to the back of my scabbard with two old hobnailed sandals on the end of it, so I'll sound like a relieving party and not a lone sentry.

"Talk," he advises as I step out into the night. "Bang a few things together."

The flagstone paving is silver in the starlight. With the extra sandals and my kit sack I sound like a junk dealer clanking along through the darkness. Every so often I stop along the wall and listen. Night sounds reverberate around the hills.

I'm relieving a pair of men. Neither seems happy to see me. They leave me an upper story lit by torches. Two pila with rusted striking-blades stand in a corner. A few old cloaks hang on pegs over some battered oval shields. A mouse skitters from one of the shields to the opposite doorway. In the story below, past the ladder, I can see the glow of the open hearth. There are two windows that look out over the heath but with the glare from the torches I'm better off observing from outside. With the moonlessness I won't have much way of tracking time.

After a few minutes I find I haven't the heart to make noise or clatter about. I untie the rawhide lead with the sandals. I don't bother with the hearth and in a short time the lower story goes dark. The upper story still has its two torches and is nicely dry though a cold breeze comes through the windows. I alternate time on the wall and time inside. It takes minutes to get used to seeing by starlight when I go back out.

Some rocks fall and roll somewhere off in the distance. I keep watch for any movement in that direction for some minutes, without success.

My father liked to refer to himself in his home as stag-hearted. He was speaking principally of his stamina on foot and with women. "Do you miss your brother?" he asked me once, on one of those winter fortnights he was hanging about the place. It was only a few years after my brother's death. I still wasn't big enough to hold the weight of my father's sword at arm's length.

I remember I shook my head. I remember he was unsurprised. I remember that some time later my mother entered the room and asked us what was wrong now.

"We're mournful about his brother," my father finally told her.

He was such a surprising brother, I always think, with his strange temper and his gifts for cruelty and whittling and his fascination with divination. He carved me an entire armored galley with a working anchor. He predicted his own death and told me I'd recognize the signs of mine when it was imminent. I was never greatly angered by his beatings but so enraged by something I can't fully remember now, involving a lie he told our mother, that I prayed for the sickness which later came and killed him.

"I prayed for you to get sick," I told him on his deathbed. We were alone and his eyes were running so that he could barely see. The pallet around his head was yellow with the discharge. He returned my look with amusement, as if to say, Of course.

Halfway through the night a bird's shriek startles me. I chew a hard biscuit to keep myself alert. The rain's a light mist and I can smell something fresh. My mother's wool tunic is heavy and wet under the mail.

When I'm in the upper story taking a drink, a sound I thought was the water ladle continues for a moment when I hold the ladle still in its tin bucket. The sound's from outside. I wait and then ease out the door and stay down behind the embrasure to listen and allow my eyes to adjust. I hold a hand out in the starlight to see if it's steady. The closest milecastle is a point of light over a roll of hills. My heart's pitching around in its little cage.

There are barely audible musical clinks of metal on stone down below extending off to my left. No other sounds.

The watchfire bundle is inside to prevent its becoming damp. In the event of danger it's to be dumped into a roofed and perforated iron urn mounted on the outer turret wall and open-faced in the direction of the milecastle. The bundle's soaked in tar to light instantly. The watchfire requires the certainty of an actual raid, and not just a light reconnaissance. You don't get a troop horse up in the middle of the night for a few boys playing about on dares.

There's the faint whiplike sound of a scaling rope off in the darkness away from the turret. When I raise my head incrementally to see over the stone lip of the embrasure, I have the impression that a series of moving objects have just stopped. I squint. I widen my eyes. I'm breathing into the stone. After a moment, pieces of the darkness disattach and move forward.

When I wheel and shove open the turret door there's a face, wide-eyed, smash-toothed, smeared with black and brown and blue. It lunges at me and misses and a boy pitches off the wall and into the darkness below with a shriek.

Behind him in the turret, shadows sweep the cloak pegs between me and my watchfire. A hand snatches up my sword.

I jump, the impact rattling my teeth when I hit. When I get to my feet, something hits me flush in the face.

On the ground I hear two more muffled blows, though I don't seem to feel them. I'm face down. Pain pierces inward from any mouth movement and teeth loll and slip atop my tongue. When my septum contacts the turf a drunkenness of agony flashes from ear to ear.

When it recedes there are harsh quiet sounds. One of my ears fills with liquid. There's commotion for a while, and then it's gone. In the silence that follows I begin to make out the agitated murmur of the detachment left to guard the now-opened gates.

Fluids pour across my eyes. Lifting my head causes spiralling shapes to arrive and depart. I test various aspects of the pain with various movements. The detachment doesn't move any farther away and doesn't come any closer. At some point, silently weeping, I stop registering sensations.

In the morning I discover they'd been pouring over the wall on both sides of me, the knotted ropes trailing down like vines. Everyone is gone. Smoke is already high in the sky from both the milecastle and the fort. When I stand I teeter. When I look about me only one eye is working. The boy from the door is dead not far from me, having landed on rock. His weapon is still beside him, suggesting he was overlooked.

The rain's stopped and the sun's out. My mother's wool tunic is encrusted and stiff. I walk the wall throwing back over those ropes closest to my turret, blearily making my dereliction of duty less grotesque. It requires a few hours to walk across the heather past the milecastle, and to the fort. I can't move my jaw and presume it's broken. Two of the fort's walls have been breached but apparently the attack was repulsed. Legionaries and auxiliaries are already at work on a temporary timber rampart. Minor officers are shouting and cursing. The Brittunculi bodies are being dragged into piles. The Tungrians rolled onto pallets and carried into the fort.

My head is bound. A headache doesn't allow me to raise it. My first two days are spent in the infirmary. My assumption about my jaw turns out to be correct. I ask if my eye will be saved and I'm told that that's a good question. A vinegar-and-mustard poultice is applied. Two messmates come by to visit a third dying from a stomach wound. They regard me with contempt, tinged with pity. Over the course of a day I drink a little water. My father visits once while I'm asleep, I'm informed. I ask after those I know. The clerk who shared my little room died of burns from the barracks fire. He survived the night and died just as I was brought in. Somehow the location of the raid was a complete surprise, despite the rumors.

It takes all of six days for four cohorts of the Ninth Legion, with its contingents of light and heavy horse, supported by two of the tattered cohorts of the Tungrians, to prepare its response. The Romans suffer casualties as if no one else ever has. There are no speeches, no exhortations, among either the legionaries or the auxiliaries. The barracks ground is noisy only with industry. The Romans, hastily camped within our walls, go about their business as if sworn to silence and as if only butchery will allow them to speak.

I live on a little porridge, sipped through a straw. No one comments on the joke. On the fifth day I report my ready status to my muster officer. The muster officer looks me up and down before moving his attention to other business. "All right, then," he says.

On the sixth day of our muster my father appears in the barracks, over my pallet, the first thing I see when I wake. He's wearing his decorations on a harness over his mail and the horsehair crest of his helmet sets some of our kitchenware, hanging from the rafters, to rocking. He's called himself up to active duty and no one's seen fit to argue with him.

It's only barely light. He tells me he's glad for my health and my mother sends her regards and good wishes and that he'll see me outside.

At the third trumpet signal the stragglers rush to take their positions in the ranks. A great quiet falls over the assembled units and the sun peeks across the top of the east parapet. The herald standing to the right of a general we've never seen asks three times in the formal manner whether we are ready for war. Three times we shout, *We are ready*.

We march all day, our advance covered by cavalry. The sun moves from astride our right shoulder to astride our left. By nightfall we've arrived at a large settlement with shallow earthen embankments and rickety palisades. Are these the men, or the families of the men, responsible for the raid? None of us care.

Their men are mustering themselves hurriedly into battle order before the settlement, unwilling to wait for the siege. They wear long trousers and have animals painted on their bare chests: Caledonii. Is this their tribal territory? I have no idea.

We are drawn up on the legion's left. At the crucial time, we know, the cavalry will appear from behind the settlement, sealing the matter. On this day with my father somewhere lost in the melee off to my right, we will all of us together become the avenging right arm of the Empire. We will execute what will be reported back to the provincial capital as a successful punitive raid. I will myself record the chronicle with my one good eye. I will write, *When we broke through the walls and into the settlement we killed every living thing. The women, the children, the dogs, the goats were cut in half and dismembered. While the killing was at its height pillaging was forbidden. When the killing was ended the trumpets sounded the recall. Individuals were selected from each maniple to carry out the pillaging. The rest of the force remained alert to a counterattack from beyond the settlement. The settlement was put to the torch. The settlement was razed to the ground. The building stones were scattered. The fields were sown with salt.* My comrades-in-arms will think no more of me than before. My father and I will continue to probe and distress our threadbare connections.

And what my mother will say about her marriage, weeping with bitterness in a sun-suffused haze a full summer later, will bring back to me my last view of the site after the Twentieth Tungrians and the Ninth Legion had finished with it, pecked over by crows and studded with the occasional shattered pilum: "We honor nothing by being the way we are. We make a desolation and we call it peace."

THE WOMAN WHO SOLD COMMUNION

by KATE BRAVERMAN

WHEN AMY CRUZ heard she had been denied tenure, she stumbled into her office and picked up her telephone directory. She leafed through the book, name by name, and the pages felt fragile between her fingers. They might be petals or antiquities. There were disasters between the lines. This was her private ritual of nostalgia and how she let herself know she was unhappy.

However, on this particular morning, she actually dialed her mother and waited for her to answer. Raven Cruz was an integral component in her arsenal of weapons of personal destruction. Raven was the core, the plutonium centerpiece. Amy needed an action to definitively express her rage and grief, something like a hand grenade or bullet. Raven could pull the trigger.

Cellular service, with static intermittent voids and uncertainties involving wind currents and angles, had finally come to Espanola. Theoretically, they could now communicate directly. But she couldn't actually talk to her mother. They spoke as if with flags the way people do at sea, where conditions are mutable, possibilities limited and primitive. She choreographed pieces of cloth. The air was so many fabrics. Raven removed language and logic. Her mother had a cell phone now, but Amy was still rendered childlike and vulnerable. She pressed the phone hard against her ear and the metal hurt. This was foreshadowing. Amy counted the rings. Twenty-five.

"They didn't give me the job," Amy began.

"You're surprised?" Raven said. "You're not a team player. You've always wanted a rank and serial number. The right uniform. Play first string for the military industrial complex."

Amy Cruz was in her office at the university where she staggered after Alfred Baxter Coleman, the ABC's of the History Department, stage-whispered the terminal news to her in the corridor. What he actually said was, "No way, Sweetie. Told you." This was true. He had been intimating this to her all year. She had ignored him.

"Do you know how long it's been?" Raven asked. "Since you called?"

"To the hour," Amy answered. Then she told her mother precisely how many years, months, and days had passed since their last conversation.

"I'm impressed," Raven admitted.

"You're always impressed by the wrong things," Amy said. She glanced out the window, palm trees stunted by sun, air oily and smeared. "Men who added fast and didn't need scratch paper. Chess players and piano players, no matter how bad. Women with trust funds who sew their own clothes and bake breads from scratch. Christ."

"I'm a simple country girl. You were always too smart for me." Raven said. "I'm just an old hippie. We sit around listening to Bob Dylan and monitoring our hep C. I'm hoping to live long enough to get Medicare."

"You have hepatitis C?" Amy asked, started.

"We all do," Raven said.

Outside was a slice of Los Angeles in early summer. The hills were a brutal stale green with brittle shrubs like dry stubble. The air seemed to be leaking away.

"You still doing that AA nonsense?" Raven asked.

"I've got it under control," Amy replied, much too quickly. "I want to see you now." Her words tumbled into the hot-stripped morning like dice hitting a wall and she wondered if she meant them. Amy thought of water in a creek, how it accommodated rocks. She considered the fluid spill.

"Get in your car now. You'll be here tomorrow," Raven said with surprising urgency. "Just check that AA crap at the border."

"I'll leave half my IQ, too," Amy offered. "As a sign of good will." After a pause in which Raven failed to construct a reply, Amy asked, "How will I find you?"

"Ask in the plaza. Anyone can tell you where."

Her mother hung up. No more details. Just anyone. In the plaza. It was like a treasure hunt. It was like dropping acid or eating peyote and letting it happen.

That's what they did for years. Let it happen. They camped in the mesas and canyons. Raven had a boyfriend with a Jeep and a sawed-off 12-gauge under the seat, a 9-millimeter in his suitcase or backpack, and a .32 semi-automatic in his pocket. A man, one man or another, who played drums or guitar in a band that had just come back from Australia or Japan. They stayed out for weeks. Finally, insect bites, sunburns and infected cuts made them return. Sometimes Raven just wanted a hot bath.

"I want perfume," Raven would laugh, standing half-dressed on a plateau, her bare shoulders sculpted as if by centuries of wind and a gifted potter's hands. "I want musk and a new hat with a feather."

They would find a town with a hotel sporting an Old West motif in Durango or Aspen or Santa Fe. Her childhood is a sequence of lead glass windows and red floral carpets, mahogany paneling and saloon doors. The air is cool and the amber of honey and whiskey. It is the color of an afternoon shoot-out.

This was the era of the commune and before boarding school. Raven's boyfriends had what they called business in town. They took sudden flights to Los Angeles and Miami. Raven drove them to and from airports. Small planes landed in the desert and Raven had flares, flashlights, and a Jeep. Amy was in the backseat wrapped in a down blanket. She was certain they were dealing drugs.

But she didn't confront her mother. They already spoke in code, in a network of implications and arrested partial sounds like passwords. Between them were flannel and denim and gingham scraps in a basket waiting to become a quilt that was never stitched. Plans for a house built of adobe on the mesa above Espanola her mother somehow owned remained a rolled-up document, a parchment hollow inside a rubber band. It was a navigational chart for a sea they would never sail. Their ideas drifted off. Soon their bodies would follow.

Amy was already leaving. She had been accepted to a boarding school in San Diego. The director pronounced her test scores impressive. He seemed convinced a university scholarship would be eventually granted. She was already studying brochures for colleges in New York and Massachusetts.

In between, during summers and holidays, she was just letting it happen. Amy remembers returning from a camping trip, a vision quest Raven called it, their clothing filthy and stuffed randomly into plastic trash bags. It was the best hotel in town and the bellman carried their trash bags to their room with the gravity afforded real luggage. It was always a suite. Her mother's boyfriend of the moment entered cautiously, his hand touching the gun in his pocket. He eased into rooms, opening closet doors and shower curtains. He glanced at the street from behind the window shades as if scanning for gunmen below.

After weeks in canyons of juniper, sage, pinion, and rock, coffeeshops and boutiques were a fascination. Amy understood this was another form of foraging. She spent afternoons in tourist gift stores. She had lost so much weight on their vision quests on the plateaus, eating only dried fruit and crackers, she could wear size twos on the sale racks in Pocatello, Alamosa, and Winslow where the women had either run away or gone to fat the way domesticated animals do.

Once she bought a hot-pink miniskirt in what felt like Teflon. Eventually Raven had to cut it off her with a scissors. Amy wore the skirt with a silver blouse that had the texture of steel wool. She bought pink spike heels. She imagined she was Brazilian. She rode a dawn bus to work from the projects. She was a clerk with ambitions. Her boss was married and took her to hotels on Sundays after mass. Through the slatted terrace windows were the sounds of birds and cathedral bells in cobblestone plazas, old trolley cars with electric spokes that sizzled, and something insistent that might have been an ocean.

We are all clerks with ambitions, Amy thought then, lounging on a brocade bedspread in a restored hotel suite in Colorado or New Mexico. She was fourteen years or fifteen years old. Raven and her current boyfriend were out doing business. They left her three hundred-dollar bills and instructed her to get an ice-cream soda and go shopping. Somewhere beyond town was thunder and the San Diego Pacific Academy. Boarding school was similar to the commune. But the sleeping and eating arrangements were superior. There were desks and electricity and a library. Bells rang and they had a specific and reliable meaning.

Now it's noon in Los Angeles. It's time to pack her office. It's the end of the semester and she won't be back in the fall. Alfred Baxter Coleman, chair of the promotion and tenure committee, has successfully convinced his colleagues they don't need her.

Amy wraps a pottery vase in the school newspaper. Ink smudges her fingers and she feels soiled to the bone. She doesn't want to put her books in cardboard boxes again. It's an obsolete rite of empty repetition. The square book caskets, carrying the dead texts from state to state, up and down flights of apartment steps with views of alleys and parking lots, bougainvillea and oleander strangling on wire fences. In truth, Amy realizes she doesn't want the books anymore, period.

What she wants is a wound that will bleed and require sutures and anesthesia. What she wants is a cigarette. Amy gathers her cosmetics and tape cassettes from her desk drawer. She takes her gym bag containing her tennis racket, bathing suit, blue jeans, diamondback rattlesnake boots, flashlight, and mace. She wraps her raincoat across her shoulders and thinks, I'm down the road. I'm out of here.

She hopes someone will say, "Professor Cruz?" Then she could reply, "Not anymore." Her response would be fierce and laconic. It would deconstruct itself as you watched. It would explode in your face. She walks to the lobby alone and begins driving.

She shoves U2's *Joshua Tree* into the cassette player. She replaces it with a ZZ Top cassette. Yes, it's time for the original nasty boys from Texas. It's time to consider an entire further dimension of the concept of garage band. After all, you don't have to just rehearse there. You could throw a mattress on the floor, invite your friends, drink a case of bourbon, shoot coke, and stage a gang rape. Maybe she should consider getting down even further. Maybe it's a moment for chainsaws and a massacre.

As she turned onto the freeway, Amy considered her final encounter with Professor Alfred Baxter Coleman. In instant replay, Amy noticed her knees wobbled and she almost went down. But she didn't. She had the presence of mind to stay on her feet and give Alfred the finger. If she had really been on top of it, she would have maced him.

Los Angeles is at her back. It feels like a solid sheet of grease and it's not entirely unpleasant. That's why she's been able to inhabit this city. The ugliness is a kind of balm. Beauty makes her uncomfortable. She instinctively averts her eyes from a flawless face the way others recoil from the sight of a car crash.

Amy Cruz has relentlessly attempted to annihilate all certified versions of perfection, she recognizes that now. The conventionally sanctioned snow-dusted peaks above wildflowers in alpine meadows that look like they should be photographed and sold as posters fill her with disgust. She is repelled by images that resemble the covers of calendars. And towns with contrived lyrical names that could be in the titles of country-western songs.

That's why she left Raven the southwest interior of the country. She took the coasts and gave her mother everything else. That was the real division of assets. She took abstraction and hierarchy, she took systematic knowledge and left Raven the inexpressible, the preliterate, the region of magic and herbs. It was a sort of divorce. Her mother could have Colorado, Arizona, and New Mexico and she would get her doctorate.

Raven accepted landscape as her due. She collected it. In her memories, Raven is perpetually staring at a sun setting in a contagion of magenta and purple. The sky seems like it's begging to be absolved. Raven nods at it, in acknowledgment, shaking her waist-length black hair at clouds passing like a flotilla above her face and pauses, as if expecting the skies to actually part.

Raven, windblown and prepared for clouds to form a tender lavender mouth and confess everything. Raven, on the third or fourth day of a peyote fast, is a pueblo priestess, accustomed to tales of routine felonies and necessary lies. Amy watches Raven taking her form of communion beneath an aggressively streaked sunset the texture of metal. Amy already knows the sky is a deceit, a subterfuge of malice.

Her childhood seems incoherent, the images stalled and stylized, somehow suspect. They might be postcards. That's curious, she thinks, they never took pictures. Even when her mother married the magazine photographer, there were no cameras, no artifacts.

"You can't paste this between album pages," Raven was saying, standing in a meadow, her bare arms stretched out like twin milk snakes, her paisley skirt wind-swirled. This what, precisely, Amy wanted to know.

Raven is topless on a mesa festooned by pinion and juniper, tilting her face to the sky, memorizing the spectrum of purple. It's an alphabet bordered by blue and a magenta that has gone a step too far, left the fold and committed itself to red. Amy wondered what could be discerned from such a sequence. You couldn't arrange it like paint on a palette, or orchestrate it to sound like flutes or bells. You couldn't put it into stanzas or paragraphs. It was entirely useless.

Her mother exists in a series of indiscriminate moments, each already framed and merely waiting for lighting cues. Raven is posed with a lagoon or a canyon as a backdrop. Amy half-expects the afternoon to dissolve into a car commercial. This is what she resists. No to the plateaus of northern New Mexico in wind. No to the vivid orange intrigues of sunsets that look designed to be stenciled on T-shirts. No to men who spend summers in sleeping bags, backpacks filled with Wild Turkey and kilos of marijuana and cocaine. No to Raven in August, scented with dope and pinion, sleeping oblivious under lightning and an outrage of stars.

"I've been tattooed," Raven laughed in the morning, making coffee over a fire of purple sage. "Look," she angled her face toward the new boyfriend, her face that was tanned peach, without a single line or freckle. Amy had a secret accumulation of invisible scratches. Those were the most exquisite. If there was an entity Raven called the Buddha, it was by these internal lacerations that you could know he was watching.

"You can live myth or be buried by it. You have a choice," Raven said. It was her cocaine voice, vague and distant and leaking light. Her mother was taking sunset like a sacrament. "I've been more intimate with this canyon than all my husbands combined," she confided. "It's had more to reveal and more to give."

Amy is on the periphery, simultaneously chilled and parched. She is not a team player. The sky is relentlessly alien. The plateaus are layered like a chorus of red mouths that have nothing to say to her.

Before nightfall and the desert, Amy Cruz stops for gas. She stands in a convenience store, fixed in the glare of anonymous waxy light, and decides, on inexplicable impulse, to change her life. She deliberately buys a pack of cigarettes, even though she hasn't smoked in eight years.

"Vodka," she says, pointing to a fifth. The word sounds inordinately white and mysterious, like something you cannot procure on this planet. It takes her breath away. I've been too long without the traditions, she thinks. Eight years. I've become estranged from my true self. I'm broken off at the root, amputated. I must graft myself back. Now she knows why she must go home.

Amy wonders if she could buy amphetamines in a truck stop. It would probably be just kitchen bennies. White crosses, manufactured in basement labs, and sold as the trucker's other fuel. Last time she copped roadside speed, she took a handful, and got a two-day stomachache accompanied by the sensation that a 747 was landing in her head.

Still, the scenarios of possible dangers excite her. Once she glided between trucks somewhere near Albuquerque, walked beside the enormous cabs oily with streaks of red and yellow like war paint on their faces. She considered the vastness of their wheels and how it felt to say, "Got any whites?" in her fake Southern accent.

Amy smoked a cigarette, drank vodka and smiled. There is no other way to cross the Mojave, she assured herself. At 3 a.m. she turned off the highway, placed her gym bag under her head as a pillow, and fell asleep, holding the mace in her right hand.

She woke stiff and feverish and drove to Santa Fe, singing with ZZ Top and drinking vodka and orange juice. She poured the vodka into the juice bottle. One of Raven's husbands had taught her how to do that. He had coached her on the Southern accent and how to carry, conceal, and shoot a weapon.

"I did all I could," he said to Raven when she left for the San Diego Pacific Academy. He sounded disappointed.

He was serious, Amy is startled to realize. He had positioned beer bottles on sand banks and taught her how to put bullets in them. He found her snakes to shoot, demonstrated how to remove the rattles and make them into earrings. He explained spoor on trails and how to determine what coyotes, raccoons, and rabbits had been eating. She remembers her mother nodding sympathetically at the man who was named Big Red or Big Sam, Jeb or Hawk or Wade.

Amy didn't encounter men with multisyllabic names until boarding school. She was stunned when strangers offered their last names. It had never occurred to her that people voluntarily revealed this information. The first time she was asked her name, she automatically gave an alias.

Amy Cruz checks into a new hotel near the plaza in Santa Fe. Everything is some manifestation of adobe, a tainted orange and pink. She has erased clay in all its permutations from her memories. That had been simple. Now she walks to the swimming pool.

The water reminds her of Hawaii. The blues are so vivid and unadulterated, the elements so participant, that landscape becomes paramount. As a child, they had lived in Maui for three years. Her mother was married to a drummer named Ed. Big Ed. The ocean beyond their lanai possessed a clarity only certain sunlight, purified currents, and cloud configurations can impart.

The swimming pool is the turquoise of Indian jewelry. There is an enticement to this blue, with its suggestion of revelation and sacrament, of opening an enormous chamber into the world as it once was, into thunder and stone and the sacrificial beating heart just as it is yanked out. Such a blue is baptismal. It announces the rising of an incandescent intelligence. It is the turquoise of time travel, camouflaged bridges at dusk, and smuggled contraband.

Yes, this terrain renders ideas and its artifacts inconsequential. That's why everyone was moving to Santa Fe and Taos, the ones who hadn't already migrated to Hawaii or Mexico. But she has no interest in being stripped by so obvious and generic a surrender. That would admit the squalor of her ambitions and what they implied about the incontrovertible value of the acquisition of systemic knowledge. Then she swims three hundred laps. It does not clear her head.

Amy puts on jeans and the red silk blouse she had worn to work two days ago and walks to the plaza. The late afternoon air is the adobe of dust and apricots. The sky is a swarm of storm clouds. Earlier, rainbows appeared in two perfect arches. It occurred to her, as the rainbows broke into fragments, that this was a DNA of the sky. Then Amy looks across the plaza straight at her mother.

"Amethyst," her mother cries, already moving towards her, awkward and determined. They embrace and Raven smells unexpectedly sweet, like vanilla ice cream and rain.

Raven's hair is entirely white and tied into a ponytail with a piece of rawhide. Raven in dusty black jeans. Her Saturday-night end-of-the-trail look. She is profoundly tanned. It is not a skin coloration one can receive through ordinary daily living. It is clearly a statement, no doubt the result of pronouncing the diminishing ozone layer an establishment rumor that has nothing to do with her.

"Too many tourists," Raven said. She seemed to be talking out the side of her mouth. "Let's go."

Amy checks out of her hotel and follows her mother's Jeep along the highway toward Taos, then off, up a winding dirt road. She parks alongside a small yellow trailer.

"It's temporary," Raven said, indicating the structure with a dismissive flutter of her left hand. "Like life."

"Right," Amy answered. They are protohumans, banging on stones. Language has barely been invented. She climbs three stairs to the trailer, and pauses, suddenly listless and disoriented.

"Old hippies don't die. They just quit drinking, take their milk thistle and liver-enzyme counts." Raven laughs.

Raven sits at a miniature formica table and rolls a joint. When her mother offers it to her Amy takes it. She left AA at the border. And half of her IQ. Hadn't that been the deal? And what had become of the Navajo rugs, the carved-oak furniture, the Mescalero Apache tribal wall hangings, Hopi baskets and masks? And where was the Santa Clara pottery?

Amy is remembering. It was the era of the Harmonic Divergence. The commune they called a tribe dwindled. First AIDS. Then the alteration no one had anticipated. Their foundation was the exploration of human consciousness. Insidiously and inexorably, their beliefs had been culturally degraded, marginalized, and then outlawed.

They were conceptual renegades, biochemical pioneers in an aesthetic frontier that was abruptly fenced. Suddenly, satellites provided surveillance. There was no glamour in being a designated leper. There were treatments for the disease. Antidepressants. Rehab. AA. Everyone took the cure.

"I'm too old for this," one of the Big Eds or Jebs said. "I'm not squatting in the mud in winter at forty-five."

Yes, there had been attrition. Drugs were now controlled by men with computers in Nassau and Seattle. Big Wade and Big Jake had arthritis and the wrong skills for the new global marketplace. The survivors dispersed, took Prozac, called themselves Zen masters and meditated in shacks with canyon views and battery-powered tape decks. There were plans for houses that didn't get built. Some found apartments in town with electricity and watched CNN on sixteen-inch black-and-white televisions.

That's how the Espanola property had accrued to Raven. She was the last woman keeping the faith in derelict rooms of kerosene lamps, incense, and candles. The buildings collapsed around her. That's why she had gotten the trailer. And what was that green square outside? Was her mother growing marijuana? Was she taking the risk alone?

"Corn," Raven seemed amused. "Subsistence economy. Tomatoes. Squash. I put seeds in the ground. I eat the plants. A simple life. Much too boring for a professor like you. But you always thought me dull."

Not dull, Amy wants to correct, just affected, predictable, and formulaic. The trailer reminds her of a boat, ingenuously compact, deceptively pulling in or out of the miniature closets and drawers. They had a boat in Maui, she remembers later, when winds rise and batter the metal sides, when there is a sudden squall with thunder and lightning. They are laying side-by-side in twin cots the size of berths, rocking. The trailer is swaying and Amy thinks, we are moving through metaphors, symbolic oceans. We make a telephone call, stand in the glaring light of a liquor store, and the course of our life is changed.

Once during the night storm, she sat bolt upright for one inconclusive moment, and thought she saw her mother standing barefoot at the tiny window, weeping. Her mother by moonlight, whitened, whittled. "I'm a moon crone," she thought Raven said, directly to the night.

Her mother sensed her movement, her intake of breath. "I'm fifty-two and haven't had a period in years. I take hormones and I'm still burning up," Raven was speaking into the darkness. "You don't have to be afraid anymore. I'm not a competitor. You've removed my nine heads. Hydra is gone. See me as I am."

"Are you lonely?" Amy may have asked, uncertain if she was awake.

"Lonely?" Raven repeated. "I have two friends. New Mexico and Bob Dylan. They say he wrote the soundtrack for the sixties. Well, he wrote the soundtrack for my life. When he dies, I'll be a widow."

Amy woke at noon. Raven had assembled sleeping bags, a tent, and stacks of camping equipment on the ground near the canopy in front of the trailer. "Let's rock and roll," Raven said. "Mesa Verde. I feel a spiritual experience coming."

This woman has absolutely no sense of irony, Amy thought. She inhabits an era of oral tradition and intuition. Science has not yet been codified. One worships flint and thunder.

They drove north, Raven taking the curves too fast. Amy composed a random list of what she hated about the Southwest. How everyone was making jewelry and searching for shrines. Santa Fe had become an outdoor theme mall. The silver was a wound that gleamed. It was a cancer. It laid itself out in strands of necklaces and belts, a glare of dead worms, obscene. The entire Navajo nation was home in some stupor, watching TV while pounding out silver conches and squash blossoms. It was sickening.

Amy suddenly remembers a town on the way to Las Cruces. Shacks where she could see lava mountains out a broken window. Her real father was coming down from the reservation to see her. He was out of prison. Amy had never met him. Big Ed or Big Jeb was buying pot. Or perhaps he was selling it. The adults were eating peyote. Her mother and a woman she had never seen before were sitting on the floor stringing necklaces and laughing. The TV was on maximum volume, picture and sound wavering and distorted. She had become dizzy, perhaps fainted. She had been carried to a car. It was a special day. She is certain. Yes, it was her fourteenth birthday and her father didn't come down from the reservation to see her after all. Later, when the woman offered her beads, silver and turquoise, Amy refused.

"Mesa Verde is a revelation," Raven said. "The Buddha must have built it."

"I thought extraterrestrials did the construction," Amy said. "Aliens from Roswell with green blood and implants in their necks."

Raven was smoking a joint. Amy Cruz turned away. She despised the concept that enlightenment could be geographically pinpointed, that one could map a route, drive there, and purchase a ticket. Spirituality had become another commodity. Couldn't Raven comprehend that? Amy experienced a disappointment so overwhelming it erased the possibility of speech. She drank from her vodka bottle surreptitiously, leaned against the car window and let the afternoon fall in green and blue fragments around her face, as if the time-space continuum was fluid and it was flowing across her skin. Or breaking across her flesh in a series of glass splinters.

They spent the afternoon in Indian ruins, peering through holes and the implications of windows, climbing reconstructed stairs and wood ladders into the cliff dwellings. The constant repetition of identical ceremonial rooms. She imagined they smoked pot there, made jewelry, got drunk and engaged in acts of domestic and child abuse. Amy crawled through a tunnel, dust settling across her forehead like another coating of adobe filigree. They stood on the edge of the rim of the canyon, their shoulders brushing. It began to rain, thunder echoed off rock.

"It's the ancient ones talking," Raven was out of breath. She was winded.

"Christ," Amy said. "You're going to end up as a tour guide."

Amy felt for the emergency pint of vodka in her raincoat pocket. When Raven wasn't watching, she finished the bottle.

"You don't have to drink like that," Raven said later. "Pot is easier on the liver. And it's more enlightening."

They stood in mud in the deserted campground. Raven was wearing a denim jacket. It had simply materialized. It was always like that with her mother, the costume changes, the inexplicable appearance of accessories, the sudden silver belt, the mantilla that was both a veil or shawl. Amy was shivering.

"West and south," Raven decided. "The first decent hotel where it's hot."

Gallup was a few blocks of pawnshops and liquor stores, a community center with windows broken, the tennis-court pavement was ripped. The net had been hacked up with knives. She imagined playing on the court, bits of glass making her footing slippery. She could fall, sprain an ankle, get cut. Amy realized that was too simple. The wound she is searching for is more profound and permanent.

"The whole infrastructure is going," Amy realizes, staring at the gutted swimming pool, the brown lawn laced with glass. "It's not just the cities."

"My infrastructure is going. But Prozac and AA won't be my answer." Raven stared at her. There was a long pause. "Listen, I had boyfriends," her mother began, voice almost a whisper. "When you were ten, I was the same age you are now. But nobody ever laid a finger on you, Amethyst. You were my jewel. Everybody treated you right. I made sure."

Late afternoon was a chasm of red that looked vaguely Egyptian. Raven sat in the passenger seat. "Your turn," she said. "Surprise me."

Amy drove west across desert. She stopped in a liquor store and bought four pints of vodka and hid them. She drank and drove until her mother woke up. They were almost across Arizona.

"What's this?" Raven asked, mildly interested. She rubbed her eyes, couldn't find her eyeglasses and opened her map. She examined it. The map was upside down.

"It's a déclassé Vegas on the Arizona-California-Nevada border. Feeds off the retirement dollar. It's nickel and dime all the way. They let them park their trailers free. Hope they'll toss a quarter in a slot machine on the way to the john. It's the fall of the Western world. It's the final capitalist terminal. Come on. We'll love it," Amy felt incredibly festive.

She paused in the lobby. Here were men who had won a minor event at second-tier rodeo. Here were men who had just buried their wives and inherited ten thousand in insurance. That's what they got for their thirty years, five of it spent going to and from chemo. Here were women who had sold their mothers' wedding rings for four hundred dollars, their divorced husbands' bass boats and tool sets. This was the new American score. It wasn't a house and forty acres with a pond and waterfall anymore. It was the world of the shrinking dollar and the failure of words. It was about having one good weekend.

On the seventeenth floor they had a view of the Dead Mountains, a swath of the Mojave and the Colorado River. Amy wondered how many people were standing at their windows, at this precise moment, drawing the curtains apart, realizing their lives were nothing they had thought they would be and feeling the sun like a slap across their mouths.

Amy Cruz feels a rising excitement as they ride the elevator back to the lobby. She listens to the bells from slot machines and the cascades of nickels falling into steel shells. Of course, this was what you heard at the end of the world. It wasn't a whimper at all. It had nothing to do with anything human, not with the mouth or the ear. It was the sound of symbol and motion. It was the sound of tin.

Raven is changing a ten-dollar bill for rolls of quarters. Raven, in a purple caftan with gold sandals and a canary-yellow sash around her waist. She is wearing oversized sunglasses and two old men are staring at her.

Amy realizes she has never had the right accessories for any of the towns or situations of her life. Standing in the lobby of the Flamingo in Laughlin, Amy wishes she had bought silver in Aspen or a squash blossom in Taos. She should have taken the birthday beads she was offered. Or even a turquoise bracelet from a pawnshop in Flagstaff where she had seen thousands in display cases. The Navajo nation was divesting itself of its semiprecious stones for gin and crack and it was horrifying. She didn't want any of it, not even for free.

Now Amy thinks she missed something vital. She should have picked up a gold lamé shawl somewhere, big brass hoop earrings, a skirt in a floral print or anything in chiffon, fall-leaf colored, a light rust, perhaps. Or maybe a straw hat with a flagrant yellow silk flower.

There is something wrong with her body. Listening to the tinny chime of bells, which are not from cathedrals or ships but from the machine proclamations of impending cash falling out, it occurs to her that no accessories could possibly be right for this occasion.

"Let's check out the river," Raven suggests. She is wearing mauve lipstick and a citrus perfume.

Outside the casino, air cracks against her face. It must be 108, Amy thinks. 110. It's a heat that rolls across the flesh, laminating it. This is how time takes photographs of you. This is how you got into the eternal lineup. It has nothing to do with INTERPOL.

Then they are walking into liquid heat. Huge insects sit on the ground. Clusters of scorpions.

"Crickets and grasshoppers," Raven explains. Her skirt is a compendium of all possible shades of purple. Her skirt is wind across dusk mesas. Her mother wears sunset around her hips. "Are you okay?"

Okay? Is that a state with borders or an emotional concept? Can you drive there, get a suite? Should she try to answer with a flag or a drum? And what is in the arc of light on the side of the parking lot? It's a confederation of hallucinatory swooping forms, too thin to be birds. They are creatures from myth. They have broken through the fabric. They have torn through time with their teeth.

"Bats," Raven says. "Can't you hear them?"

Everything is humming. It's some corrupted partial darkness, too overheated and streaked with red neon to be real night. It's grazing above the river that is surprisingly cold. Amy touches it with her hand. They are standing on a sort of loading dock. The terrain is increasingly difficult to decode. What is that coming toward them? A sea vessel? Yes, a mock riverboat calling itself a water taxi.

Raven reaches out her tanned arms, helps her climb down the stairs. "You look like you're going to vomit," her mother whispers. "You're drinking too much. You could never maintain."

The boat motion is nauseating. It simply crosses one strand of river, disgorges silent passengers, takes new ones on and crosses back again. They ride back and forth, back and forth, ferrying gamblers from Arizona across the river to Nevada where it is legal. Everyone is somber.

She closes her eyes and counts the rivers she has been on or in with her mother. The Snake, the Arkansas, Rio Grande, Mississippi, Columbia, Missouri, and Wailua, and now this ghastly Colorado in July where she doesn't have the right accessories, not a scarf or bracelet or shawl. Do they call this the Styx?

"You're not smoking," Amy realizes, looking at her mother.

"Even the bank robbers quit," Raven replies. "Even guys in the can have quit."

It's the last ride of the night. The driver tells them this twice. They've been in the boat for hours, Amy with her head in her mother's lap. Amy has finished her last emergency pint of vodka. She stands, and then pauses on the dock. There is anomalous movement in the river. Two young boys are doing something with white flowers. They are tossing bouquets into the muddy cold water and the flowers are being savagely ripped apart.

Amy bends down, startled by an agitation beneath the surface. Enormous fish circle in the shallows around the wood planks. They must be three feet long. There are severed palms in the water. People have removed their hands and these grotesque fish are eating them. The hideous dark gray fish. It's a ritual. They must supplicate themselves.

"My God," Amy says, wondering if she should jump in. This is the moment. She understands that. She's an excellent swimmer. She knows CPR. She takes a breath.

"Just carp," Raven seems tired. "Hundreds of carp."

"But what are they eating?" Amy feels an ache that begins in her jaw and runs through the individual nerves of her face. Fine wires are being pulled through her eyes. Perhaps they are going to use her skin for bait.

"Bread," her mother says. "Look. Pieces of bread."

Yes, of course. Slices of white bread. It is not the torn-off hands of virgins. It's not the orchids the Buddha promised. It's bread from plastic bags. And we are released. We are reprieved. Enlightenment does not announce itself on the map. It is random, always.

"Where are you going?" Raven demands. "You're sick. Let me help you." She sounds frightened.

"I'll come back," Amy says.

"You haven't been back in ten years," Raven says. "You left too soon, Amethyst. Fifteen was too early, baby. And you're not going anywhere now."

She is moving through the lobby and she is way ahead of her mother. She's been way ahead of her since the beginning. That's why her attention wanders. It's always been too easy. Amy passes machines with glittering gutted heads. She possesses the secret of this age. It's about the geometry of cheap metal. And she knows where the parking lot is and she has the only set of keys.

Amy Cruz stops, paralyzed. She understands this moment with astounding clarity. No. She is not going to pack her office at the university. She is not going to carry books through corridors, one cardboard box, one square casket at a time, across any more parking lots. We decide the components of our necessities. We design our ceremonies of loyalty and propitiation. History does not explain the necessity of accessories.

Raven is reaching through the garish neon, her palms open, waiting to receive something. The original pages from the Bhagavad Gita? The UFO invasion plan? An Anasazi document inscribed in glyphs on bark in a lime ink thought centuries extinct?

"Give me the keys. Give me the booze and cigarettes," Raven commands. "I'm taking you home."

Her mother is a predator bird who was never captured. She's an albino, infertile, arthritic. She has no claws and osteoporosis. She has liver disease and refuses antidepressants. Her nest is lit by kerosene and candles. Amy will be safe there. She will receive the correct instructions and this time she will listen. When they drive through the Four Corners, through the region of the Harmonic Convergence, this time she will hear.

Her mother is driving, wearing eyeglasses, white and stiff in the darkness, a woman with lines like dried tributaries in her face. She gave birth to a daughter named for the distillation of all known purple. Raven has wrapped a shawl gold as a concubine's solstice-festival vestment around her shoulders. This woman loves her. Raven will give her tenure. Amy leans against her mother, her eyes close and she is completely certain.

The architectural drawings can be revised. They can build with hay bales now, it's cheaper. They could do it themselves. Some vestigial survivors would help with the foundation and carpentry. After the adobe walls and kiva-style beams, they'll tile the floors. Later they'll plant chilies. Then half an acre of lilies, calla lilies. They will have a roadside stand in April at Easter. They will be known throughout the northern plateaus as the women of the lilies. They would become famous for this the way some women are for their turquoise bracelets and hand-painted gourds. They will be called the women who sold communion. They will be known by rumor. It will be said that the solitary raven of the mesa received a miracle. There was a brutal severing and a long season of mourning. Then, inexplicably, since this is the nature of all things, the unexpected occurred. Hierarchies are irrelevant because they do not examine central and recurring events. As there is lightning and cataclysm, so too exists the inspired accident. Are we not reconfigured as we cross rooms, strike matches, catch moonlight on our skin? On the mesa above Espanola, where the Rio Grande is a muddy creek you can't even see from the highway, it is said that one day a lost daughter with the name of a sacred stone was somehow returned.

CIVILIZATION

by RYAN BOUDINOT

WHEN I TURNED eighteen I was among the kids who received notice that it was time to make some sacrifices and fulfill our duties as Americans. My family had been receiving letters from the government since we'd registered as a nuclear unit. We had learned to discard the notes asking us to watch certain shows, skim the flyers with health and hygiene tips, and set aside the forms having to do with money or the variety of multiple-choice quizzes that gauge our happiness. I know that those of you living in less regulated earlier eras are probably raising your freedom-loving eyebrows at the idea of the government telling you what to do. But grant me the benefit of the doubt, because the time in which I reside is infinitely more complicated yet more peaceful than yours, as anyone like my grandparents, who straddled the ages, can confirm.

"Those were some hella shitty times," my grandfather says from his vibrating barcalounger at The Home.

"Fer sure," says my grandmother.

I'm a profiled procrastinator, and knew I had two months before I had to report to my Duty Manager to perform the terms of my duty. I tried to pretend that the remainder of my senior year was unburdened by what I had been asked to do. I imagined that the texture of my daily existence—hanging out with friends, eating bad-for-me food, petting heavy with a girl in the backseat of my dad's Buick—was the template from which everyone's life took cues. Yeah, but I had this "thing" hanging over me, this immense, democratic responsibility. I tried to ignore my looming duty by pouring stolen porn-rock and Coca-Cola Classic Classic ("The cocaine is back!!!") into my head. But no matter which distraction technique I attempted, I could not escape the malformed, rotting mass of fear sitting on my chest every time I remembered that the USA had asked me to murder my parents.

Because I liked them well enough. They'd given me some great presents over the years, made me some fine meals. And while I didn't feel ready to perform what was expected of me, they nonetheless provided the same unwavering support they always had, like when I wrestled freestyle a whole season and never won a single match.

My dad, short, wearing a tie, by way of description, offered me a beer and made some noises about personal responsibility. My mom, who unlike my dad had been called to duty back in the day, said it was really a quick procedure, that I'd have my choice of instruments, and that she'd try not to make too much noise. Then we sat down as a family to watch the Homeless People Channel, and seeing those guys pushing their shopping carts around really made me feel like I had a lot of resources—natural and otherwise—to be thankful for.

My friends, of whom none had yet received duty papers, intensified my nervousness with stories of kids who'd only half-killed their folks, who'd had to chase them down stairwells, hunt them in cornfields, even deal with their moms and dads fighting back. (Both my parents had assured me they wouldn't struggle.) Or the stories about brothers and sisters of duty-bound kids who'd strangled their siblings in the night to spare their folks. Luckily I was an only child, and one of the benefits of performing my duty was a paid-in-full scholarship to the college or university of my choice. I wasn't going to blow it like the stupid kids who signed up for Harvard and dropped out during the first semester, thereby losing their free ride. I already had my eye on a little East Coast college no one had ever heard of that had a fantastic Egyptology program. Call me weird, but I've always had a thing for mummies and pyramids, I guess.

At school, my teachers let me slack that semester, aware of the enormous responsibility weighing so very hippo-like on my formative young mind. I openly smoked the cheeb in the back of class and they didn't even make me drop Western Civ and take Rehab or Home Ec instead. You could get away with shit like that at my high school when you were assigned the task of preserving American democracy.

After school one day I went to pick out caskets with my folks, and even though I would be tapping into my own grieving-stipend to foot the bill, I let them choose any style they wanted.

"Are you positive? We really shouldn't spend so much," my mom said. I could tell she had her eye on the "Freedom through Strength" model, the curly maple one with the engraving of an American eagle clutching a bouquet of nuclear missiles in one talon and an Osama bin Laden head in the other. My dad picked the classic American flag model that plays the song of your choice when opened and "Taps" when closed, even though he was never in the service. My dad told the casket coordinator that he wanted it to play the patriotic hit song written by the software band Mugwump 2.0. While I usually clashed with my dad over our music tastes, that song, "Lightning Will Strike Our Enemies," had been a real cross-generational hit and had even kicked the hypothetical Francis Scott Key's ass in the reality show *National Anthem Smackdown*.

Afterward, we went out to dinner at this Italian-themed restaurant called Il Italiano and talked about my future plans, but really the only thing in my head was a loop of the following words: gun, knife, poison, blunt instrument, gun, knife, poison, blunt instrument. On top of that—Keerist!—I still hadn't taken the frickin SATs. Even though they were a formality at this point, I still had promised my parents to shoot for at least an 1100. To make myself feel better, I kept reminding myself they'd be dead when I got the results in the mail.

Our waitress, Pam, came by with the salad and breadsticks. "Who wants pepper?" she said, bearing her mill. "Just tell me when." None of us were stepping up to the responsibility of being the pepper when-sayer, so Pam kept cranking over the mound of iceberg, olives and pepperoncinis. "Whoa. You folks must-a really like-a the peppa!"

"Enough," my dad said, raising his hand. For a second I allowed myself to believe he was referring to this me-killing-them business.

"Fantastico," Pam said, "We have two specials tonight, a pesto radiatore with grilled salmon fillet and a raquetella with creamy Gorgonzola sauce and peas. Now, I don't expect you to know all these fancy Italian pasta names, so let me tell you that raquetella are little tennis raquet shapes. The peas are supposed to be like the tennis balls. Can I get you started with some artichoke-spinach dip or ranch cheesy bread?"

"I don't care what we have," I said.

My dad cleared his throat. "Our son has been called upon to perform his duty for this great land of ours."

"Oh shit," I said, knowing what happened in these kinds of places when they learned you'd been served duty papers. And sure enough three minutes later the entire waitstaff of fifteen was crowded around our table clapping rhythmically and singing one of those dippy patriotic songs from the employee manual.

"This is bullshit!" I shouted, "I don't want to kill you! I love you!"

"*Please*," my mom said through lips stretched to the point of losing blood, "We're in a *restaurant*."

My father nodded to the restrooms and said, "Go take a chill pill, Craig, and come back when you're ready to have a mature discussion about performing your duty."

As I tearfully left the table I heard my father nervously chuckling, telling the assembled waitstaff that it was just some to-be-expected performance anxiety on my part. I was starting to see how seriously fucked my situation really was. My parents would never see things my way, because in their mind I was still just a kid. And if I didn't go through with the killings, the government would tax my family into poverty and I wouldn't get a chance to study Egyptology at the college of my choice.

The Il Italiano men's room had one of those urinals that played "Flight of the Valkyries" when you peed into it, which I hated. Eating at Il Italiano over the years had conditioned me to race to the bathroom during one of my favorite scenes in that classic movie *Apocalypse Now Redux II*.

I popped one of my chill pills from its foil wrapper and washed it down with warm water from the sink. After I freshened up I returned to the table, apologized, and had some on-the-house house salad. My parents pretended my outburst never happened.

My parents had a lot of things to take care of before they died, and their final weeks were crammed with meetings with the title company, insurance agents, accountants, lawyers. In between all the meetings, though, they still managed to spend quality time with me. One afternoon my mom was cool enough to suggest that I skip fifth period and meet her for coffee. When I arrived at the place, she was talking to two of her friends from the State Lottery Commission, ladies who I suspected I could have gotten in the sack had older chicks been my thing.

Catherine, the tall one whose nipples always showed through her blouse and bra, ruffled my hair when I sat down at the miniature table. "Gloria, will you take a look at this young man," Catherine said, "Just a couple-three years ago he was playing army men in the conference room and now he's about to do the shit work of making America proud."

"Your mom and I were just talking about when we had to perform the duty," Gloria said. She was one of those cat-lady types who is disappointed if visitors to her condo fail to comment on the endearing wackyness of her Elvis shrine. "I must have bashed my pop over the head fifty times before the son of a bitch gave up the ghost."

"They gave you blunt instruments?" I said.

"Honey," Gloria said, "Back in the day we didn't have no arsenic pills. We had to do things the hard way, isn't that right, Sally?"

My mom looked down and smiled, as if she was embarrassed about how she'd shot my maternal grandparents. I got the sense she considered her duty easy compared to Gloria, and didn't want to appear too smug about it.

"Yeah, Mom, tell everyone how you offed Grandma and Grampa," I said.

"It's not worth telling."

"Oh sure it is," Gloria said, "Go on, Sally, your own son is old enough."

"He sure is," Catherine said, winking at me over her macchiato.

"It was easy," my mom said. "It's not that interesting. They gave me a choice of a Mach II machine pistol, a .44 Magnum, and a .38 Special. Since I was a girl they made all the plastic hardware pink with flowers on it."

"Pathetic," Catherine said.

"My duty officer told me the best bet was the .38, but I wanted to really do some damage, you know, just to show off. So I chose the .44."

Chuckling, anticipating the punch line, Gloria said, "Come on, that's not all."

My mom sighed. "Okay, sure, I was nervous. And in those days let me just tell you, I know it's hard to believe, but I weighed a hundred pounds in the rain. Don't give me that look; I'm serious! So unfortunately I blanked out on all those shooting classes I'd taken to prepare for this very special day, because I must have locked my elbows and the thing just kicked and knocked me flat on my rear end."

Catherine and Gloria howled, slapping the miniature table we were gathered around.

"So there I am, on my back, with a big bump on my head, and it turns out I missed my dad by a mile. My mom is cussing up a storm, my duty officer is leaning over me asking how many fingers he's holding up, it was just a mess. In the end I went with the machine pistol and that was that."

"Didn't you feel bad?" I asked.

"Well, sure, for a little while. But they gave me the pill."

Gloria made a face. "I heard in the early days they didn't give kids the pill. I can't imagine. Whatever you do, Craig, *take the goddamn pill!*"

"What's the pill?" I asked, worrying that I had missed mention of it in the brochure I'd been sent.

"The pill makes it all better," Catherine said. "It makes it impossible to feel like shit about what you just did. I feel funny saying this, but it's real Orwellian in a way."

"You're thinking of Huxley," Gloria said. "*Brave New World* was the one where they were always popping pills. Like that part when they all go to spring break and party with the Beatles."

The three ladies laughed, and I felt as though I had stumbled into some foreign and primal feminine ritual. As they continued to talk, their voices faded away like they sometimes do on TV, when they want to indicate a character has just been slipped something in a drink.

Poison, shotgun, length of chain.

They abducted my parents while I slept, allowing them time to gather some personal effects and leave me a note on a Post-It on the kitchen island. "Good luck, Craig! Don't let your nerves get to you!" read my father's blocky handwriting. I would have a day to contemplate my upcoming actions. I spent it like many teens who've been selected for duty, moping around the house, trying to chill out to the Sleeping Babies channel. My friends called to razz me because I'd been mentioned on the news and the anchorman had hilariously bungled the pronunciation of my last name. I attempted to will into being a series of events that would save my parents and me, a string of happenstance and luck that spiraled outward into a self-generating parallel reality. In my daydream my parents were rescued from their confinement by some kind of paramilitary freedom-fighter guys that in this reality only existed as contestants on reality shows. I left my house through the back door, jogged across the yard, climbed over the fence, and ran through the wheat field abutting our property, and this wheat field, instead of ending at Parkway Road with the Deli Mart that has the porno mags, extended uninterrupted across this grand continent, and while I ran, naked now in my imagination, a farmer on a tractor would occasionally tip his hat and call out, "Way to go, son! You keep on a-runnin'!"

And it was maybe indicative of my own maturing process that I quickly pressed Pause on this fantasy and declared it stupid and infantile in my head.

The Duty Officer who arrived at my house in her midsized sedan looked not much older than me. Her name was Tisha and she smacked her gum as she wore a red, white, and blue tracksuit.

"All right," Tisha said, "Looks like we're ready. Are you totally psyched? I went through the procedure myself and can't tell you how much it has positively changed my life. Don't worry, you're going to do fine. I met your parents this morning at the center and can tell you they're really swell folks. They want you to do a good job. They'll be so proud of you up to the moment they die."

As we pulled out of the driveway I declined Tisha's offer of Juicy Fruit.

"You read *1984*, right?" Tisha said, taking a free right. "Ha! I know you did, I reviewed your school transcripts. Well anyway, I tell people who are maybe a little nervous just to think of that one part where Winston Smith kicks down the door of his neighbors and catches them smoking crack. Then the part when he turns to the hidden camera and says, 'Time to unleash a lil' whoop-ass, don't you think, Big Bro?' and then he smokes those dirty hippies with his Glock! I know, you're going: like what does this have to do with sending Mom and Pop to the boneyard. So what I'm saying is, you're going to have a real genuine American kind of moral authority real soon here, unleashing your own personal whoop-ass on your mom and dad for the sake of all our heterosexual liberties."

The midsized sedan took a couple sharp turns and we passed the historic district with the office parks and brick-and-mortar schools, then the stadiums and the focus-group factories where people like my soon-to-be-retired parents worked. And the flaming sun was a chariot racing across the sky and I thought how incredible it would have been to be an Egyptian engineer shepherding gigantic blocks of limestone across the desert. How a guy with that kind of mindset would not be capable of comprehending such things as terrorists who hate us for having a movie-rating system that includes P for Penetration.

We got to the Duty Center, which used to be a post office. They even had a faded poster for commemorative Marilyn Monroe and James Dean stamps in one of the windows. When I couldn't or maybe wouldn't get out of the sedan two beefier-style duty officers named Mike and Otto extracted me. Inside, they handcuffed me to a waiting room chair. There were three other kids sitting in the dusty semi-dark next to a table piled with old *Reader's Digest*s with all the naughty parts censored with felt pen. We all looked nauseated and miserable, which struck me as ironic given that we were all recipients of free-ride scholarships. I read a little "Humor in Uniform" to pass the time. After a few minutes a door opened and a kid appeared with his designated duty officer. The kid was my age, with blood spattered on his seriously grinning face. It was the kind of grin that looks fused in place, a grin accompanied by laughter generating in the back of the throat. As soon as the girl sitting beside me saw him she put her head between her knees and puked into a receptacle one of the duty officers had thoughtfully provided.

One by one the kids ahead of me were called back by their own personal duty officers, and one by one they returned about twenty minutes later clutching their college-admissions paperwork, weeping, shaking, or passed out in a wheelchair. I told myself I was just going to get it over with and keep thinking of the pyramids. Then my name was called and I followed Tisha, who now had a more serious demeanor, down a hall that seemed longer than the building we were in. At the end of the hall was a door that had been painted over many times, as if the room behind it had served many purposes over the years. Tisha opened the door onto a tiny, well-lit room where my parents sat back-to-back in foldout metal chairs, arms bound behind them. My mom's makeup was smeared down her cheeks and my dad's hair was ruffled. On a nearby table sat a fillet knife, a meat cleaver, and some kind of Oriental sword. Dammit. I'd been hoping I'd be one of those kids who lucked out and got a selection of poisons and a pair of syringes.

"You are about to perform an essential function of preserving American democracy for generations to come," Tisha said. "I'll be out here in the hall if you need me. Just holler."

Here we were, then, a family. My mom made a choking sound and her lips were quivering.

"Just get this over with, Craig," my dad said.

"I don't want to do this," I said.

"Do it!" my dad shouted, the same kind of shout he used when he was tired of reminding me to mow the lawn.

I approached the table and considered my weapons. "The fillet knife is the sharpest," my mom sobbed, "but the blade looks flimsy."

"If you want my honest opinion, I'd go with the sword," my dad said.

"It's too heavy and dull," my mom said.

"Craig can handle it. He'll just have to use both hands."

"I think this is Craig's decision."

"I'm not saying it isn't, honey. I do think, though, that the meat cleaver is out of the question."

I selected the fillet knife and stood in front of my mother, and my admiration for her having performed this duty twenty-odd years ago grew.

"Just do it," my mom whispered. I stabbed her in the chest. She gasped a deep, rattling breath. I took a step back and left the knife quivering, lodged between two ribs. She slowly looked down, her eyes ripped wide.

"Oh my god," I said.

"You're not done…" my mom gasped.

"I can't!"

My mom scowled, blood sliding out the corners of her mouth. "Craig, you pussy, finish the job."

What followed I guess was just some sort of blacked-out murderous rage. There was some missing footage and then I was sitting in a corner of the room, the three bloodied instruments lying on the floor, my folks slumped dead in their chairs.

After awhile Tisha leaned down and offered me the pill and a glass of water. The pill was stamped with a picture of the president's face with a cartoon word-bubble containing the words, "Say No to Terror."

"It'll make it impossible for you to feel remorse for this later on," Tisha said. "Trust me. Taking the pill is the most important part of the process. Not taking it will turn the rest of your life into a nightmare."

Things turned out swell for me after fulfilling my duty, and I have to admit I'm a little embarrassed about how big a deal I made of it at the time. I write these recollections two years later in an encampment south of Cairo, where I am in charge of cleaning the equipment for a dig. The remains of a teeming city lie just beneath the shifting sands. The camels tonight are especially flatulent. An occasional fighter jet drags a contrail across the sky on its way to bomb countries that stubbornly refuse to let us help them achieve the American dream. I have watched a man lose his leg after falling off a train. I have smoked hashish and found myself in bars speaking to German textile-plant owners trying to sell me their daughters. I have gazed upon the freaking Rosetta Stone. Digging through this barren landscape to uncover cities where real people once worked and raised families thrills me. I can't imagine going back to America. My life's true pleasures I have found in the remains of this lost, proud culture, in the solitude of their beautiful tombs.

We are pleased to present

THE AMANDA DAVIS HIGHWIRE FICTION AWARD

to

JESSICA ANTHONY

THE AMAZING RAPUNZLE FINELLI HANGS BY HER HAIR

Here's what Amanda liked: stories that grab you and take you for a ride, characters you want to know better, or think you know but you're wrong, language that is precise and fresh (but not writers who "masturbate with language"). She mystified students by scribbling in the margins of their stories things like "yeah, I do that," "oooh, gross" or "I like this—it's strange." She told them: "Write like your life depended on it." She focused on basics: What is the story you're telling? Whose story is it? Where does it take place? But most of all, she exhorted writers to probe: "Write until you write about what makes you uncomfortable."

Amanda was the harshest critic of her own work and everyone else's best editor and ally. Those of us she read or line-edited were, to use a phrase she liked, lucky fish. She could bore a hole through a sentence, knock the stuffing out of an idea. She could find the nerve you were pussyfooting around and ask you why you were scared of it. She could talk about it until three in the morning, feed you tea and ginger snaps and just enough resolve, then make you laugh about it all. She could say, "know that I like it," or "this is good," and when she did you knew you had done something worthy. Yes, the girl who penned email subject lines like "you smoke crack with your bottom" could speak the truth, quietly, calmly, with a smile and a hand on your knee, and you just knew it was oracular guidance.

I have some of her journals. Amanda, the writer, to herself: "WRITE, motherfucker." And: "I'm doing a lot of sitting and staring." She asked herself the tough questions, kicked her own ass when she didn't write, even nagged: "Back to work, lady. Come on."

Hail to the Amanda Davis Highwire Fiction Award. And welcome Jessica Anthony. Congratulations on being a writer Amanda would call the real thing. Now write like your life depended on it. Back to work, lady.

—ANTHONY SCHNEIDER

THE DEATH OF MUSTANGO SALVAJE

by JESSICA ANTHONY

L'amour est un oiseau rebelle
Que nul ne peut apprivoiser.
Et c'est bien en vain qu'on l'appelle
S'il lui convient de refuser.
—Carmen

UNO. THEY SAY that it's amazing: I am not only a woman-bullfighter, but the best bullfighter that ever lived. No one can believe it. Reporters stand packed around me, arms waving like flags. They're asking the usual questions. Where did I come from? How was I trained? Blah, blah, blah?

"Cristina," they say. "Tell us how it feels to fight in the ring."

I say, "As soon as I enter the ring, I only concentrate on the bull. I appraise its agility, intelligence, sight and, most importantly, whether it favors one horn or the other."

Now they're getting excited.

Papers rustle. A microphone becomes unplugged.

"How large are the bulls you fight?" they ask.

"Not less than four years old," I say, "with a weight somewhere between five and eight hundred kilos. The same as any fighting bull."

A woman steps forward. She asks me if—because of my female sensibilities—I ever feel sympathy for the bull.

I say, "If I have made a clean, quick kill, I will be applauded. I will do a lap of honor, and be showered with flowers, hats, and cushions. If the bull has put up a good fight, its carcass will also receive a lap of honor."

"*Mustango Salvaje*," they beg, "Strike a pose!"

They, the conduits to the people, call me "Wild Mustang." And it isn't long before they start getting impatient. They would prefer it if Wild Mustang didn't answer the questions in the traditional way. They would prefer it if she tossed her brown ponytail over her shoulder and pinched her cheeks to make them blush and maybe did a little *Olé!* on the pavement. If she pretended to twirl her cape.

They are frequently disappointed.

When Wild Mustang doesn't strike a pose, they turn away glum, microphones swinging at their hips. This makes her feel bad for them, so she holds her fist in the air and shouts *Toro!* so they get to cheer and scribble on their writing tablets. I do this now and there is the sound of a thousand popping bulbs. Their cameras flash, illuminating the parking lot. Two men yell, "Love me, Cristina! Love me!" They clap to my name: "Bar-re-ra! Bar-re-ra!" Little children who do not understand names go, "Oo! Oo! Oo!" The boys hold their fingers to their heads and play bull. The girls toss petals at my feet. The air smells like coal and perfume.

"The people are calling your name, Cristina," cries my father, Eugenio. "They're calling your name over and over!"

We're making way to our sport utility vehicle. Eugenio is red-faced with joy. He waves at the reporters, his grin stretching tight as rubber. "Barrera!" he shouts, half to the crowd, half to himself. He's tickled by the sound of his own name.

"Bah-ra-ra," I mumble. "*Maw-maw-maw*."

Eugenio shoots me a scathing look. What's important to Eugenio is not important to his daughter. What's important is that today I, Cristina Barrera, stabbed and killed a bull more cleanly and swiftly than any bullfighter in the history of the Real Maestranza, the largest bullfighting ring with the largest bullfighting crowd in Seville, the largest bullfighting city in Andalusia.

For my final maneuver, I employed a dramatic *farol*, kneeling, with the cape spread out in front of me. When the bull charged, I swung the cape over my head, around to my back, and he barreled past. I rose slowly and positioned my sword forward and held him low. Entranced. Then I stabbed him. I thrust my sword deep between his thick-boned shoulders and pushed and threw back my hands, gasping from the feel of it. A wave of sound rose from the stadium. The bull's knees buckled. He tipped forward and then fell to his stomach. A breeze kissed my neck, tilting me forward with the bull. The spectators—the twelve thousand five hundred—took this as my bow. Flowers began to pour: roses, chrysanthemums, zinnias, roses, violets, roses, begonias. And more roses. Roses full stem, and just the simple heads, soared. The sweet of the bull-blood and the torrent of the floralia overwhelmed me. I dropped to my knees. The people who were closest, the ones standing in the *callejon,* the first row of the *plaza de toros,* threw their hands in the air and wept.

The people love their Wild Mustang. Their cape-swinging, bull-puncturing she-matador. Their Madonna. But there are some men that are less in love. These men see Wild Mustang and they want to possess her; they want to watch her and at the same time possess her. She wants to tell them that possession is not love: owning talent is not like owning a pretty vase: this is not the first time she has killed.

Nor will it be the last.

Then people rushed the ring. In seconds, I was lifted high in the air and paraded like a trophy around the perimeter. I caught a rose as I was carried from the ring to the waiting room, where Eugenio was waiting to greet me.

The people dropped me to the floor. I handed the rose to my father.

"Cristina," Eugenio said, beaming. He glowed from head to toe. "Do you realize how much money we made tonight?" He clasped his hands together, and ushered me to the changing room. "Everyone will pay to see you fight now. Even if you are a woman."

(This is my father.)

I changed out of my Suit of Lights—the *Traje de Luces*—and into my street clothing: blue jeans and cowboy boots and a T-shirt tucked into the jeans. Eugenio thinks I should wear more elegant streetwear, but Eugenio thinks a lot of things. Since my mother left us, I am his only concern. He's concerned for our finances. He's concerned for my image. He's concerned that since I am a bullfighter, I will never find a man and settle down and live in the country. Hence, my father's paradox: to reap the benefit of his daughter's success or to stay true to the traditions of our Andalusian geography; we have mountains. We are embraced by oceans.

Lately he's been enjoying the success.

"Let us walk out together," he said. "So the reporters can see that you belong to a family. That you are not a woman out of nowhere."

"Yes, Eugenio," I said.

"It will be less awkward that way," he explained.

Eugenio is frequently in awkward positions because Wild Mustang does not have *cojones*, what the men call "cushions of courage." It's common knowledge that cojones allow a bullfighter to fight and fight well—beyond that—survive. Wild Mustang does not believe cojones are something a bullfighter needs to survive. In fact, she believes that the tight pants she must wear in the ring are less tight because she does not have to maneuver around a bagful of coins. So there's that. And there's the litany of *fatalidades*, the cojones-bearing bullfighters whose tiny cushions did absolutely nothing for them in the ring when they took a horn someplace crucial and died. There have been forty-eight fatalidades in Andalusia: ten were named Jose, nine, Manuel.

None were named Cristina Barrera.

Eugenio and I walked outside arm in arm. (In this way, we were less awkward.) As soon as they saw us, reporters rushed forward and hurried toward the parking lot, which is where we are now. The Traje de Luces, which only moments ago sparkled in the center of a dusty ring, is now wrapped in a black plastic bag. It hangs lifelessly over my arm.

There have been the usual questions. We're about to load in when one reporter shouts, "Cristina, show us the *oreja!*" So I remove the bull's ear from beneath the smothered Traje de Luces. But as I do, the same reporter asks, "Cristina, are you in love?"

I turn to look at this reporter. He's very short, wearing a jacket much too large for him. The sleeves are rolled.

I look at Eugenio. "I have no *time* for love," I say.

Eugenio grabs my hand tight. "Say yes," he seethes. "If you are in love they will treat you like a human being and not a cold idol."

So Wild Mustang faces the reporter. She lifts one eyebrow. "Okay," she says, "I *am* in love," and holds up the ear.

A dozen bulbs flash.

"With who!" the short reporter screams. "What's his name?"

"What's your name?" she says.

The reporter laughs. "Jaime Ostos."

"Then I am in love with Jaime Ostos," she says, and closes the door to the sport utility vehicle.

*   *   *

Dos. The following week I'm fighting in the Baena ring, in the Córdoba Province. It is close to my hometown, Hinojosa el Duque, so Eugenio and I don't have far to travel. We wake at first light. Eugenio dresses and makes the coffee and rolls and slices oranges. I yawn and lean on my elbows at the windowsill to watch our neighbor, Victor Liria, dig up potatoes that do not exist out of the earth in his backyard with bare hands.

Victor will hold a clump of dirt in his thick paws and smell it as if it were salted and fried and served hot with tomatoes. Then he will grin, wide, like a madman. There are, of course, no potatoes in his yard, but several dozen lines of lemon trees that are never harvested. I fall asleep listening to the whump of lemons dropping in the night. During the day they rot in the sun, stinking with sweet and sour. The smell carries easily on the breeze from his house to our house. I've gotten used to the smell of rotten lemons. When I travel, it reminds me of home. Eugenio is not as understanding. He'll hear them drop and shake his fist out the window and shout, "Curses to you and your lemons, you madman!"

This morning is like any other morning. Victor holds the imaginary potato in both hands above his head and shakes it at the sky that at this very moment is breaking into a thousand yellows. He cries, "Once again, God has given me great pleasures!" then drops the ball of dirt onto the ground.

I shout, "Victor, got a big one?"

Victor is short, but wearing those brown trousers that only reach mid-calf he looks even shorter. Around his thick arms he wears a loosely assembled boar pelt. Victor likes pretending he's a shepherd. An imaginary flock of ewes follows him everywhere, even to the toilet. Sometimes he gets so fed up with the ewes he curses and spits, and has to slam the door. Then he feels bad about this treatment, and has to make up with each and every one of them.

This can take all week.

For a false shepherd, Victor is very serious-looking. The boar pelt is supported with leather straps that cross his stomach, and underneath the pelt he wears a blue-and-white-striped sailor shirt that he says he got in Irkutsk. We all know that he's never been anywhere, but Victor says he was in a war with Russians and the Russians gave him the shirt and a small crown of flowers when he saved the lives of their village people.

Some days Victor is a soldier. Other days, a shepherd.

Wild Mustang likes Victor immensely.

Victor stands up and squints. His face is heart-shaped and rough, like the backside of good leather, and his eyes perpetually squint, even in our darker, Andalusian winters. Today he holds his hand over his eyes to block the sun. When he sees me, he clasps his hands together. "*Matadora!*" he cries, and runs to my windowsill.

Victor knows more about bullfighting than any man alive. It was not Eugenio who trained Wild Mustang to flick her wrists in a hard left when performing swirling *mariposas,* making the cape look like a butterfly; nor was it Eugenio who sat with her in the lemon trees telling her stories of famous matadors, like José Cándido, who in 1771 jumped over the bull's forehead and was the first to die in the ring; or "Fortuna" Diego Mazquiarán, who in 1928 slaughtered a bull that had escaped from the corrals; or Luis Freg, who was gored fifty-seven times; or "Gafe" Marcial Lalanda, the "Bad Luck Sign" who fought alongside four other matadors on the day they were killed; or Wild Mustang's favorite matador, "Manolete."

Manuel Rodriguez y Sánchez, the highest-paid *torero* for eight years in the 1940s, only ever employed one single maneuver with the bull: a simple *verónica,* or pass of the cape, that beckoned the bull to a ninety-degree angle, which, the newspapers noted, he had mastered with "an elegant, cold perfection."

Victor arrives at the windowsill, breathless. "How big was the *toro bravo?*" he asks. "Half a ton?"

"Bigger," I say.

"A large one," he says, rubbing his palms. "And the kill?"

"Swift," I say. "Clean."

His eyes shine. "And the men," he says. "They love you now?"

"The people love me," I say.

"The people will always love you, *Mi Batata,*" says Victor. My Sweet Potato, he calls me, and puts his rough hand on mine. He looks at me. "You're not happy?"

"I'm fighting today," I say. "At the Baena."

"So soon?" he says.

"We need the money."

Victor leans in, very close. "Tell Eugenio that a famous bullfighter needs her rest," he says.

I shrug.

"Tell Eugenio," he says, "that there is more to life than money."

Victor spits on the ground, then resumes digging. So I turn on the television set to watch the morning episode of *Yolanda!*

Hinojosa el Duque: the apex of modernism. We have female bullfighters. We have television. The only television station we get in this area is

Channel Two, which alternates *El Lobo*, the newssource, and the Spanish-American program out of New York City called *Yolanda!*

This morning there are two Spanish-American women fighting on *Yolanda!* Both of them are wearing suits with silver breastpins in the shapes of dung beetles. The Spanish caption tells me they are sisters. They are extremely fast-talking sisters. I'm impressed; my English is only acceptable, and they spit out the syllables like a machine gun.

Yolanda! herself is named Yolanda Thomas. Yolanda Thomas is an incredibly fit woman with large breasts. She only wears pink suits with padded shoulders. Yolanda Thomas tells us that *Yolanda!* is designed to aid the plight of the Spanish-American people. She interrupts the discussion with extreme gestures, alternating faces of perplexity and disgust. One woman says she's sick and tired of all this crazy American life and misses Spain. The other responds that the Spanish people who live in America must work through the craziness to achieve their goals. Yolanda Thomas agrees with the second woman and then points menacingly at the camera with a long white fingernail and then they go to commercial. *Yolanda!* is the number-one program in Andalusia.

In America, it is number three hundred and fifty-seven.

Sometimes Victor will leave his potato-digging to join me at the window and we will watch together. Victor is very puzzled by *Yolanda!* He doesn't understand what kind of a show it is.

"It's not drama," he says, wringing his hands.

"No," I say.

"It's not comedy," he says, "and it's not news."

"No."

Victor shakes his head. "Then what is it?"

"It's just people talking," I say. "It's American."

This always makes him laugh. But not now. Now Victor's far too absorbed in his potato-collecting to watch television. So I gather together my fighting garments, my Traje de Luces and my white shirt, black tie, green sash, black slippers, and my black *astrakhan*—the two-sided hat—in boxes and long plastic bags and go downstairs to greet my father.

"*Buenos dias,* Eugenio," I say, and peck him on the cheek.

He coughs. "Good morning, Cristina."

My father is sitting at the breakfast table in the middle of his morning ritual of sucking oranges. It takes a half hour. He wakes up early to do it. He slices the oranges in eight pieces and puts an entire slice in his mouth—rind and all—and sucks so hard his normally round cheeks draw inward. He holds them in for a good twenty seconds or so, until his cheekbones begin to show, and his chin and his eyes bulge from their sockets. Once the rind is dry, he picks it out of his mouth with his thumb and middle finger, and drops it into a blue bowl. The rind, rounded. The flesh, emaciated. Eugenio eats the oranges so he can take his anti-anxiety pills. He's always taking the little white pills because he says that I give him anxiety.

We're quiet at the table. I nibble on a roll.

"What's the matter," Eugenio says, his mouth full of orange.

"Nothing, Eugenio," I say.

"Nothing, Eugenio," he says, as if I exhaust him.

He flicks the newspaper.

My father is nearly sixty. His eyebrows arch in points off-center from each other. His cheeks, I imagine, were once full, but age has pulled them and now they sag low around his mouth. His nose presses flat against his face, and rises up thick to a pair of eyes so rounded they barely have visible lids. The eyes are startling; people who don't know him think Eugenio is staring wide-eyed at them. As though glaring.

After breakfast, Eugenio and I pile into the sport utility vehicle with my garments and sword. There's a tense moment when I accidentally slam the door on my Traje de Luces, but after a long inspection and a few harsh words, Eugenio sees that no damage has been done and I'm forgiven.

The Barreras arrive at the Baena. I'm tired today. The sun is too bright. I'm too hot. Eugenio dresses me in the light of a small white room. A plastic cross of Jesus the Savior hangs on the wall above a cluster of red silk flowers. Outside we can hear the people stir, and the smell of the fried pancakes they sell to the spectators on paper plates seeps in through the open window. There is a noticeable absence of a breeze.

Wordlessly, I pull on the tight satin pants. Eugenio designed the whole thing. He chose deep pink, with hand-stitched panels of gold that rise up each leg and divide my waist, just below the breasts. The suit was made ten years ago, after I took my *alternativa* and graduated to matadora. It took six people a month to create and cost Eugenio over a million pesetas, the sum of which Wild Mustang made in three fights, and promptly returned to his bank account. Ten years later, the Traje de Luces still fits like a glove. My body is firm anyway, but wearing the bottoms of the suit, I am invincibly so.

"Victor was pulling potatoes again," I say, because—

"Hmpf," says Eugenio. There's a pin in his mouth. He holds onto it with his mouth, his lips pinched as tight as an asshole. He removes the pin and his pointed brows furrow. "Victor's an idiot. If we're lucky, he'll be dead in two years like the doctors say." He pulls my hair back tightly into a single ponytail and brushes until the tail shines. He tugs the small coat of the Traje de Luces tightly over my shoulders so the gold frames my neck. "Then," he says, "we can buy out his property. Then we won't have to listen to those infernal lemons."

(Eugenio Barrera: humanitarian.)

He sighs, and pulls the coat rough and tight. "There is tension today, Cristina," he says. "You need to be focused."

"Yes, Eugenio," I say.

"You are fighting with Pepin Romero and Antonio Mondejar."

"Yes, Eugenio."

"They have both won the Real Maestranza, and the women love them."

"There are men in the audience too, father."

"Yes, but a man only watches the bullfight to pretend that he is the matador. How can a man pretend to be a matadora?"

Wild Mustang! The children go, Oo! Oo! Oo!

Eugenio pulls the tie close to my neck and exhales loudly from his nose. It's an annoying habit that started only recently. With it he looks and sounds a decade older than he really is. He holds me firm at the shoulders, then reaches down to tie the strings that hang from the pants. These are my *machas*.

"Cristina," he says, "this is serious business. There are reputable men out there that want to roast you on a spit. You are a rarity: not all women are beautiful. Not all women have talent. To them, you are spitting in the face of tradition."

"Talent," I tell him, "isn't something you have, it's something you use."

"Serious business," he repeats, and stands up to give me the once-over. "You look tired," he says. "Take this." In his hand is a small white pill. He places the pill in my hand. "For your nerves," he says.

"I don't have any nerves," I say, and hand back the pill.

He starts to say something but changes his mind. He replaces the pill in a bag he keeps in the small pocket of his vestcoat. Together, we enter the Doma Crucifixione, the small church that has been a part of the Baena for years. Together, the old man and I kneel before the wooden altar of Jesus the Savior. Eugenio's eyes are closed very tight, and he whispers with an impassioned urgency. Eugenio never looks at me while reciting his mantras, but always says them loud enough so I can hear him.

"Please," he begs, "first let the girl fight well. Then let her marry well and live in the country."

But that isn't even my favorite part. My favorite part comes right—

"Above all, let her recognize You and thank You for bringing her to this moment of stardom."

Stardom? Wild Mustang didn't earn her stardom. Once day, when she was just a girl, a stranger passing her by on the street gave her a piece of cloth and said it was a cape. He said if she learned to use the cape a certain way, she would be able to talk to the animals. And since she grew up in the country without a mother, animals were Cristina Barrera's only friends. "How marvelous," she marveled, "to talk to animals." And she flicked the cape right. Clouds swung together, and the birds shut up. The cape flicked left. Whisper: *toro*. And she lay in bed that night holding the cape in her fists, listening across the countryside; listening to the collective sigh of the souls of a thousand bulls.

I sigh. I do the North/South/West/East and silently thank my father's God.

The old man stirs. He snuffles out of penitence for mistakes he never made, and rises. "Now," he growls at his only child, his daughter, "*lucha.*"

I look him in the eye and say, "Of course, Eugenio."

There will always be a fight.

Tres. Eugenio and I walk down a narrow corridor with a cement floor that smells of steel and mold. The Baena's not in the best of shape. The water that runs through the drainage pipes gurgles overhead, and if we're not careful, pellets will drip onto the Traje de Luces. Eugenio has brought along a sliced plastic bag which he places over my head and shoulders until we get to the waiting area, where Pepin Romero and Antonio Mondejar are waiting on the waiting couch sporting their Trajes de Luces. They're watching *Yolanda!* on a small TV that hangs from a ceiling in the corner of the room.

I've seen this one. It's about mothers and prostitutes, and prostitutes that are mothers and the mothers of the prostitutes. There's a lot of crossed arms, loud voices. General hooting.

Pepin has his girlfriend, Lola Baroja, with him. Lola is wearing a traditional white dress with a red rose over the breast, and is quite beautiful. Her black hair falls loose around her shoulders. She's a dancer in the *romeria*, the dance that leads a pilgrimage to the shrine of a saint. She's half-gypsy, and also a dancer in the gypsy caves of the Sacro Monte in Granada, which used to be only for the real gypsies who lived there, but now has been taken over by half-gypsies like her who make a bundle from the tourists as a marketable attraction. I see her and think of one word only: plucked. Lola is extremely tan and extremely fleshy and can't be older than nineteen. She eyes me as though terribly bored by my presence, but behind the boredom is a flicker of curiosity that she is too inexperienced in life to hide.

Pepin and Antonio used to stand up to greet me—like all men in Andalusia rise to greet a woman—but now when they see me, they just go back to watching *Yolanda!* Perhaps I'm too pale, too wan. (I'm a skeleton compared to Lola Baroja.) Perhaps I am just Cristina Barrera. But mostly I think it's because Antonio Mondejar and Pepin Romero are both very handsome men, and I would imagine that if you are handsome, there is nothing more irritating than someone else soaking up what should be your God-given attention.

"Pepin," I nod. "Antonio."

Pepin waves, absently. "You remember Lola," he says.

The fleshy thing bats her lashes, long as handheld fans.

Eugenio pulls me aside and whispers, "They're only competing for your attention." Then he holds my head tight, like a vice, and kisses me dry on both cheeks. He bows to the boys on the couch and departs for the entrance of the ring to watch.

I stare at the matadors. We're all sweaty, and pushing thirty. Pepin has been performing wonderfully. Audiences love him. He invented a move called the *adalia* after his last girlfriend who became pregnant with his baby. Both died in childbirth. They had never married, but Pepin named the move after her, which seemed to suffice for him. The adalia is a swift move, where he slides the cape over the bull's head while holding a posture like a statue, making it look like the cape is more human than he is. Pepin would be the top moneymaking matador if I were not around. About this, I have no doubt.

Antonio is married, has two children, and has not been getting good reviews. During his last fight he stumbled and the bull charged. Antonio, possessed by an irrational fear, jumped over the fence into the *callejon.* Audiences are skeptical of his talent, but enjoy his fights for nothing if not their unpredictability. His wife is not as understanding. Antonio and I have fought together a dozen times before; I have always received top billing.

Now he watches both me and the television, simultaneously. There's a mother on *Yolanda!* with four children who are about to be taken away from her. The caption says she's a prostitute. I'm skeptical of this, because she's largely overweight, wearing nothing but a bra and a miniskirt. Her thighs roll out onto the chair like dough, and she's screaming like a large, wronged bird. I've heard that Americans hire actors to go on television and pretend they have problems in real life.

Quietly, I admire her chaos.

"Whore," seethes Antonio, and dry-spits at the TV. He stands up and stares at me and fluffs his cape, sending a wave of heat rippling in my direction. His Traje de Luces is dark purple with gold beading. "I have never *seen* such a whore."

Antonio looks at Pepin, and then they both look at me.

Lola smiles, and nuzzles her head against Pepin. They murmur at each other. Sweat glistens along the crown of her head like tiny diamonds. Pepin kisses them off one by one and runs his tongue over his lips to taste her salt. Then Pepin and Lola rise and leave the room. Lola walks with her head against Pepin's shoulders and he lowers his hand to her ass. They close the door behind them.

What people won't do, Wild Mustang always marvels, for something as commonplace as sodium.

Antonio parades to the other end of the room to groom himself in front of the long mirror. "They're going to fuck, don't you think?" He looks at me.

I shrug.

"Are you offended?" he says. "Have I offended you?"

Antonio is a large, square presence. He should have been an actor. He picks at his dark hair and runs his tongue across his teeth. He stands up as tall as he can with his feet together, arms swung across his chest as though assuming the first position we take with the bull. His toes are too close together for the proper stance, but I don't say a word. He breathes in deeply through his nostrils. Above us, the Baena roars and then dies down.

"I'm not offended," I say.

Antonio laughs like he didn't hear me. "You behave like a man. Why shouldn't I treat you like a man?" He makes a vulgar gesture with his tongue and two fingers. Staring at him, I'm suddenly curious as his head begins to grow. His chin extends outward. The round of his head rises up like a back. Then his ears point, becoming two sharp horns. The horns grow sideways for a few thick inches, then take a sharp turn north and sprout up toward the ceiling. Antonio is an extremely silly-looking bull. His horns are imbalanced. His eyes, cocked.

The children go, Oo! Oo! Oo!

I look up. The ceiling is threatening to drip condensation from the cold water pipes, just centimeters from the bull's satin jacket. One large drip hangs like a plumb then falls in slow motion, staining a dark crescent onto a flank of the glittering, purple material.

"Shit!" shouts Antonio, a full octave above his normal register.

Pepin returns from the room without Lola. "What happened?" he says.

"My jacket," Antonio cries. He is red-faced, and shakes his fist at the ceiling. "Shit!" he cries again. He stomps his foot.

Pepin ignores him, and goes right for the floor-length mirror. He adjusts his coat, and turns to look at his butt. He changes position, alternately standing on one leg and then the other, trying to get a glimpse of how his butt might look from any angle. He alternates back and forth for a while, then opens a crack in the small window above the mirror. The pancake smell pours in with the sun. It's bright out there, and it's hot. It's hot and bright.

Our *Trajes de Luces* blaze.

Rafael Camino comes in with the papers. He's the manager for the Baena and always likes to gives us a copy of the papers with the announcement of the fight. We all rise and look at the papers. Wild Mustang has once again received top billing. Today Antonio has received third billing, in the smallest print. He will be paid the least out of all of us, even though he will fight the same fight. Usually when Antonio sees that I have received top billing, he throws a fit. He will glare at me and say something like, "This is fucking ridiculous," and slam the paper on the couch. But today there is no fit. Instead, he calmly strides over to the couch, reaches in his bag and opens a Diet Coke. He's careful to hold it away from his suit, though now with the stain it hardly matters.

"It's too hot to fight," Pepin says to Rafael, and shakes his head. His face is bright red. He shifts his tie, uncomfortably. "Look at Cristina. She looks like hell."

I look at Pepin.

Rafael beams. "Wild Mustang," he says, lovingly, like he never gets to say it.

Rafael Camino is a squat man with arms like rolled sausage. He smells of chicken, the only thing he ever eats. His fingernails are stained bright orange from paprika. He approaches me and reaches out to touch the sash on my Traje de Luces with one hand. From the other, he holds a burning cigar. An inch of ash slips to the floor.

"Cristina," he warbles. *"Bella."*

"Get away from her," Pepin says, crossly. "You'll burn the suit."

Rafael backs away but keeps staring at me. His eyes well up. "Cristina," he gushes, "I can't believe that you would come to my little Baena after your incredible win at the Real. I thought you'd be touring around Europe and

America by now. I can't tell you how much it means to me. It's—unthinkable. I don't have enough room for all the spectators!" He clasps his hands together and kisses air.

(In his eyes, he's counting the pesetas.)

"You've ruined my suit," cries Antonio, and rushes up to show him. "Look what your broken ceiling has done to my suit! This place is a dump!" He dry-spits. "I'm never fighting here again!"

Rafael gestures with pinched fingers like an Italian. "It's an old place, Antonio. The bones of your ancestors are buried in the cemetery next door. Why don't you keep yelling and disturb their peaceful slumber?" He turns to me. "Now," he says, "are we ready to fight?"

"What about the *sorteo?*" I say.

We usually draw lots on which bulls we fight, numbers written on cigarette papers.

"There's no time for lots," says Antonio.

"No time," says Rafael.

Pepin fusses with his tie. "It's too hot to fight," he says again. "Dammit."

I'm about to complain to Rafael that this is not professional, not professional at all, but then the trumpet sings for the entrance of the bullfighters.

There's no time.

We line up. Our friends and close family are gathered at the entrance. As we pass, they stare nervously at our frail bodies. Eugenio rests his back against the wall with one foot propped up. He sees me and his brow drops. He holds his hands together, tight. "*Lucha,*" he whispers.

The Baena chants above us. We step forth to the berth of the ring. The crowd sees us, and the noise breaks. The sand of the ring is smooth. Six bulls in the cage to our right swallow thickly.

Cuatro. The bullfight, like any bullfight, begins with a *paseo*, the parade of all of us involved: the matadors, the picadors, the banderillos, the peones, the mulillas. We enter into the ring, the open desert, in three long lines, dressed in our costumes, waving. It's dusty out there, and hot as fire. The sun makes us blink, it's so white. The contestants and bailiffs salute the president, the man who controls the fight. This president is a small man seated in the president's box, in mid-bleachers. He's wearing tan slacks and a cool-looking hat for shade, and sunglasses and a red scarf tied around his neck.

Immediately, I don't recognize this president, which is strange because I have fought here so many times and could recognize one of them on the street if I had to. I look over and see Pepin salute the president in the traditional way and I place my feet together to ready myself. But Antonio, to my left, has not saluted the president properly. Instead of raising only one hand to his brow, he has raised both hands, a gesture that any normal president would find self-serving and offensive. But this president does not seem to mind. He acknowledges Antonio's gesture and even brings his fingers to his mouth and kisses them.

I look at Pepin.

"It's his uncle," Pepin says, and shrugs.

We retreat to our waiting space. The next three stages take place to weaken and tire the bull, and prepare him for killing. In the meantime, I watch my bull. All bulls must be between the ages of four and six, and my bull looks an even five. The horns are distinctly *playero;* the two points lay wide across the top of his head. I don't envy my peon, Manuel, who works very hard to exhaust the bull. Manuel is a boy from the outskirts of Hinojosa el Duque. He's grown up on a farm, working with cattle and horses, and is an excellent peon. Antonio's peon is his cousin, Luis. Luis grew up in the city, is very fat, and uses the cape like he's bored with it. It's a disgrace. Such sloppy performance is an insult to the animal, the spectators and, most importantly, the matador.

"Antonio," I want to say, "look at your peon. He's a mess!" But I never do, because Antonio is a man driven by private inner rages that, like dangerous fish, are disturbed by the slightest tremor in their waters. And at this particular moment, the dangerous fish is not even watching; he's lying with his back against the wall, examining his fingernails.

Then Pepin says, "Cristina." He points at my bull.

We are in the third stage, the *Tercio de Varas*. A circle is drawn in the sand. The picadors ride blinded horses, holding a long lance with a spike at the end. They prick the bull's neck to lower the head for the kill, but always keeping at the circle's distance. The problem is that my bull isn't responding to the taunts of the horse or the picador. He's just standing still, leaning slightly to the right. Then he shifts his weight to the left. It looks like he's waiting in a grocery line. Because of the bull's reluctance to go to the picador, the president gives permission to cross the circle and go to the bull.

The picador gallops past and pricks the neck.

From the unexpected puncture, the bull lifts his head and quickly looks left and right for the picador but cannot seem to find him. The picador goes by again, closer, and gives the bull a second prick, this time deeper.

The bull growls, his head lashing north.

The final time the picador rides by, he rides as close as a picador can ride next to a bull. It's an extremely dangerous maneuver, and I sense that given this bull's unpredictable behavior, it's a bad idea.

Pepin has noticed this too. "Don't do it!" he shouts.

The picador gallops right up to the bull, at which point the bull kneels down and lifts his head sharply skyward, forking the horse straight up the gut. The horse collapses, bucking the picador, who crashes hard on his head.

"*Tumbos!*" shouts the audience.

The bull disengages his horns from the body of the horse and makes for the picador, who rushes over the fence that lines the entire ring, and into the callejon. The bull trots to the place where the picador suffered his fall, pulls his hooves together, sniffs, and continues standing completely, and oddly, still.

Usually if a bull does not appear to want a fight, the president will raise a green flag and the bull will be removed. But this president, Antonio's uncle, is flagless.

Pepin looks at me. "I'm going to tell the president to pull it," he says. He motions for Rafael. They argue about the bull. Pepin accuses Rafael of accepting bulls from poor breeders. Rafael accuses Pepin of snobbish perfection.

"Just back out," Pepin says to me.

But Wild Mustang cannot back out. She will be seen as a coward if she backs out now. Worse, a woman. No: she will own the bull. She will make him fight. She will dazzle him with her elegant, cold *verónicas* until he can't help but bow his head and walk headlong into her sword.

"I'm fighting," I say, and that's the end of it. I look to the president who, at the moment, is enjoying a face-full of pancake. Is there a green flag?

There is not.

So I remove my hat and salute him, asking permission to perform. He waves his hand, absently. I begin matadora-ing. I use a series of passes with my red cape, none of which succeed in bringing the bull closer. I'm hot and constricted in my Traje de Luces. A bead of sweat travels from my neck down to the small of my back in one long ride. I take a deep breath and hold it. I stride closer to the bull. The banderillas hang across his back as though yoked; I hold my cape forth and flick it quickly to the right. Now he sees it, and charges madly. He even froths at the mouth. But once he gets a few meters beyond me, he stops and looks quickly around the perimeter of the Baena, licking his lips.

My bull, my *toro,* can't see beyond a few feet in front of him.

I glance at Antonio, who sees me seeing him, and smirks. No *sorteo?* Somehow Antonio has arranged with his uncle for Wild Mustang to be ridiculed. It's a good one: she could kill this bad bull, she could run up from behind him and slam her sword into his back, but an improper death is worse than no death at all. Lesser violations have killed whole careers of some matadors. For a matadora, they barely even need a reason.

I motion for Rafael, who scuttles into the ring.

"This bull," I say, "is blind."

"That's impossible," he says.

"I'm not going to kill a blind bull," I say.

Rafael puts his hands out. He reeks of sour chicken. "This is your bull. You must kill him. Besides, the fight has already begun. Look at him! He's suffering. It would be less humane to let him live."

"Get me another bull," I say, "or I'm never fighting here again."

Rafael goes to the president. The president gestures angrily toward Rafael and then angrily toward me. The crowd's restless. Even the people not sitting in the sun-side of the stands look hot. I know how they feel: my neck sweats, my toes burn. I'm having trouble breathing. The president decides to remove my bull from the ring while they make their decision. They send in Pepin's bull instead.

Pepin has a good wrangle with his bull. He executes several veronicas and adalias close enough to warrant an *Ole!* from the audience. Soon the bull is charmed. Pepin holds his sword high and thrusts it neatly into the back. The bull rises on his hind legs, cries out in a terrifying song, and then collapses.

The audience thunders appreciatively.

When Antonio's bull is ready, he kisses his hands and bows to the crowd. It doesn't take long to win. This bull, thick with fat, is lulled to the cape like a drunk. So Antonio begins performing all sorts of ridiculous adornos with his spotted Traje de Luces to garner attention from the crowd. First he touches the bull's horn with his finger, then he kisses the bull's forehead, then he does *telefono,* resting his elbow on the bull's forehead with his hands to his head as though speaking on the telephone. There's moderate applause. He gets so carried away that he performs what with a regular bull is the most dangerous adorno there is: he lines himself up in front of the bull and tips his head forward, so the edge of his chin rests on the spike of the horn. He lingers there for a moment, perched on the horn, then rises slowly, as though it were dramatic, as though there was anything *remotely* dangerous about what he'd just done, and drives the sword in. The bull buckles forward, hissing like a deflated balloon.

The president applauds, wildly. But the people always know a cheap performance when they see one. A few flowers are scattered, then Rafael returns with the message: I am to kill the bull that was allotted to me. But if I'm afraid, the president will understand, and I may withdraw.

If I withdraw, I'm a coward. If I fight, it will be an improper fight. I look to Eugenio, standing by the entrance of the ring. He glares at me and slowly slices a finger across his throat.

So I enter the ring. I salute the president with a smile. The people roar with pleasure. They cheer, "Mus-tan-go! Sal-va-je!" They stomp their feet.

My bull reenters the ring. He tears in lopsided. The froth at his mouth has thickened. His eyes look glazed and confused. This bull cannot be charmed. It could turn at any moment. I keep my distance, but examine him as closely as possible. There's a marking on his rear of a circle with another smaller circle inside it:

This is the marking of the Félix de la Corte ranch in Córdoba. It's a small ranch, but dates from 1845, specializing in the Saltillo breed of bull, the foundation stock of most Mexican ranches, which are highly regarded in Spain. These bulls are extremely bright, and extremely dangerous. But the Félix de la Corte ranch also produced the famous Civilón, the bull that was tame as a cow. It's a story Victor told Wild Mustang when she was only eight years old:

"It was the early 1930s," Victor said. "A magical time for the *corrida*."

The small girl sat next to him, listening. Her knees at her chin.

"Civilón was owned by a man named Isidoro Tirado," he continued, "a matador-turned-farmhand. Isidoro observed that Civilón seemed calmer than the other bulls on his ranch. He didn't have the same inner rage. So Isidoro fed him tender branches to eat from horseback. He kept a safe distance until eventually he felt comfortable enough to dismount from the horse and feed him like a regular farm animal. He was so tame, children were allowed in to pet him."

The girl smiled.

"But when Civilón was five years old," he said, "it was decided that his time to fight had come. He was sent into the ring. When the cape danced in front of him, nature took over. Civilón's instincts ignited. He charged, wildly! And then Isidoro was dared to enter the ring and pet the bull, to see if it truly had been domesticated."

"What happened?" said the girl.

"He entered."

"And?"

"Civilón saw his old master and headed right for him."

The girl gasped.

"But instead of attacking," he said, "the bull nuzzled Isidoro's coat, and followed him out of the ring."

"Then what happened?" said the girl.

"Then the audience rose," said Victor, "demanding that the bull be discharged and his life spared. Everyone agreed. It was decided that Civilón would be a stud for future fighting bulls, but would remain at the arena until he had recovered from the fight."

"That's good," said the girl.

"I'm not finished," said Victor. "A few nights later, rebel soldiers entered Barcelona. Desperate and hungry, they went to the ring in search of beef. There was Civilón. He was shot to death, and butchered."

"Civilón!" whispered the girl.

"So you see," said Victor, "there are many different uses for a life."

I move in closer, standing just a few feet in front of the bull. I look at him; at the odd way his feet turn inward. I drop my cape. A murmur floats through the crowd. No one understands why Wild Mustang has dropped the *capa.* From the stands, the spectators block their eyes, but not from the sun: it's the glow of my Traje de Luces.

"Civilón," I whisper.

The bull turns his head, fast.

"No, Cristina," Pepin yells. "It's suicide!"

I look again at my father. He glares back. "*Lucha,*" he whispers. But next to my father, a little further on down the wall, is a short, shadowy figure with cropped trousers. It's Victor. He leans against the wall by the entrance, smoking a cigarette. He sees me seeing him and smiles.

"*Mi Batata,*" he whispers.

I gesture for Manuel to bring me my sword. He hurries back with it. I take the sword and place it on the ground next to the cape.

"Civilón," I say, this time louder.

The bull snorts, disagreeably.

A shout goes out: "Someone rescue the woman!"

There's commotion in the stands. The president doesn't like what he is seeing. The kill is always performed with a sword thrusting through the back of the bull. There are even certain classicists who believe the bullfighter should keep one foot on the ground as the sword is placed. It does not appear that Wild Mustang plans to do either. "This fight will not be counted," the president announces. "This is not skill! This is not talent! She is breaking all the rules."

But Wild Mustang cannot hear him. Capeless, swordless, I drop my hands into fists. "God has given me great pleasures!" I shout, as the bull rushes blindly forward.

I'm well aware of my surroundings:

Antonio has fallen to his knees in shock. He doesn't know it, but this is his last fight and no one will remember him. His wife will leave him. He will die only a dozen years from now, poor and alone, from a messy and uncomfortable digestive disorder. And Pepin? Who stands nearby, ready with his own sword? He doesn't know it, but he's about to become the best matador in the world. He'll step into the shoe like it was his all along, garnishing many accolades from many respected bullfighting officials. He will retire, rich and respected, to a large house with many mirrors from which he can view his butt from any angle. Someplace lovely.

Italy, perhaps.

Then there's Eugenio. Eugenio sees the bull charge and grabs his chest so hard he crushes the anti-anxiety pills into powder. He's having a mild heart attack. Oh, he'll live. Only after today, there will be no more bullfighting. No more money. What will he do? He will continue listening to the lemons. He will continue to be an average man, which will make him angry. Angrier than he's ever been. Because from now on he will have to live with what happened to his daughter.

And there are simply not enough pills in the world for that.

Then there are the rescuers. The brave, brave men. They make their way down from their seats and, in a spectacular display, tumble over themselves to jump over the callejon and be the first one into the ring to save me.

There is no need.

In a flicker, I slide to the ground, reach for my sword with both hands and lie flat on my back. I angle the blade up, holding steady with both hands. When a bullfighter places a sword into the back of the bull, the blade slices not the heart itself, but only an aorta. It is a slower death, designed purely for the drama of the kill. So when this bull gallops over me,

I catch him underneath; the sword slides deep into the center of his heart, and he dies instantly. It is illegal, but the quickest way, with the least pain.

In this way, Wild Mustang dies too.

I suffer only a few cuts and bruises.

EXECUTORS OF
IMPORTANT ENERGIES

by WELLS TOWER

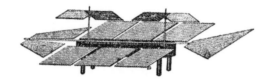

MY SISTER WAS under her house again, at 6:00 a.m., calling me up. "Do you ever think about all the ones who you didn't let them relish you? I wish I could get another crack at all of them, even the nastiest ones."

She said she felt undesirable. I threw a pencil and it made a tiny blue chevron on the wall. I told her plenty of people desired her.

"Well, nobody desires me to my face," she said.

"How is your dear husband, by the way?"

"He's like those microbes in the Amazon that rocket up your urine stream. Touch him in even the littlest way, and *zthhhhht!* He's all over you."

The day was beginning to pale. I'd been looking at the inside of this room for three years and still I couldn't have drawn a picture of it. What a sorry little warren it was—one hundred and fifty square feet—an indescribable waste-shape of crannies and recesses left over when the rest of the building had been sectioned off into more reasonable places to live.

"Anyway," she said. "Even though I *knew* it was bulljive you were coming down tonight, I stayed up till two for the train."

"Don't give me this, Lucy. I very clearly told you Wednesday."

"Sure you did. So I went over to the platform and you weren't there, and then I kept walking around all night. Except for the man in that glass thing on Person Street, I was the only sign of life in this entire town. I was thinking of you and I walked all the way over to the orange light zone, and I sat on some wood until the sun came up, which is now." She was talking about a giant gravel freight lot near our old house, where an orderly forest of vapor lamps went on forever. We spent evenings there as children because the light was alien and monstrously orange and had a way of making you feel good.

"Things are going to turn around for you, Lucy, I know it."

"What's your proof of that?"

"For one thing," I said, "keep doing like you're doing out there, all night long on Person Street, and somebody's going to relish you to a pulp."

The man who invented the sonic pest dispeller is one of our wealthier citizens, which is a sorrow to me. I bought his machine from a catalog, and for a time I took comfort in its honest ruby eye, glimmering from the dark corner by the stove, where a Norway rat patrolled. The rat found comfort in it, too. The vibrations did something pleasing to his brain. He would pick his way through a maze of traps just so he could cozy up to the speaker and sail into a mellow high. I knew the man who came up with this terrible box. He had condominiums in Manhattan, Malibu, and Dubrovnik, and young action on the couch. Yet he was obliging and decent and frustratingly hard to despise. His secretary was a sardonic beauty with an underbite and a hairless golden sacrum. She made her living murmuring into his ear, assuring him of his genius.

I had just received a royalty payment for an item of mine, a novelty silo that melted down your spare plastic grocery bags and poured them into interchangeable molds (golf tee, pocket comb, flatware, etc.). What would you think the take might be, in dollars and cents, for an appliance featured in a nationwide, full-color circular? $430.42. I could hardly bear to show such a melancholy check to the good girls at the bank.

I did not leave for my sister's house on Wednesday. Instead I took the Icepresto to a trade show in Connecticut. I snugged a foam shipping sleeve around it and boarded the morning train. There was an atmosphere of worry on the platform in Westport. The clouds' upholsteries had ruptured badly, and citizens were fleeing what would surely be an awful rain.

I lingered for a moment to arrange my things at a sheltered bench where two men were sitting. One was wearing a T-shirt of the New Mexico license plate.

"*Land of Enchantment,*" said the man's friend. "Now what exactly do they mean by that word 'enchantment'?"

"You don't know 'enchantment'? Now that's ridiculous," the first man said. He sighed. "You know what 'charm' is?"

"Yeah."

"Well, it's about like that."

The second man gazed at the violent green immensity above the trees and power steeples. "*Land of Charm,*" he said.

My booth cost me three hundred dollars, and I stood at it for six hours with very little luck. My Icepresto was essentially a commercial coffee cistern with a copper heat-transfer coil in the base so that freshly brewed tea or coffee came out tepid. Today, I planned to sell the prototype and patent for several tens of thousands and hurry to the Gulf to cram an inexpensive boat and a big-titted stranger into the hollow places in my heart. All day long I had poured cool tea for men from large concerns. They drank of the Icepresto and kept one hand in their pockets so I couldn't snap my card into their palms. At five o' clock, with the hubbub of dealmaking dying out, and the rain falling thickly on this great glass cavern, I slid the Icepresto back into its sleeve.

I went to a party in the Fo'c'sle Lounge. Everyone there was in a good mood already, except for a walleyed little ladybug from the Beatrice Corporation. She was complaining about how somebody had stolen her glass of drink, and I took the opportunity to recommend an item of mine: a Styrofoam cooly-cup fitted with a clap-triggered alarm for just this sort of difficulty. "You might have seen it around," I said. "They've got it all over QVC."

She said it was the stupidest thing she'd ever heard. Three seconds later she was up on a table eating a hot wing and beaming a shit-eating grin at all who cared to glance her way.

Good ideas sell and bad ideas sell. Ask the fellow with the rat beguiler. In Japan they have a method for turning turds back into food.

Tim called to say he and Wendy hadn't heard from me in a while and they were worried. I wouldn't have worried about Tim if I'd seen him eating an ember, and also, who was Wendy?

*   *   *

I woke up in the afternoon, and the rat was sprawled in front of the dispeller, whose merry pomegranate seed still blinked in vain vigilance on and off and on. I rose from the bed for the first time today, and tiptoed toward him with a hammer in my hand. I nearly had him in murdering range when someone opened the door, and the rat flowed back into the wall. It was my good friend Aubrey Brunious. He said, "Gyah!" when he saw me. "I was thinking you were gone."

I put the hammer down. "I was getting ready to be, Aubrey," I said. "But then a couple of ducks slipped out of line on me."

"Yep, yep," he said. He bit off a kernel of pinky nail and worried it with his front teeth. He began making a little wheedling noise.

"What's wrong?" I asked him.

"Ah, jeez, well I'm not going to dress it up for you," he said, galloping his fingers on his clipboard. "There's this thing with the apartment." Aubrey was part-owner of a small-potatoes real-estate firm, and he part-owned my terrible apartment as well. His brother, Wes, was Aubrey's partner, and because of the largeheartedness of the Brunious boys, I had not paid rent here in some time.

"Oh, jeez," Aubrey said. "I was thinking you'd left town, and Wes's got some guys coming in pretty soon to do some things around here."

"When, soon?" I asked. "What kind of things?"

Aubrey pursed his lips.

"A couple of things, tomorrowish, I think."

I looked around at all my stuff spread out everywhere. "Wow, tomorrow. Interesting."

"You know how it is with Wes," he said apologetically. "'Hey, Aubrey, ASAP! ASAP!' Don't sweat it. We'll work something out."

He would have been within his rights to order me off the premises right then, but he was an old friend, and he understood he owed me something for having endured his company when things had not been so fine for him. There are plenty of stories that illustrate what an unpalatable person Aubrey used to be. Here is one example:

He was a sophomore in college when a tiny patch of blemishes sprouted on his cheek, and he somehow thought that these were responsible for every difficulty he'd ever had with the human race. He more or less quit eating, and you never wanted him to come across you during a meal because he'd make you drop everything so that he could sit there and smell your lunch. Yet the problem persisted. He begged dermatologists to punish his skin with a laser, but his acne was so minor that all they would give him was liquid soap. At last Aubrey convinced a psychiatrist that he was going to blow his own head off unless his condition improved. The psychiatrist wrote him a prescription for some drastic curative tablets, known now to cause feeble-mindedness and suicide. The pills cleared up the acne and at the same time turned Aubrey's face into a brittle, cracked disaster, crazed chin to forehead with little crimson wounds. He spent two semesters avoiding well-lit places and lathering himself with so many creams and unguents that he looked as though he was sweating lithium grease.

I remember I was crossing the campus with him one day when a member of the groundskeeping staff, a man I liked, who was moderately stricken with Down's syndrome, made the mistake of asking Aubrey to explain the mystery of his face. Aubrey was gingerly carrying a brand-new lightbulb back to his dormitory room. It took a moment for Aubrey's fury to gear up, but when the man was still not quite a sporting distance down the path, Aubrey turned the lightbulb loose. Aubrey was craven even in a rage and fled for the bushes as soon as the lightbulb left his fingers. It flew more purposefully than you might think. It shattered musically against the man's canvas jacket. He turned around unharmed. Then he peered at his feet and browsed the airy lightbulb flak with the toe of his rubber shoe. He looked at me as though we were sharing a great discovery. "Well, well," he said happily. "How is this for snow?"

There were worse, weirder stunts Aubrey pulled, both on me and near me. For years it nagged at me that I had stayed friendly with him in those ugly days, unlike wiser friends of mine. We were both glad, I think, that he'd been able to pay me back a little bit with a free apartment, even if it was this awkward little belfry.

"Yeah, I don't think anybody can come in here tomorrow," I said. "There are a couple of packages I'm trying to roll out before I split."

"Oh, they can work around you," Aubrey said. "They're Wes's people. Oh, they're awesome. They can do anything."

Tim explained that Wendy had a sister who was wanting to get dated. I said I would date her within an inch of her life, if that's what she was looking for.

Tim said she was free on Friday. Would that work? Frankly it wouldn't. I needed to be gone from here by then. But in recent years the episodes where I'd been allowed to touch a woman had been getting farther and farther apart. This was a pattern that worried me. I had to strain to remember the last time. What I did recall was a lot of talk and hard work and a sunrise beside a stranger who was quaking with loneliness. I reserved a table for Friday at Red Morocco.

Sister Lucy on the phone again, back under her home, down in the hideout, inhaling bongloads. Her husband forbade her habit, with good reason. Under the fevered clarity of reefer, her favorite thing was to savor his inadequacies—the girlish overdrive of his singing voice, his moist, offended silences, his delicate heron-manner in bed. Still, tough luck if he thought Lucy was going to listen to anything he said. Times that I had visited, I'd found it strange to be among them. Whenever he'd leave the house, the second the door shut behind him, she'd go, "Move! Move! Move!" We'd hustle down into the hole, turn very rapidly on, and douse ourselves with Visine and Binaca, which she'd hidden down in the earth. She was like the Navy SEALs when it came to running deceptions on her husband.

"What are you doing?" said Lucy's voice, close in the clay and soft stone.

"Just sitting here breathing."

"You're somehow still not here."

"Yeah. Sorry. Tomorrow for sure."

"Well, I'm fucking hurting."

"I gave you an apology," I said. "I'm doing my best here, Lucy."

"No, I mean my head, my skull is hurting. Big Iranian girl on my volleyball team. Absolute sasquatch. Most ungraceful bitch you've ever seen. Stuck her finger down my eye and touched me on the mind. Seeing double now."

I said I was sorry to hear it.

"Beer helps. Anyway, is all your shit packed up? You're not going to screw me on this, are you? If you flake out out again I'm going to lose it on you in a major-type way."

"I promise, mostly," I said. "In fact, I've got a woman I'm supposed to catch up with. I'm going to see what she has and then get the late train."

It turned midnight, and all up the street security shields rattled down over shop windows.

"You better. This is really sucking down here. Bart and Joanie Duene are still upstairs with Dennis. I know they're popping shit. Hey, did I tell you I saw another armadillo come in here? They are the craziest things. I really, really love 'em. All they care about is digging. They've got these shovelish-type whatchacallit—tallions—and they only dig and dig. At least that's all I've ever seen 'em do."

"Bart and Joanie who, now?"

"Oh, Duene. The *Duenes*—if you asked me for the two biggest rod-ons in the state and I gave you the Duenes, you'd owe me back some change."

First thing in the morning, Wes Brunious was in my face. "Okay, what the fuck is this?" he said. "Aubrey, can you explain what this asshole is still doing in my property?"

In my opinion, Wes was one of those people who more than anything needed somebody to come along and break him down with a piece of steel cable. That kept not happening and every time I saw him he needed it more.

I stood up in my underpants. "All right, Wes, just take a breath. Let's just try and figure out how to the handle this."

"Shut your fucking mouth," Wes said. "Now look, Aubrey, I don't know what the hell you're doing, but I'm trying to run a business here. I don't have time to stand around jawing with some washout friend of yours. Tell him to get his shit and get out."

A handyman appeared, grunting under the burden of a sleek black commode. Then another guy shouldered in with a sawsall and a bucket of joint compound. A third fellow was out in the hall. I couldn't see him, but I could see the end of some long lumber bobbing around through the door.

Aubrey did his old tic, a trembling reverse-yawn, as though he was gnawing at a washboard. "Hey, Wes, come on."

Wes kicked at a box on the floor. Something inside made a chimey fracturing sound. "Okay," I said. "Now you're starting to get me a little mad here. What I want you to do—"

Wes put a big brown finger in my face. "I said for you to shut your mouth. Now, Aubrey, this is on you."

Aubrey was going red as a cranberry. "You get this joker together and get him out of here," Wes said. "However long it takes, it's coming out of your ass. The crew's getting what, a hundred fifty an hour? That's coming out of your end."

Aubrey punched the wall. A wound in the plaster a few feet away coughed out a spray of dust. Wes glanced at Aubrey and chuckled. He checked his watch and gave me fifty minutes. He explained that they were going to attach one of those refuse chutes to the window. Whatever I left was going down it. His mood seemed to lighten when he talked about the chute. Then he nodded at his handyfolk, and they all thundered down the stairs.

Aubrey went over to the sink and poured himself a drink of water.

"Well, that wasn't all that cool," I said.

"He's fine most of the time," Aubrey said. "It just sucks when he gets a bee in his bonnet." He rubbed his thumb and forefinger together and flicked something away. "Do you have anywhere you can go?"

"Sure," I said. "I've got a couple of options, but thanks," even though he hadn't offered anything. He hung around the sink for another moment, trying to work up a goodbye. At last, he just dropped his glass into a shoebox on the counter, nodded at me, and jogged off to find his brother.

I filled my large duffel-pack with clothes, specs, a chef's knife, a photograph of my mother holding a leggy ten-year-old who was unknown to me, and a jar I knew contained at least $200 in small change. I thought of calling Tim to cancel this evening's get-together, but then it registered that I might not get a crack at anything else for quite some time. I jammed the bag into a secret cubby space above the closet where I could come and get it later. There was no room for the Icepresto, so I carried it in my arms.

It was 11:00 a.m., and a cowl of pale clouds was receding over the river. I walked past a vest-pocket park where young people were making a movie. It revolved around a single special effect: a skinny youth with a mail of birdseed glued to his nude chest. Cameras were poised but the pigeons were not cooperating. Too much free seed was falling off of him, and none of the pigeons wanted to bother pecking him on the skin. I walked for three hours north, then three hours south again. The Icepresto was so cold that it turned my palms gray. Frost was growing on the street. I bought hot almonds cloaked in sugar. I peered into a plastic barrel and watched huge green frogs striving on each other in the waning sun. Then I went to Red Morocco. I stashed the Icepresto in the cloakroom and awaited Wendy's sister.

She arrived on time. Wendy's sister must have once been very lovely, but she was still perfectly all right. Strong bones, thick hair, lipstick bleeding into hairline crevasses around her mouth. She was of higher quality than any woman I'd sat down next to in an awfully long time. She made me uneasy. I cannoned her with foolish questions.

She replied:

"Anything? I think I would wish that my psyche were divided into twenty or thirty different, wholly realized egos scattered all across the planet. We would all be distinct, but we'd be able to share a common fund of knowledge and experiences, so that at any time I could slip into another ego totally capably and let someone else take over mine for a while. Either that or shrimp where you didn't have to remove that disgusting poo-vein."

"Anywhere but Maryland."

"I don't think I've seen that channel, though it sounds like quite an achievement." She continued: "Interestingly," she said, "it was an uncle of mine who designed the Lippes Loop, the I.U.D. He's a fairly famous man."

I mentioned an idea I'd been thinking of, and immediately wished I hadn't. It was not one of my better ones: a broad-coverage prophylactic, thigh to belly button. You applied it like a spray-on bedliner for a pickup truck.

She listened patiently. "With an aerosol can? Actually, I try to not to have much to do with aluminum—you know, Alzheimer's."

"Do you want to hear a funny story?" I told her about my grandfather, the last time I saw him. He lived in Florida and he'd been married to my grandmother for sixty-five years. I didn't know what his aluminum appetites had been, but when he got old, Alzheimer's struck him suddenly, and soon a day came when he didn't recognize his wife. To him, she was just a strange lady who'd shown up on his property. He kept calling the police to come and take her to jail. My sister had sent me down there to check on him. He'd looked fine to me. "You look all right," I said.

"I am all right," he said. "Fine in every way, except the doctor says I eat too much calabash. Also, there's a crazy woman who's moved herself in here with me."

"I heard about that," I said.

"Yes, well, can I tell you something in the strictest confidence?" he said.

"Sure," I said.

"I've been thinking this one over," he said, his voice full of fever, "and I believe I'll try and fuck her."

Wendy's sister's face assumed the puzzled, faintly terrified look of someone anticipating a sneeze. She said, "Oh. Oh, no."

We sat in silence for a while. "Tim says you have a book coming out," I said. "Tell me the name so I can look for it. I'm a very big reader."

Wendy's sister said: "Oh, that? It's embarrassing. Okay, well I called it *Now You're Talking: Toward a Pedagogic Praxis of Dialogue-Constitutive Universals*, if that gives you any idea."

"Sure, sure." Then I said, "You see, the thing about my work—as I see it, the human appetite for convenience is a force of nature, a massive, tectonic power. Our longings, our wants—they shape the world to fit their own exigencies. People who do what I do, we're the executors of important energies, the energies of human desire."

I kept filling up my wine glass, hoping that if I drank enough, I might find a way to shut up. If she noticed, she didn't say. She was eager, as I was, to get us to a point where we could start behaving like animals with each other.

Together we labored to steer the conversation toward a topic with some erotic promise. I asked her to relate a memory from summer camp, something her parents never knew. She grew melancholy and talked about a gorge in New Hampshire with rocks as smooth as water. Walking barefoot along the creek she'd come across a livid trail of fresh blood and followed it across a beach of white stones to a thicket of dark junipers, into which she didn't want to go.

I put my hand on hers, which seemed to make us both unhappy.

We stood on the pitted sidewalk and shivered in the unyielding December wind. We lost the flickering instant where we might have grabbed each other by the face, and instead watched a child working his fingers up the change slot of a newspaper machine. No cordial kiss, just a crisp goodbye and the morbid clasping of cool hands. When she left, I went back inside, and retrieved my machine.

I rummaged in my pocket, where I found a goofball that had once belonged to my sister. I ate it, and then my brain began to marble up with fat white veins of optimism. I headed east and then west. I stopped into a number of establishments, and I must have cut a suspicious figure with the Icepresto because people looked at me and drew into themselves, as though it would be bad if I found out anything about them.

I stopped for an orange hand pulsing at a crosswalk. I waited beside a man with a dirty bag on his back and a less dirty bag on his front. Along came a squad of guys in leather car coats and skinfade haircuts, hooking their thumbs in their pockets and grinning at one another with asymmetrical longshoremen's grins. Their broad, braying camaraderie was exciting for me to hear. They moved in close around us, giving off the eye-watering store-bought whang of north New Jersey malehood. "Let me ask you a question," one of them said to me. "Does he suck your dick, or do you suck his?"

"They think we're friends," I said to the man beside me.

"You people better vaporize," he said. "Unless you want to see a nigger go nuclear."

Perhaps something exciting would have taken place, but police cars came rolling down the boulevard at one mile an hour, escorting a sirenlight parade of oversized loads. The men sauntered off, sneering and bawling loud New Jersey swears as they bumped along the street.

Now it was just the man and me, the two of us together. "Jack, you are looking out of shape," he said. "And what is that, a tin watermelon?"

"This is part of my business," I said.

"Yeah, cool," he said. "Well, let me tell you this. I'm the victim of some unforeseen hassles at the moment. I'm not proud to tell you that I will be staying on the street tonight, but those are the facts of the situation. What I'm wanting right now is maybe fifteen or twenty dollars for transportation and other expenses, if you could help me out."

I gave him four quarters from my pocket, which lingered in his palm for half a second before they vanished into his jacket. "That's it," I said. "That's a hundred percent of my resources."

"As long as it spends," he said. "I bless you for it, because to look at you, I can tell you don't have too much to spare. You seem to me like Li'l Abner. I mean, look at me. Talking 'bout Girbaud, Karl Kani, Gucci, Dick-Knee. You see, no matter the condition of my circumstances, I always present myself with respectable style."

I said, "You've got something on your chin, a snot-booger or some filth, it looks like."

He wiped his chin with his fingers. "C'mon, now, be nice," he said. He reached out with his wiping hand, and I shook it.

"All right," I said. "Kenneth is my name," I told him, although this was a lie.

I asked what I should call him, and I heard him say, "Jarmoos."

Jar*what?* I wanted to try saying the word but I wasn't sure what would happen if I did.

Two human greyhounds in immaculate white jackets stepped from a restaurant door, hatchet heads swiveling in their fur collars, estimating the chill. The man went and spoke to them and they gave him eighty cents to make him leave.

"Don't cross your eyes at me," he said to me. "Just because I know a few hustles, that doesn't affect my value as a human being. You are in the presence of an artist, a musician. I blew horn for Kenny Loggins on a European tour. I blessed his outfit with very beautiful backing vocals. I know the private number of his home telephone. Call him up and he'll tell you how it was."

He mimed a flurry of saxophone riffs and his fingerings looked fairly professional.

He said he lived a ways away, but he was visiting here on business. "I'm here to get my masters from Aristedes. You know this man? He's young, but he gets respect as a producer, so I shared some compositions with him. But at this point in time, it's become necessary for me to terminate our relationship. He sold three hooks for me, but he's delinquent on my dividends, which puts me in a bad understanding of his character. We are going to get into a problem about all this. I'm an artist, and I don't hurt people, but I'm afraid when I find this Aristedes, I will whip his ass until the Lord tells me to lay off of him."

"I understand," I said. I offered to buy us something at a bodega. I got a thing of gin and a beer and he got a bottle of liquid yogurt that cost four dollars. We sat on a narrow lip of concrete below a row of iron palings. He sipped the yogurt and sighed. Then he began to talk about his music. He said he'd written a lot of songs, but he had one in his head right now that was making him miserable. He didn't know the words or the notes, but he knew the shape of it, he said, and the way it made him feel. "I been trying to creep up on it all week, but the vision is so strong that it always whups my ass." He pointed at his temple. "I always got a war going on up here. That's just how it is in the mind of a genius."

I told him what I did, and he immediately interrupted me with an idea he'd been working on.

His idea, he said, was that a cell in the human body was like a circuit in an electrical matrix. He said this meant that people could actually withstand electrical shocks of infinitely high voltages. If you modulated the shocks correctly, the electricity would let you live forever, he said, and enable all sorts of extraordinary new organ transplants, even brains or entire living hides.

"But if nobody dies," I said, "the world is going to be completely clogged with people."

He said, "No, it won't, because human beings are still gonna be killing each other and whatnot."

"But I thought that with the electricity and the organs you could you could cure every injury known to man."

"Yeah, but look at it like this," he said. "All that modulation and such ain't gonna do nothing for you when somebody hits a lick with a durn machete and chops your head off."

"Why is somebody going to chop my head off?"

He said, "Because in this age I'm talking about, they are really gonna want to *kill* you, man!"

Jarmoos sucked the last of his yogurt into his mouth with a brusque mucosal clatter. He shook my hand and said he was going his own way, out to Queens to settle his score.

"Look," I told the man. "I'm going to help you out, but I don't want you to kill me. You can come over to my house. The heat's good. They crank the boiler. We could have a conversation. I wouldn't mind doing that, but if you think you might want to make it or rip off my things, just tell me up front. That's what that dollar was for, and that drink I got you, the truth."

He shut one eye and looked at me. "All right, now you starting to vex me. Why am I gonna try do some stuff to you? How do I know what type of shit you might be wanting to do to me?"

I said he didn't, and yet he came along.

The air in my room had a high clean reek of fresh solvent and spackle. I mashed a brand-new rheostat and hidden halide lamps threw cold blue light into the room. The Bruniouses had made a new apartment here, sumptuous and germ-resistant: white lacquer cabinets; beige granite counters; a hard milky polymer had been sprayed over the ruined wooden floors and was perfectly slick and dry. Everything I owned had gone down the refuse tube, which yawned in the window and bellowed traffic sounds and voices from the street.

Jarmoos sat and leaned against the wall. The workmen had left some saws and things. Jarmoos rummaged in a bucket and found a nail puller. He slicked his thumb along its pudgy cleft and grinned. "Know what this reminds me of?"

A flurry of rat's nails whispered in the new ceiling tin and then fell silent.

"I used to have a wife who I loved deeply with my soul. Everything about it was the way it was supposed to be, except one thing."

"Hm?"

"Man, there was something hectic with her rig. I was allergic to it, and that got me mixing with other girls. Bless her, she went and took it to a friend of mine who was better built to hack it, I suppose."

A woman's screaming blared up through the tube. On Fridays, they had "faggot bingo" two blocks up the avenue. Afterward, it was a regular thing for the lesbians to stop by and use the west wall of my building to beat each other up against. They broke each other's hearts on schedule, always in the same indigo half-hour of the morning.

Jarmoos dozed under the bright light. The soft tissues in his throat bleated faintly. His hands lay in his lap, forefingers hooked together. This was something pretty good. How long had it been since this man had been between four walls? You could see from the asphalt texture of his cheeks and the tall, sun-nourished moles around his eyes that he'd spent a lot of uncomfortable time out of doors. But no alleyways or steam grates for him tonight, no sir. I got a good feeling in my chest—a painful feeling, actually, as though a sea urchin was swelling there. I felt suddenly fierce with it, and let me tell you this: anything I owned, I would have given it to that man right then. Was this not something rare? Hadn't we stolen something back from this uncharitable town tonight? Two good people coming together with no secret greeds or intrigues in either of our minds—that was a triumph. A *minor* triumph, one that no one would remember a week from now, but at this spot, for these brief hours, a tiny human victory was taking hold. I could see that Jarmoos knew this as I did. The corners of his broken lips were hoisted in a dozy smile, and I was overcome with the urge to give him something valuable. Instead, I reached over and touched his shoulder. His eyes snapped open. "*Watch your business!*" he yelled. I had made a mistake.

It was late, and I did not feel well. I went to sleep, and I woke up a minute or an hour later to the sound of singing. It was Jarmoos going into "How She Boogalooed It," but at a third the tempo. He hummed an overture, and even that hum was good, trembling with a kind of ethnic insouciance, spiralling around the homely old melody. He got into the words, and it filled up whole room. You could hear an entire crowd of people singing in his one voice—a husky, howling tenor up front, a brassy feminine volume chiming in the chorus, and a gang of weary men who grumbled in the gaps between the phrases. Music this good had never happened so close to me before. I opened my eyes and he stopped.

"No, man, please keep going."

"I'm gonna need about three dollars," he said. "This is how I make my living."

I threw up into the new toilet. When I came out of the little cupboard where the bathroom was, he was standing in the middle of the room, watching me.

I slept again. When I stirred, he was close, staring at my face.

"You still breathing?" he said. "You starting to worry me, man. You need to sleep more careful. Roll over on your side."

That didn't sound too smart to me. "I'm going to stay like this," I said. "Why don't you go over there and lay down."

"Nah," he said. "I already did my resting. But I'm not trying to disturb you, man. I'm just gonna sit here and consider some lyrics, turn some things over in my mind."

When I heard him head for the john, I grabbed my bag from the cubbyhole. I laid my head down on it, but first I got the chef's knife out and held it in my fist.

When Jarmoos came back out, I was straight with him. "So I'm hitting the hay. I'm sleeping on everything I want, but if you want to take those tools or whatever, I don't care."

He started to laugh. "Kenneth. *Ken-nay.* Right now, I'm reminded of a song written by a colleague of mine called 'Killing Me Softly,' because you are hurting me with this."

"I know. I was just saying. Also—" I waved the knife at him. "—I've got this, just in case you're waiting to rob me or do whatever. I don't mean anything by it, but just to let you know."

I started nodding off. Then I felt the toe of his shoe nudging my ribs. "Open your eyes, motherfucker," he said. He was standing over me with a huge bulge of money in his hand, a five-dollar bill on top. He held the money so tightly his hand shook. He seemed to wish there was a way of killing me with it. "You see this? This is two hundred and seventy dollars, you ignorant piece of shit."

"What am I supposed to do about it?" I asked him.

"Respect it," he said, and the door clicked shut behind him.

I slept poorly. All night long a sharp splinter of streetlamp light was sticking straight into my eye.

When the buzzer rang, it was dawn, and the carpentry dust floating in the room was turning blue. I was instantly afraid. The buzzer bleated in steady bursts and got me off the floor. I went to the box and pressed listen. I heard the gruff gray static of the street and the warning song of a reversing truck.

"Kenneth!" a voice said. "It's Craig."

"Who?"

"Fuckin' *Craig,* man, from last night. Buzz me in. My gear's all up in there."

The man called Craig was looking rough today. The whites of his eyes were so yolky and pebbled up with broken capillaries it seemed as though his eyelids would make a scraping sound going over them. On the side of his neck was an inch-long gash where his ear met his cheek. A dark varnish of blood had dried on his neck, but he was in a sprightly mood. He hoisted his bags. "All right, my man," he said. "I am square with Aristedes, and today I'm on the move," he said. He claimed to have a car, and he said he was going to drive it immediately to Dinwiddie, Virginia, a town whose name I was happy to hear, and which was not so far from where I needed to be. I thought of my sister, down in the dirt, and of the Bruniouses advancing. I asked Craig, "What would you think of helping me out with a lift?"

"That'd be a big inconvenience to me," he said. "I have some things to think about, and I couldn't have you disturbing me with a lot of extra chatter. But what kind of cash have you got on you?"

The car he had was a brand-new white Mercedes with deep leather seats, but when I tried rolling up my window, a crumbling horizon of broken glass rose in the pane. Outside, the gray winter was viciously underway. I said, "I'm going to freeze to death riding like this."

The mouth of the tunnel gaped in front of us. Craig touched his ear, put his finger to his tongue, and told me, "This is how we roll."

AN INVESTIGATION INTO
XINJIANG'S GROWING SWARM OF
GREAT GERBILS

which may or may not be
LOCKED IN A DEATH-STRUGGLE
with the
GOLDEN EAGLE
with important parallels and/or implications regarding

KOALA BEARS	CANE TOADS
THE PIED PIPER	BLACK DEATH
SPONGMONKEYS	TEXT-MESSAGING

by JOSHUAH BEARMAN

IT WAS EARLY last spring when people started noticing. There was a late thaw, ice still on the ground, and already a lot of gerbils—numerous, fat, and healthy-looking. Then came heavy rains, and the seasonal pastures around the edge of the Junggar Pendi desert bloomed with taller and greener grass than usual. These were the makings of a really bad gerbil year. By early summer, it was. Changji, Tacheng, the Altay foothills—half of Xinjiang province was overrun by swarms of oversized gerbils.

There are now so many—at least a billion by some estimates—that they have affected around five million hectares, or an area the size of Costa Rica. They've eaten the grass, attacked crops, killed trees by tunneling through the root systems, and even undermined roads and railways. This is because gerbils are fossorial, meaning they dig a lot, excavating as many as two thousand holes per acre. And these gerbils are so big—about a foot long, sixteen inches with the tail—that their extensive burrows weaken the earth, making it unsuitable for agriculture or grazing, and even dangerous, because when the nomadic herders who live in the area come through with their goats and camels and wild asses, they and their livestock can fall through the ground into the gerbil-warren sinkholes below.

The Chinese government, always quiet on catastrophe, revealed the problem to the world only after it was beyond control. And what little information that did circulate about the gerbils was contained in only a very few short reports in the BBC World Service, Reuters, and the *China Daily*, an English-language Chinese government newspaper. By then, vast areas had been destroyed entirely, and the focus shifted to trying to save what grasslands they could in the region. It was turning out to be, in the words of Xiong Ling, a local government official quoted in all the news items, "the worst rodent disaster since 1993."

Xiong's authority rests on her employment with an office called the Regional Headquarters for Controlling Locusts and Rodents. They're the local entity responsible for addressing the gerbil problem with force. They laid out poison, gassed the burrows like trenches at the Somme, and offered bounties to the locals to kill as many gerbils as possible. The gerbils continued to thrive. When the traditional arsenal failed, the government turned to a new weapon. They decided to breed a massive convocation of eagles to fight the gerbils the way nature intended—from the skies.

The Chinese word for gerbil is *sha shu.* This literally means "desert mouse." I turned to *Walker's Mammals of the World, Volume II* to make sure the news reports weren't conveying some kind of mistranslation. They weren't: *Rhombomys opimus* is the beast in question, and he is indeed a gerbil, the Great Gerbil of Central Asia by his full familiar name—the largest member of the many gerbil genera, and monotypic, meaning he's somewhat unique in evolutionary terms as the only species within his genus.

The great gerbil inhabits the sandy and clay desert steppes areas throughout northwestern China, Afghanistan, Pakistan, and the former

Soviet Republics of Central Asia, such as Kyrgyzstan, Uzbekistan, Tajikistan, and gigantic Kazakhstan. This is the kind of environment favored by all gerbils: arid, desert areas where the soil is loose enough to burrow easily and they won't get washed out by too much rain. For this existence, gerbils are well equipped with bodies that require little water and do not sweat, so they reabsorb their few liquids. They also have strong hind haunches that allow them to cover large distances, and jump quickly from shrub to shrub in a harsh habitat full of predators. Many sources on gerbil physiology describe how gerbils produce infrequent, small amounts of thick urine, and that their droppings are always bone-dry. But only one—Helga Fritzsche's *Hamsters, Golden Hamsters, Dwarf Hamsters, Gerbils: A Complete Pet Owner's Manual*—also points out that when gerbils excrete their dusty pellets and rare urine concentrate, they do so entirely without sound.

Trying to find out the gerbil status in Xinjiang, I called China. A rough business when you speak no Chinese. Via a dogged and expensive effort of extreme international telephony, I did make it as far as Urumqi (pronounced Oo-ROOM-chi), the capital of Xinjiang, where the trail went dead. Noted: the number for information in China is 114, the exact opposite of our number for information. Also noted: whenever I called information, the operator-people on the other end just kept asking for my number. Like so (from a partial transcript of one such call):

Urumqi 114: [Chinese greeting!]

Me: Yes, hi, I'm terribly sorry—do you speak English?

Urumqi 114: Please.

[Silence, as operator fetches someone. The full sound of the crowded room behind Urumqi's information hotline comes through clearly. They discuss at length who should speak with me.]

Urumqi 114: Yes?

Me: Hi. I am looking for an office.

Urumqi 114: …

Me: A phone number for an office.

Urumqi 114: …

Me: The Regional Headquarters for Controlling Locusts and Rodents—

Urumqi 114: Yes?

Me: —for Xinjiang?

Urumqi 114: …

Me: Is this information?

Urumqi 114: Information! Yes!

Me: Yes. Telephone for Regional Office—

Urumqi 114: Region?

Me: Yes. The Region Office for Controlling—um, okay, how about this: Foreign Liaison Office.

(I was asking for the Foreign Liaison Office not because I knew what it was, but because that's what was recommended to me by one Mr. Gao, National News Editor of the *China Daily*. I reached him at his office in Beijing. He spoke English and was the reason I made it as far as Urumqi at all. He himself did not have any updates about the gerbils, or even know what I was talking about at first. "Remember?" I said. "Over the summer—the horde of gerbils eating the interior of China?" "Oh yes, yes, I do recall," he said. "And they were breeding eagles. I wonder what happened.")

Urumqi 114: Number please?

Me: Yes, I was—yes, I need a telephone number. For the—

Urumqi 114: Number?

Me: Yes. A number, that's right.

Urumqi 114: Please—take number?

Me: My number? I'm in Los Angeles.

Urumqi 114: Yes, number please.

Me: What, like, my phone number here?

Urumqi 114: Please.

Me: Okay, I guess. It's 626…

Urumqi 114: 6… 2… 6…

Through similar interactions, at least half a dozen people in Xinjiang now have my cell-phone number, including someone who answered at 011-86-991-2842262, which I think may have been some kind of animal husbandry facility. It later occurred to me that perhaps one or more of these people was taking a message, maybe even for Xiong Ling.

There are many types of gerbils, including:

The Baluchistan Pygmy Gerbil (*Gerbillus nanus*), from northern Afghanistan;

The Duprasi (*Pachyuromys durpasis*), with a fatter tail and native to northern Africa;

The Charming Dipodil (*Gerbillus amoenus*), a cute little fucker ranging in the same area;

Wagner's Dipodil (*Gerbillus dasyurus*), from the salty Sinai, land of Moses' crossing;

Shaw's Jird (*Meriones shawi*), medium-sized, and smart enough, say breeders, to respond by name; and

The Mongolian Gerbil (*Meriones unguiculatus*), which is the relatively small, variably colored gerbil known from pet stores and the glass-enclosed wood-chip habitat of the American household.

Size comparison: Mongolian gerbil (left) vs. great gerbil (right)

In the long history of pet domestication, gerbils are a recent entry. The first gerbils ever to leave Central Asia were a small group of "yellow rats" sent by an adventuring man of the cloth named Armand David to the Musée d'Histoire Naturelle in Paris in 1866. That's when the Mongolian gerbil entered into modern taxonomy. In 1935, about twenty breeding pairs imported from northern China into Japan became the ancestors of all pet gerbils living today. In 1954, gerbils arrived in the United States, and ten years later they made it to the United Kingdom and beyond.

Such is the progression of what has become an elaborate realm of wild gerbil enthusiasm. For the hundreds of thousands of devoted aficionados, there are gerbil breeders, gerbil associations, gerbil magazines, gerbil newsletters, gerbil product catalogs, and an international circuit of gerbil competitions. The American Gerbil Society leads the way, and their judging standards have also been adopted by some of their "sister societies, including but not limited to, the National Gerbil Society and the Swedish Gerbil Association." According to their standards, championship gerbils have well-proportioned tail and tuft, and eyes that are bright, widely set, large but not bulging. Their ears shall be fairly small, not too rounded, and carried erect. In temperament, they will be mellow; "hard nipping" results in immediate disqualification. But the real magic arises from the quality and color of the coat. Breeders[1] have thoroughly documented the genetics of fur shading, and they forever try to manipulate the gerbils' six loci of color in just the right combination to get an animal that meets the ideal of gerbil aesthetics:

---

[1] The dirty secret of the gerbil world, if there is one, is that the constant breeding and the narrow genetic origins of today's pet gerbil population means that they can be physically troubled animals. The most common problem is that they are prone to seizures, which are euphemistically referred to as "fits." Some gerbil enthusiasts like to claim that the seizures, rather than evidence of genetic abnormality, are actually a clever evolutionary mechanism that in the wild helps gerbils to "confuse predators."

distinctive markings with a striking contrast of colors—but with gradual shading, "pleasantly blended away from all points, except the ears... and darker towards the ends of the animal." Nowhere, according to the AGS, should a gerbil's color change suddenly.

Xinjiang is a place of lonely scale. It is big, mostly deserts and mountains. I used to read about it as a kid in Victorian travelogues like *Visits to High Tartary* and old history books that referred to the region as Chinese Turkistan or the Central Asian Oases. What they called oases were the stops along the Silk Road, the path Marco Polo took to visit Kublai Khan, and the path of passage-making caravans before and since. I remember particularly lik-

ing the accounts of Turfan, a rainless outpost below sea level that remains important to this day and draws its fresh drinking water from a series of deep wells called *karez* that all connect to a vast underground river network 150 feet below the desert floor.

More than half the area is basically empty. The Tarim Basin, or Taklimakan Depression, a desolate tract bigger than the Gobi, is one of the world's most severe environments. Only a few isolated oases support small populations there. Most of the people—a nomadic, Muslim, linguistically Turkic people called Uyghurs[2]—live to the north, on the other side of the T'ien Shan, or Heavenly Mountains, whose major peaks rise higher than twenty thousand feet and always bear snowcaps. The forested, northern slopes of the T'ien Shan give way to another desert depression, smaller and milder, called the Junggar. It's the foothills and edges of the Junggar, enclosed by a belt of true pasture naturally watered by snowmelt from the T'ien Shan and the Altay mountains on other side, that support the traditional herding economy of the Uyghurs.

---

[2] There is also a smaller population of Kazakhs and other Turkmen groups. But the region has long been the object of Chinese colonialism. Although Xinjiang is also officially called the Uyghur Autonomous Region, it is a titular autonomy only, and the central government has been for decades systematically settling ethnic Han in the area to tip the demographic scale toward the Chinese. Today, there are almost as many Chinese as Uyghurs.

As well as the traditional hoarding economy of the great gerbil. To ensure survival, gerbils cooperate. Unlike most rodents, who are solitary roamers—a trait that has helped solidify the poor reputation rodents have developed over time, typified by Templeton the selfish rat in *Charlotte's Web*—all gerbils, including the great gerbil, are extremely social animals, with complicated underground societies.

And the Junggar is a natural setting for gerbil society to flourish: a predominantly dry area of easy burrowing, but with enough water from elsewhere to provide a stable food supply. The gerbils lie low in the winter, and get most active in the spring when there is a bounty of fresh grass and other vegetation to exploit. Below ground, they manage their extended families, which can range in size, sometimes including a male with several females or a kinship of related pairs. Females are called sows; males are boars. And everyone cares equally for the pups, which come into the world as furless, blind, deaf, little nubs that weigh a fraction of an ounce. In high times, gerbil families can be large, up to fifty or sixty animals—true communal enterprise on the rodent scale of sociability. Together, they all live in a complex array of tunnels, which include multiple nests and subterranean pantries for storing all the food collected in the spring.[3] It's that group-pantry system that allows the gerbil to beat the mean season—a blistering long summer, during which they emerge only at dusk or dawn and only when necessary. This is how the gerbils have made their way for a long time in the Junggar depression, and when the nomads showed up a few millennia ago, they learned to survive similarly, by relying on the terrain and rain runoff and by storing calories, in their case in the form of livestock.

The golden eagle of the steppes is a formidable bird. Central Asia is still mostly wilderness and there are a host of marauders that may hunt the great gerbil—wolves, lynxes, polecats, weasels, snakes and huge monitor lizards— but the golden eagle is the champion predator. And the most handsome, according to ornithologists, who affectionately call their subjects "goldies."

---

[3] When it comes time, young males will leave home and start digging a new burrow elsewhere. Or re-inhabit an empty one. Because of the flux of the gerbil population, there are times, like now, when hordes of venturing juveniles have to strike out and dig their own burrows; and then there are easier times of cheap real estate, with plenty of empty burrows ready for turnkey living. Carbon-14 dating suggests that some burrow compounds have been in use for thousands of years.

The golden eagle's wings can span up to 1.8 meters, or five feet. They get their name from the fair hue of their napes. Males and females are hard to tell apart, but—and this seems a measure in my mind of a badass species—the females are usually bigger.

Golden eagles usually attack prey from upwind. The speed of their descent is often compared (with some exaggeration) to lightning. But this I do remember from a report in third grade: the peregrine falcon is the fastest animal on earth, with a vertical dive approaching two hundred miles per hour. Cold jacking rodents with a quickness! Golden eagles are slower, but still fast; the time between eagle-eye recognition,

The golden eagle

swoop, and gerbil-in-talons is usually a matter of seconds. They have, in fact, several methods of airborne hunt, each of which have names, such as the "high soar with glide attack," "glide attack with tail chase," and "low flight with sustained grip attack." Each tactic targets a different type of prey. The preferred method for surprising colonial prey, like the great gerbil, is called the "contour flight with a short glide attack."

According to Fritzsche's *Pet Owner's Manual,* Mongolian gerbil pairs live in life-long matrimony. Like swans. Don't own just a single gerbil, she says, unless you want that gerbil to be very sad. And if you do have a gerbil couple and one dies, be careful not to let the other plunge into depression. You can avoid this by "showing great concern for the survivor. [You] must not only feed her but also stroke her and give her companionship and frequent excursions outside the cage. Otherwise, she will languish, and grow fat and apathetic."

Gerbils are not hamsters!

As any gerbil fancier will tell you, gerbils are way better than hamsters because gerbils are intelligent, happy creatures who enjoy life, whereas hamsters are boring misanthropes. But another central dogma among gerbil fanciers is that gerbils' love for each other is matched only by their love for people. Hamsters don't need one another, and they don't need you. But gerbils specifically enjoy human interaction. And, they say, gerbils know and care for their human captors, who in turn can tell when their gerbils are happy because gerbils like to wink at their people friends.

So strong is the perceived bond between people and the Mongolian gerbil that the American Gerbil Society maintains an Internet memorial called

Prairie dog w/ reporter, Los Angeles Zoo

Gerbil Heaven, where countless mourners have shared tales of loss about their beloved gerbils, who, as the memorial says, "have passed over the 'Rainbow Bridge.'" That includes: Leaper; Peanut; Final Fantasy; and Sugar Cookie, who only weeks before her age caught up with her had won the Outstanding Senior Award in the Self Class of the 2003 AGS Virtual Gerbil Show. Sugar Cookie's epitaph: SLEEP TIGHT LITTLE ONE!

"I never saw one of my prairie dogs wink at me," said Mike D.,[4] the curator of the Los Angeles Zoo. There are two important institutions of rodentia in Los Angeles, the Museum of Natural History and the prairie-dog exhibit at the Los Angeles Zoo. The main attraction of the prairie-dog exhibit is that you can go underneath the prairie dogs' terrain and then surface in these plastic bubbles that allow you to observe the little guys at their own vantage.

For a zoo curator, Mike D. didn't seem that interested in animals. "That creature of yours sure is a weird one," he said when I met him at the gate. "I looked him up in the book." Mike started pronouncing the taxonomical name and after stumbling on the specific epithet *opimus*, he shrugged, laughed, and trailed off with, "Oh, you know, some Latin deal."

Mike also suggested that the great gerbil might be "what's in those Quizno's commercials." For the uninitiated, Quizno's is a sandwich chain that markets itself as the down-home version of Subway, the main feature of their down-hominess being that they toast their buns. Quizno's recently launched an ad campaign in which a duo of curious little furry things with human eyes and mouths sing like Daniel Johnston about how the Mesquite Chicken and Bacon Sub is "like a toasty tasty heaven" and creates "big joy in our hearts."

---

[4] This is how he introduced himself.

"Hell, I was watching TV with my wife and those things came on, and I said, 'What the hell is that?' Hamsters? Or a couple of albino tarsiers? Could be it's your gerbils!"[5] Mike was only casually interested in the actual gerbils in Xinjiang, about which he said, "You'd figure over there, if they got too many gerbils, they'd just BBQ 'em,"—adding with a chuckle— "I don't call that a disaster; I call that a bonanza!"

Mike did confirm that prairie dogs are rodents too, and share with the great gerbil the atypical habit of living in large groups. Back when there was much more prairie, the prairie-dog colonies, or "towns" as they're colloquially known, could be huge. One prairie-dog town on the Texas high plains a hundred years ago was recorded to be two hundred miles wide. I asked Mike what would cause such an explosion in the population of a rodent like the great gerbil. Mike responded that he'd never heard of such a thing, and then added, as his primary advice: "All I know is, if you're planning to go to China with all those gerbils, be sure to tuck your pants into your boots…"

Rodent disaster is not confined to the distant regions of Mongolia. In 1929, the town of Taft, in the San Joaquin Valley of Southern California, was invaded overnight by millions of mice. The battle against them lasted months, beginning with the locals driving their harvesters and combines through mice by the acre—a tactic that quickly failed when the blades of the machines became clogged with dead mice and stopped working. Here's an account from an observer, William Rintoul, that describes how rapid rodent disaster can unfold:

---

[5] The rodentlike things singing bizarre ditties about Quizno's are not hamsters, gerbils, or albino tarsiers. They're called spongmonkeys, and, if you believe the trades, they are at the center of an advertising phenomenon the likes of which have not been seen since 4' 11" Clara Peller lifted the burger buns of Wendy's rivals back in 1984 and asked about the whereabouts of her beef. The spongmonkeys were created by a British internet animator in London named Joel Veitsch, whose website had been forwarded to one of the advertising executives on the Quizno's account. "Advertising gold" is how one admiring writer described Quizno's subsequent bold attempt to challenge Subway for the top ranking in the "sandwich segment of quick-service restaurants" by using a national campaign that is confusing and/or disgusting to the average viewer. It's a heterodoxy that seems to be working. There is a school of advertising that says ads work best when polarizing the nation; love 'em or hate 'em, people are talking about the spongmonkeys, and by extension they're talking about Quizno's. A hundred thousand people have downloaded the screensaver that puts the two spongmonkeys on daily view on their desktops. Both children and adults come into Quizno's singing the songs. Even Bob Goldstein, the grouchy critic of *Advertising Age,* applauded the spongmonkeys for "break[ing] through the clutter as few ever have."

Advancing to the southwest, [the] mice killed a sheep and devoured the carcass in less than a day. A column slipped past the poison-filled trenches to touch off an exodus of women from Ford City, an unincorporated community adjoining Taft. Another column captured the golf course, encountering only token opposition from fleeing golfers. To the north, hordes swarmed the highway, where thousands were ground to death beneath car wheels, making the highway dangerously slippery.

This is the kind of thing immortalized in story of the Pied Piper from Hamelin, and in fact the Taft paper advertised "Fabled Pied Piper Needed," after which the U.S. Bureau of Biological Survey promptly sent in their number-one wildlife poison officer, a man named Stanley E. Piper. A veteran of many a rodent disaster, Piper assembled a team of recruits—called the "Mouse Marines"—to begin the extermination campaign. Unlike his namesake, Piper could not subdue the mice. But after three months, the mice were defeated by nature. First, rodent *septicemia bacillus* swept through the population, weakening their numbers. Then, the sky filled with birds; hawks, owls, gulls, herons, ravens, shrikes, and golden eagles dove down for days to get their pick of mice. Shortly thereafter, the mice were gone, and the infestation ended as abruptly as it began.

There are no great gerbils in the United States. At one time there were some specimens living in the United Kingdom, having been imported by the BBC to play bit parts in a television series called *Realm of the Russian Bear.* Today, the only great gerbils in captivity are at the Moscow Zoo.

The Museum of Natural History in Los Angeles has many stuffed rodents, but no great gerbils. They only acquire rodents indigenous to California, explained Jim Dines, the head of the Mammalogy Collection. And, he added, it is unlikely any other major museums would have great gerbils either. But Jim did know something about the population dynamics of rodents, having studied the biogeography of an obscure member of the order in the Pacific Northwest called the mountain beaver—an animal, he said (because scientists love to say such things), that is neither a beaver nor lives exclusively in the mountains. "Beavers are rodents," he said, "but this rodent's not a beaver." He drew me a map of the scattered dwellings of mountain beavers around Washington state.

So what causes rodent disaster? "It's mysterious," Jim said. He explained how some rodents, like lemmings and voles, have a very regular boom-bust cycle. Every few years, a static, small population surges, plateaus, and then crashes. Plotted on a graph, the reliability and scale of these swings are impressive. Yet other rodent populations don't do this. Why? People have studied these cycles for a long time, and still find it difficult to identify precisely what causes them. The obvious elements, like food, are well-known; harder to pin down are the many ancillary factors, their thresholds, incremental

Mountain beaver dwellings (rough sketch)

changes, and combinations thereof, that cause a population of animals to oscillate between two points of stability an order of magnitude apart.

Or suddenly shoot out of control. Because in much of the natural world, things aren't regular at all. The unpredictability and density of causes behind population dynamics are what make the field a very technical business, the province of data and its interpreters. It is, in fact, precisely the kind of inquiry where the theoretical and heavily mathematic fields of chaos and complexity are supposed to lend insight, because they help describe non-Newtonian systems—that is, systems where looking at current conditions don't seem to predict what the conditions will be down the line. And what are the conditions to measure anyway? From a scientific perspective, an actual forest or desert steppe is so full of unknowability that most population-dynamics work is done in a lab so the variables can be limited and controlled. Or inside computers, where biogeographers produce enormously detailed mathematical models, trying to factor in anything they can think of: predators, moisture, landscape, rainfall, sunspots. Consequently, when you open the discipline's scholarly texts, even James Tanner's *Guide to the Study of Animal Populations*, a book meant as a primer, it's not yet page six before the hieroglyphic narrative of equations begins. The first of these equations I actually de- and re-focussed my brain to understand in a heroic exertion of mental retrieval after which I turned the page, saw ten more equations, closed the book, and said: fuck it. The one mathematical statement about the great gerbils we do need to know is they have such reproductive potential— two to three litters a year; quick, twenty-four-day gestation; between four to seven (but as many as fourteen) pups per litter; three months until the pups can bear their own pups, and so on—that, if unimpeded, they can multiply exponentially in a short amount of time—a set of arguments that we may as well relate with the precision of an equation like thus:

$$\text{Favorable conditions in Xinjiang } \times \text{ reproductive potential } =$$
$$\text{one assload of great gerbils.} \qquad (1.1)$$

In the bulletins last August, Xiong Ling claimed that the great gerbil does go through a multiyear reproductive cycle, and that this year was a peak. She also said that the great gerbil's cycle used to be smaller and regular, every four or five years, until the phase was broken when her office implemented more aggressive rodent control in 1990. But such a cycle has never been documented among great gerbils. And a thousandfold increase is beyond cycles, anyway. This is Hamelin territory—an unexpected, dramatic population spike, hinting that something has gone haywire.

A Chinese cell-phone call costs one Yuan per minute. But a Chinese text message sent between cell phones is much cheaper, at .2 Yuan per message. This cost differential has created a hugely popular, wide-scale instant messaging network, called *duan xin xi,* which translates as "short information." Everyone uses it as a regular means of communication, for quotidian purposes like movie listings as well as for sharing very intimate, important information. A friend of a friend of a friend of mine told her boyfriend that she was pregnant by means of duan xin xi*,* and back came a text message from the boyfriend saying he wanted nothing to do with it. No more than fifty words were exchanged, in under five minutes, and the whole business was settled. Like email, the text messages can be forwarded to multiple people, so in addition to companies picking up the network as a new outlet for advertising, duan xin xi has also flourished as a frictionless vector of information, both good and bad.

Because of the lack of open news sources, China is a massive churning rumor mill, and so the bad tends to prevail. During the SARS season, while the Chinese government and local media kept mum, the invisible membrane of duan xin xi was alive, spreading mass paranoia among China's citizenry. Like, for example, the erroneous belief that household pets were SARS carriers, which caused panicked pet owners to throw their dogs and cats out the window. And another rumor that the government would send planes to spray disinfectant against SARS over all of Beijing on a certain date that led people to stay home and seal up their windows and doors.

To find out what duan xin xi had to say about the great gerbils in Xinjiang, I asked a friend of mine in Beijing (the third and closest "friend" in the list above) to put out a feeler through her cell phone. She sent a message to several friends, who forwarded it to their friends, and so on.

CALABRIEN

Regio

SICILIEN

Messina

The port of Messina

Theoretically, the query could get around the country quickly, perhaps as far as Urumqi, and—who knows—maybe even to Xiong Ling. With the net cast, she waited.

In October of 1347, a fleet of twelve Genoese merchant ships was quarantined in the port of Messina in Sicily. The merchants had fled with their families from war on the Black Sea coast, and while underway they began dying of an unknown malady, described by a Sicilian observer at the receiving end as a "sickness clinging to their very bones." Clinging to their bones was *Yersinia pestis*, the bacterium that causes the Bubonic Plague, and they were the patient-zero population that brought the Plague to Europe.

The Genoese merchants had been infected while under siege by Tatars in Kaffa, a city on the Crimean Peninsula. The Tatar army failed to breach the city walls, partly because they started dying. Before departing, the Tatar captains used catapults to volley their diseased corpses into Kaffa. It was the first modern use of biological warfare. And the most effective: two months after the Genoese arrived in Messina, half the city was dead. Thirty days later, Marseilles was infected. By the summer, the Plague had reached Paris, and was spreading east and north, arriving in London in December 1348. When it was over, a third of Europe had succumbed to what came to be known by the English as the Black Death, by the Germans as *das Grosse Sterben* (the Great Dying), and among medieval scholars by the cataclysmic-sounding Latin designation: *Magna Mortalis*.

The Tatar armies had been in the path of a Plague outbreak fanning westward through the Lower Volga, the Middle East, and the Caucuses—all territories with overland caravan routes leading back to the Silk Road and

Xenopsylla cheopsis

the desert steppes of today's Xinjiang. It was there that the Black Death originated, among the marmots, the hares, and indeed, the great gerbils. In fact, the various great gerbil populations in Central Asia are what epidemiologists call inveterate foci of *Yersinia pestis*—permanent reservoirs for the Plague. Which they remain to this day. *Y. pestis* resides in the gut of *Xenopsylla cheopsis*, a hardy flea that prefers rodents. Normally, bacteria and flea live together in an equilibrium, and the whole operation cohabitates peaceably on the unaffected rodent; but sometimes the flea's *Y. pestis* population rapidly swells, escapes the flea's gut, kills the rodent, and sends the flea packing to find a new host. Likewise, the great gerbil normally lives in equilibrium with its environment; but its population also sometimes rapidly swells—as in Xinjiang—and the gerbils, eating themselves out of house and home locally, go looking for greener pastures. Here is danger. It's this dual population dynamic that allows fleas regurgitating *Y. pestis* to hitch that ride—from remote desert burrow to exploratory juvenile rodent to urban rodent to human—and create devastating pandemics.

And not just in the fourteenth century. The same thing had occurred eight hundred years earlier, in 540 CE, and after the Black Death there were substantial flare-ups around the world as *Y. pestis* resurfaced episodically. In both absolute and relative numbers, Plague has been the most destructive scourge in history. The last major pandemic shot out of Central Asia in the mid-nineteenth century, and killed thirteen million people over the next fifty years.

It was during this time that Plague entered the United States, through ships with Chinese manifests mooring in the San Francisco bay. Eighty-nine people died of a small run of the Plague there in 1907–1908. The longer-term consequence was that *Y. pestis* established itself among the wild rodent population in the American West. From the raiding mice of Taft to the friendly squirrels and perky chipmunks begging gamely at our camp-grounds, rodents are all potential Plague vectors. In spring, when there are vehicles from the Centers for Disease Control criss-crossing the mountains and deserts of the Southwest, it's usually the Vector Control Division on the move, evaluating rodents for the incidence of *Y. pestis*. Up in the Angeles National Forest above Pasadena, where I camped in high school and sometimes hike today, such surveys always turn up infected fauna. And it was in Los Angeles in 1924 that the last urban plague in the United States erupted.

Traditionally, agriculture has been secondary to pastoral herding among the Uyghurs. When Chinese settlement in the region increased, the government began using runoff from the mountains to irrigate for crop-based agriculture. Agriculture has been a preoccupation of modern China, since there are so many people to feed. Collectivization, the Great Leap Forward, the Four Modernizations, the "free-market" reforms of 1978—all were partly conceived as grand schemes to increase agricultural productivity. Xinjiang was not exempted from this process. Dams, ditches, and canals were built. A lot of pasture was converted to farmland. A lot of desert was converted to farmland. Pictures from the region show moist fertile fields whose edges draw a sharp line against sandy dunes. Today, juicy melons from rainless Turfan are enjoyed by millions of people across China.

The rise of agriculture in Xinjiang has locked its people in an elevated-stakes duel with the great gerbil. The gerbil is now more of a pest, because there are valuable crops to eat, and because there are crops to eat, there are more of them to be pests. Hence the Regional Office for Controlling Locusts and Rodents. Those frequent rodent explosions in recent decades referred to by Xiong Ling were probably caused by the availability of agriculture as a food source. Similar great gerbil populations in areas that are still true desert, according to the literature, don't seem to swing so rapidly. In Xinjiang, the irrigated fields have become the perfect growing medium for rodents, and all it takes is for a few colonists to find their way in for a surge to take hold. In fact, this is what set the stage for the great mouse war in Taft, where a few mice became a hundred-million-strong swarm by living unmolested nearby in the once-dry bed of Buena Vista Lake that had been irrigated and planted with eleven thousand acres of grain.

In 1859, a man named Thomas Austin released twenty-four rabbits from his house outside Victoria, Australia, on Christmas Day. Fifteen years later, the rabbits had spread fifteen hundred miles. Another fifteen years after that, they were all over the continent, eating up all the vegetation and leaving nothing for the native species. It was one of the world's worst environmental disasters. Australians of grandparenting age can tell stories about the peak years of the 1940s when the yards in the evening would be undu-

The rabbit fence (detail)

lating carpets of furry little bunnies. The plague of rabbits grew so dire that the government erected a giant fence that spanned the entire continent longitudinally: eighteen hundred kilometers from Starvation Boat Harbour to Cape Keraudren. But by the time the fence was finished in 1907, there were already enough rabbits on the other side that it was all but ineffective.

In the 1950s Australia afflicted its rabbits with a disease called myxomatosis, which caused them to go blind and/or die. But not all of them. And it doesn't take very many rabbits to form the seed of a horde, which is what reappeared, as multitudinously fluffy and hungry and horny as ever. Recently, the Australian government returned to biological weapons. They developed the Calici virus, a lethal disease specific to rabbits, at an experimental research station on an island off Australia's coast. The authorities were reluctant to release it before they knew it would not affect other animals, but a few years ago the disease mysteriously appeared on the mainland and quickly destroyed the rabbit population. It created a riotous scandal: environmental sabotage that was, in the end, applauded by environmentalists.

And that's just one of example of ecological woe in a place that acts like a perpetual laboratory of creatures run amok. Like the proliferation of grey kangaroos when watering holes were built for cattle. Or the koala infestation on Kangaroo Island. Can koalas infest? Well, koalas had never been to the island in the Gulf St. Vincent near Adelaide. Soon after crossing over a few years ago, they took to the resident gum trees like nobody's business and now there are too many of them. This of course raises the philosophical question: can there be too many koalas? To which my answer would be no, since when I imagine even an infinity of koalas, what I am really imagining is heaven, as I dive amongst them and snuggle and kiss and hug them and sing how very much I love them! In fact, I hereby declare that I would pay a thousand dollars to snuggle with a room full of koalas for one hour.

But this is not how Kangaroo Islanders see koalas. They say the koalas are overeating their welcome, to the point that the "invaders" may soon exhaust the forests and starve themselves to death anyway. "We're in crisis mode," says the local government in Kangaroo Island, and as preventive measures it is considering biological control (a golden eagle–type method), sterilization, and even allowing people to shoot koalas out of the trees.[6]

Here's what gerbil news *duan xin xi* turned up: not much. So meager is the available information about Xinjiang's rodent disaster that the text-messaging chatterbox can't come up with even unfounded gossip on the topic.

> From: Andrea Hill
> Subject: re: Gerbil Fury 2004
> Date: March 27, 2004
> To: Joshuah Bearman
>
> Dear Josh,
> I'm sad to report few solid leads. Nobody here knows much about these gerbils. A few people remember the story from last summer. That's it. The text messages I got back all asked me to tell more about the gerbils. I did also do a search of Chinese-language news sources, but there's not much there either.
>
> P.S. No word from Xiong Ling.

Andrea did turn up one report, more recent than those I'd seen, from November 19, 2003, which updated the affected area from five to six million hectares. At least some bureaucratic progress has been made, because this new intelligence was attributed to something called the Autonomous Region Locust and Rodent Elimination Command Post.

In the fourteenth century, no one understood disease or pathogens like *Y. pestis,* so when every other person in Europe started dying, Europeans laid blame everywhere else:

1) On the Jews. It was obvious to all that the Jews had poisoned the wells, so pogroms broke out all over Europe. Tens of thousands of Jews were killed, many burned alive, and even those conventionally slaughtered were incinerated for good measure.

---

[6] NO!

2) On the stars. At the request of King Philip VI of France, forty-nine medical masters at the University of Paris studied the problem and published their findings in the *Paris Consilium*, which concluded that the plague was probably caused by the conjunction of Saturn, Jupiter and Mars in the 40th degree of the moist, miasmic sign of Aquarius at precisely 1 p.m. on March 20, 1345.

3) On themselves. Incredibly, Pope Clement VI quite reasonably declared the plague not to be God's wrath against sin, but no one listened. Local clergy preached divine punishment, and in early 1348, the defunct Order of Flagellants was revived. These were Christians who wandered from town to town, flogging themselves with metal-tipped leather whips until their bodies were covered in blood. Their painful public penance was supposed to deliver absolution to onlookers and confessors—for a fee. The flagellants managed to identify the source of the plague as both Christian transgression against God *and* the sinister doings of Jews, so they incited anti-Semitic riots wherever they went. It was these "Brethren of the Cross," forbidden as they were from bathing, washing, sleeping in a bed, or changing clothes, who actually brought plague with them on their "processions." The word *scourge,* which today refers to widespread disease, like the Plague, or its path of transmission, like rodents, originally described the whipping of the flagellants.

Jan Randall, a field biologist with a quarter century of desert-rodent study under her belt, is the English-speaking world's foremost expert on great gerbils. For the last ten years, she has sojourned each spring, first to Turkmenistan and now Uzbekistan (always carrying a heavy regimen of Tetracycline in case of Plague), to observe great gerbils in their natural habitat. That entails spending a lot of time watching gerbils munch seeds and grass while standing on their hind legs and looking around in various directions. "That's what they're up to much of the time," she said. They also sometimes do maintenance on their burrows, and so an active workday might find the steppe punctuated by petite dirt plumes being expelled over areas of construction.

"Do they ever wink at you?" I asked.

"No. Great gerbils don't wink at people."

"Are you sure?"

"Yes. And I've worked with the Mongolian gerbil in the lab and they don't wink either."

Jan's main research interest is gerbils' genuine social behavior. She believes that the great gerbil is a keystone species, meaning that it plays a central role in the area's ecosystem, and has a theory that its adaptive social structure enhances survival during environmental changes. Jan also listens to the gerbils. They're a chatty lot, twittering, peeping, and chirping away while interacting intimately and cleaning each other. But what Jan has been writing about is the long-distance exchanges. When the gerbils are standing, eating, and looking around, they are also acting as sentries, and when danger appears, they make alarm calls with foot drummng and whistles. "We're not sure exactly how it works," Jan said. "I've worked on drumming in kangaroo rats, which is my earlier expertise. Kangaroo rats are just trying to scare predators; they're not talking to other kangaroo rats, since they travel alone. But *Rhombomys*' antipredator behavior is group communication. It sends messages to the rest of the burrow." What does gerbil song sound like? "They're not really songs," Jan said. "And their drumming doesn't change that much."

I asked Jan for the scuttlebutt in the great gerbil scientific community about the state of affairs in Xinjiang. She replied that there is no scuttlebutt, both for lack of enough scientists studying the great gerbil to constitute a community capable of scuttlebutt, and because none of those scientists have been to Xinjiang in the past year. The only concrete information she could provide was that a local contact of hers "checked it out and said the population is very high."

And the eagles?

"I heard about that," she said. "I don't know if they put that in place. But the eagles are what got National Geographic interested."

National Geographic?

"They contacted me recently and asked me to accompany them to Xinjiang to do a documentary. They want to film the gerbils. It will be the first time I've been there. They're planning to go in June."

And until then?

"No one knows how many gerbils there are now."

No one at all?

"No one knows."

Here are some theories. Refer back to equation (1.1). Let us examine those favorable conditions. Jim Dines, from the Museum of Natural History, described the usual suspects for broad factors behind volatile population growth: food abundance, the elimination or lack of natural predators, and human activity. And these days, Jim pointed out, the first two factors are usually direct results of the third. Or, as he phrased it: "Fuck with Gaia… and she'll always come back and bite you in the ass."

Last year, the wet spell yielded rich pasture. There's also the agricultural growth, which entails wildlife control and with the rains created an unprecedented motherlode of cultivated food. That all follows a couple years of drought from the Buran, a hot summer wind that blows across Central Asia and sets the stage for some rains to shake things up. (It was desert flooding that provided the actual spark for the Taft's mice; when the Buena Vista Lake bed became inundated, they fled en masse and set to colonizing the town itself and areas beyond.) It may even be that weather patterns, together with the rodent-control program itself, helped lay the foundation for the worst rodent disaster since 1993 by interfering with the natural balance between predator and prey. When the rodent population plummets from drought and extermination, the predator population follows. This creates a predator vacuum, and when conditions especially congenial to rodents return, there is nothing to keep a burgeoning generation of gerbils in check. By then no amount of human pest control on its own is effective.

But here's another idea. An intrinsic characteristic among great gerbils that can suppress their population is territoriality. What biologists designate as family units are called clans by pet owners and breeders, and that better expresses how defensive gerbil groupings are in relation to one another. With domesticated gerbils, two males from different clans in the same terrarium will invariably fight, usually to the death. Even brothers may chew each other's tails off if they're feeling surly. In the wild, each gerbil clan will stake out a homestead and fight off intruders. Other clans can't come along and buddy up or share resources. Theirs is a community divided, and that usually restricts expansion. Which suggests, then, that this particular expansion in Xinjiang might represent a truce between the clans—if they're advancing so fast through the fields, they must not be wasting any time fighting with one another. I.e.: the gerbils have unified against us.

This has happened before, with the ants. All those little black ants that so resourcefully seek out lost bits of bacon from behind the stove are not just ants; they're members in good standing of a colonial confederation of *Iridomyrex humilis,* or Argentine ants. Unlike other ants, who fight intramurally, those little black ants are so successful because they've colluded together and turned their attention toward the common enemy. In Europe, entomologists recently discovered the Argentine ants had organized themselves into the largest single ant colony in the world: 3,600 miles long, from the Italian Riviera to Northwest Spain. It's a sensible strategy: why fight each other when you can fight the Man?

Which brings us back to the golden eagles. Because if the gerbils are indeed united, all the more reason why you need to fight them with eagles, right?

There are two problems to consider here. The first is logistical, since the gerbils reproduce so quickly, while it takes some time to come up with a lot of eagles. But the wider predicament posed by using one animal population to control another—integrated pest management, they call it—is that it often backfires. Everyone points to the well-known successful use of ladybugs to eat aphids, employed by backyard gardeners and commercial horticulturalists alike. "But now," as Jim Dines said, "people are quick to reach for this solution. They bring in one species to eat another one that is going insane. But then the new one goes insane and they need something else to eat the one they brought in."

Except sometimes there is no "something else" higher up the chain. As in the case of the amphibious horror called the cane toad. Again we turn to Australia, where *Bufo marinus* was introduced deliberately to eat the cane beetles that were seen as pests by the local sugarcane growers. Since 1935, a hundred tadpoles have become who-knows-how-many millions of indestructible cane toads, spreading steadily and vying with rabbits as an unmatched environmental disaster. This is because the

Bufo marinus

cane toad eats anything and can be eaten by nothing, since every life cycle of the thing is poisonous. The cane toad parotoid glands create a potent venom that, if ingested directly, causes cardiac arrest in minutes. And if the cane toad empties its glands in water, it turns the aquatic area around it into poison.[7] Now, across Australia, a creature that was supposed to help out by eating some beetles is marching along the coast, creating vegetative carnage

---

[7] Observers who have spent time among stoners of the American Southwest and Floridian peninsula may notice from the cane toad's scientific name that it is related to the local *Bufo alvarius*, otherwise known as "this fuckin psychedelic frog, dude, that Tim licked last night out in the desert, fuckin bufo man, and seriously he was still trippin' this morning, swear to God," which is the lay description Matt Devonshire gave me the first time his brother came back from Joshua Tree. As part of their dermatological defense, both *Bufos* excrete an alkaloid called Bufotenine 11, which is indeed an extremely potent hallucinogenic. So don't take too much, and if you do, smoke it, otherwise it may be the final voyage: every so often someone straight up licks too much bufo and dies right there, toad in hand, wrapped in a bandana.

and rendering dog bowls, wells, and entire wetlands toxic. Greetings... from Gaia?

Think about those eagles back in Xinjiang again. A quick calculation tells you that if the typical golden eagle can eat about a gerbil a day—the figure I got from the ornithologist on staff at the Museum of Natural History—you'd need an armada of eagles to make a dent in this rodent disaster. Like a million. Perhaps two. And do you really want a couple million eagles circling overhead? What if they finish off the gerbils and start in on something else?

Or worse. The sagacious editor of this article, upon first hearing the subject matter, asked what may be the critical question: what if the eagles and gerbils become friends, like Milo and Otis, and go on exciting adventures together? Sounds silly, but perhaps not in light of the clever Argentine ants and the possible alliance of gerbil clans last summer that helped bring on the rodent disaster in the first place—which would be how much worse with the gerbils and eagles in league? The first time Xiong Ling steps off her porch and sees a majestic goldie soaring overhead with a gerbil riding shotgun, she'll realize maybe the eagles weren't such a hot idea after all.

The possibilities spiral outward. One reason the multiplying gerbils haven't yet left Xinjiang is that the terrain surrounding the Junggar depression is harsh enough that they can't traverse it on their own. But: what if they have air transportation? With no news from the area, who can say what will or has already happened? Are the gerbils spreading, or in abeyance? Are the eagles locked with the gerbils in a deadly *pas de deux* over the desert? Or have they together laid waste to the Regional Headquarters for Controlling Locusts and Rodents and are now making for the rest of China? As Jan said, no one knows. She could arrive there in June and find no gerbils. Or no Xinjiang. And we might have to wait for answers until she gets back.

Unless in the meantime my number has floated around Xinjiang long enough, through 114 outposts or the channels of duan xin xi or the corridors of the local wildlife bureaucracy, and I wind up getting a call from the Elimination Command Post.

"Is this Josh Bearman?"

"Yes?"

"Xiong Ling speaking. You want to know about our gerbils?"

HOW IT FLOODS

by PIA Z. EHRHARDT

SAY I'M CRAZY about Roger who works in my office building. He gets off on the twenty-third floor, so he must have a job with the Army Corps of Engineers. The first minute is mine. When he enters the lobby, I walk toward him and brighten my eyes. I show him I've seen him. He stops to talk to an associate, so I sit in one of the leather chairs, like I'm waiting for someone. He looks again at me over the guy's shoulder on the chance I'm still looking at him. I am. He's trying to listen. I think the guy's his boss, by the way Roger's mostly nodding, and his concentration's shot to hell. I stare. He moves his briefcase to the side and puts his hand in his pocket. His boss finally moves off.

The second minute is his. He walks over to me, says, "I saw you at the grocery." I know he did, but I say, "Oh? What did I buy?" He smiles, says, "Cereal."

Sometimes he has a drink at Pete's Pub after work. I walk up to him at the bar and say, "Hey, again." I ask questions. "What do you do?" "Were you a happy kid?" "Did you marry the woman you wanted, or the one you were engaged to?" He laughs knowingly. It's an interview with no hostility. He gives me answers. He says, "Most women don't listen." We talk some more. When he looks at his watch because he's got to get home, I ask him what he was like in college, and what his wife does, and we have another drink. She's a nurse.

When I was young, my dad taught me about men by telling me how he was with women. He'd talk about these things at dinner and my mom would nod, but I understand now that she had her own ideas, and the only way to keep them hers was to be quiet.

"I married your mother because she couldn't wait any longer to have sex."

This was more than I wanted to know and it made me wonder about my mother. She was a bad girl. He'd kept her a good girl, but they didn't seem close, more like irritable siblings. She seemed a little bored with him. I wasn't.

He approved my bikinis. We had a pool in the backyard. He checked tight shirts before my dates—"If it's in the window it's for sale." When I was in junior high I would break up with boyfriends, sometimes, just for him. It was my gift. He dropped whatever he was doing to give me help. He'd tell me love was easy to get over, and there was more of it—even better love—right around the bend, but it was a moving target, not something that settled down and rested, and neither should I.

In the cafeteria line, I brush the back of Roger's hand with my thumb. I follow behind him and dust against the fabric of his shirt. I can almost not be there at all, so slim, and still burn into his memory.

I walk with him to the elevator. I show Roger I am serious by standing too close, not touching him, but my clothes will be on him, and my perfume. The body warmth is so present, I want to ride all day.

I liked my father's friends. They were lawyers who liked classical music, and they'd come to our house and sit in opposing chairs to do comparative listening in the study. They'd drop the needle on different recordings and listen to this or that pianist play Bach, or Rachmaninoff, and argue about who was pure, who was a showman and a charlatan. I liked the showmen, but that was the wrong answer. So, I'd walk in and out of there and bring them beer and chips. That was the right answer. My dad told me on the way to class one morning, in a coy, almost girlish way, that one of them, Christopher (the one I liked most), had said my ass was so high you could balance an ashtray right there. And he showed me how Christopher had used both of his hands, like he was placing the ashtray on me.

Roger stops by my office to say hello, leaves notes under my windshield wiper. I try to look undersold, but worth his effort. It must've been great when guys came to your door to sell encyclopedias and knives that cut through brick, some unexpected company in the morning. How could a woman not fall in love? I am ready to fall in love with anyone at any time, even if it's just for a couple of minutes, because this is the only feeling worth having. It is so good. It is thick syrup.

Roger rides a motorcycle. We sneak out of our jobs early, tell our bosses our kids are sick. We head for River Road and follow the line of the Mississippi River. I am pressed against him like Velcro. We're weaving in and out of cars, and it feels so great, all that air pushing against me. Folks get out of our way and I think how lucky we are. What's to be afraid of when the day's just starting? Roger looks at me over his shoulder and laughs. I touch the back of his neck with my fingers.

I go to my mother's during my lunch break. She's out of town. My parents have been divorced since I was eighteen, but she kept the house I grew up in.

She likes me to visit, but not leave a trace. I am comfortable here. I toast half a bagel, put on butter and cream cheese. I lick my finger and press away crumbs, then put everything back in the fridge.

I go up to my room and look at my books. I underlined everything in college that I didn't want to forget. I should've underlined what wasn't important because the pages are a smudge.

There's a note on the bathroom mirror, reminding me to turn on the exhaust fan if I shower. I do. She has white towels everywhere and I hate to use them. I use a little washcloth to dry myself. I'm okay here. I know the drill. I don't want her to change a thing. I write her a note of thanks and put it beside hers.

* * *

One afternoon, when I was a senior in high school, my father came in my room and sat on my bed. I was lying on my side, studying, and he put his hand on my hip, and while he talked he moved his hand over my ass, like I was a bronze and he wanted to warm the metal. I told him I was in love with my boyfriend, Larry, and he said, no, I wasn't, because he knew my mind. I thought: if you know what I'm thinking then don't, please. He put his finger through the belt loop on my Levi's, and then he touched the skin between my jeans and shirt, ran his fingers under the top of my jeans. He made a sound, like he was the wounded one, stood up and went to my door, blocking the light and blocking my way out. He looked at me, brought his hand to his lips.

Saturday morning, Roger and I go for a longer ride on his motorcycle across the Bonne Carre Spillway. There are bald cypresses to admire, and crooked bands of ducks fly over. I want more, so I urge stuff out of Roger. We pull into a truck stop to get some coffee and pie. I make him tell me he cheated on his wife before they married. That he killed too easily in Viet Nam. That the scar on his mouth was from getting pistol-whipped in the French Quarter when he was twenty-five.

I tell him a few things about men, about the client I screwed while I was married to Larry. We had been shooting a video in a forest. We were done and drinking beer, and I walked off with him to look for blue-heron rookeries. The moon was full and this lake his company managed was a plate of silver. Pretty. He had to get home, and I told him to go on then, and men hate to hear that because it reminds them they are whipped. We kissed hard and knelt down and there was moss, on cue. When we walked out, my crew was finished packing, and the guy shook hands and said goodbye, and I told my crew to go ahead, too, because I felt good. I was making a change. I was leaving my jealous husband Larry tomorrow. Not for this guy, but because of this guy. I sat in a clearing and listened to barn owls chastise each other. They were as big as mini-fridges. I yelled at one, said, "Can I get a fucking word in edgewise? You owls will be okay. You're paired for life."

Roger looks at me upset, like he's Larry. "You gave him up that fast?" he says.

"What?" I say, and the surprised look on my face makes things worse.

He reports that he hit his wife once when she got in his face and goaded him, dared him, and she hit him back. I say, "Sounds like that's between the two of you, right?"

I ask if I should find another ride home with a trucker, but he says, no, get back on.

Roger's working long hours. A hurricane's in the Gulf of Mexico right now, a few days away. He's a civil engineer, a levee specialist. I can look out my window and see the local news stations in the parking lot setting up for interviews with the Corps of Engineers. Everyone's worried more about flooding than they are high winds. The storm is coming in at a bad angle for New Orleans. Privately, Roger says I should prepare to leave. He describes the worst-case scenario with bright eyes: high winds push gulf into river, river crams into lake, hurricane comes in left to right, and Lake Pontchartrain gets picked up like a frisbee, tossed onto New Orleans, and we're fourteen feet under water.

I like men who know things.

Later that night, Roger's boss is on the ten o'clock news, reassuring people that the Corps is doing everything possible to make sure the levee system holds. All of the openings are being sealed. They haven't done this in fifty years. I listen to him. I don't care about the water.

Roger calls me from his car and asks if I want to go out and check on the sandbagging that's going on around the clock. It's a free night for us, he says, because his wife thinks he's working. I stay in the car while Roger talks to his staff and the volunteers who've come out by the dozens to help.

Most of the night, though, we drive down quiet streets. The music is on loud in the car and we're drinking giant daiquiris and we have all the time in the world.

My son is sleeping out at his friend's, so we stop at my house at two different times during the night and screw, and at dawn we go there again and rest for a few hours.

I take his money. I don't want to and I don't need it. But when I have trouble some months paying my rent and he leaves five one-hundred-dollar bills on my pillow, it's okay to go ahead and feel like a call girl for a second. We joke about how sex with me is worth more than that. I put a tip bowl by the front door as a prop.

The next day, Roger talks to me in the parking lot after work. He needs to calm things down at home, spend more time at home. Sandy doesn't believe he was working all night. She has a small bruise on her jaw. Sandy hit him in the stomach while he was sleeping His eyes were closed. He thought he was having a bad dream, and he said he hit her back. Reflex. The kids have been doing lousy in school. They hear him and Sandy fight. Every day is an argument. I notice that Sandy's name is in a lot of sentences.

Roger's boss passes me in the lobby and doesn't give me a second glance. I take this as a challenge. I tell him I'm a good friend of one of his employees, Roger. He comments on what a good-looking family they are, how great Sandy is. He asks if I have time to grab a beer at Pete's Pub.

I say, fine, Pete's is a place I like. Roger has gone home early to help his wife prepare for the storm. His boss and I watch the TV behind the bar. The hurricane's in the Gulf and they've drawn a red box on the map that includes New Orleans. The wife and kids and Roger are packing clothes and stuff they love, in case it floods. Roger has a motel booked in Jackson. I tell his boss I'm staying put, I'll ride the storm out. It's me and my son. He acts concerned, and offers to come by and help and I look at him like, yeah, sure, but he's writing down my address, and he says he will, really, and he says he's gonna stop by Wal-Mart and buy me some flashlights and Spam and batteries for the radio.

It's the morning of the hurricane and I'm having coffee with Roger at Denny's. I say to him, "Would you hit me?"

He says, "No. It's the way Sandy and I fight. The bad fights."

I say, "Is there anything I can do to make you hit me?" and he says, "Just be quiet, okay? I'm working things out."

I say, "Your temper's bad," and he says, "Yeah, my dad," and I say that's a cliché, maybe he just feels like hitting her.

He says, "It doesn't happen often."

I figure he might enjoy knowing who I could fuck in Pete's Pub if I wanted to. I say, "Well, someone's been enjoying drinks with her lover's boss."

He blinks like I've air-punched him close to his eyes. "It's good," I add, "to hear off-the-record stuff—funny anecdotes about you and your pals around the cooler."

Roger plays with the ends of my hair and twists a piece around his finger. "What else?"

"Oh, job performance."

"So, how am I doing?"

"Fast-tracker," I say.

Roger's boss and I sit on the couch in my den and watch television. He's in no hurry to leave. We've made the house as safe as we can. Raised my furniture on bricks, and put sandbags in front of the doors so water doesn't come in. There's a crazy star of masking tape over every window. Drapes are pulled. Both bathtubs are filled, and the kitchen wall is lined with gallon jugs of water. I flip around to see the local news stations. They keep cutting to the hurricane center in Miami, to the expert with the flattop, who says it's five miles slow of being a Category Four. And then they show black-and-white footage of Hurricane Camille, a Category Five, battering the Mississippi Gulf Coast in 1965.

Roger's boss puts his arm through mine. "They like to whip things up," he says.

"We'll be all right?" I ask. My son is in a sleeping bag in the hall, away from windows.

"It'll turn," he says. He's been tracking the coordinates on a map I got at Exxon.

I'd like to believe him.

There are long lines of traffic leaving the city. I point at the TV and say, "Suckers." Cars are going twenty mph on the interstate. At this rate, it will take a day to get to Jackson. I think Roger's kids are sleeping in the back, and his wife is sleeping in the front.

I check on my son, kneel beside him and kiss his hand. He brushes me away. I pray that he falls in love the way other people fall in love, where it's just a gift offered by a man and a woman at about the same time, where their hearts are flying toward one another, sure and scared.

In the middle of the night the storm turns for Galveston.

Roger calls the next afternoon and says he's coming by to help me pick up fallen tree branches.

I don't want this anymore. It's in my eyes. That's what taunts him. Roger raises his hand so quick I don't even budge. He crushes my nose. My face feels bigger. I lean over so blood drips on the grass. I grab my nose and look around for a towel, but there's no towel. Yards don't have towels. I watch him back quickly out of my driveway. Roger's boss is pulling up to help me with fallen tree branches, and Roger waves at him through the window, acts normal, but Roger also runs through the stop sign at the end of my block. "What's he doing around here?" his boss asks, and I run to him and lower my face, ask for some help, and he takes off the sweatshirt he's wearing, because that's all he has to stop the blood.

We drive to the hospital. I tell him it's only a nosebleed, and he doesn't say anything, but he stops the car and stills my head with his hands, and his eyes look frightened and confused. "What the hell is going on?" he says. I beg him to get there, please, because I can't see anymore.

He wants to fire Roger. I say, "Don't."

He brings me home from the hospital. It's dusk and there's no traffic. Most of the city evacuated. A splint is on my nose. Some giant clip held in place by adhesive.

I ruin things. That's what I want him to know. Tricky girls find men who trick them. I say it, but he shakes his head, says he doesn't care about that, can he get my prescription filled at Walgreen's? I tell him some more about how it works, and he just shakes his head and takes my hand and opens it and presses my palm against his chest.

The radio's on and people are calling in, cheerful and ready to talk for days about the near miss of the hurricane, poor Galveston.

He walks me to the door. His face is white, and I know it all looks worse than what I can explain to my son. I ask him in but he says no, get some rest, and he puts his face close to mine but only kisses my hair goodbye, and all I can say is thank you, thank you, George, and goodnight.

THE ANIMAL KINGDOM

by JESSICA LAMB-SHAPIRO

THE WHOLE WORLD was afraid of mother: the trees shivered in the wind, the bushes hunched together, trying to hide, the grass lay flat and silent on the ground. Even the air shrieked. Eat your peas, mother said. Thanks very much, but no. No thank you, I said. Why, she said. *They made me nervous. They felt alive on my tongue.* I pressed my lips shut tight, but she fisted them in my mouth.

When we had visitors she asked me to pretend I didn't exist. Why, I said. She made me hide in a box in the attic. I wasn't allowed to go to the bathroom. I wasn't allowed to read since they might hear the pages turning. If you have to cough, swallow, she said. There was dust in the box. I could hear their voices downstairs. Murmur murmur, the man said to my mother. They laughed softly. Then no noise. I sneezed so loudly my ears hurt.

I heard a scream from downstairs. Bloody murder.

Consequently, she put my hands into scalding dishwater. I said, it's awfully hot. Also I said, ow you're burning me. She said, do something helpful for a change. I did the dishes, and I dried them. But mostly, I practiced the art of being invisible. I made myself small and quiet. I practiced slipping in and out of doors. I could flatten out almost entirely. I walked like I was skiing. I thought if I believed I walked an inch above the ground, it would actually appear that way.

I was exactly the speed of air.

WHAT IS KNOWN OF KANSAS

I would spy on fathers from my window. Fathers threw round objects at sons and sons threw back. They slapped palms and fisted playfully. They whispered things, what things I didn't know. A round object landed on my lawn and a boy came after it. He was red.

I slipped out of the window at the speed of air and wished myself visible. I picked up his ball and handed it to him. I said to him, hello I have no father. Everyone has a father, he said. Not me, I said, I have no father. What happened to him, he said. I don't know, I said. Maybe he died, said the red boy.

Ask your mother, said the red boy.

You don't understand, I said.

Mother was in the kitchen. I was brave because she was holding a knife.

Who is my father, I asked her. She said, the wind is your father. I said that's impossible. She said the grass is your father. Where is my father, I said. She said, your father lives in China. I said, then take me back to China. She said, you needn't shout.

Your father was a man, she said. She said:

This area was a land of Opportunity for him
He was dedicated to certain Basic Rights of Mankind
He was a Real person, as real as you or I

I was doubtful. She said: George was man, he was everything man. He was all man and he was George.

I was still doubtful. She grabbed my hands and put them into the scalding dishwater.

I said, that's not so hot. So she gave my arm the iron grip.

Doesn't hurt, I said, also a lie because it did really hurt. I thought to pick up the knife but did not. She was tired. She was dry.

PILGRIMS

My mother said, the state of Georgia was named after King George the Second.

I AM FORGOTTEN

On my fifth birthday, I was invited to a secret wedding. It was secret from me. My mother married a sallow and heavy man who giggled through the ceremony. At the end he wept and blew his nose loudly into a giant handkerchief.

"Who are you?" I asked the man.

"I am your new father," exclaimed the man.

I said, leave us alone new father. He said, ha ha! little man, and fisted me on the head.

The man moved many boxes into our house. I was moved out of my room to make room for the boxes. There were so many boxes it was hard to find my new father. Once when he was out I walked into one of his secret rooms. It was filled with medium-size boxes. I opened a box. It was filled with smaller boxes. I opened a smaller box. It was filled with seeds. I ate three seeds and waited to see if I would die.

A TWO-FOLD NAKEDNESS

I had so much water in my body it was always falling out. If I stepped outside into the dry cold air my eyes would leak until I could not see a thing but patterns of light. I had so much water in my mouth my new father called me Saliva Kid. He was always giving me napkins to clean myself up with but they were not enough. One eye could soak a napkin in two minutes, dripping wet. He said he would invent a sucking tube that might take the water out of me but I never saw anything. A false promise. I dripped all around the house until they limited my movement to one area. When I walked I left a glistening trail in my wake.

I had extra skin on my fingers. It looked like I had an extra finger but I didn't, it was just extra skin. Meaning, no bone; graceless.

I don't think I had lips; my mouth just began. I felt my teeth but could not discern anything of their character. I tried to dry them with napkins, but it never lasted. I was grateful to them, for they ensured that my mouth was not a black foreboding hole. I counted them, one two three, and I hoped to God they were white and fine.

My hands and arms tingled when it was very sunny, especially my hands. For this reason I became convinced I had magic hands. I would face my palms towards my new father and concentrate on the idea of explosions. When this did nothing I pointed my magic fingers at him and tried a few magic words. I said:

Fregentia!
Libinia!
Massacrititia!

None of these words had any effect, but perhaps I just did not know the right coda. Still my hands tingled, hard, all the time. I put my hands on the floor to see if the floor would crack but it did not. I tried to punch a hole in the wall but could not. New father had punched many holes in the wall quite well, but he did not have the magic hands. I began to look around for dead things to touch. Maybe my magic was healing, not destructive. I found a sick bird. I used my own hairbrush to massage its tiny head. I fed it from my own baby's bottle, milk that I had stolen from our table. The bird began to strengthen and I was proud. I knew what it was to be a mother, and I was a better mother than my own.

But one day the bird was gone. I did not know if it was healed and had flown away to be with other birds, or if my mother had stolen and destroyed it. I asked her, have you seen my bird? She said, if I had seen your bird your bird would be dead. I locked myself in the bathroom and leaked water for two days straight.

I knew a word that could upset her: testify. I used to whisper it through her keyhole at night to disturb her sleep. Once I shouted it to her face. She turned white: actually white. I tried other forms: testimony, testification, testinninny. I could make my own language. I said, mother your conscience you must keep, or it must be kept for you. She said, shut up little bone. I said, you did harbor covenance. She said, shut up slimy. I wiped my eyes. It was true, I was covered in water. I tried to dry my mouth with my shirt but it only made my shirt wet.

Well, look at you, I said.

Not a drop of water on her.

She was a dry woman, mother, all dried up.

A LITTLE KEY MAY OPEN A BOX
WHERE LIES A BUNCH OF KEYS

On my mother's birthday I made her a card. I didn't have any paper but new father had many papers so I took one to draw on. The paper already had some drawings and notes on it. There was a drawing of a big chair and a little man. The little man's eyebrows were raised to make him look scared. He did look scared, probably because that chair was so big; it was twice his size.

I knew what it was to feel dwarfed and I felt sorry for him. Everyone was bigger than me, and most chairs were bigger than me too. My advantage was limited.

New father had drawn many wires coming out of the chair and going into the man. This is also perhaps why little man was scared. I would not like to have many wires going into me. I used the other side of the paper to make my mother's card. I was only four years of age but I could write a little. I copied some of the letters that new father used when he wrote, and I guessed at the rest of it. I knew that certain letters corresponded to certain sounds. So I wrote some letters on the page. Happy Birthday Mother, I wrote. Love George, I also wrote. I made the George bigger than the other words so that she would get the idea.

I was not as small as I looked, that was the idea.

When I gave her the card she looked confused. She handed it to new father. New father laughed and patted me on the head.

"Little idiot," he said. "This isn't even English."

I looked at the words and I was pretty sure they were English. I read aloud, "Happy Birthday Mother Love George." New father just laughed harder and mother smiled. New father put his fat hand on my head, making the worst hat. He squeezed my brain and repeated, "Little idiot."

New father wanted to pretend like he was the only person in the world who could read and think. He was not. There was me, too, and I was getting smart.

On my fifth birthday, my mother gave me a present. She said it was something of my old father's. I opened the box. Inside lay an unfamiliar object: hard, white, and oval. I did not know what it was. I held it in my hand; it was cold. I smiled at it for a while.

"What is it?" I asked her.

"Take it to the river," she said. She would not come with me for she hated the water.

It was a cold day and I didn't like to be outside. I sat by the river all day with the white father object. It didn't change. By nightfall, I still didn't know what it was.

"Nothing happened," I said to my mother.

"Take it back," she said.

I went the next day and sat again. Again, nothing happened. I talked to the object, it did not respond. I smelled it, it smelled like dishes. I was starting to hate the object, for it evaded me.

"Nothing happened," I told her.

"Take it back," she said. "And don't drop it."

I went the next day and sat by the river. The air was freezing and the river was fast. There was dirt on the object, and it needed washing. I held it tight in my fist and plunged it into the river. The hard cool object became slippery in my grip. It jumped out of my hand like a fish and swam down the river. Goodbye to old father, quite fast.

"I dropped it," I told my mother. I was ashamed. "What was it?"

"Now you'll never know," she said.

But several years later I did come to know. My new father had one just like it.

"You have the father object," I observed smartly. No praise for me. Instead my new father looked confused and annoyed.

"This is a bar of soap," he said, and used the father soap to fist me on the head.

THE GENERAL OBSERVATION OF FOUL

I woke up one night to find my new father chewing on my arm. "What are you doing?" I asked him.

"I had a dream that I was chewing my way out of a sack. I am free now?"

"You are free."

"Good boy," he said, and dissapeared behind some boxes.

I didn't sleep for a week.

But there was a loveliness too, wasn't there? The feel of hard teeth on a soft arm.

WHAT IS KNOWN OF GEORGIA

I sometimes dreamed that my old father would come to rescue me. In the dream he was carrying two large crates, tied up with purple velvet ribbons. He would put his hand on my shoulder and tell me to open them. I would open them and see rows and rows of perfect white soap.

I knew we would be a very clean family.

In reality, only once did a man ever come to visit. He was a big man, so big, with white hair. His name was mine and he wore a crude crown fashioned out of string and stone. It looked kid-made and sad. There was a question to which he did not know the answer. I did not know the answer myself. When the man opened his mouth to speak, water had spilled out. My mother gig-gled. I had never heard her laugh before. New father sighed, and gestured towards the back room.

Then the big man said, "Wait. Wait. Wait. I am a man, I am every-thing man."

More water.

This sounded familiar, but was apparently unsatisfactory, answer-wise. New father took him by the sleeve and led him in a a room with many boxes and I heard a great cracking.

I heard new father say, "He is not your son."

My mother followed them into the room. I heard my mother say, "He is no one's son or he is everyone's."

I heard the man say, or I think I heard him say, "Have you never remarked on the similarity of the names George and George? Has it not occured to you that they might be the same?"

There was another cracking noise. This time light flickered. I heard my mother say, "You could have been a great man," but I did not know which man she was speaking to. Then I heard a man say "I am a great man," but I did not know which man it was that spoke. Then there was silence. Soon my mother returned, closing the door behind her.

Water seeped through the crack under the door until there was a small lake in our front room.

This was also the day I first saw my mother cry. She didn't do so great a job. Truly, it was the worst cry I had ever seen. She was clutching a bar of soap, useless. Her face was pulled into a tight ball and she made no sound. She couldn't so much as muster a single teary drop. I cried better with my eyes closed.

Oh mother, all dried up.

"What's the matter," I asked her, though I didn't care so much. I knew it was my time to be angry.

"No one really loves me."

"Well, why do you think that is," I said in my most adult voice.

AFTER THAT, I WAS THE DOG

They built me a little house to sleep in, outside.

THE DOUBTFULNESS OF WATER

MADAM KNIGHT'S JOURNEY TO NEW YORK, 1702

by T. CORAGHESSAN BOYLE

Boston to Dedham

THE ROAD WAS dark, even at six in the evening, and if it held any wonders aside from the odd snug house or the stubble field, she couldn't have said because all that was visible was the white stripe of heaven overhead. Her horse was no more than a sound and a presence now, the heat of its internal engine rising round her in a miasma of sweat dried and reconstituted a hundred times over, even as she began to feel the repetition of its gait in the deep recesses of her seat and that appendage at the base of the spine her mother used to call the tailbone. Cousin Robert was some indeterminate distance ahead of her, the slow crepitating slap of his mount's hooves creating a new kind of silence that fed off the only sound in the world and then swallowed it up in a tower of vegetation as dense and continuous as the waves of the sea. Though it was only the second of October, there had been frost, and that was a small comfort in all of this hurt and upset, because it drew down the insects that a month earlier would have eaten her alive. The horse swayed, the stars staggered and flashed. She wanted to call out to Robert to ask if it was much farther yet, but she restrained herself. She'd talked till her throat went dry as they'd left town in the declining sun and he'd done his best to keep up though he wasn't naturally a talker, and eventually, as the shadows came down and the rhythmic movement of the animals dulled their senses, they'd fallen silent. She resigned herself. Rode on. And just as she'd given up hope, a light appeared ahead.

At Dedham

Robert her cousin leaving her to await the Post at the cottage of the Reverend and Madam Belcher before turning round for Boston with a hundred admonitions on his lips—she should have gone by sea as there was no telling what surprises lay ahead on the road in that savage country and she was to travel solely with trusted companions and the Post, etcetera—she settled in by the fire with a cup of tea and explained her business to Madam Belcher in her cap and the Reverend with his clay pipe. Yes, she felt responsible. And yes, it was she who'd introduced her boarder, a young widow, to her kinsman, Caleb Trowbridge, only to have him die four months after the wedding and leave the poor woman twice widowed. There were matters of the estate to be settled in both New Haven and New York, and it was her intention to act on the widow's behalf, being a widow herself and knowing how cruel such divisions of property can be.

An old dog lay on the rug. A tallow candle held a braided flame above it. There was a single ornament on the wall, a saying out of the Bible in needlepoint: *He shall come down like rain upon the mown grass: as showers that water the earth.* After a pause, the Reverend's wife asked if she would like another cup.

Sarah's eyes rose from the fire to the black square of the window. "You're very kind," she said, "but no thank you." She was concerned about the Post. Shouldn't he have been here by now? Had she somehow managed to miss him? Because if she had, there was no sense in going on—she might just as well admit defeat and find a guide back to Boston in the morning. "But where can the Post be?" she asked, turning to the Reverend.

The Reverend was a big block of a man with a nose to support the weight of his fine-ground spectacles. He cleared his throat. "Might be he's gone on to the Billingses, where he's used to lodge."

She listened to the hiss of the water trapped in a birch stick on the fire. Her whole body ached with the soreness of the saddle. "And how far would that be?"

"Twelve mile on."

At Dedham Tavern

She sat in a corner in her riding clothes while the Reverend brought the hostess to her, the boards of the floor unswept, tobacco dragons putting their claws into the air and every man with a black cud of chew in his mouth. The woman came to her with her hair in a snarl and her hands patting at her hips, open-faced and wondering. The Reverend stood beside her with his nose and his spectacles, the crown of his hat poking into the timbers overhead. Could she be of assistance?

"Yes, I'd like some refreshment, if you please. And I'll need a guide to take me as far as the Billingses to meet up with the Post."

"The Billingses? At this hour of night?"

The hostess had raised her voice so that every soul in the place could appreciate the clear and irrefragable reason of what she was saying, and she went on to point out that it was twelve miles in the dark and that there would be none there to take her, but that her son John, if the payment was requisite to his risking life and limb, might be induced to go. Even at this unholy hour.

And where was John?

"You never mind. Just state your price."

Madam Knight sat as still as if she were in her own parlor with her mother and daughter and Mrs. Trowbridge and her two boarders gathered round her. She was thirty-eight years old, with a face that had once been pretty, and though she was plump and her hands were soft, she was used to work and to hard-dealing and she was no barmaid in a country tavern. She gazed calmly on the hostess and said nothing.

"Two pieces of eight," the woman said. "And a dram."

A moment passed, every ear in the place attuned to the sequel. "I will not be accessory to such extortion," Sarah pronounced in an even voice, "not if I have to find my own way, alone and defenseless in the dark."

The hostess went on like a singing Quaker, mounting excuse atop argument, and the men stopped chewing and held the pewter mugs arrested in their hands, until finally an old long-nosed cadaver who looked to be twice the hostess' age rose up from the near table and asked how much she *would* pay him to show her the way.

Sarah was nonplussed. "Who are you?"

"John," he said, and jerked a finger toward the hostess. "'Er son."

Dedham to the Billingses

If the road had been dark before, now it was if she were blind and afflicted and the horse blind too. Clouds had rolled in to pull a shade over the stars and planets while she'd sat listening to the hostess at the tavern, and if it weren't for the sense of hearing and the feel of a damp breeze on her face, she might as well have been locked in a closet somewhere. John was just there ahead of her, as Cousin Robert had been earlier, but John was a talker and the strings of his sentences pulled her forward like a spare set of reins. Like his mother, he was a monologuist. His subject was himself and the myriad dangers of the road—savage Indians, catamounts, bears, wolves, and common thieves—he'd managed to overthrow by his own cunning and heroism in the weeks and months just recently passed. "There was a man 'ere, on this very spot, murdered and drawn into four pieces by a Pequot with two brass rings in 'is ears," he told her. "Rum was the cause of it. If I'd passed by an hour before it would have been me." And: "The catamount's a wicked thing. Gets a horse by the nostrils and then rakes out the innards with 'is hinder claws. I've seen it myself." And again: "Then you've got your shades of the murdered. When the wind is down you hear them hollowin' at every crossroads."

She wasn't impressed. They'd hung women for witches in her time, and every corner, even in town, seemed to be the haunt of one goblin or another. Stories and wives' tales, legends to titillate the children before bed. There were real dangers in the world, dangers here in the dark, but they were overhead and underfoot, the nagging branch and open gully, the horse misstepping and coming down hard on her, the invisible limb to brain her as she levitated by, but she tried not to think of them, tried to trust in her guide—John the living cadaver—and the horse beneath her. She gripped the saddle and tried to ease the ache in her seat, which had radiated out to her limbs now and her backbone, even her neck, and she let her mind go numb with the night and the sweet released odors of the leaves they crushed underfoot.

At the Billingses

She would never have known the house was there but for the sudden scent of wood smoke and the narrowest ribbon of light that hung in the void like the spare edge of something grander. "If you'll just alight then, Missus," John was saying, and she could feel his hand at her elbow to help her down, "and take yourself right on through that door there."

"What door?"

"There. Right before your face."

He led her forward even as the horses stamped in their impatience to be rid of the saddle. She felt stone beneath her feet and focused on the ribbon of light till the door fell inward and she was in the room itself, low beams, plank floor, a single lantern and the fire dead in the hearth. In the next instant a young woman of fifteen or so rose up out of the inglenook with a contorted face and demanded to know who she was and what she was doing in her house at such an hour. The girl stood with her legs apart, as if ready to defend herself. Her voice was strained. "I never seen a woman on the road so dreadful late. Who are you? Where are you going? You scared me out of my wits."

"This *is* a lodging house, or am I mistaken?" Sarah drew herself up, sorer than she'd ever been in her life, the back of a horse—any horse—like the Devil's own rack, and all she wanted was a bed, not provender, not company, not even civility—just that: a bed.

"My ma's asleep," the girl said, standing her ground. "So's my pa. And William too."

"It's William I've come about. He's the Post, isn't he?"

"I suspect."

"Well, I'll be traveling west with him in the morning and I'll need a bed for the night. You *do* have a bed?" Even as she said it she entertained a vision of sleeping rough, stretched out on the cold ground amidst the dried-out husks of the fallen leaves, prey to anything that stalked or crept, and she felt all the strength go out of her. She never pleaded. It wasn't in her nature. But she was slipping fast when the door suddenly opened behind her and John stepped into the room.

The girl's eyes ran to him. "Lawful heart, John, is it you?" she cried, and then it was all right, and she offered a chair and a biscuit and darted away upstairs only to appear a moment later with three rings on her fingers and her hair brushed back from her forehead. And then the chattering began, one topic flung down as quickly as the next was taken up, and all Sarah wanted was that bed, which finally she found in a little back lean-to that wasn't much bigger than the bedstead itself. As for comfort, the bed was like a mound of bricks, the shuck mattress even worse. No matter. Exhaustion overcame her. She undressed and slid in under the counterpane even as the bed lice stole out for the feast.

The Billingses to Foxvale

She arose stiff in the morning, feeling as if she'd been pounded head to toe with the flat head of a mallet, and the girl was nowhere to be seen. But William was there, scooping porridge out of a bowl by the fire, and the mistress of the house. Sarah made her own introductions, paid for her bed, a mug of coffee that scalded her palate and her own wooden bowl of porridge, and then she climbed back into the rack of the saddle and they were gone by eight in the morning.

The country they passed through rolled one way and the other, liberally partitioned by streams, creeks, freshets and swamps, the hooves of the horses eternally flinging up ovals of black muck that smelled of festering decay. There were birds in the trees still, though the summer flocks were gone, and every branch seemed to hold a squirrel or chipmunk. The leaves were in color, the dragonflies glazed and hovering over the shadows in the road ahead, and in the clearings goldenrod nodding bright on a thousand stalks. For the first time she found herself relaxing, settling into the slow-haunching rhythm of the horse as she followed the Post's back and the swishing tail of his mount through one glade after another. There were no houses, no people. She heard a gabbling in the forest and saw the dark-clothed shapes there—turkeys, in all their powers and dominions, turkeys enough to feed all of Boston—and she couldn't help thinking of the basted bird in a pan over the fire.

At first she'd tried to make conversation with William (a man in his twenties, kempt, lean as a pole, taciturn) just to be civil, but talk seemed superfluous out here in the wild and she let her thoughts wander as if she were at prayer or drifting through the mutating moments before sleep comes. *You should have gone by sea*, Cousin Robert had said, and he was right of course, except that the rollicking of the waters devastated her—she'd been once with her father in a dinghy to Nantucket when she was a girl, and once was enough. She could still remember the way her stomach heaved and the fear she'd felt of the implacable depths where unseen things—leviathan, the shark, the crab and suckerfish—rolled in darkness. She'd never learned to swim. Why would she, living in town, and when even the water of the lakes and the river was like the breath of midwinter, and the sea worse, far worse, with men falling overboard from the fishing boats and drowning from the shock of it? No, she would keep the solid earth under her feet. Or her horse's feet, at any rate.

Sure progress, the crown of the day: there was the sun, the solemn drapery of the forest, birdsong. She was lulled, half asleep, expecting nothing but more of the same, when suddenly a small thicket of trees detached itself from the wood and ambled out into the road so that her mount pulled up and flung its near eye back at her. It took two catapulting moments for the image to jell, and then she let out a scream that was the only human sound for twenty miles around.

The thing—the walking forest—was bearded and antlered and had eyes that shone like the Indian money they made of shells. It produced a sound of its own—a blunt bewildered bleat of alarm—and then it was gone and William, taciturn William, was there at her side. "It's nothing to worry yourself over," he said, and she saw that he was grinning as if he'd just heard a joke—or formulated one. He had a story to tell at the tavern that night, that's what it was, and she was the brunt of it, the widow from Boston who wouldn't recognize a—what was it, a moose?—if it came right up and grazed out her hand.

At Foxvale

The board was primitive, to say the least, Sarah sitting at table with William while William discharged his letters to Nathan, the western Post, and the hostess bringing in a cheese that was like no cheese she'd ever seen. Eating was one of her small pleasures, and at home she always took care with the menu, serving up fish or viands in a savory sauce or peas boiled with a bit of salt meat, fresh roasted venison, Indian corn and squashes and pies—her speciality—made from the ripe fruit of the season, blueberry, raspberry, pumpkin, apple. But here the woods gathered close so that it was like night in the middle of a towering bright day, and there were none of the niceties of civilization, either in the serving or the quality. The cheese—harder than the bed she'd slept in the night before—barely took to the knife, and then it was a dish of pork and cabbage, which looked to be the remains of dinner. She found that she was hungry despite herself—ravenous, actually, with the exercise and air—and she took a larger portion than she would have liked.

"Tucking in there, Missus, eh?" William observed, giving her that same grin even as he nudged Nathan, and here was another story.

"We've been on the road since eight in the morning," she said, wondering for the life of her what was so amusing about sheltering in a shack in the woods fit only for a band of naked savages, "and it's now past two in the afternoon. A woman has got to eat, if only to keep up her strength." She was throwing it back at them, and why not—that was how she felt. And she *was* hungry, nothing to be ashamed of there. But the sauce was the strangest color—a purple so deep it was nearly black—and the thought came to her that the hostess had stewed the meal in her dye kettle.

William was watching her. As was Nathan. The hostess had vanished in the back room and the sound of the fowl scratching in the dirt of the yard came to her as if she were standing there amongst them. Very slowly a branch outside the sole window dipped in the breeze and parted the dense shadow on the wall. She hesitated, the spoon hovering over the dish—they were both of them grinning like fools—and then she plunged in.

Foxvale to Providence

This was the leg of the journey that wore on her most. The new man—Nathan—rode hard and she had to struggle to keep up with him, or at least keep him in sight. Though he'd seen her discharge William handsomely enough and pay for his refreshment too, he didn't seem in the least solicitous. He was a hat and a pair of shoulders and a back, receding, always receding. Her mount wasn't much taller than a pony and tended to lag no matter how much encouragement she gave him, running to his own head and not a pace faster. The clouds closed in. A light rain began to awaken the dust. Nathan was gone.

She'd never been out alone in the wilderness in her life. When she was younger she'd gone berrying on the outskirts of town or spent a warm afternoon sitting by a cool brook, but the wild was nothing she wanted or recognized. It was a waste, all of it, and the sooner it was civilized and cultivated, the sooner people could live as they did in England, with security and dignity—and cleanliness—the better. To her mind, aside from the dangers that seemed to multiply with every step they took—a moose, indeed—it was the dirt that damned the wild more than anything. She hadn't felt even remotely clean since she'd left town, though she'd done her best to beat the soil from her skirts, brush her shoes of mud, and see to the demands of her hair. And now she was wet and the horse was wet and her baggage and the road before her, and every leaf on every tree shone and dripped.

She tried to concentrate her thoughts on easeful things, the tea set in her parlor and her daughter and Mrs. Trowbridge pouring out the tea and artfully arranging the pastries on the platter because it was teatime now, and if it was raining there they'd have built up the fire to take the damp out of the air—but she couldn't hold the picture long. Her thoughts kept coming back to the present and the dangers of the road. Every stump seen at a distance seemed to transform itself into a bear or wolf, every copse was the haunt of Indians mad with rum and lust, the birds fallen silent now and the rain awakening the mosquitoes that dove at her hands and face where they'd coarsened in the sun. She'd thought she was going on an adventure, a respite from town and gossip and all the constraints of widowhood, something she could look back on and tell over and over again to her daughter and the grandchildren she saw as clearly as if they'd already come into existence—but she wasn't foolish, and she wasn't blindered. She'd expected a degree of hardship, an untenanted road, insects and the like, wild animals, and yet in her mind the road always ran between inns with reasonable beds and service and a rough but hardy and well-tendered fare. But this was impossible. This rain, these bugs, this throbbing ache in her seat that was like a hot poker applied to her backside by one of Satan's own fiends. She hated this. Hated it.

At Providence Ferry
It got worse.

Nathan's silhouette presented itself to her at the top of a rise, unkempt now and dripping. Slowly, with the testudineous progress of something you might crush underfoot, she made her way up the hill to him, and when she got there he pointed down at the lashing dun waves of the Seekonk River and the distant figure of the ferryman. She didn't say a word, but when they got there, when the water was beating to and fro and the ferryman accepting her coin, she held back. "The water looks doubtful," she said, trying to keep her voice from deserting her.

"This?" Nathan looked puzzled. "I'd call this calm, Missus," he said. "And the quicker we're over it, the better, because there's worse to come."

She closed her eyes fast, drew in a single breath and held it till they were across and she knew she was alive still and climbing back into the saddle even as the rain quickened its pace and the road ahead turned to sludge.

Providence Ferry to the Havenses
They hadn't gone on a quarter of an hour when they came to a second river, the name of which she never did learn. It was dark as a brew with the runoff of the rain and ran in sheets over the submerged rocks and boiled up again round the visible ones. She felt herself seize at the sight of it, though Nathan assured her it wasn't what it seemed—"No depth to it at all and we're used to ride across it even at spring thaw"—and when they were there at the crossing and Nathan's mount already hock-deep in the surge, she just couldn't go on. He remonstrated with her—they were late on the road already, dusk was falling, there was another crossing after this one and four-teen miles more to the next stage—but she was adamant. There was no inducement in the world that would make her risk that torrent.

The rain had begun to let up now and a few late faltering streaks of sun shone through the clouds across the river. But wasn't that a house there on the far shore? A cabin, crudely made of logs with the bark peeled back and smoke rising palely from the stacked stone of the chimney? The current sang. Nathan swung his horse round on the shingle and gave her a look of hatred. "Does someone live there?" she asked. "In that cabin there?"

He didn't answer. Just thrust his horse into the current and floundered through it with a crashing like cymbals and she was so furious she would have shot him right through his pinched shoulder blades if only she'd had the means. He was deserting her. Leaving her to the wolves, the murderers and the haunts. "You come back here!" she shouted, but there were only his shoulders, receding.

That was her low point. She tried, at first, to screw up her courage and follow him—it wasn't so deep, after all, she could see that—but the way the water seemed to speak and hiss and mock her was enough to warn her off. She dismounted. There was a chill in the air, her clothes wet still, the night coming down. She should have stayed home. Should have listened to Robert and her daughter and everyone else she talked to—women simply did not travel the Post Road, not without their husbands or brothers or kinsmen there to guide and protect them, and even then, it was a risk. Something settled in the back of her throat, a hard bolus of self-pity and despair. She couldn't swallow. One more minute of this, one more minute of this water and these trees, these endless trees, and she was going to break down and sob like a child. But then, out there on the naked back of the water, she saw the envelope of the birchbark canoe coming toward her and a boy in it and Nathan beckoning to her from the far shore.

What to say? That the crossing—eyes tight shut and her grip on the papery gunwales like the grip of death—was the single worst moment of her life, at least until the next crossing, through which they plunged in a pit of darkness so universal that it was only the tug of the reins, the murmur of the current and the sudden icy stab of the water at her calves to let her know she was in it and through it? Or that the fourteen miles remaining were so tedious she could scarcely stay awake and upright in the saddle despite the horripilating shivers that tossed her from one side to the other like a ball in a child's game? Say it. And say that she thought she was dreaming when the Post sounded his horn and the snug, well-lit house of the Havenses materialized out of the night.

At the Havenses

As weary as she was, as worn and dispirited, she couldn't help feeling her soul rise up and shout when she stepped through the door. There was Mr. Havens, solicitous and stout, and Mrs. Havens beside him with a welcoming smile, the fire going hard in the hearth and a smell of broth to perfume the air. She saw immediately that these were people civil and clean, with a well-ordered house and every sign of a demanding mistress, a picture on one wall of the sitting room and a glass vase of dried flowers set atop an oiled sideboard on the other. Chairs were drawn up to the fire and a number of people cozily ensconced there with their mugs and pipes and they all had a greeting on their lips. Mrs. Havens helped her off with her riding clothes and hung them up to dry and then asked if she could get her anything by way of refreshment, Sarah answering that she had a portion of chocolate with her and wondered if she might have some milk heated in a pan. And then she was shown to her room—small, but sufficient and tidy—and the door was shut and she felt as if she'd come through a storm and shipwreck and washed up safe.

She must have dozed, because she came back with a start when Mrs. Havens rapped at the door. "Yes?" Sarah called, and for a moment she didn't know where she was.

A murmur from the other side of the door: "Your chocolate, Missus."

The milk had been boiled with the chocolate in a clean brass kettle, and there was enough of it to give her three cups full. And there were corn cakes, still warm from the griddle. This was heaven, she was thinking, very heaven, dipping the cakes into the chocolate and warming her hands at the cup, but then the voices began to intrude. It seemed that her apartment, separated from the kitchen by a board partition, wasn't quite as private as she'd supposed. Next door to her—just beyond that thin rumor of a wall—were three, or was it four, of the town's topers, and all of them arguing a single point at once.

She listened, frozen on the starched white field of the bed, and she might as well have been right out there amongst them.

"No," a voice declared, "that's not it at all. Narragansett means 'briar' in the Indian language, and the patch of it was right out there on Peter Parker's place, thirty feet high and more—"

"I beg to differ, but it was a spring here—and that's where the country gets it name. Waters of a healing property, I'm told."

"Yes? And where is it then? Why aren't you drinking the waters now—why aren't we all?"

A scuffle of mugs, the scrape of chair legs. "But we are—only it's been distilled out of cane." Laughter rang out, there was a dull booming as fists pounded the tabletop, and then someone followed it up with a foul remark, in foul language.

And so it went, for what seemed like hours. Exhausted as she was, there was no hope of sleep as long as the rum held out, and she began to pray the keg would run dry, though she was a practical soul who'd never had the calling and she never expected her prayers to be answered since there were so many worthier than she calling on the same power at the same moment. But the voices next door grew thicker, as if they'd started chewing maple sap boiled to gum, and the argument settled into a faintly disputatious murmur and then finally a pure drugged intake and outlay of breath that formed the respiratory foundation of her dreams.

The Havenses to the Paukataug

The next knock came at four in the morning, black as pitch and no breakfast but what was portable, and here they were, back out on the road in the dark and cold, deep in the Narragansett country now, which to Sarah's mind was just more of the same: the hard road, the shadowy trees and the reptatory murmur of the waters that were all running underfoot to gather in some terrible place ahead. "Narragansett," she whispered to herself, as if it were an incantation, but she had to be forgiven if she couldn't seem to muster much enthusiasm for the origins of the name.

They'd been joined at the Havenses by a French doctor, a slight man with a limp and a disproportionate nose, whose name she couldn't pronounce and whose accent made him difficult to understand, so that they were a party of three now for this leg of the journey. Not that it made a particle of difference, except that Nathan and the doctor rode on at such a furious pace as to leave her a mile and more behind, alone with her thoughts and whatever frights the unbroken wood might harbor. From time to time she'd spy them on a hill up ahead of her, waiting to see that she was still on the road and not lying murdered in a ditch, and then they'd tug at the reins again and vanish over the rise.

The Post had warned her that there was no accommodation or refreshment on this stretch of the road—no human habitation at all—for a full twenty-two miles, but as the morning wore on it seemed as if they'd gone a hundred miles before she saw the two figures poised on a ridge up ahead, looking back at her and pointing to a tight tourniquet of smoke in the distance. She'd been down on foot and leading her mount at that point, just to ease the soreness of her seat and thighs, but now she remounted with some effort and found her way to the source of the smoke: an ordinary set down beside a brook in a clearing of the trees.

Painfully she dismounted and painfully accepted the refreshment the landlady had to offer—stewed meat and Indian bread, unleavened—and then sat over her journal she'd determined to keep while the landlady went on to the doctor about her physical complaints in a voice loud enough to be heard all the way to Kingston town and back. The woman spoke of her privates as if they were public, and perhaps they were, but just hearing it was enough to turn Sarah's stomach and she had to take her book and sit out in the courtyard amongst the flies, which were especially thick here, as if they'd gathered for some sort of convention. She sat on a stump and swatted and shooed and blotted her precious paper with the effort until the Frenchman and the Post, still chewing a cud of stewed meat, saddled up and moved on down the road, and she had no choice but to rouse herself and follow on in their wake.

The country was unremarkable, the road boggy, the sun an affliction. Her hands and face were burned where they were exposed and the pain of it was like being freshly slapped every ten seconds. She saw a pair of foxes and what might have been a wolf, loping and rangy, with something dangling from its jaws. The sight of it gave her a start, but the thing ignored her and went about its business, which was slipping into a ravine with its prey in order to feed in some dark den, and then she almost wished it would emerge round the next bend to attack her, if only to put an end to the ceaseless swaying and battering of the horse beneath her. Nothing of the sort happened, however, and at around one in the afternoon she found Post and doctor waiting for her on the shores of a broad tidal river she knew she would never get across, not in this lifetime.

At the Paukataug

"Well, the road ends here then, Missus, because the doctor has his business in Kingston town and I've got the letters to deliver." The Post was leaning across his saddle, giving her a look of indifference. He was going to desert her and it didn't bother him a whit.

The doctor said something then about the ebbing tide, but she couldn't quite fathom what he was getting at until Nathan translated: "He says it's easier crossing at low tide—"

"Well, when is that, pray?"

"Three hour. Maybe more."

"And you won't wait?"

Neither man spoke. They were both of them like the boys she used to teach at school, caught out at something—doing wrong and knowing it—but unequal to admitting it. She felt her jaws clench. "You'd desert me then?"

It took a moment, and then Nathan pointed an insolent finger at what at first she'd taken to be a heap of flood-run brush, but which she now saw was some sort of habitation. "Old Man Cotter lives there," he said, and at the sound of his voice a great gray-winged bird rose out of the shallows at river's edge and ascended like a kite on the currents of the air. "He'll take you in."

Stunned, she just sat there astride her horse and watched the Post and doctor slash into the current until the water was at their waists and all that was visible of their mounts were their heads and a flat sheen of pounding rump, and then she made her way to the ramshackle collection of weathered boards and knocked at the door. The old man who answered gave her a startled look, as if he'd never seen a woman before, or a lady at any rate, but she steeled herself, and trusting in human kindness, offered him a coin and asked if she might shelter with him until the tide drew off. Very slowly, as if it were coming from a long way off, the old man discovered a smile and then stood back and held the door open for her. She hesitated—the floor was bare earth and there were animal skins on the wall, the place as dank and cold as a cellar. She turned to look back at the river, but the Post and his companion were already gone and the day was blowing away to the east in a tatter of cloud. She stepped inside.

The Paukataug to Stoningtown

There was a wife inside that hut and two children, both girls and ill-favored, and the whole miserable family dressed in rags and deerskin, and no furniture but for the rounds of logs cut for stools, a bed with a glass bottle hanging at the head of it for what purpose she could only imagine (decoration?), an earthen cup, a pewter basin and a board supported on rough-cut props to serve as a table. The hearth was a crude array of blackened stone, and as Sarah stepped through the door the wife was just setting a few knots of wood to the flame. "I don't mean to intrude," she said, all the family's starved blue eyes on her, "but I've been deserted here at the river and I don't know what else to do—"

The wife looked down at her feet and murmured that she was welcome and could make herself at home and that they were very honored to have her. "Here," she said, "you just sit here," and she indicated the bed. After that, no one said a word, the girls slipping out the door as soon as they could and the old man responding to Sarah's questions and observations ("It must be solitary out here" and "Do you get into Stoningtown much?") with a short sharp grunt of denial or affirmation. The dirt of the floor was pounded hard. The fire was meager. A draft flowed continuously through the gaps in the river-run boards that made the walls of the place. She was cold, hungry, tired, uncomfortable. She closed her eyes and endured.

When she opened them, there was a new person in the room. At first she took him to be a wild Indian because there was no stitch of civilized clothing about him, from his moccasins to his buckskin shirt and crude hat tanned with the fur of some creature still on it, but she gathered from the conversation—what little of it there was—that he was the son-in-law of the old man and woman and living off in the deeper wild in a shack of his own with their daughter, also named Sarah. No introductions were made, and the man all but ignored her, till finally Mr. Cotter rose to his feet and said, "Well, the river'll be down now and I expect it's time you wanted to go, Missus."

Sarah began to gather herself up, thanking them for their hospitality, such as it was, but then wondered aloud who was to escort her across the river? And beyond, on the road to Stoningtown?

The old man gestured toward his son-in-law, who looked up at her now from out of the depths of his own cold blue eyes. "If you'd give him something, Missus, I'm sure George here could be persuaded."

Stoningtown to New London Ferry

It was past dark when they limped into Stoningtown and her guide (no, he hadn't murdered her along the road or robbed her or even offered up an uncivil remark, and she reminded herself the whole way not to judge people by their appearances, though she could hardly help herself) showed her to the Saxtons, where she was to spend the night in the cleanest and most orderly house she'd yet seen since leaving Boston. Will Saxton was a kinsman on her mother's side and he and his wife had been expecting her, and they sat her before the fire and fed her till she could eat no more. Oysters, that was what she was to remember of Stoningtown, dripping from the sea and roasted over the coals till the shells popped open, and a lobster fish as long as her arm. And a featherbed she could sink into as if it were a snowdrift, if only the snow were a warm and comforting thing and not the particles of ice flung down out of the sky by a wrathful God.

She left at three the following afternoon—Thursday, her fourth day on the road—in the company of the Saxtons' neighbor, Mr. Polly, and his daughter, Jemima, who looked to be fourteen or so. The road here was clear and dry but for the dull brown puddles that spotted the surface like a geographical pox, but they were easy enough to avoid and the weather was cool and fair with scarcely the breath of a breeze. They looked out to the sea and moved along at a reasonable rate—Mr. Polly, a man her own age and cultivated, a farmer and schoolmaster, setting a pace to accommodate his daughter. All went well for the first hour or so, and then the daughter— Jemima—began to complain.

The saddle was too hard for her. The horse was lame and couldn't keep to a regular gait. She was bored. The countryside was ugly—or no, it wasn't just ugly but what you'd expect to see on the outskirts of hell. Could she get down and walk now? For just a hundred yards? Her backside was broken. Couldn't they stop? Couldn't they buy that man's farm over there and live in it for the rest of their lives?

Finally—and this when they were in sight of New London and the ferry itself—she got down from the horse in the middle of the road and refused to go a step farther.

Sarah was herself in a savage mood, wishing for the hundredth time that she'd stayed home in her parlor and let Mrs. Trowbridge worry over her own affairs, and each second she had to sit on that horse without moving forward was a goad to her temper. Mr. Polly gave her a look as if to say, What am I to do?, and before she could think she said that if it was her daughter she'd give her a whipping she'd never forget.

Jemima, big in the shoulder, with a broad red face beneath her bonnet, informed her that she wasn't her daughter and glad of it too. "You're an old hag from hell," she spat, her face twisted in a knot, "and I wouldn't live with you—or listen to you either—if I was an orphan and starving."

The trees stood still. In the near distance there was a farm and a pen and a smell of cattle. Then the father dismounted, took the daughter by the arm and marched into a thicket of the woods, where both their voices were raised in anger until the first blow descended. And then there were screams, raw, outraged, crescendoing, until you would have thought the savages had got hold of her to strip the skin from her limbs with their bloody knives. The blows stopped. Silence reigned. And Jemima, looking sullen and even redder in the face and probably elsewhere too, followed her father out of the thicket and climbed wearily back into the saddle. She didn't speak another word till they arrived at the ferry.

At New London

She would just as soon forget about that careening ride over the Thames on the ferry, with the wind coming up sudden and hard and the horses jerking one way and the other and Jemima screaming like a mud hen and roaring out at her father to save her because she was afraid of going overboard and Sarah's own stomach coming up on her till there was nothing left in it and the certainty that she would die stuck there in her throat like a criminal's dagger, because here she was handsomely lodged at the house of the Reverend Gordon Saltonstall, minister of the town, and he and the Reverend Mrs. Saltsonstall entertained her with their high-minded conversation and a board fit for royalty. Her bed was hard, the room Spartan. But she was among civilized people now, in a real and actual town, and she slept as if she were stretched out in her own bed at home.

New London to Saybrook and on to Killingworth

For all that, she awoke early and anxious. She felt a lightness in her head, which was the surest sign she was catching cold, and she thought of those long hours in the rain on the road to the Havenses and the unwholesome night airs she'd been compelled to breathe through the traverse of a hundred bogs and low places along the road, and all at once she saw herself dying there in the Reverend's bed and buried in his churchyard so many hard miles from home. She pictured her daughter then, pale, sickly, always her mother's child and afraid of her own shadow, having to make this grueling journey just to stand over her mother's grave in an alien place, and she got up out of the bed choking back a sob. Her nose dripped. Her limbs ached. She was a widow alone in the world and in a strange place and she'd never felt so sorry for herself in her life. Still, she managed to pull on her clothes and boots and find her way to the kitchen where the servant had got the fire going and she warmed herself and had a cup of the Reverend's Jamaica coffee and felt perceptibly better. As soon as the Reverend appeared, she begged him to find her a guide to New Haven, where she could go to her kinsmen and feel safe from all illness and accident.

The Reverend said he knew just the man and went out to fetch him, and by eight o'clock in the morning she was back in the saddle and enjoying the company of Mr. Joshua Wheeler, a young gentleman of the town who had business in New Haven. He was educated and had a fresh look about him, but was crippled in the right arm as the result of a riding accident when he was a boy. He talked of *The Pilgrim's Progress, Paradise Lost* and the Holy Bible as if he'd written them himself, and though her acquaintance with all three was not what it was once or should have been, she was able to quote him three lines of Milton—"And fast by, hanging in a golden chain, / This pendent world, in bigness as a star / Of smallest magnitude close by the moon"—and he rewarded her with a smile that made the wilderness melt away to nothing. He was like her own husband, the late, lamented Mr. Knight, when he was twenty and two, that was what she was thinking, and her nose stopped dripping and the miles fell away behind them without effort or pain.

Until they came to the bridge near Lyme. It was a doubtful affair at best, rickety and sway-backed, and it took everything she had in her to urge her mount out onto it. The horse stepped forward awkwardly, the bridge dipped, the river ran slick and hard beneath it. Her heart was in her mouth. "Get on," she told the horse, but she kept her voice low for fear of startling him, and the animal moved forward another five paces and froze there as if he'd been turned to stone. From the far side, where the trees framed him on his mount and sun shone sick and pale off the naked rock, Mr. Wheeler called out encouragement. "Come ahead, Sarah," he urged. "It's as safe as anything." If she hadn't been so scared, suspended there over the river and at the mercy of a dumb beast that could decide to stagger sideways as easily as go forward, she might have reflected on how easy it was for him to say since he was already over on solid ground and didn't have her fear of water. Or bridges. She gave him a worried glance and saw from the look on his face that he could have dashed across the bridge time and again without a thought and that he knew how to swim like a champion and trusted his horse and was too young yet to know how the hurts of the world accumulate. A long moment passed. She leaned close to the horse's ear and made a clicking noise. Nothing happened. Finally, in exasperation, she resorted to the whip—just the merest flicker of it across the animal's hindquarters—and the horse bucked and the world spun as if it were indeed hanging from a pendant and she knew she was dead. Somehow, though, she'd got to the other side, and somehow she managed to fight down her nerves and forge on, even to Saybrook Ferry and beyond.

She must not have said two words to Mr. Wheeler the rest of the way, but when they disembarked from the ferry he suggested they stop at the ordinary there to bait the horses and take this opportunity of refreshment. It was two in the afternoon. Sarah had had nothing since breakfast, and that she couldn't keep down for worry over falling sick on the road, and so she agreed and they found themselves at a table with one respectable diner and three or four local idlers. The landlady—in a dirty apron, hair hanging loose and scratching at her scalp with both hands as if to dislodge some foreign thing clinging there—told them she'd broil some mutton if they'd like, but as good as that sounded, Sarah couldn't muster much enthusiasm. She kept thinking of the landlady's hands in her hair, and when the dish did come—the mutton pickled, with cabbage and a bit of turnip in a sauce that was so ancient it might have been scraped together from the moss grown on the skulls of the Christian martyrs—she found she had no appetite. Nor did Mr. Wheeler, who tried gamely to lift the spoon a second time to his lips, but wound up pushing the dish to the corner of the table while Sarah paid six pence apiece for their dinners, or rather the smell of dinner.

They pressed on after that for Killingworth and arrived by seven at night. It was Friday now, the end of her fifth day on the road. She didn't care about the bed or the food—though the former was soft and the latter savory, roasted venison, in fact—but only the road ahead and the sanctuary of Thomas Trowbridge's house in New Haven. If she could have flown, if she could have mounted on the back of some great eagle or griffin, she would have done it without a second thought. *New Haven*, she told herself as she drifted off to sleep despite the noise and furor of the inn and the topers who seemed to have followed her all the way from Dedham, *New Haven tomorrow*.

Killingworth to New Haven

They set out early after a satisfactory breakfast, and though there were the Hammonasett, the East and West Rivers to cross and a dozen lesser waters, the fords were shallow and she barely hesitated. It was overcast and cool, the breeze running in off the sea to loosen her hair and beat it about her bonnet, Mr. Wheeler giving her a second day's course in literature, the way relatively easy. And what did she see in that country on the far side of the Connecticut River? Habitations few and far between, a clutch of small boats at sea, two Indians walking along the roadway in their tatters with scallop shells stuck in their ears and dragging the carcass of some dead half-skinned animal in the dirt behind them. She saw shorebirds, a spouting whale out at sea, a salt-water farm on a promontory swallowed up in mist, and, as they got closer to their destination, boys and dogs and rude houses and yards chopped out of the surrounding forest, stubble fields and pumpkins still fat on the vine and scattered like big glowing cannonballs across the landscape. And then they were arrived and she was so relieved to see her cousin Thomas Trowbridge standing there outside his considerable stone house with his wife Hannah and a sleek black dog that she nearly forgot to introduce Mr. Wheeler properly, but they were all in the parlor by then and tea was brewing and something in the pot so ambrosiac she could have fainted for the richness of the smell of it.

At New Haven

She stayed two months, or one day short of it, having arrived on Saturday, the seventh of October and leaving for New York on the sixth of December in the company of Mr. Trowbridge. In the interim, she vanquished her cold, wrote in her journal and prosecuted her business, at the same time taking advantage of this period of quiet to learn something of the people and customs of the Connecticut Colony, which to her mind at least, seemed inferior in most respects to the Massachusetts. The leaves brightened and fell, the weather grew bitter. She spun wool. Sat by the fire and chatted with Mrs. Trowbridge while the servants made a show of being busy and the slaves skulked in the kitchen to escape the cold of the fields. There were savages here aplenty, more even than at home, and they were a particularly poor and poorly attired lot, living on their own lands but suffering from a lack of Christian charity on the part of the citizenry. And the people themselves could have benefited from even the most rudimentary education—there wasn't a man or woman walking the streets who was capable of engaging in a conversation that stretched beyond the limits of a sow's indigestion or the salting of pilchards for the barrel.

One afternoon she happened to be at a merchant's house, looking to acquire a few articles to give the Trowbridges in thanks for their hospitality, when in walked a rangy tall bumpkin dressed in skins and Indian shoes and with his cheeks distended by a black plug of tobacco. He stood in the middle of the room, barely glancing at the articles on display, spitting continuously into the dirt of the floor and then wiping it over again with the sole of his shoe till he'd made his own personal wallow. The merchant looked inquiringly at him, but he wasn't able to raise his eyes from the floor. Finally, after what must have been five full minutes of silence, he blurted out, "Have you any ribbands and hatbands to sell, I pray?" The merchant avowed he did and then the bumpkin wanted to know the price and the ribbons were produced; at that very instant, in came his inamorata, dropping curtsies and telling him how pretty the ribbon was and what a gentleman he was to buy it for her and did they have any hood silk and thread silk to sew it with? Well, the merchant did, and they bartered over that for half the hour, the bumpkin all the while spitting and spitting again and his wife—if she was his wife—simpering at his arm.

That night, at supper, she remarked to Mrs. Trowbridge that some of her neighbors seemed to lack breeding and Mrs. Trowbridge threw her eyes to the ceiling and said she didn't have to tell *her*.

New Haven to Fairfield

The saddle again. If she'd begun to harden herself to it on the long road from Boston to New Haven, now her layover with the Trowbridges had softened her and the pains that had lain dormant these two months began to reassert themselves. And it was bitter out of doors, a taut curtain of iron-gray cloud pinning them to the earth even as the wind stabbed at her bones and jerked loose every bit of chaff and ordure in the road and flung it in her face. The breath of the horse was palpable. Her fingers and toes lost all feeling and never regained them, not for two days running.

There was a brief contretemps at the Stratford Ferry—water, more water—and she froze upright with fear and at first wouldn't budge from the horse, Thomas Trowbridge's wide lunar face floating somewhere beneath her as he pleaded and reasoned and tried repeatedly to take hold of her hand, but in the end she mastered herself and the expedition went forward. The water beat at the flat bottom of the boat and she buried her face in her hands to keep herself from screaming, and then she thought she was screaming but it was only the gulls, white ghosts crying in the gloom. After that, she was only too glad to dismount at the ordinary two miles up the road and sit by the fire while the horses were baited and the hostess served up a hot punch and a pumpkin/Indian bread that proved, unfortunately, to be inedible.

By seven at night they came to Fairfield, and lodged there.

Fairfield to Rye
They set out early, arriving just after noon at Norowalk, where the food, for once, was presentable and fresh, though the fried venison the landlady served up could have used more pepper in the seasoning and the tea was as weak as dishwater. The road from there to Rye was eight hours and more, a light snow swirling round them and the last four hours of the journey prosecuted in utter darkness, with only the faint tracks of a previous traveler to show them the way through the pale gauze of the night. And here she had a new sensation—her feet ached, aside from having gone numb with the cold, that is. For there was a prodigious high hill along the road, a mile or more in length, and they had to go afoot here, leading their horses behind them. Her legs took on all of her weight. They sank beneath her. She couldn't lift them. Couldn't breathe. And there was Thomas Trowbridge plodding ahead of her like a spirit in his winding sheet and his horse white too and the snow still falling as if it been coming down since the beginning of creation and everything else—the sun, the fields, high summer and green crops—had been an illusion. "Is it much farther yet?" she asked, gasping for breath, and she must have asked a thousand times. "Na much," came the reply, blown back in the wind.

A French family kept the ordinary at Rye, and this was a novelty to her.

She sat by the fire, shivering till she thought she would split in two, and then, so famished from the ordeal of the road and the cold and the weather she could have eaten up every last scrap of food in the county, she asked for a fricassee, which the Frenchman claimed as his speciality. "Oh, Madame," he told her, all the while pulling on his pewter cup, "I can prepare a fricassee to fit a king, your king or mine." But when it came it was like no fricassee she'd ever seen or tasted, its sauce like gluten and spiced so even a starving dog would have spat it out. She was outraged and she told him so, even as Thomas Trowbridge shoveled a simple dinner of salt pork and fried eggs into his groaning maw and pronounced it as good as he'd ever tasted. "I won't eat this," Sarah said, piercing the Frenchman with a look. "You'll cook me eggs."

"I will cook you nothing," the Frenchman said. "I go to bed now. And so do you."

Rye to Spuyten Duyvil

The night was sleepless and miserable, the bed an instrument of torture, Thomas Trowbridge and another gentleman making their beds in the same room and keeping her awake and furious with their blowing and snorting till she thought she'd have to get up and stuff rags down their throats, and they were away at first light, without breakfast. The previous day's snow had accumulated only to three or four inches but it had frozen hard during the night so that each step of her horse groaned and crackled underfoot. To say that she ached would be an understatement, and there was the cold—bitterer even than yesterday—and the scare her horse gave her every two minutes when its feet skewed away and it made a slow, heaving recovery that at any moment could have been its last. Did she picture herself down beneath the beast with her leg fractured so that the bone protruded and the unblemished snow went red with her blood? She did. Repeatedly.

By seven in the morning they reached the French town of New Rochelle, and her previous experience of Frenchmen notwithstanding, had an excellent breakfast at an ordinary there. She was so frozen she could scarcely lift the fork to her mouth and found she had no desire to leave the fireside ever again, no matter that her family would never more lay eyes on her and the widowed Mrs. Trowbridge would die in penury and the life of Boston—and its gossip—would go on without Sarah Kemble Knight ever seeing or knowing of it. But within an hour of their alighting, they were back on the road even as she cursed Thomas Trowbridge under her breath and her horse stumbled and slid and risked her life and limb with every clumsy faltering step.

They rode all day, through an increasingly civilized country, from time to time meeting other people on the road, people on foot, on horseback, in wagons. Cold, sore and miserable as she was, she nonetheless couldn't help feeling her spirits lighten as they came closer to their destination—here was real progress, in a peopled country, the wilderness falling away to the axe on both sides of the road. She took it all in and thought to memorialize it in her journal when they were arrived at New York late that night. All well and good. But then came the final crisis, the one that nearly prevented her from laying eyes on that recently foreign city with its Dutchmen pulling at their clay pipes and playing at draughts in hazy taverns, the women in their foreign dress and jeweled earrings—even the dogs that looked to be from another world—and the amenable society of the Governor Lord Cornbury from the Jerseys and the solid brick buildings built cheek to jowl all through the lower town and a hundred other things. The sleighing parties and the houses of entertainment in a place called the Bowery and the good drink—choice beer, metheglin and cider—and a standard board that consisted of five and six dishes served hot and steaming from the fire. All this. All this and more.

But when they came to Spuyten Duyvil, the Spitting Devil, at the crossing to the north end of Mannahatoes Island, with the night coming down and the wind blowing a gale and the waters surging as if it were the Great Flood all over again, she couldn't go on. There was a bridge here, narrow and unreliable, perched high up out over the waters, and it was slick with a coating of ice that lay black and glistening in the fading light. She got down to lead her horse, because if she led him she'd be lower to the ground—or the planking—and wouldn't be at the mercy of his uncertain footing. Thomas Trowbridge, hulking in his coats, paid the gatekeeper the sixpence for the two of them, and started across, mounted and oblivious; Sarah held back.

He was halfway across to the far shore, nearly invisible to her in the accumulating dark and the hard white pellets of ice that seemed to have come up with the wind, and the gatekeeper was huddled back in his hut giving her an odd look. All she could hear was the thunder of the roiling water where the river hit the surge of the tide even as the skin of it, black and unforgiving, stretched taut beneath her and exploded again. She was going to die. She was certain of it. She'd come all this way only to have the horse panic and trample her or bump her over the rail and into the spume or the bridge collapse beneath her. Thomas Trowbridge was gone now, enfolded in the mist, and he hadn't even so much as glanced back. The city was on the far shore, somewhere to the south of the island, and it was what she'd come for. Die or not, she stepped out onto the bridge.

It quaked and quailed. The wind thrashed. The horse jerked at her arm like a dead weight come to life. But she steeled herself and put one foot in front of the other and never looked down, a whole eternity passing till she made the other side in a hard pale swirl of spray thrown up off the rocks and frozen in midair. For a long while she just stood there looking back the way she'd come, the bridge fading away into the blow till it might not have been there at all. But it was there, because this was no child's tale struck with magic, and she knew, even as she turned her mount and swung out onto the road, that she would have to cross it again.

THUMB IN EYE

[CESAR'S THUMB / SADDAM'S ARM / WEIHAI'S FRAME]

by LAWRENCE WESCHLER

YOU CAN BE coming round the corner there at the world's loveliest and most beloved museum (Louisiana, of course, in Humlebaek, Denmark—but then that's a whole other story), and suddenly find yourself face-to-face with it— or rather face-to-nail, or rather face-to-face-in-nail. Your own face, that is, as presently becomes evident, reflected back at you with funhouse distortion, slightly abashed, in the broad shiny fingernail of a massive, exuberantly erect, meticulously realized bronze thumb. An exact replica, as it turns out, of its creator Cesar Baldaccini's *own* thumb, pantagraphically blown up to the size of that full-standing, gallery-trawling human, yourself—just under six feet in height. Obtruding there in the midst of your gallery walk, the thumb's a decidedly aggressive presence—it seems, as it were, to be giving the entire world the finger—but then, on second glance, it seems to be offering forth a decidedly more playfully benign and affirming gesture: a simple thumbs-up, after all. The perfect token, in other words, of the larkish place and time of its conception: Paris in 1968. (And indeed, back in Paris, to this day, you'll find the piece's big brother, an equally meticulously rendered monolith rising up stupendously out of a tree-lined plaza in the La Defense quartier, to a height of almost forty feet!)

But in fact the piece's associations go well beyond the timebound political.

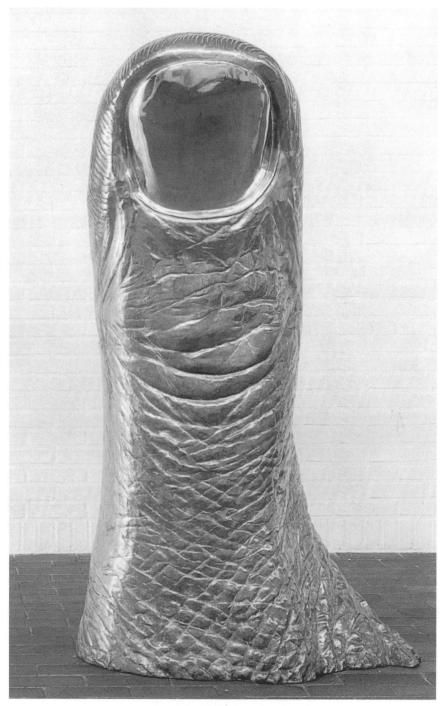

Cesar: Le Grand Pouce *(1968)*

For at another level, Cesar's Grand Pouce is simply playing off that hoary old art-historical cliché—the master painter (or sculptor) pausing in the midst of his labors, extending his arm straight out toward his subject, cocking his thumb skyward, taking the measure of his quarry, getting everything into perspective. Only, for this artist, or so we are invited to surmise, his own thumb has become endlessly more absorbing as a subject of contemplation than anything that might be transpiring in the backdrop beyond. My God, it's as if he's suddenly exclaiming, look at *that*—that structure, those folds, those whorls, those lines upon lines! What could possibly be more amazing? "When I point my finger at the moon," the zen teaching instructs, "don't mistake my finger for the moon." To which the ecstatic Cesar would seem to be responding, "Oh yeah, *why not?!*"

1968: Same year: another city. And a whole other kind of Caesar.

For that was the year, too, that the Baath party, in anything but a lark, came hacking its way back to power in Baghdad, with the thirty-two-year-old Saddam Hussein already lurking serpentine in the wings, putatively in charge of internal security. Within ten years, through a murderous series of purges, he would consolidate absolute power, and within a few years of that he would launch out on a horrifying war against neighboring Iran, a blitzkrieg that presently bogged down terribly into what was arguably the most devastating siege of trench warfare since Stalingrad, poison gas wafting over the wasted dunes night after night after night.

Several years into the debacle, with thousands and thousands of dead on both sides and no end remotely in sight, the Dictator hit upon the idea of commissioning a gargantuan celebratory monument, a wide parade ground flanked on either side by huge scimitar-wielding arms, with the bronze arms erupting sixty feet out of the ground and the clenched steel swords converging into an arch over the middle of the parade ground a further eighty feet above that. And here was the genius of the scheme: no artist was going to be required to realize the Dictator's exalted vision, for the arms and fists would be pantagraphically extrapolated from out of plaster casts of the Dictator's very own, exact down to the last pimple and follicle.

And while the French Cesar's gesture, twenty years earlier, came welling up, positively pickled in irony, even the slightest tincture of the ironic had been squeezed out of every last pore of the Iraqi master's conception. Hussein's entire regime, after all, consisted in a veritable paroxysm of the literal-minded, and anybody else's arm, let alone anybody else's exercise of

Saddam's Victory Arch (Baghdad, Iraq, 1989)

imaginative interpretation, would have undermined the entire conception. (And indeed, in a similar seizure of the literal-minded, no matter how awkward the resultant effect, it was decreed that the arms on both sides of the parade ground would have to be *right* arms, since how could His Exalted Majesty be seen wielding such incomparable power, on either side, from his left?)

It took four years to realize Saddam's vision, and indeed the work had to be farmed out, no Iraqi metalworks proving up to the task. But the Morris Singer Foundry in Basingstoke, England—one of the art world's largest and most distinguished—proved only too willing to lend itself to the Dictator's grotesque vision (just as in those days American administration emissaries, such as Defense Secretary Donald Rumsfeld, were all too willing to pay sycophantic calls on Baghdad to extend their support on behalf of the Dictator's wider war aims).

It was through the happenstance of that Basingstoke connection, however, that one of the Saddam regime's most fervent critics in exile, the London-based Kanan Makiya (pseudonymous author of that seminal chronicle of the Dictator's deprivations, *Republic of Fear*) first caught wind of the whole scheme, presently becoming almost as obsessed, in his way, with the monument as was its patron, and eventually penning an entire treatise on the subject, under his regular pseudonym of Samir al Khalil.

The meatgrinder of a war dragged on and on, finally expiring in an inconclusive cease-fire in the summer of 1988: no one had won, nothing had been resolved, hundreds of thousands had perished and thousands beyond that were left severely injured. Notwithstanding which, in a splendidly triumphant ceremony the following summer, the Dictator inaugurated his Victory Arch, as he had taken to calling it. And in a final fit of morbid inspiration, he scattered about the bases of the erupting arms thousands of literally actual Iranian helmets, many of them pierced by the holes of the very bullets that had felled their onetime wearers.

Time moved on, and vaulting from triumph to triumph, the Dictator invaded Kuwait, was pushed back, savagely suppressed the ensuing rebellion that his internal opponents (egged on and then abandoned by the first President Bush) attempted to mount, hardened his regime yet further, only to be removed from power, a decade later, when he became the collateral object of the second President Bush's post-9/11 fixations. Throughout the bombings of that decade, however, the Americans made a point of steering clear of the Victory Arch, and it indeed survived the Allied capture of Baghdad unscathed. At which point, in a sublimely opportune *volte face*, the folks over

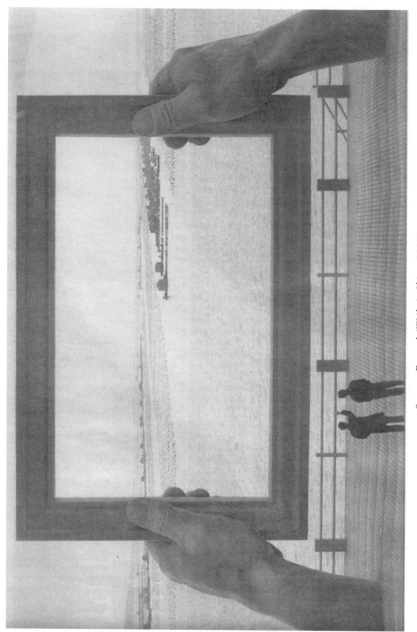

Scenery Framed (*Weihai, China, 2000*)

at the Singer Foundry patriotically volunteered up the thumbprints from their original Plasticine cast, preserved lo these many years in the company vault, to the Coalition Forces, as a potentially useful aide in someday ID-ing the suddenly fugitive Dictator. Turned out not to be needed: a swab of saliva from the mouth of the eventually captured, decidedly bedraggled malefactor having done the trick. But here's a piece of post–Iraq War trivia for you: Who today owns the Dictator's erstwhile Victory Arch?

Why, Kanan Makiya, who has in the meantime returned to Baghdad, the city of his birth, and taken out a lease on the whole hideous thing. He wanted to see it preserved as testament to the Dictator's entire terrible tenure, and he is currently raising the funds necessary to slot a museum documenting the horrors of that tenure into the base of the Arch.

One morning, a few months after the World Trade Center disaster, in the period building up to the eventual invasion of Iraq, I happened to open my hometown paper to an entirely different though equally startling image of monumental hands—a Reuters news-service photo, as its caption explained, of "Chinese tourists in the seaside city of Weihai standing at a bronze sculpture measuring 30 feet by 60 feet." There was no further elucidation of the structure, and nor have I been terribly successful in the months since in scaring up much more by way of explication.

Weihai, at the easternmost tip of the Shandong peninsula, facing Korea across a relatively narrow strait (and beyond Korea, Japan), turns out to have seen some fairly dramatic history of its own, having been the site where the Japanese Navy completely scuttled an entire Chinese imperial fleet during the Sino-Japanese War of 1894–95. Though it doesn't appear that this shameful episode is what the framed perspective of the monument in question is intended to be honoring. Rather, or so I was able to glean from a series of Google-forays, the past several years have seen a decided intensification of efforts to increase tourism in Shandong in general and Weihai in particular. Among other kudos, or so its website boasts, Weihai was recently proclaimed a National Sanitation City, and "in 1999, approved by the Ministry of Construction, it became a State-level Civilized Scenic Spot."

There are apparently all sorts of lovely vistas in the coves and islands scattered about the Weihai region, and a celebration of the "scenic" itself is clearly what this sculpture intends: *You want scenery, we'll give you scenery: Look! See! Presto! Scenery!*

Which is odd, since it's a peculiarly Western sense of the scenic. After all, Chinese art, in its whole magnificent sweep over many thousands of years, is famous for having eschewed the crimped and cramped aesthetic of the framed (Chinese art having historically reveled by contrast in scrolls, in their endless unspooling) or the trope of the window (as David Hockney has pointed out, Chinese art historically evaded that model entirely, having reveled instead in doorlike screens)—or, not to put too fine a point on it, the very fantasy of one-point perspective embodied, in the West, by the pervasive suggestion of the artist's outstretched thumb.

A thumb. A fist. A frame. The moving finger writes, and having writ...

THAT WHICH I AM

by Silvia DiPierdomenico

I AM A WOMAN of medium height. My eyes are hazel. My hair was reddish brown and wavy. I am now bald and completely hairless. My eyebrows and eyelashes remain as stubborn artifacts upon my face, strangely mocking as they begin to recede and fade. My right eye carries an acrylic foldable interocular implant Model Number MA60B, serial number 560531.018. My left eye carries a cataract that awaits ripening in order to be removed and replaced by the same interocular implant. My right eye twinkles when it picks up glare from street lamps and soft dim lighting. In my left chest I carry a BardPort with an open-ended catheter Product Code 0602610, lot number 22ELA 895. A round protrusion the size of a C-battery head, the port allows direct access to the vena cava, the large vein that returns blood from the body to the heart.

I carry in my wallet three identification cards: a Massachusetts driver's licence (I do not drive), a medical-alert card for the BardPort, and a patient lens-implant card complete with diagram for the acrylic foldable interocular implant. I hold three degrees that grant me the titles BA, MA, and MPhil after my name. I am married to an art critic. He carries in his wallet two identification cards: a New York state driver's licence, number 110-777-337, which he uses to legally operate his car to and from work, and a press pass which he uses as a means of persuasion to enter museums for free. He has blue eyes and two moral victories against the Department of Motor Vehicles. In August 2001, while he spent time on the beaches of Provence, I spent time in the emergency room of a Brooklyn hospital. As my blue-eyed husband refreshed his French, I became acquainted with the curious jargon of the medical world.

The first word I encountered was "mediastinum." This is the term used by radiologists and doctors alike to describe the space in the middle of the chest between the heart and lungs. (Medical Record Number 1074491, CT Scan of the Chest: "Extensive heterogeneous soft tissue is noted to fill the anterior mediastinum... extensive soft tissue is noted to surround the ventral and left lateral surfaces of the heart. Within the area of soft tissue opacity, subtle areas of enhancement with central low attenuation is noted, suggesting the possibility of necrosis. Findings suggest a large soft tissue mass and/or matted lymphadenopathy.") The second word I learned was "lymphoma," and all of its conjugations applicable to my newly discovered diagnosis: large cell, B-cell, intermediate grade, stage 2A, non-Hodgkin's. (Clinical Indication: large anterior mediastinal mass measuring six inches by nine inches.) The third word I learned was "bulky."

I have not made nor declared my last will and testament. Since being introduced to the medical world I have been advised to create a Living Will. I shall assemble and publish one when I get time. I live on a tree-lined street in Brooklyn. My apartment is situated on the third floor of a nineteenth-century brownstone. The number of the apartment is number 3; the number of the house is 191. The night of my hospital admission I reckoned up my belongings so that I might decide what things I would take with me. I began the task with a black-and-tan long-handled tote. It has a green tag sewn into its seam. The tag serves to identify the tote's producer as well as its city of origin and the materials used in the making of other totes of its kind. The tag reads: Hervé Chapelier, Paris, 100% Polyamide/100% Nylon, Fabrique en France/Made in France. It is a new tote and in it I placed the following: one pair Brooks Brothers (established 1818) 100% cotton men's pajamas (size small), one pair orange Dr. Scholl slides (size 8), two Victoria's Secret 100% cotton bikini panties (size small), one black Petit Bateau tank (size 14-year-old / 156 cm), one black Eres under wire bra (size 90 / 34B), that week's issue of the *New Yorker* magazine (the contents of which I have forgotten but which I hope to remember sometime soon), one black wallet with a gold zipper stamped Comme des Garçons and measuring 5 1/2 inches by 4 inches, one Alain Mikli spectacle case (for one pair of spectacles). In a small toiletries case I deposited the following articles: Clarins light activated Extra-Firming Day Cream, Lac-Hydrin Five (an alpha hydroxy acid lotion prescribed by my general practitioner to combat the "hyperkeratosis pilaris"—chicken skin—from which my upper arms suffer), Flonase—fluticasone propionate—nasal spray, 50 mcg (I spray one inhalation into each nostril, each night, before bed), Johnson & Johnson dental floss (unwaxed). After placing this case into the long-handled tote, I placed myself into a sedan marked Tel Aviv Car Service that waited outside. It would be later that night, at about midnight, on August 2, 2001, that I would become a patient.

The word *patient* arrives to the medical world from Middle English via Old French. They borrowed it from the Latin *patiens –entis*. It is the present participle of *pati*, which means "suffer." The process of becoming a patient entails receiving and wearing an Identification Bracelet. The ID bracelet is white, plastic, and above all, computer-generated. Its role is to distill each patient to his or her vital facts: Surname, Forename, 5-Digit Identification Number (which works both with and against the Patient's Full Name as a means of identification), Physician's Surname and Forename, the Patient Account Number, Date of Birth (MM/DD/YY), Sex (M/F), Age, and Admission Date.

I was hospitalized for eight days before receiving a diagnosis. My hospital room, complete with a large glass window overlooking the Brooklyn waterfront, boasted a view of the Statue of Liberty. I traded my street clothes for a blue faded hospital gown stamped LICH that I in turn traded in every two days over the course of my eight-day stay for a freshly laundered one of the same design. For each meal my art-critic husband, who was just two days and one night back from France at the time of my admission, arrived to my room smelling of roadside-diner ashtrays and carrying large I Love New York plastic bags of food. The meals were divided according to the following schema: Dawn, Midday, Dusk. The rations for Dawn (meal number one) included 1 large (tall) black coffee from Peet's Coffee and 2 croissants: one plain, the other chocolate. The menu for Midday (meal number two) consisted of grilled salmon, 4-6 oz.; steamed asparagus, 8 spears; and watercress, 1 sprig. For Dusk (meal number three) I consumed one 6 oz. grilled bison burger, a green salad with olive oil and lemon juice, and 1 slice sourdough bread. There was a cheese course. It consisted of a single cheese selection—Selles-sur-Cher, a goat's-milk cheese from the Loire in France. Because this cheese has been approved by the French government it carries the AOC label (L'Appellation d'Origine Contrôlée). I ate 1 apple, either Golden or

Gala and then drank Long Life organic green tea from a white Styrofoam cup. (Styrofoam is a North American trademark version of expanded polystyrene). Every other day I partook of dessert: 2 squares Lindt chocolate (70% cocoa). I did not consume supplements or vitamins. I did brush my teeth with the miniature toothbrush provided by the hospital. Each night before retiring I read approximately ten pages of Herman Melville's *Moby Dick*. I slept alone.

On the third day but before the third night of being a patient my sensible husband decided that it was time to inform others of my indeterminate and undesirable stay in the very desirable cardiology unit of the aforementioned Brooklyn hospital. From the park surrounding the hospital said husband dutifully placed phone calls to various friends and family. The rules were clear. The standard hospital room telephones allowed for no reciprocity: long-distance calls incoming only; local calls outgoing only. There were large placards noting "No Cell Phones" and patients like me were restricted to the floor that was subjected to twenty-four-hour surveillance by the pink-outfitted, predominantly West Indian female nurses. (Some useful pro-woman relationship tips I learned from one of these nurses: never place your shoes above your head and never leave your purse below your feet.)

When the calls came in they came in one after the other. Here is a sample:

"Hello, dear, it's Ma. George [my blue–eyed husband] tells us you are probably really sick." There was air on the line and then more words. "But no one knows yet what it is."

"Yeah, I'm sorry."

"Well, you know your father and I can't come to see you—with the long journey and this heat wave."

My mother has brown eyes and is a housewife. My father is a man of less than medium height with a penchant for outdoor labors. They live jointly (as they have always lived) in a white colonial house with green shutters surrounded by a grassy yard dotted here and there with a ceramic and wooden menagerie. Their house is situated in a small town in Massachusetts near the city of Boston. They own two cars that they do not drive in the rain, the snow, or in the evening. I was born in Saint Vincent's Hospital, in Worcester, Massachusetts. I have three sisters and no brothers. The youngest child lives in Connecticut with her husband and a dog. I am the second child to my older sister, who is the first child. She lives in New Jersey. The third child, who is also the middle child, lives in New York City on the Upper East Side. She too is a woman of medium height. Before I became a patient, strangers thought we were twins.

"You know that we can't make that kind of a long drive. Your father was recently diagnosed with night-blindness, you know."

I do not ask questions of my parents. That time, euphoric from a diminished supply of oxygen, I hazarded a query: "But why can't you?"

"I will call you back."

My art-critical husband with fading summer tan and jet-lagged blue eyes is of the opinion that I begged.

Like the calls, when the doctors came, they came one after the other. My team included but was not restricted to a seasoned cardiologist whose wife moonlighted as his office nurse, a lung specialist of Spanish descent with a penchant for romantic descriptions, and a rheumatologist who appeared threatened by others of his kind.

On my sixth day as a patient they arrived together after a brief huddle around the nurses' station down the hall. In the days following my admission each doctor had put forth his professional opinion. The lung specialist officially ruled out Pulmonary Embolism, favoring Thymoma, while the rheumatologist dismissed Scleroderma, wagering instead Thymoma. It was the cardiologist's role as the Attending Physician to venture no guesses.

As it turns out, Nuclear Medicine knew the truth. The Gallium Scan, a molecular test that has been replaced by the PET Scan, spoke thus: "On 8/7/01 the patient was given 8 mCi of Gallium 67 Citrate intravenously. Subsequently, anterior and posterior whole-body images were obtained at 48 hours post injection. In addition, SPECT images were obtained 72 hours post injection and reconstructed in axial, coronal, and sagittal planes. Impression: (1) Large area of intense increased uptake in the anterior mediastinum extending to the left hemithorax. The finding is consistent with lymphoma." The binding nature of a diagnosis hinges upon both the Attending Physician's verbal pronouncement of disease and upon the patient's receipt of the Physician Attestation Form. This form serves as an inventory of all of the procedures and diagnostic tests that were performed under the supervision of the Attending Physician in order to arrive at a diagnosis. It reads like this: "Admitting Diagnosis: 780.2 Syncope and Collapse; Principle Diagnosis: 200.02 Reticulosarcoma Thorax; Secondary Diagnoses: 443.0 Raynaud's Syndrome, 253.8 Pituitary Disorder; Procedures: 87.41 CAT Scan of Thorax, 34.25 Percutan Mediastinal BX; 92.14 Bone Scan; 92.15 Pulmonary Scan; 88.76 DX Ultrasound—Abdomen."

I was discharged and released on August 10, 2001. After declining the dispensation of "God's Love and Mercy" offered free of charge by a man of plump width who kept his bibles in a small suitcase gripped in his right hand, I signed my Discharge Résumé. It verified that I had received a copy of my Discharge Instructions (specifying limited strenuous exercise and minimal food and drink.) While the middle-aged woman who had taken up residence in the bed next to my bed accepted the complimentary solace and prayed, I waited for further instructions. These came five days later when I met and chose my oncologist. I was admitted to another hospital, a Manhattan hospital, where I received my first chemotherapy treatment. The admission date was August 20, 2001. That hospital stay lasted five days.

I am a woman of medium height. Once a month for five days I take 80 mg of Prednisone, two red gelatinous pills, each containing 100 mg of Docusate Sodium, U.S.P. (a stool softener), and 1mg of Ativan (a controlled substance for which my oncologist carries a special licence). Although Ativan is not regarded as a narcotic (it is considered a sedative) I must present the pharmacist with the official pink Practitioner Prescription Form stamped I 5744049 in order for the pills to be dispensed. After dinner I take 1 tablespoon of Milk of Magnesia (a stimulant-free laxative) and my good-natured husband injects me in the abdomen with Neupogen, a recombinant granulocyte colony stimulating factor [rG-CSF] derived from E Coli bacteria. This hormone promotes the growth of white cells in the bone marrow. The Neupogen burns as it goes under the skin and seems to experience an after-life of sorts in which it causes bone and joint pain. Between certain specified chemotherapies (numbers four and five and after number six) I receive two doses of Rituxan. Aside from rare sudden death there are no dangerous side effects associated with taking Rituxan save for high fevers and shaking chills. (I have been experiencing shortness of breath.) The pre-medications are an attempt to prevent these effects. The analysis of my prescribed pre-medications is guaranteed; the schedule is as follows: 1,000 mg Tylenol, 25 mg Benadryl (which has been reduced from 50 mg) and Decadron (a gluco-corticoid like Prednisone). In an inspired demonstration of recalcitrance I have refused the two extra-strength Tylenol.

The infusion of Rituxan takes four hours. The infusion of chemotherapy takes three hours. The pre-medications for chemotherapy include Decadron, Kytril—an anti-emetic with the generic name Granisetron HCI—and Ativan (also prescribed to treat anxiety). In the hours following my chemotherapy I take regular 1 mg doses of Ativan and Kytril until the next morning in order to avoid becoming violently ill every three hours for the entire day and night into the next day. At the beginning of the day of my chemotherapy I will be a thinking woman of medium height. By the evening, as the drugs accumulate, I will be an unblinking biomedical Stepford wife obediently swallowing sedative after sedative.

Each week I visit my oncologist's office in order to have blood drawn from my port into two plastic tubes. From a lavender-topped tube the complete blood count is measured. This includes the exact number of red blood cells, hemoglobin, white blood cells, and platelets that comprise the blood. From a black-and-red-speckle-topped tube (more fondly known as a "tiger top") my blood is sent out to a lab for a Comprehensive Panel, which measures the levels of particular indicators for damage to the organs of the liver and kidneys. Because there is no tumour marker for lymphoma as there is for numerous other cancers, my blood is monitored instead for such cancer indicators as LDH, Lactate Dehydrogenase level. Occasionally, I accept a shot in the left upper arm of a hormone called Epogen that stimulates the growth of red blood cells. This morning I opened and read a letter notifying me of my insurance's review of my case and their subsequent certification of my use of Epogen. The letter informs me that this certification has been entered into my file, and my authorization is valid through the fourth day of December in the palindromic year of 2002. I understand now that the New York State Empire Prescription Drug Plan's Prior Authorization Program "requires all prescriptions for Epogen to be certified for coverage under the Empire Plan's prior authorization protocol and that Express Scripts administers the program in conjunction with CIGNA—Connecticut General Life Insurance Company—the insurer for the New York State Empire Plan." Because I have entered into a personal account with the manufacturer of these drugs I receive a monthly billing statement from Vitality Pharmaceuticals in Roslyn Heights, New York. My Patient Code is DIPISILV.

When I finish what I am today writing it will be eleven days from my birthday. It will be twelve days from chemotherapy number 6. On the morning of the day after the day of chemotherapy (and by nine a.m.) I swallow four pale orange-pink pills, Code Number 5443. I see that the medicine bottle advises the patient to consume the chalky pills with milk and food in order to prevent nausea. In studying the cartoonish drawing of a hamburger on the pink-and-orange warning label affixed to the edge of the Prednisone container, I reflect momentarily upon medicine-bottle design and find myself queerly nostalgic for the previous bottle (after chemotherapy number 4), which featured a bright yellow sticker depicting a loaf of bread. The side effects of gluco-corticoids are divided into two groups: musculoskeletal changes and affective or behavioral changes. The former includes muscle weakness and loss of muscle mass and the latter includes such disparate problems as insomnia, mood swings, euphoria, and possible psychosis. While flipping through the "recipe book" doctors use to calculate drug doses for patients, I discovered that the official characterization of psychosis in this instance has been defined as "ineffective coping and role-relationship problems if patient unprepared."

Each morning I drink one liter of Evian mineral water and four cups of coffee. Alone in the kitchen I read aloud the dedication to the consumer: "It's easy to know where we're coming from, a pure, natural spring tucked in the foothills of the French Alps." Encouraged by the slogan "Untouched by man. Perfect by nature," I consume one St. Joseph's 81 mg Adult Low-Strength Aspirin to prevent a blood clot from forming in my port. I brush my teeth with a Butler G.U.M. soft-bristle toothbrush Number 430, USA. I don bathing suit TYR size 36 each morning for my daily swim. I wear foam goggles by Barracuda. My swim cap is a gray Speedo which is composed of silicon and not latex. My flip-flops are by Dr. Scholl. I shower with L'Oreal HydraFresh foaming cream and am able to contact them for advice by ringing 1-800-322-2036. I wash my bald scalp with PhytoVolume, a French volumizer shampoo (Yarrow extract, 40%). It boasts the advantage of Chitosan, a shellfish-derived ingredient that keeps curly hair smooth. I moisturize my face with Doctor's Dermatologic Formula (DDF) Moisturizing Photo-Age Protection Cream. It contains SPF 30. It does not contain oil or fragrance. Last year, in an attempt to prevent breaking strands of my fine hair I purchased a Mason Pearson (Junior) nylon and horsehair bristle brush. At the moment I have no need for such an item nor for the following items: a comb, hair gel, hair conditioner, a hairdresser, hairspray, a blow dryer, straightening balm.

My husband and I owe various friends and family thank-you cards for wedding gifts. The wedding was on the first of December, 2000. I was twenty-nine years old and had reddish-brown wavy hair. I smoked light American Spirit cigarettes recreationally. I swam five days a week at the local YWCA. I spent long weekend evenings out in smoke-filled bars and restaurants. I never ate dessert. Kiosk vendors carded me for cigarettes. In New York City the V train had not yet replaced the F train, causing all manner of head-scratching confusion. In my wallet I carried two identification cards: my Massachusetts driver's licence (I do not drive) and my intraocular implant card. I did not know then that my thymus gland had begun to metamorphose into a mediastinal tumour.

WHAT IT AIN'T

by SUSAN STRAIGHT

BECAUSE IT WASN'T nobody else, okay? You gon ask me that question, straight up, now that you thirteen, and you haven't looked around all your life? Who you saw?

Lafayette. Fine brother. Played football when we went to school. Uh-huh. Left Clarette cause she workin and he ain't. Like she jumpin for joy about that situation. Like she ain't scramblin. Tryin to keep up with her boys.

They met at the basketball court. Same as we did. Me and your daddy. We didn't go to the movies. Ain't had no car or money half the time.

Didn't call it Dating. You sound like some old lady.

People just said, You mess with Lafayette now? And you said yeah or no. Then you just hung out. House party sometimes. Or the park.

Nobody said it was Louisiana or Alabama. Now you need to close your mouth, cause you edgin over to rude and I ain't readin that map now. Not while I'm drivin your behind to another birthday party where I gotta hear you talk about how our party is you go shoppin with your daddy and then I take you out for etouffee. Creola's where my mama always took me for my birthday, and if you don't like it you can make yourself some eggs.

No, I ain't stayin. Sonia bring you home when she get Trinette.

Cause by the time they hit that piñata it feel like they crackin my skull.

Cause it's February, okay? What does that mean?

Right. It means tax time. It means I got five returns to do today.

Here. Take the present.

What? When you buy instant chai? Thanks, baby. Go.

What do you mean, Give up? Why did we give up?

What? Why did I give up on him? Like it's my fault he—

No. I ain't doin this now. Wait til we get on the freeway, please, before you start the game show.

Yeah, I heard you. Trinette's daddy was there. And—

So Sonia gave him some cake. I know what he did. He probably got to the rink late, stood around with Darnell and Nacho and them, watched y'all untie your skates, said y'all were gettin too big and he could hardly stand lookin at you, and then Sonia gave him some cake and pizza and they talked for a couple minutes and then y'all did presents.

Why wouldn't I be right? You think this is a movie?

So Sonia supposed to scream at him about the past and throw cake in his face, right in front of Trinette?

And he would move back in with Sonia and be a daddy like you see on TV? Turn into Damon Wayans or some shit like that?

Yeah, I cussed.

Don't even think about it.

Cause that's half of Trinette. And I ain't sayin a damn thing more, so you can turn up your Walkman and turn your face out the window.

When I see y'all walkin around, it's like seein me and Sonia and Glorette and Sisia in some crazy fun-house mirror.

What you mean, where? Everywhere. The fun house is every street. Every walkway in the damn mall. *That '70s Show*. Girls have afro puffs and those puckery shirts we used to wear. But the belly. We didn't show ourselves like that.

Yeah, you seen Chaka Khan, on that first Rufus album. Those big bell-bottom jeans and a little T-shirt. Okay. Her stomach flat and her navel look like it's laughin.

Yeah. Y'all can call em flares.

I looked like Nona Hendryx. Patti LaBelle's runnin buddy. No, you ain't gon find no album cover with her. Not unless you look through all the albums your daddy took with him.

Eight years ago.

Navel string. You know what? The old ladies on Jacaranda Street, when I was so little, they used to tell my mother and them, "Bring the navel string home from that dang hospital so we can bury it by the porch. Else you gon lose your child."

They lost most of us anyway.

But you girls. No, you ain't gettin left here by yourself. I'll wait for you. No, I ain't goin into Payless. Not today. Cause my feet hurt. I ain't lookin at shoes today. Mall benches hard as sittin on a curb.

We had little baby-doll shirts, too. But we didn't have the bra strap danglin out in a special color. Belly rollin over the jeans, the diamond hangin on a chain out the navel, pubic hair practically showin. That blonde girl—I can see her hipbones way above her jeans. Like she went and sewed rocks under her skin.

We used to see those ads for Wate-On in *Ebony*. So you could get your womanly curves and the brothers would want you. But we didn't have no trouble with them wantin us.

You got Darnell, the brother you see with the landscapin truck. Three girls. He ain't run away. But it's somethin about him. He likes that truck, likes his house, likes comin home and Brenda makes gumbo and he drink a beer and sit on his porch. Cause that's what he does.

Esther ain't had nobody since Killer Joe. Cause she do hair all day, got ten people in the house, and all her kids. You see her across the street sittin on the porch at night. Glad to be alone for a few minutes before somebody want somethin.

I know you see them. I see them. I'm sittin on the porch with you, okay? You. All your clothes clean, and your hair braided, and your homework done, and my pile of 1040s sittin there waitin for me when you take your narrow behind off to bed.

That's enough questions.

No.

You ain't watchin *Law and Order*. Then I gotta hear why I ain't hooked up with that fine brother work for NYPD. Cause he don't exist, okay? And if he did exist, he sure wouldn't live on this street. Wrong side of the whole continent, okay?

Plus I'm too old.

Don't even go there. Thirty-five and you think it's a miracle I can still walk.

No.

You ain't grown. Go.

Sonia. You tired?

How's Trinette?

Yeah. I know it's late. What you mean, What I want?

I know you still waitin on that dryer to finish. Don't play like you done.

Remember when we used to say, What it is?

You forgot? Lafayette and Nacho and them say, What it is? We used to say, What it ain't, what it never will be.

Okay. Trinette twelve now, right? She asked you about JT yet? Why y'all ain't together?

I heard. He came to the party and made his appearance.

Melisse gon ask me why I ain't married somebody responsible. Somebody stayed around. Why I had to mess with somebody like Chess.

Yeah. Even gotta talk about his name. "How did he get a stupid nickname like that? Didn't guys back then ever call each other by regular names?" Uh-huh. After I told her not to disrespect anyone grown like that, she gon get mad about her own name! Told her for the hundredth time she called for her grandmere and she gon say she got a old-fashion name and everybody make fun of it. Told her that's disrespect too and sent her butt to her room.

Yeah, again. What, Trinette turn into an angel this week?

See? I don't take away TV cause we don't have cable anyway and accordin to Melisse, Ain't nothin on.

Yeah, I'm tired. Got two returns to do tonight. Mr. Harper and Mr. Walters.

Mr. Harper seventy now. I been doin his taxes ten years.

Look, all I'm sayin is your time gon come. Trinette ain't jammed you up, she will. Then you get to say what I did. Damn. Melisse gon tell me she can't believe wasn't nobody like Theo from *The Cosby Show* around. She saw *Tribute to the Cosbys* on TV last week and now she think we just in the wrong place. We should be livin in New York. In a brownstone. She like to say brownstone. Says stucco a foolish word anyway. Must be Italian and here we are in California.

Well, yeah. Why Theo didn't come on vacation over here to Rio Seco? Coulda shown him the Westside. Coulda taken him to Oscar's for ribs.

Girl, he probably didn't eat pork.

What you mean did I play chess?

They call me that cause when I was on the court I got everybody movin just where I wanted em to and then I made my move and took the rock to the hole.

That all you called for?

Go on to bed, now. Your mama probably think you talkin to some fool.

Cause they always want somethin.

Even when they say they don't.

Put on your seatbelt or your mama gon kill me with her eyes.

Why you gon ask me that, Melisse? Your mama told me you ain't allowed to go out with no fools til you fifteen. Got two years to figure it out your ownself. Why you gon ask me?

Melisse. This ain't my job. My job for you to pick out them clothes for school. Summer last too long for you. You got too much time to be thinkin if you askin all these questions.

You asked your mama?

What she say?

What you mean, She say what she said. You gettin a mouth?

Cause they always want somethin. Look, you want clothes right now. And your mama know every August I buy the clothes.

Watch your mouth. You ain't half grown, okay?

Look, it's too goddamn hot in this parkin lot to argue. Cause we didn't have nothin back then. And we was playin ball, or whatever, playin three on three, and then the girls come around and want to hang out. And everythin costs money.

I'm talkin about, Buy me a ice cream from the truck. Give me a ride. You don't think gas cost money? And everybody ain't had a car, so we had to borrow a homey's ride, and he gon want five dollars for gas. And then she gon say, Why you ain't got me nothin for Christmas? And you just hung with her on the court three, four times. You want somethin and she want somethin and you think what you want free but it ain't.

No free lunch? Your teacher say that? Ain't nobody wanted lunch.

Sonia.

Hey.

I heard Glorette got herself killed. The alley behind that taquería. She was still workin Palm Avenue. Girl, she still looked so good, and I swear, I would see her walkin and think, How she gon live her life like that, doin all them drugs, and her hair halfway down her back and her legs like Tyra Banks?

Well, yeah, it was a lotta exercise. Sonia, you too cold.

But we all the same age. She used to sit in front of me in math class.

I used to think I would meet somebody, sittin at the mall waitin on the girls or in New Hong Kong at lunch when I was takin a break from returns.

Not Melisse and Trinette, but shoot, those older girls, they pass by with everything hangin out and their hair perfect. And thongs. At the top of the jeans. Them boys have little-girl twists like we did when we were in diapers. Pants hangin down past sweats hangin down past gym shorts hangin down past boxers.

Melisse say she don't know how they carry all that weight at school. And the girls got goosebumps like—like chickens. When my mama used to pluck them in the back yard.

That ain't Dating. I don't know why she calls it that.

Well, they're twelve. Melisse say plenty twelve-year-olds already goin to the movies, out to eat.

I'm hip. Chess never took me out to eat until we were married.

Shut up.

Well, yeah, after that I cooked. So did you. These girls probably go out more at twelve than we did at twenty.

Cause Chess always say nothin free. I wonder what he told Melisse. I wonder did she ask him.

She told me, "Cause people do date. They go to the movies, to the mall. Tisha's boyfriend bought her a celly and one a those Italian charm bracelets and that coat she got on."

That's what she told me, Sonia.

Sonia. She said they would never settle for what we settled for. How I'm supposed to tell her?

Trinette still up? Alright then. Later.

Sonia.

Sonia.

Why he had to stand out there? Sonia. Why? He knew them kids was dealin around the Launderland and Sundown Liquor. He knew they been fightin. He used to always tell me, Bullet got no name on it—meant for whoever in the way.

Sonia. Why he have to have Camels? Midnight and he gon stand out there like it's some goddamn movie from the old days. Foxy Brown. He *knew*, Sonia. What I'm supposed to tell Melisse? Oh, my God. Dear God.

You comin now? What about Trinette?

Sonia. Sonia.

Sonia. She mad at me. At *me*. Keep askin me why I had to be with him. Why. Why I had to have her with him.

She mad at me. Like it's my fault he's dead.

I heard them kids. Talkin about He got gotted. That's how they call it. And Melisse in her room screamin at me. Why you had to be with him?

Because it wasn't nothin but him.

How you gon look at me like that?

Like that.

Like you want me to die, too. Right now, on the way to Target. You think I want to be goin to Target to buy you a black dress? You think I want to stay up all night makin pound cakes for your grandmere? Your daddy's mama can't make enough food for all them people, and it ain't nobody else to help her.

I heard you. I always hear you. Just cause I don't say nothin don't mean I didn't hear you.

Sonia.

Now she ain't said nothin to me for days. Since the service. All them people, and she ain't said nothin about none of em. Ain't asked me about a single one. Ain't made fun of their names, ain't talked about the funky clothes or how old we all look.

Nothin.

Now that you in the front seat I can't help but hear you. Drivin all over God's creation for you. Practice and Christmas shoppin. What you gon put on his grave?

Big Hunk bars and a basketball? You know what? I think that's perfect.

Melisse.

Don't cry.

Melisse. If I hadn't met him, you wouldn't be you.

Yeah, I know that's junior-high biology. But it's true. Your eyes, your fingers, all that.

Well, yeah, you got my thighs. Way of the world, baby.

Melisse. Come on.

Okay. Must be better if you talkin cellulite. See, we didn't even have that word. We just said must be jelly cause jam don't shake like that. And back then, with your daddy and them, that was a compliment.

Yeah, I know you find that hard to believe.

Where's practice? Isn't it at the school gym? Why didn't you tell me?

Yeah, I washed your socks. Don't I always?

Yeah, you smell fries. You think I never have to drive during work? I eat in the car half the time so I can get my prescription or whatever you need at the store.

Why you care what I eat? I know what you eat. Whatever they got at school.

Sometimes Mickey D all I have time for. Drive thru.

Well goddamnit. I know it ain't good for me.

I know it's got too many calories, and I know where they go.

You know what? Close your mouth for a while. Til we get off the damn freeway.

We ain't off.

Let me tell you what you told me this month. You said, Mama, look at *People*. Check this out. Foxy Brown got a necklace and some dog tags all covered with diamonds. Worth $250,000.

You said, Mama, Tyrese top lip longer than his bottom lip. What that tell you about a person?

You said, It says here the shortest celebrity marriage on record was eight hours.

I ain't seen you get all mad about that.

I heard you.

I heard you, but when you keep askin me Why you pick him? Why weren't you smarter? And I said Wasn't no pickin really, back then, things just happened. And you got all smartass and said Excellent. Good plan, Mama.

And my mama woulda slapped the pink off your lips.

Yeah.

You ain't heard Auntie Clarice and them talk? You ain't listened. You hear them at Christmas, every year, talking bout X-Box and GameBoy, start with Girl, back in 1946 we sure didn't get nothin but a orange and a scarf. Maybe two hard candies.

Cause oranges why they all came here. California. Oranges. They made the boxes for the groves out here in Rio Seco.

Yeah. Now he's buried with his people. And you here. With the ones you got left.

Sonia.

Sonia. She gon ask me, Why couldn't you pick somebody like that guy who came to our school to talk about college loans? He was nice.

Probably from LA.

I don't know how I feel. It ain't like I thought he would ever touch me again. Ain't like he looked they way he used to. But I remember crazy things—how can I still remember somethin like what his shirt felt like? When we danced?

I know. On my cheek. They don't even dance like that. Never will. No Isley Brothers.

Well, yeah, I heard their new song, but it ain't like the old ones. Not like ours.

Melisse roll her eyes when I change the station to Soul Oldies. She say I should be ashamed to listen to somethin with the word "old" in it. Then I go in her bedroom and she's sleep, and I smell perfume on her sheets where it rubbed off—that new glittery body spray all the girls wear? And I can see sparkles on her pillow. Make me cry right then. She don't know. All the times we talk, right, and she don't know.

Sonia. Girl. We didn't know.

I didn't.

Hold up—mine's done, too. Them damn socks. She's got practice twice a week, but look like them socks tangle up into a knot every night.

Alright then. Tomorrow night.

What it ain't. What it was.

GOOD MONKS

by MALINDA McCOLLUM

A DELIRIOUS MOMENT. Picture this. Pale man shouting, "I am drunk on water and the bitterest love!" In the near-empty diner his voice surprising as a first drop of blood.

Severa eyed the man from her booth along the glass wall of Andy's Eats. She was stretching a cup of coffee into the infinite, sip by sip.

"Water!" the pale man shrieked. "Love!" His table was in the center of the diner. On it, onion rings and a red malt, untouched. Two streaky-haired kids seated at a long chrome counter spun on their stools and waggled their boots at him. Severa recognized them as sophomores from school. They were just chippers, occasional flyers, not too hardcore.

"Kool-Aid!" one of the kids yelled.

"Insanity!" said the other, cracking up.

A waitress tending to a candy display at the register sighed. Her eyes looked like cranberries. Her arms disappeared into a carton of Zagnuts.

"Water!" the pale man screamed again.

The waitress withdrew from the Zagnuts and started toward him.

Severa shouldered her heavy leather bag and walked to the man, arriving just before the waitress. Coming right up, mister.

"He's mine," she said, grabbing the man's arm. "I'll take him."

"Yours?" the waitress said.

"For now and maybe always." She worked her hand up the wide sleeve of the man's coat. He quieted in her hold.

"Why weren't you all at the same table?" the waitress asked. "Why were you letting him scream?"

"You have beautiful eyes," Severa told her.

"So you're going to pay for him? Since he's yours and all?"

Severa tugged on the man until he stood. "I can let him sit here and scream," she said, "or I can get him out of here."

"You can't pay for him?"

"Let's see if he can pay for me." She spoke loudly to the man. "Do you have money? Can you settle your debts?"

The man reached inside his jacket and came back with three perfectly folded bills.

"There. Now we're all square." She placed the money on the table. The waitress seemed uncertain, so Severa repeated, "You have beautiful eyes."

The waitress's face dimmed as she worked the question: complimenting or making fun?

"If you weren't on duty," Severa cooed, "I'd ask you home. I have this peppermint lotion I could rub on your feet."

For some reason, that decided it. The lady's whole body went stiff.

"Bitch," the waitress said, "get out now."

Outside, beyond the nimbus of the diner's floodlight, the night was its darkest, hoarding all. Someone somewhere was playing bad chords on a guitar. Severa bit her lip. Doubt and worry, worry and doubt. In the diner she had made more waves than was good for her.

"I'm drunk on water," the man said, softer now, on the sidewalk. Under his coat his arm was fleshy and bare. Severa gave it a few squeezes.

"Goes down easy don't it," she said. So all right: she needed money. Her boyfriend Doug had left her. Alone, she had nothing. A few weeks ago she'd spent most of their savings on a nose job. And now she needed to eat, didn't she? She did!

"You like my face?" she said to the man. "You see symmetry there?"

"Water," the man said dully, "oh, oh, water."

"What about bitter love?" she said. "Don't forget that."

The man stumbled forward a few steps, but she didn't let him go. There was a slat bench up against the diner wall, and she led him to it, to get a better view. A slight guy, gentle-looking, with smooth skin and single-lidded eyes.

"Where you from, man?" she asked. "Your face ain't like mine, for real."

"Laos," the pale man said. His voice oozed through the air like something liquid. "Bordered by five different countries on all sides."

"No way to the sea," she said. "I relate."

"Somvay," said the man.

"Lola," said Severa.

Somvay placed his hands in prayer position and nodded. She sat next to him. A thick wig, a bandanna stretched over her head like a mantilla, dark glasses, and lots of makeup, but still she nuzzled into Somvay's arm when a car drove past them, casting its white pitiless light. Better safe.

"So I heard they have prostitutes in Laos that jerk guys off with their feet." She lifted her feet and rubbed her kicks together. "Look, Daddy, no hands!"

Somvay stared at her. "Most sacred," he said finally, gesturing to her head. "Least sacred." He pointed to her feet. Then he slapped his cheeks lightly and drew a deep breath.

In her bag was a roll of duct tape and a thermos of beer with codeine stirred in. The idea came from Doug. He used to go ganking with his ex-girlfriend. The ex-girlfriend would dress tarty and lure a drunk weakling somewhere lonely. Then she'd drug him or Doug would hit him and they'd take everything he had. To Severa, it seemed heavy on effort as compared to reward, but Doug was convinced it was worth it, with a low chance of getting caught. When the mark awoke, disoriented and embarrassed, he was unlikely to go to the police. And even if he did, his story would be fuzzy. Doug didn't want to go back to jail.

Somvay touched her arm. "What happened here?" he asked, lifting her bandaged wrist.

"I fell," she lied. She had punched through a window. "I was running after my dog and I tripped."

"Where did you get your dog?" He let her go.

"The shelter," she lied again.

"Good. Good for you. You saved it from death."

She studied him. "Buddhist?"

"Yes."

"Me too! I have some books. Later on, we should chant chant chant."

A hick girl in tight jeans swung past the bench then, massaging the neck of the boy walking with her.

"Fuck him!" Severa yelled. "I did!"

The girl turned quickly, like she might start something, but then she kept walking. That's right, chick.

"I'm drunk," Somvay announced.

"So why you drinking tonight?" Severa asked him.

"My girl," he started, "my flower, she won't let me go. In Laos, where I am from, I bicycled to her house every day, to help her learn to read. We sat upon the hill behind her house and she stared across the river at Thailand. I had to take her hand and place it on the page to bring her attention back."

"Here," Severa said and gave him the red thermos from her bag. "Some beer to cut that water's power."

He unscrewed the cup cap and poured himself a drink.

"One night my mother awakened me in the dark. I took my soccer ball, and a small bag of clothing, and followed my mother to the banks of the river. When I saw the barge there, I tried to run away, back to my flower. But a man grabbed me, and took my mother's hand, and we floated across the Mekong."

"Mekong," Severa said, trying it out.

"For many months after we lived in an earthen hut in a Thai camp. There was a well at the edge of camp, but it ran dry quickly. I would go with my mother, and I still remember the fear as we came to it, that this time we would be too late." Somvay paused. "And then the taste of water on my tongue, sweet as something sugar."

He sipped from the thermos cup.

"Here there is plenty of water and I still am not satisfied. I drink and drink and I am still thirsty. I have lost my way."

"I know how you feel," Severa said. She patted his leg. "My boyfriend and I just broke up."

Above, the moon peeked out of a neat envelope of clouds. Then the air was heavier and heavier until it started to rain down upon them.

"Oh no," Somvay said. "No, no." His shoulders sagged.

"Close your mouth," Severa commanded. "We don't want you anymore drunk."

The taxi driver was as tanned as a detasseler. Severa put Somvay in the rear of the cab and settled in the front seat. She figured the driver would look at her less there than if she sat in the back, with him working the rear view mirror.

"So I heard that fat prostitutes let johns get away with more," she told the cabbie. "The rule of the marketplace makes it like that."

"The rule of the marketplace is one hell of a bitch," the cabbie said slowly. "The rule of the marketplace kicks your ass good."

"The market is a bitter and suffering place," said Somvay from the back. "Take the marketplace away."

"Oh, don't mind him," Severa said. "He's a major Buddhist. He talks big. Me, I'm the kind of gal that appreciates works way more than faith." She drew close to the cabbie's ear. "What good things you done lately?"

"I've done a few."

"Please," she said, "tell me about your good things. At length."

"Well," the cabbie drawled, "well, there is a certain length I could tell you about."

"I'm drunk," said Somvay.

Severa passed back the thermos.

"So about that length," the cabbie said. His voice was easy, but she could hear the meanness underneath. All right.

"How long?" she asked.

"Until what?" Somvay leaned into the space between the front seats. "What are you saying?"

"I'd have to say I've never measured," the cabbie said. The moon had moved and now lit the bronze hollows of his face.

"What they say," Somvay broke in, voice thick, "is that pain is what it is you measure pleasure by."

"No, pumpkin," Severa corrected him, "pain is what it is you measure pain by."

"Both of y'all are wrong," the cabbie said. "Pleasure is what you measure pleasure by." And then his heavy fingers were up on her thigh.

Right on. "Stop the cab!" she yelled. The cabbie, unbothered, pulled to the curb. Severa threw open the door and called for Somvay to join her. He did, stepping gingerly out of the car. The rain was almost nothing now.

"You owe me ten bucks, girlie," the cabbie said.

Severa helped Somvay lower himself to the sidewalk, then marched around to the driver's side. Smiling her wicked smile, she bent to his open window. "I owe you shit. You're lucky I'm not reporting you. You'd never drive a cab again."

The cabbie grasped her head. His hands covered her whole ears. "Listen, honey," he said, pulling her in, fingering the bones of her skull, "I'm giving you this one for free. This little lesson. It's real easy picking up a bruise. It's real tough getting rid of it."

"Thanks, working man!" she said, jerking away. She danced to the sidewalk and threw a rock at the cab as it drove off.

The rock missed. She cursed. It was a bad sign.

Severa and Somvay made their way through dense woods to a clearing all the kids called the Lost Planet. Not easy—first a slick weedy ravine, next train tracks, then a faint path to the Planet's rocky beach. A lime pit there foamed purple, Des Moines's own small terrible sea.

Severa removed her dark glasses and held fast to Somvay by the loops of his jeans. He stepped tentatively with not enough bend in his knees. When they arrived at the bank of the lime pit, she let go of him for a moment, to squeeze some dampness from her wig. Somvay tripped and ended up on all fours.

"Come on," she said impatiently, kneeling, "let's attempt to remain upright." His face was flushed, so she untied the bandanna from her hair and wiped his cheeks and ears. Sweat wet her fingers through the cloth. When she was little her dad had worked summer construction, and when he came home sweaty, he shook salt onto his palm and licked it off. He said it was to replace what he lost during the day. She loved seeing him do it. It seemed smart. One hot August she ran around the block in a wool sweater so she could come in and eat salt straight, like her dad. Instead she fainted and broke her head on the sidewalk and a neighbor had driven her to the hospital to get stitches.

"I am in trouble," Somvay said. "I am drunk and I have lost my way."

"Oh no," she said. "We're going to have some fun is all."

"I do not want to be here."

"Lie down." She gave him a little shove and he sat, heavily. "Lie back."

When he did, his shirt rode up, revealing his smooth belly, the aching cut of his hips. He really was beautiful, and for a second she considered changing plans, letting him take her home, cook her something spicy, wake her in the morning with a kiss as long and clear as a ringing bell. But instead she set her bag on the ground and straddled him, pushing his arms over his head.

"Here," she said, "here in America, we free ourselves by getting totally confined." She retrieved the roll of tape and taped his wrists together.

"Ah, a Baci ceremony," he said, and it was the happiest she'd seen him. "Make three knots: one for good health, one for prosperity, one for joy."

"Let me help you off with your shoes." Severa slid back and pulled his canvas kicks from his feet. No socks, so she applied the duct tape to his bare ankles. She was starting to sweat under her wig so she removed it and put it on the ground.

"You can kill me," Somvay said suddenly, "but not yet."

She stopped her preparations. "Not ever," she said, annoyed. "Who do you think I am?" She repositioned herself on his stomach, knees close to his body. He wore a delicate silver chain high on his throat, and when she touched it she felt his pulse against her thumb.

"Relax," she said. "Tell me more about Laos."

He obeyed. "When I was a boy I played ball around the *wat* with my friends. Beautiful trees there, and the temple's golden roof. My mother warned me to be very careful about kicking the ball, because if I were to lose control of it, and if it were to hit a monk, I would lose merit. We were careful, but we were boys and one day I kicked the ball with the top of my foot so it would fly over my friend Thong. It flew, but when it came down it hit a monk. In the head!"

Behind her, the terrible sea gurgled and breathed.

"I froze," he continued. "And the monk looked at me, eyes black, and then bowed and said, 'Thank you. For the opportunity to practice patience.'" Somvay brought his arms up an inch from the ground, and she felt him shift beneath her. "And now I say thank you. For this. For the reminder that I own nothing, not even my body."

"Cut it out," she said, truly nervous now.

"*Bo pen nyang,*" he said. "Never mind." He laughed, and it was like a red scarf in the air.

She kissed him on the mouth, just once, hard, and when she stopped his eyes were shut, his breath light. She taped his mouth and reached under him for his wallet. Inside, a credit card—she could use that tonight at least—and thirty-five dollars cash. Behind the bills was a cracked photograph, and when she removed it she saw a young monk in orange robes, lacquer bowl in hand, standing beneath a well-leafed tree. Somvay, of course, same soft eyes and flat cheeks. She slid the photo and credit card into her jeans. She laid the wallet next to her wig. She rose and circled Somvay's still body. The lime pit taunted her, that terrible sea. For a second she imagined floating across it, away from her dirty little life, hitting Thailand, super-green, on the other shore.

But everything's working, she reassured herself. I'm alive. Isn't that the real truth?

Then she heard. The growl of an engine, a dark beat pumping through bad speakers. She grabbed her wig and bag and reached under Somvay's arms. He was out. Holding her breath she dragged him to a spread of brush, dirt funneling into where his jeans gaped from his waist. When she heard the vehicle pop over a log blocking the Planet's secret path, she dropped Somvay and moved away into other weeds.

A truck careened into the Planet. Two men in the cab. And then she saw Somvay's wallet near the bank of the pit. And his bound ankles, not quite in the weeds, shined on by the big moon.

Severa huddled in the dirt. The men were first-class cranksters, she could see right away, scabby and bone-thin. Just skinny little zipheads, she told herself. And hadn't her dad once showed her some killer judo moves? But then again the crank had probably made the men vicious and paranoid enough to pack heat.

Still: the wallet. The ex-monk in the woods. Severa closed her eyes and slowed her breath and tried to tap into the vibes of any good forces that might be lurking, able to help.

The men had left the truck's headlights on which lit the clearing nice and bright. One of the them, a blue-skinned guy with long arms, hurriedly fired a camp stove and unloaded boxes of chemicals and a collection of small empty jars. The other, small and hairless, cut open a series of Vicks inhalers, removed the cottons, and mixed them with water in a glass meatloaf dish.

"I bumped into this girl last night," she heard the bald man say, "this South-of-Grand girl, and she goes, 'Trade you the rings off my fingers for a gram.'"

The blue man sprayed starter fluid into a jar and shook it until there were clouds inside. "I'd have said, 'How 'bout you give me your fingers instead.'"

The bald man frowned.

"I'd bite off a finger and use it to get her wet!"

"Nice," the bald man said. He dumped a cupful of clear fluid into the meatloaf dish and balanced it on the camp stove. A smell like nail-polish remover made Severa's eyes tear.

Something rustled the high grasses around her, something stronger than wind. When she looked, Somvay was squirming. She slid toward him, keeping an eye on the clearing. In their rush to cook up, the men had missed the wallet and the ankles both, but now Somvay was getting noisy.

Kneeling behind him, she pulled his body—slowly, slowly—farther into the weeds. His eyes blinked open. A sound burbled in his throat. Could he breathe? Watching the men, Severa held one finger to her lips and untaped his mouth.

"Water," Somvay said.

The blue man looked up.

"Quiet," Severa whispered fiercely. "None here."

"Who's there?" the blue man said. He started toward their hiding weeds, and Severa saw the gun in his pants. So she retaped Somvay's mouth and stepped into the clearing. It was exactly like going on stage.

"Hey, you all seen a giant black guy out here?" she said. "I lost track of my boyfriend somewhere in these woods."

The men appraised her. She tried to look ugly and old.

"You're not law, right, dressed like that?" the blue man asked.

She made herself giggle stupidly. "No, no, these are date clothes. My boyfriend and I come down here on weekends and practice with his gun."

"Glad to hear it," the blue man said. "Because I've been in jail once and I'd kill somebody first before I went back."

"You mean you'd kill yourself before going back," the bald man corrected him.

"Is that what I said?" the blue man asked Severa, smiling. "Did my brother hear me right?"

She ignored the question. "You two are brothers?"

"We're brothers," the bald man said. "You can call him Luke and me Pat."

"But we're not like your brother," blue Luke said. "That's one crazy brother, leaving a little girl alone in the woods."

With men, Severa knew, the key is to not let them think they scare you. Don't give them anything. Just get away.

"Enjoy your crappy redneck heroin," she said. "I'm gone."

"Wait a minute," Luke said. "I don't want to chase you."

She stuck in her place.

"If you're lost, it's no good to run all over," he said.

"Really is better to stay still," advised Pat.

"All right," she said, voice light, "I can hang for a time." She found room for herself between a pile of Prestone cans and a box of Red Devil lye.

Luke took a step toward her and sent the cans clattering with his foot. Then he settled into the empty space he'd made. His neck was dirty above the collar of his shirt. His pupils were big as dimes.

Severa stared back, trying to be cool. She had a plan. If he made a move, she'd yell, "Thank you Lord for sending him!" If he kept going she'd whisper, "Praise Jesus for every act you do." That might make him lose his nerve.

In the meantime, she yawned and twisted away from him, pretending to stretch. She cast a quick glance toward where Somvay was. Her stomach wobbled when she saw him sitting head above the grass line, arms untaped. He was going to free himself and leave her. Then where would she be?

Her spine cracked, and she twisted back to center. Pay attention, girl. That's everything now. Her best hope was that these guys fixed and left fast.

"Can I see your gun?" she asked Luke sweetly, to distract him.

He took the gun from his waistband and pointed it at her.

Not so scary. In fact, something about a gun in her face made her feel like she was exactly where she was supposed to be.

"Come on, man," said Pat. "That's uncool."

"You think?" Luke let the barrel hover eye-level a few seconds more and then stood and replaced the gun in his pants. "Well, that's all right. Night's long. Besides, I got to go drain myself of poisons before I put new poison in."

"I have to piss too," said Pat.

"Why don't you first stay with her," Luke said. "We sure wouldn't want anybody to be alone." He loped toward the truck, slow and easy as a cop.

Severa watched to make sure he didn't veer toward Somvay. Then she turned back to Pat. He avoided her glance, scrambling up to gather the cans his brother had scattered. His ears were dull yellow and scarred.

"What's with them angry ears?" she said.

He stopped and used a can to poke one lightly. "Used to be a firefighter," he said. "These days they got helmets with protectors. Back then, your ears were all out."

"Poor you," she said, pretending sympathy.

"Better before," Pat said, "with your ears like antennas. Hot ears meant it was time to bail." He let the cans fall from his arms into a brown Hy-Vee bag. "Fellas today are so covered up they can't feel it. It's too late before they know trouble's there."

Severa eyeballed him sharply. Was this iced-up tweaker making metaphors? Was he, in fact, a bright guy?

Pat wasn't saying. He wasn't even paying attention to her anymore. He knelt by the camp stove, warming his hands and scanning the black sky. "I loved that job," he sighed. "I loved my chief like he was my own daddy. If that man pointed me to the Gates of Hell, I would have grabbed a hose and charged in."

"You know," she said, trying to play his sudden softness, "I think bald guys are the smartest and most soulful of all guys. It's like without hair to worry about they have more time to think deep."

Pat massaged the sweat on his face up to his scalp. She watched him try not to be pleased. "You're putting me on," he said finally. "But still. I ought to let you run right now. But what Luke would do…" He whistled. "Go along nice is all I can say. Don't make things harder than they got to be."

Her blood sped up, getting her dizzy. She took a deep breath and watched the dish on the fire steam. Over the summer she and Doug had tried to make raisins by drying grapes on a blanket in the sun. While they waited, Doug had her do bong hits. Pretty soon she was all over that blanket, popping hot fruit with her teeth.

"My turn," she heard Luke say. He squatted next to her, smelling like a sick cat. Pat got to his feet and jogged toward the truck.

Severa prepared to fight.

But Luke had other things in mind. He arranged his works on a rock, then took a packet of crystal from his pocket and fixed a shot. His muscles tensed. A rare red came to his cheeks.

"So," he asked when he finished shooting, "where do you think your brother is now?"

She was rethinking the whole boyfriend tale. Luke might like the idea of having to use force on her. Best plan was to get the brothers beating on each other, in the wild of their after-shot flash.

"I'm talking to you," Luke said. He leaned closer and toyed with the hem of her skirt. His finger bled from the nail bed. When it brushed against her, her quadriceps flexed against her will.

"Stop," she said. "I don't want your poison blood on me."

"I asked you a question." He moved the finger to her wrapped-up wrist. She already had a story made up about spraining it during karate lessons, but Luke didn't ask. He touched her neck, and she cleared her throat and spoke.

"You seen right through me, guy. You know I don't have a boyfriend. I'm just playing coy."

"Playing coy," Luke said softly. Then he grabbed her head and kissed her. It was like jumping into a pool of dead fish.

"Your mouth is trash!" she spit, pushing him away.

Luke grinned, eyes strobing. "Anyhow I'm too speedy to fuck. At present."

She made herself chuckle. "Oh, who am I fooling. I saw something with you and me right away. The thing is your brother's coming on real strong."

"Yeah?" Luke knuckled his eyebrows and then gazed at her sadly. "That boy always wants what's mine. But I cut him slack again and again. You know how it goes. Next to water, blood's thick."

"Next to water, everything's thick," Severa said. "But then, like, you have this lime pit, for example. Compared to what's in there, blood's real thin. Plus there's more you should know." She leaned in, bolder. "Your brother said we ought to gank you and snatch the crank and run."

Luke's face darkened. "One night…" he started. "One night my brother died three times. Three! But I kept bringing him around. I sat him in a cold tub and kept him alive." He ground his teeth. "This is how I get paid back?"

"He said you barely had enough brains to keep your body breathing. He said it's like your head's full of meat."

Thank you, Crank, for how fast you turn a person upside-down mad! Luke began a scratching and grumbling spree, clawing at his cheeks and the inside of his arms. He kept at it until his brother returned and sat cross-legged, folding his hands nice in his lap.

"You talk to this girl?" Luke demanded right away.

"Sure I did," said Pat.

"You say anything I should know about?"

"I might have made a suggestion." Pat polished his head, sheepishly, with his sleeve. "But forget her. Let's get to work."

Luke's chest heaved like some tacky romance starlet. His nostrils blew out like a bull in a ring. It worried Severa some. Had she pressed the guy too hard?

"Why don't you turn on the music in the truck first," Luke said, super steely. "I'll get you fixed up."

Pat struggled to his feet. "All I do anymore is get up and walk," he complained.

As his brother left, Luke dumped a half-spoon of lye into a bottle, added water, and shook until the pellets dissolved. A dark path appeared in Severa's mind—why fix liquid lye?—but she tried not to take it. She stared past the pit to where the downtown flickered pink, like it was on fire. When she looked back, Luke was pressing his blue lips together as he drew the straight lye into a syringe.

Hard Spanish rap boiled out of the truck. Pat jittered back, shaking his fists like maracas. Luke handed him the dirty shot and a length of brown tube.

"Hey, don't," Severa started, but Luke clapped his hand over her mouth, hard enough to make her cavities ache.

"You can go next," Pat told her, tying off. He got ready and pressed the plunger down. "I feel bad," he said after the needle hit the vein. Then the plunger broke off in his fingers. He pulled the shot away. There was a mark where the needle had just pierced the skin. He stabbed at it with the broken syringe.

Luke let go of Severa and grabbed the shot and threw it into the lime pit.

"Don't waste it!" Pat groaned, white and woozy.

Luke wiped new tears from his eyes. "Oh Jesus," he said. "I did wrong."

Pat dragged himself closer and touched Luke's shoulder. "It's okay," he said. "Just hurry and fix me one more."

"My own only brother," Luke moaned. "How could I?"

Severa knew the right move now was to bolt, before Luke turned and said, "Look what you made me do." But when she rose to leave, he drew the gun.

"Take it," he ordered. "Shoot me in my brain. If he goes, I want to go too."

"Stop," objected Pat. He tried to stand, then went ghosty and sank to the ground.

Luke spoke only to her. "Shoot me in my brain before I shoot you."

Severa took the gun from him. Holding it made her hand so much bigger. She was so much bigger. Even raising the gun to her temple didn't shrink her. Even the barrel against her weak pulse.

"Not you!" Luke insisted. "Me!"

She'd always imagined a real peace would come just before kicking. Now she waited for it, toying with the trigger, but not firing. She waited for something, but nothing appeared. It surprised her. Was dying as black and white as anything? Until the very instant it happened, did you stay right here?

"Who's that?" Pat said suddenly, before falling into a full faint. Luke let loose with a sob and hunched over his brother in the sand.

Severa turned to see Somvay approaching on bare feet. Silver tape flapped at his ankles. His coat hung wrinkled and loose. The lipstick on his chin from when she'd kissed him now—of course—looked like blood. Still, he seemed calmer. She felt awful.

"I probably shouldn't have done all this," she said, lowering the cold gun.

Somvay's cheeks glowed. Did the moon make him look like that?

"Will you again?" he asked.

"No," she said. But then thought: how true is that? So she said, "At least not exactly in the same way."

Somvay nodded and reached for the gun. Wary, she swung it behind her.

"Are you still drunk?"

His arm was steady. "Please."

"Nononono," Luke crooned. Severa checked him from the corner of her eye. Pat was flat out, maybe asleep, maybe something deeper. Luke brushed a stripe of sand stuck to his brother's head. He kissed his brother's nose. Then he stopped and glared at her.

"You better shoot me fast," he said. "You better."

"Don't listen," she said, turning back to Somvay. "Talk to me. Tell me more about Laos."

"Please," he said, palm out. "I do not want to be here."

The gun stayed in the small of her back. "Are you a monk anymore?"

Behind her, she could hear Luke lurch to standing. "Who's a monk?"

"He is," Severa said, trying to change the air's flavor. "A monk," she repeated, like just speaking it could chill the scene.

"Not now," said Somvay.

Luke pushed past her and bellied up to Somvay. "If you're a monk, do something," he demanded. "Wake him up. Bring him back."

Somvay's voice was low and even. "You cannot return to a place unless you first leave it. First go away, then come back and learn more."

Luke stepped off, sort of shocked, like he'd just seen sun after a whole week of moon. "You're telling me," he began, "you're saying everybody's got to die before things get better?"

"The fuck he is," said Severa. "What kind of monk says that?"

Somvay sighed. "I am no monk," he said. "I am no more than a lonely man."

A wet, horrible sound interrupted them. They all looked at flat Pat. Pink bubbles gushed past his teeth to his chin.

"Guy?" Luke was pleading with Somvay now. "You got anything? Any power prayer words you can say?"

But Somvay was saving his last word. He relaxed his shoulders and let his head fall. Severa felt her arm jerk wildly in its socket, spinning her around as Luke stripped the gun from her. He pointed the gun at his face. Then he took dead aim at her.

"You got warned," Luke said, shaky. "Didn't you?"

Beside her, Somvay dropped to his knees. Severa shut her eyes and waited for the world to break. Just one more second and it breaks.

Run, Somvay whispered.

So she ran. Through mud and pale-barked trees. Then she heard three shots, each ringing the same truth to her: *It's not me. It's not me. It's not me.*

THREE PIECES OF *SEVERANCE*

A COLLECTION OF HEADS IN PROGRESS

by ROBERT OLEN BUTLER

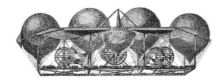

After careful study and due deliberation it is my opinion the head remains conscious for one minute and a half after decapitation.

—Dr. Dassy d'Estaing, 1883

In a heightened state of emotion, we speak at the rate of 160 words per minute.

—Dr. Emily Reasoner, *A Sourcebook of Speech*, 1975

THOMAS MORE
Lord Chancellor of England, beheaded by Henry VIII for opposing his divorce, 1535
his arm is around my neck the king out among my roses the Thames sliding heavily along just beyond the rosemary hedge *you never fail me* he says, tugging me closer in the crook of his arm his breath on my face smelling of pheasant and ale from my table *let's speak now of the stars spinning round the earth* he says, and I sit in a palace hall the king and Katharine the queen beside him and the plates are of gold and the servants are backtreading softly and there is not a sound we wait for Henry's hands to open from the fists beside his plate and the peacocks are before us their bright plumes vanished their flesh darkened by the fire and waiting, the king loosens his right hand and takes up a knife and he places his left hand on the back of the bird and

the knife comes down, the body comes apart, and he lifts the meat and he says *eat,* but my hands are folded before me, I am kneeling, I wait—where now?—there is only darkness *eat* I open my mouth *Corpus Domini nostri* his arm is round my neck he twists me to him his hair a fiery crown *I am your king* he says, and it is dark again and I lift my eyes to a body torn *Jesu Christi* the bread on my tongue I eat my king

DAVE RUDABAUGH
Outlaw and, briefly, member of Billy the Kid's gang, beheaded by townspeople in Parra, Mexico, 1886
that first set of eyes some old Johnny Reb ready to throw down on me and I'm young and twitchy and into my hand comes my 1860 Colt Army my first sweet thing walnut in my palm black powder and paper-wrapped cartridges eight-inch barrel coming out and it's been around a long time and knows what to do the bluing near all rubbed off but you can see the big-masted ships etched on the cylinder the Texas navy blowing up the Mexicans their dark faces around me hands grabbing and a later Colt in my hand my Peacemaker barks like a stable dog a fat Mex flying back from the table his sombrero spattered from my bullet in his brain and Billy touches my shoulder, the Kid is dead but there are his eyes, as blue as noonday, and his tiny hand on my shoulder, he has the smallest damn hands, like a girl, Billy whispers *let's ride* and I lift my own hand to touch his and I'm holding my first Colt now all sassy and sweet and long and it thumps and kicks and goes hot and Johnny Reb is falling backward and I say to him *here's me,* and all at once I see my life ahead my hand full of pistol my trigger finger touchy as my cock and I'm riding hard and I'm lying under the stars and Billy's sleeping nearby quiet as a girl

BENITA VON BERG
German baroness, beheaded by Adolph Hitler for espionage, 1935
my cell at Ploetzensee full of tobacco smoke I light this cigarette with the dying stub of my last and fill my lungs holding very still, woolen socks on my feet prison trousers and shirt if I could but whiten my face and trace my lips in scarlet we lean together and sing Brecht the club full of smoke and bodies the emcee in tails and white tie points at me—*welcome to Kabarett madam but free that red fox about your neck he is our comrade*—and it is Munich now a woman in a swirl of silk, her body naked beneath, she leaps onto our

table and her womansmell fills my lungs I leave my cigarette in my mouth my hand falling the sound of weeping from some other cell I slip my hand inside these rough trousers to my own cleft like hers flashing above me on the table and her face is white her lips scarlet and Friedrichstrasse is ablaze with electric light passing in a cab his clumsy Polish hand between my legs I whisper *Captain your country is in danger*, as if I loved him, and our voices swell through the smoke and we sing *there was a time and now it's all gone by* and I move down the corridor into the room of the ax and the executioner turns to greet me and he is dressed in tails and white tie *welcome*

DEEP WELLS, USA

by CHRIS BACHELDER

I

CELEBRITY: This just in from our Deep Wells Bureau... It seems there is... a... a *baby*... in a *well*.

CONSUMER: No!

CELEBRITY: An unconfirmed report. Of a baby. In a well.

CONSUMER: Hot *damn*. I love well babies. What's its name?

CELEBRITY: As yet unknown.

CONSUMER: Is it real or fictional?

PROFESSOR: Please discuss the respective functions of real well babies v. fictional well babies.

STUDENT: Well, the function of a real well baby is to draw us together as a community—

PROFESSOR: A *tight-knit* community—

STUDENT: —yes and to help us put our dismal lives in better perspective. A fictional well baby is a shadowy doppelganger of a real well baby. Its function is to *raise the stakes*. A kid in a pit's got altitude, stakes-wise.

EXPERT: Literary stake-raising gimmicks include:

    War
    Bad Step-Parents

Cancer (some forms)

Secrets

Toxic Airborne Events

Infidelity

Lame Horses

Thwarted Things

Unrequited Things

Delayed Things

Mercutio's Death

Babies in Wells

Babies in Mine Shafts

Babies in Sewer Pipes

Babies under Futons

POLLSTER: Which do you prefer, then?

CONSUMER: Well, real well babies of course, but I'm not going to look down my nose at the mouth of a gift horse. (Baby in a well, pass it on.)

II

CELEBRITY: When did you realize that something was wrong?

EYEWITNESS: When the baby fell in the well.

CELEBRITY: Can you describe what you saw?

EYEWITNESS: The baby was enormous with tattered clothes. It was drunk. I saw it stumbling toward one of those boxes with sand in it—

CELEBRITY: A well?

EYEWITNESS: No, a—

CELEBRITY: A sandbox?

EYEWITNESS: Yes. It stumbled forward and then just fell right in.

CELEBRITY: That's not a baby in a well. That's a wino in a sandbox.

EYEWITNESS: Listen, muckraker, I know what I saw.

III

EYEWITNESS #2: I saw the baby come out of its house this morning in a shirt and tie. It was 8:24. Then I saw the baby get in the well and drive away, staring straight ahead with spooky, soulless eyes...

IV

MAYOR: Listen, people, we all need to simmer down and really think about our breathing for a minute. That's it, relax, think about that special place. Are you there? Darrell, leave Loretta alone. Can you all visit your special place? Good. *Good.* Okay, listen. I was awakened this morning, from sleep, by a concerned citizen claiming that we had ourselves a baby in a well. Yes, I know, it's big news. *Please* don't hit each other. Just don't even touch each other. Now look, I'm as excited as you all are about the possibility of a well baby and I assure you we're doing everything we can to make sure there is one. The sheriff is on the case, and as you well know, when the baby hits the well, there is nobody finer than Sheriff Buddy Highstakes. Nobody. Tommy, get your hand out of your pants. Breathe, that's it. But we have got to deal with the facts, and the facts are, people, that we don't know if we're talking about a baby here or an infant or a toddler or a tyke or what. We don't know if this little baby is even *weaned*. We don't know if it's got a little tiny pecker or one of those other things. Knock it off, all of you! We don't know the location of the well, the depth of the well, or the number of snakes within it. So I just want to urge everyone—*Nigel!*—yes, urge everyone here to just be patient and wait for the cold hard light of reason to shine. Down. On the cold hard facts. Thank you.

V

CELEBRITY: Is the well-baby rumor an embarrassment to the sheriff?

SPOKESPERSON: No. No, why would it be? No. I don't know why it would be. He's not embarrassed, are *you* embarrassed? Why would he be embarrassed? *I'm* not embarrassed. Babies are not embarrassing. Babies are beautiful and miraculous. Even when they're trapped. They don't embarrass the sheriff.

CELEBRITY: Well, it's just that in the sheriff's recent campaign for re-election he surprised everyone by promising to rid the town's wells of babies once and for all with a three-phase, eleven-step plan based on *deterrence*.

SPOKESPERSON: You're twisting his words around.

CELEBRITY: He spoke passionately about nets and fences and smaller wells and bigger babies and prophylactics and public service spots.

SPOKESPERSON: You're taking his comments out of context. He said *acceptable amounts*. He said *virtually*.

CELEBRITY: No. He said *zero tolerance*. He said *abstinence*. He said *money-back guarantee*. He said, and I quote, "Re-elect Pierre 'Buddy' Highstakes for Baby-Free Wells."

SPOKESPERSON: This interview is just about complete.

CELEBRITY: Tell the town: does the sheriff hate well babies?

SPOKESPERSON: Listen to me. Sheriff Buddy Highstakes has nothing against babies and he has nothing against the compelling human drama or the pathos or the archetypal oppositions that accrue like snakes around well babies. It's just that his opponent was promising a car in every garage and a baby in every well and—

CELEBRITY: But isn't the *middle road* the best?

SPOKESPERSON: Yes, yes, yes. Middle road. Middle. Steering a moderate course through a valley of moderation between extreme and radical mountain ranges. We are very much in the middle. Think of Buddy as the dotted white line of the law.

CELEBRITY: Would the sheriff agree that babies are a precious natural resource?

SPOKESPERSON: Of course.

CELEBRITY: Any last words for Deep Wellians?

SPOKESPERSON: Yes. To the good people of Deep Wells let me say this. Buddy Highstakes's record speaks for itself. He was a decorated Baby Retrievalist in the Marines and he has a proven commitment to plucking out subterranean youth. He doesn't have any children personally but he thinks of all the trapped children of Deep Wells as his own. He's a family man. The current well baby, if there is one and especially if it dies, is a direct consequence of the policies of the previous administration, the rippling-out effects of which cannot simply be made placid overnight. Sheriff Highstakes wants you to know that if there is a well baby, then he loves it as much as you do, but in a very manly, special-forces type of way, and he will do everything in his power as president—

CELEBRITY: Sheriff.

SPOKESPERSON: —as sheriff to see that the baby is brought to justice. I mean to the ground. Out of the well.

VI

NIGEL: Gimmeuh *B!*... Gimmeuh *A!*... Gimmeuh *B!*... Gimmeuh *Y!*

SHERIFF: Who is that child on the lawn?

AIDE-DE-CAMP: That's Nigel, sir.

SHERIFF: What is his problem?

AIDE-DE-CAMP: He's excited, sir.

SHERIFF: What the hell's on his head? Do I want to know?

AIDE-DE-CAMP: It's a Styrofoam well, sir.

SHERIFF: For God's sake. Might we *detain* him?

VII

WELL BABY (COMPUTER-SIMULATED): Help me! Help me! I'm too young to heed TV warnings and I seem to have fallen down a well! My soul is spotless! I am the nation's most precious natural resource! I have an innate curiosity about my world that has yet to be extinguished by schooling! My innocence and my human status and my claim to basic needs are at this point irrefutable! Right? Please use the available resources to pull me toward the light! Oh the snakes! The snakes!

VIII

CELEBRITY: Several citizens have come forward as the possible parents of the well baby. Now Mrs. Jenkins, you say you are missing a child?

MRS. JENKINS: Yes, several.

CELEBRITY: And how long have they been missing?

MRS. JENKINS: Well, let's see. Ernie went away to vocational school in aught three. Learn a trade, you know, like his father. Bullfrog was drafted a year later. And Lizzie ran off with a gandy dancer not long after that. It's just me and Hank now. In that big house.

CELEBRITY: Do you fear that your babies are down in a well somewhere tonight?

MRS. JENKINS: Well, yes. It's a fear that every parent has to live with in Deep Wells. You just have to trust that you brought them up right.

IX

YES-MAN: Aren't you going to strap on the gear, Chief? For old-time's sake?

SHERIFF: What?

YES-MAN: You know… hit the wells…

SHERIFF:

YES-MAN: Or not. I could see how you might be needed here. In the office.

SHERIFF: Has anyone found that goddamn baby yet? Do we have any leads?

YES-MAN: No, sir. But we've got all our people on it, sir. If there's a well baby, we'll find it, sir.

SHERIFF: Just find it. Just. Find it. You'd *better* damn find it. Meanwhile keep the press off my back and I mean find the damn munchkin, even if it means throwing a kid in a hole and calling out *Bingo*.

YES-MAN: Yes, sir.

SHERIFF: If I wake up tomorrow—*listen,* if I wake up tomorrow morning and the front page has got some pansy-ass National Guarder holding up *our* wan and snakebit but relieved and smiling baby, some heads are gonna damn roll.

YES-MAN: Yes, sir.

SHERIFF: And do something with these flowers. And get me a drink. And some of those—mother of God would you look at all these flowers? Has everyone in the nation sent a freakin' bouquet? For a hypothetical well baby that may not be real? What is going on? Is it just me?

YES-MAN:

SHERIFF: Is it me?

X

PROFESSOR (TENURED): A baby is drawn to a well like a moth to moth food. Call for papers!

EXPERT #1: A baby hurling itself down a well is reenacting its own conception.

EXPERT #2: A baby plummeting down a well is making a utopian return to its womb.

EXPERT #3: A baby falls down a well because of the social construction of gravity and also a sort of hardwired insouciance.

PROFESSOR: Last call!

EXPERT #4: Historically, babies fall.

XI

CELEBRITY: It turns out that the current well baby, known now simply as Baby Well Baby until we learn its real name, is really nothing new. Joining me now from the Institute of Historically Innocent Victims is a Historian. Welcome.

HISTORIAN: It's a pleasure to be here.

CELEBRITY: Give us a historical perspective on well babies.

HISTORIAN: Our records indicate that Baby Well Baby is the eleventh well baby of the Modern Era. Interestingly enough, none of these babies perished in the wells. All were saved by human ingenuity and community spirit and a fierce, maniacal belief in the sanctity of baby life.

CELEBRITY: That's fascinating. Let's take a look at a list of the previous well babies and find out where they are now:

> Baby Charlie, prison
> Baby Icky, deceased (drug overdose)
> Baby Marla, deceased (suicide)
> Baby Ray-Ray, mental-health institution
> Baby Finkerton, deceased (suicide)

Baby Mercutio, deceased (homicide)

Baby Candi, deceased (unsolved)

Baby Khan, state senate

Baby Dread, ?

Baby Michelle, coma

GHOST OF BABY ICKY: The thing you have to keep in mind is like the incredible pressure on you when you're a well baby. One minute you're playing unsupervised, the next minute you're in a well, and the next minute, you know, you're like a millionaire. I was just a baby, I didn't know how to handle the fame and the attention and the endorsement deals. It was just one big party for two solid weeks, then Baby Marla fell in a well and I was all of a sudden a nobody. My dad mishandled all my money and I had nothing. I turned to the streets. You know the rest.

XII

NIGEL: BAY-*BEE!* BAY-*BEE!* BAY-*BEE!*

AIDE-DE-CAMP: You okay, Sheriff?... Buddy?...

SHERIFF:

NIGEL: Here *baby baby baby!* Here *baby baby!*

AIDE-DE-CAMP: It's the prisoner, sir. He's unruly.

SHERIFF:

NIGEL: There once was a baby who fell

Down a deep, snake-covered well

La LA la la LA

La LA la la LA

This little fat baby in a well!

AIDE-DE-CAMP: Sir? Permission to use force, sir?

XIII

EXPERT: There are many ways to extract a baby from a well:

    Chewing Gum and String

    Harpoon

    Dogs

    Black Magic

    Mashed Carrots

    Plastics

    TV

    Boyle's Law

    Long Stick

Prayer
Community Spirit
Winch (or Windlass)
Tractor Beam

XIV

PRE-ADULT IN SUPPLIES CLOSET:

XV

CONSUMER: Do you see it?

CONSUMER #2: Where?

CONSUMER: Right there.

CONSUMER #2: I still don't see it.

CONSUMER: Look. See the sparkly mobile?

CONSUMER #2: Okay.

CONSUMER: All right, it's directly beneath that. Just look straight down.

CONSUMER #2: …That's not…

CONSUMER: See it? Let's call the news and the sheriff and—

CONSUMER #2: Todd, that's a *crib*. That's a crib baby.

CONSUMER: I've never been on TV before.

XVI

AIDE-DE-CAMP: Buddy, look, at some point today, you're going to have to put on pants.

SHERIFF: Would you *please* not speak so goddamn loud? Please?

AIDE-DE-CAMP: The people need you. They're grabbing each other's hair and hyperventilating. I think you should say something to them.

SHERIFF: *Shhhhh.*

AIDE-DE-CAMP: Reassure them. Let them know that if there's a well baby we'll find it and everyone will get a chance to touch it.

SHERIFF: What's the latest?

AIDE-DE-CAMP: We just got a call from the boonies. Seemed promising at first but it turns out it's just old Curty Olson. Down in a well.

SHERIFF: Christ on a *goal*/post, who let old Curty Olson out?

AIDE-DE-CAMP: He snuck out this morning and fell almost immediately into a deep well.

SHERIFF: Damn Finlander.

AIDE-DE-CAMP: Apparently old Curty's crying real bad. Wants out.

SHERIFF: Well, he's not a baby now, is he? *Jesus.*

AIDE-DE-CAMP: He's kind of bawling. Had people thinking baby.

SHERIFF: Old, crazy, multiply divorced man in a well is just *embarrassing*.

AIDE-DE-CAMP: No power to unite the community. Low stakes.

SHERIFF: Just deal with it.

AIDE-DE-CAMP: What's protocol?

EXPERT: It's 291.23.3: *When two citizens are trapped in separate wells at the same time, first priority and all resources are to go to the citizen baby. If neither citizen is a baby, priority should be given to a dog in a well. If there are no dogs or babies, opt for the non-dangerous mentally handicapped.* You get the idea.

DEVIL'S ADVOCATE: Just, all I'm saying is what *if* you had like a real innocent well baby, right? And then someone came along, someone like Stalin or Jimmy Carter or a drug dealer and they like tried to save the baby but they *also* fell in the well, on top of the baby, so that in order to save the baby you'd have to save Carter, too. What would you do?

SHERIFF: I am going to *fire* someone, watch me.

XVII

CELEBRITY: Shouldn't you be at work right now, sir?

CONSUMER: I took the afternoon off. I wanted to see what was happening out here.

CELEBRITY: What have you seen?

CONSUMER: Some looting. Some rioting. A real festive-type feel to the downtown area. Some guy put on diapers and dove into an empty swimming pool. Some freelance baby-looker got shot with a *arrow* is what I heard. You look familiar. Are you on TV?

XVIII

CELEBRITY (IN THE FIELD): Authorities say they have not yet found a well or a baby, but the good news, Rick, is they say they have reason to suspect—nay, to expect—that there is a baby shivering in a well tonight. Back to you.

ANCHORMAN RICK: In other news today, nine people were gunned down in a Detroit shopping center. Mannequins spray-painted with blood, etc. Mall police say they haven't seen anything this grisly since November of last year.

TOSHA: Were the victims all adults?

ANCHORMAN RICK: As far as we know, yes.

TOSHA: Do the police have a suspect, Rick?

ANCHORMAN RICK: The suspect is a former mine-shaft baby who

couldn't get his life turned around. Police are not releasing his name at this time. He is being referred to simply as Former Mine-Shaft Baby Who Couldn't Get His Life Turned Around.

TOSHA: At least there weren't any baby victims.

ANCHORMAN RICK: I love babies, Tosha.

TOSHA: Oh I do also.

XIX

THINK-TANK MEMBER: Okay, just go with me on this one. We're in the brainstorming stage here. What if we had like little well-shaped snack cakes with sort of babyish cream filling in the middle?

XX

CELEBRITY: This just in: good news and the opposite of good.

CONSUMER: Okay, give me the bad news first.

PRE-ADULT IN SUPPLIES CLOSET:

CELEBRITY: The good news is that authorities have located the baby in the well.

CONSUMER: *Hoo* doggy. I got a pawnshop harpoon and I smell *re*ward.

CELEBRITY: The bad news is it's not really a baby and it's only a well if you define "well" pretty broadly, as like "any enclosed space that's dark."

CONSUMER: I am not liking what I am hearing here.

CELEBRITY: The *baby* is really a pre-adult, a third-grader at Canning Factory Elementary School in the Dirtytown section of Deep Wells.

CONSUMER: Need more than a harpoon you go to Dirtytown.

CELEBRITY: The *well* in question is a supplies closet at C. F. E. S. The young man, eight, reportedly shut himself in the closet two days ago and won't come out. Won't talk, won't eat, nothing.

PRE-ADULT IN SUPPLIES CLOSET:

CONSUMER: Is he mongoloid or like *special* in any way?

CELEBRITY: No. Average kid.

CONSUMER: Let the fraud rot.

SHERIFF: Call off the dogs, then. Get that Finlander out of the well. Get me a drink.

CELEBRITY: The young man has a home life that social workers might refer to as *bad*.

CONSUMER: At some point you just got to take responsibility for the actions of your parents. Am I wrong? Yes it hurts but it's called growing up. Did Custer just lay down at Waterloo? No he did not.

CELEBRITY: The young man reportedly told a classmate that he was quote tired of black eyes and dog food unquote.

CONSUMER: It's a matter of if you can't stand the food, then get your ass out of the kitchen. And don't let the door—of the kitchen—hit you on the way out. Hit your ass. And don't come crying to me when things don't go your pathetic little way. God I *hate* that tiny little man in the supplies closet.

CELEBRITY: The thing is, the door's not even locked. The supplies-closet door.

CRITIC #1: A supplies closet, archetype-wise? Just not that sexy.

CRITIC #2: Fiction's cockpit's dials waggling as stakes plummet... vulgar didacticism... paroxysmic style... bathos...

CURTY OLSON: I can't feel my *legs*.

CRITIC #3: Role model! School vouchers! Rap music!

ANCHORMAN RICK: These chinos are not flattering. They sort of pooch out. Right here. And *here*.

AGENT: Not interested. The closet door is all wrong. You get me a *locked* door and then a daring rescue by a guidance counselor and a vice officer, I could have that kid pushing Beef Stew and Diet Water next week. That's *if* he's white and has straight teeth. He's white, right?

MRS. JENKINS: Lizzy? Bullfrog?

FLANNERY O'CONNOR: If it looks funny on the page, I don't read it.

GHOST OF BABY ICKY: Could be worse, pal. You could have been a well baby.

PRE-ADULT IN SUPPLIES CLOSET:

XXI

CELEBRITY: This just in from our Whirring Blades Bureau. It seems there is a baby... stuck in a *reaper*...

MAYOR: People! *People!*

EPILOGUE

SHERIFF: *Hi, Baby.*

SHERIFF'S WIFE: *You sound tired, Pierre.*

SHERIFF: *Ah I'm fine.*

SHERIFF'S WIFE: *I saw on TV.*

SHERIFF: *Yep. Just another coward in a closet.*

SHERIFF'S WIFE: *Sort of sad, though.*

SHERIFF: *Well, it's over. For now.*

SHERIFF'S WIFE:

SHERIFF: Any… news? Sweetheart?

SHERIFF'S WIFE: It came out burnt spring loganberry.

SHERIFF: I forgot what burnt spring loganberry means, Baby.

SHERIFF'S WIFE: It means no, Pierre. It means no.

SHERIFF: That's what I figured.

SHERIFF'S WIFE:

SHERIFF: You okay?

SHERIFF'S WIFE: I'm fine. Things could be a whole lot worse.

SHERIFF:

SHERIFF'S WIFE: We'll just try again. We'll just keep trying.

SHERIFF: It's difficult. To be hopeful.

SHERIFF'S WIFE: Well we've always got each other, Pierre. And that's a lot.

SHERIFF: Hey Honey, do you remember Baby Finkerton? When I came out of that
    well with him strapped to my chest? The way he looked at me once his eyes had
    adjusted to the light?

SHERIFF'S WIFE:

SHERIFF: God.

SHERIFF'S WIFE: Why don't you come on home now, Pierre. It's been a long day.

SHERIFF: A few things left here. These goddamn reports.

SHERIFF'S WIFE: They can't wait? Couldn't they?

SHERIFF: I suppose they could.

SHERIFF'S WIFE: They can wait. Come on home now.

SHERIFF:

SHERIFF'S WIFE:

SHERIFF:

SHERIFF'S WIFE: Buddy?

SHERIFF: I'll be there soon, Baby.

Saddam's thumbs, further discussed on page 181. (Photo courtesy of Morris-Singer Foundry.)

TORSO AS FACE

The New York Times Magazine *(November 14, 1998)*

YET ANOTHER CONVERGENCE

by LAWRENCE WESCHLER

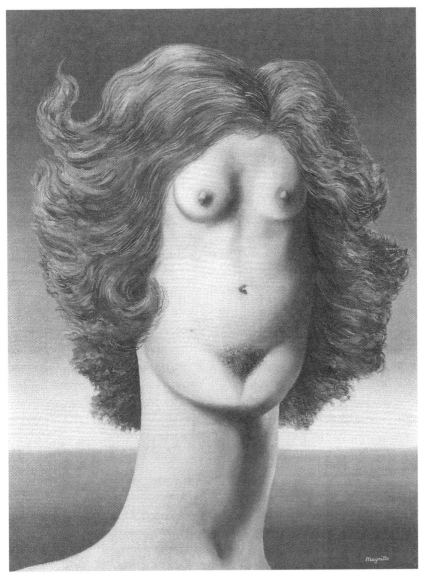

Rene Magritte: Le Viol *(1934)*

YET ANOTHER CONVERGENCE
TORSO AS FACE
{*TIMES MAGAZINE* / R. MAGRITTE / D. MORRIS / R. M. RILKE}

by LAWRENCE WESCHLER

OR, FOR INSTANCE, this. What are we to make of this?

The former, the startling and quite memorable cover of a *New York Times Magazine* from about five years back, designed by the late Claude Martel (featuring a photo of the model Shalom Harlow by Andrew Eccles) and ostensibly intended to introduce a special issue on What Clothes Reveal and Mask about Identity—though clearly charged with associations far more primordial, indeed an image almost salacious in its clotheslessness, in its curious (yet inescapable) suggestion, that is, of an entirely *naked* female body. And an unabashedly knowing body at that, one, in turn, that has us (with our cereal-filled spoons arrested halfway to our opened mouths) completely nailed in its gaze.

Though an image not entirely original for all that. Surely Mr. Martel must have had Mr. Magritte rattling around somewhere, at least in the back of his mind. (I mean, even down to the rhyme in the siren's sex-tousled hair.)

Magritte perpetrated his astonishing painting in 1934, just a year after Man Ray's celebrated lips-hovering-in-the-sky image, *The Lovers, or The Hour of the Observatory*, and shortly after he himself had made his so-called "Elective Affinities" breakthrough. Prior to that, Magritte's surrealist juxtapositions had tended toward the confoundingly, if oddly evocatively, arbitrary (a woman with her head swathed by a cloth standing beside a table on which sit a tuba and a valise, for example, or one man's head pronouncing the word-bubbled phrase "The piano," while another's replies, anything but self-evidently,"The violet"). But then (likewise in 1933), Magritte had hit upon the image of an oval birdcage with, inside it, filling it almost to the brim, a huge solitary egg. Magritte thereafter positively reveled in these sorts of "secret affinities" between objects. The process of conceiving such affinities, Magritte said, was difficult (and here I am following the account of Dawn Aves in the catalog to the Tate's marvelous 2001 "Surrealism: Desire Unbounded" show), but the solution, once found, was self-evident, with all the certainty of a fact and the impenetrability of the finest conundrum. And it was in the thrall of this new method that, the following year, he contrived the striking image we are considering today, which he entitled, unsettlingly, *Le Viol*. Meaning, on the one hand, "The Viola," thereby inversely aligning his painting with the Picasso/Braque tradition of portraying musical instruments (guitars, violins, cellos, etc.) as metaphorical stand-ins for the female body. But, more directly, meaning, "The Rape." In attempting to explicate the latter, Ades notes how "the neck is elongated beyond the demands of erotic sinuosity to become an ironically maternal phallus" (we speak, of course, of the head of a penis), going on to observe how, in this context, "the head of hair becomes pubic in texture, penetrated by rather than crowning the face/body." Which, come to think of it, it sure does seem to be doing.

But I want to return to the central discovery of the painting, that inspired recognition which the Magritte shares with that *Times* cover photocollage, the insight that a woman's torso, in the arrangement of its features, somehow does recapitulate the splay of features in a face—and in fact that, as such, it *stares* at us, it *hold us in its gaze*. I am reminded of the delightfully loopy theory advanced years ago by the zoologist Desmond Morris in his wildly controversial blockbuster of a book, *The Naked Ape* (1967), his notion that the size and shape and allure of the human female chest hearkens back to the moment when our primate ancestors first began to move about upright. Prior to that, Morris theorizes, among our ancestor's ancestors—as was and remains the case with all other primates—the males had approached and copulated with their females from the rear, the female buttocks in turn constituting a primary token of sexual display and arousal. Once humans began to walk about upright and approach each other (sexually, as otherwise) face-to-face, however, Morris suggests that the seductive work of the buttocks would have needed to be transferred to the front of the female body, a feat accomplished through the genius of natural selection by the progressive expansion and rounding of human female breasts beyond anything previously (or, for that matter, currently) seen anywhere else in the animal kingdom.

Well, I don't know about that—about breasts as buttocks, I mean (and I sure as hell don't know about how such tendrils of perverse speculation get lodged and stay lodged in my own poor hyperventilating head; what in god's name is going on in there?)—but as for breasts as eyes and bodies as faces, it seems to me that Magritte and latterly Mr. Martel of the *Times* are onto something. Our gaze—and I would suspect anybody's gaze, male or female—gets drawn to and held by the female body (or, alternatively, finds itself compelled to turn away in abashed embarrassment) precisely because of the bald directness of the way that body is staring back.

And maybe not just female bodies.

Didn't Rilke, after all, launch the second volume of his *New Poems*, in 1908, with that invocation of an "Archaic Torso of Apollo," in which he noted (in Edward Snow's superb translation) how

We never knew his head and all the light
that ripened in his fabled eyes. But
his torso still glows like a candelabra,
in which his gazing, turned down low,

holds fast and shines. Otherwise the surge
of the breast could not blind you, nor a smile
run through the slight twist of the loins
toward that center where procreation thrived.

And otherwise, as Rilke notes, "this stone would stand deformed and curt" and, a few lines later,

...not burst forth from all its contours
like a star: for there is no place
that does not see you.

This, of course, being the poem that ends (and, as I suddenly just remembered, being the poem with which Philip Roth ended his own startlingly unsettling surrealist 1972 romp, *The Breast*)

You must change your life.

To which all I can add (with reference to myself, anyway) is, I'll say.

PIGS IN SPACE

by CLAIRE LIGHT

FROM WHERE I SIT, strapped down in this seat, I can see most of the Earth through the porthole. Daryl has on his Sunday face—part complacency, part celebration, no calculation. He's bouncing, naked, hands free, around the quarters, singing his Making the Omelette Song. The Making the Omelette Song is pretty much the same as the Strap on the Toilet Song or the Mix the Slurry Song or the Wait for the Rations Song: it comprises two notes, as many words as the title, and endless repetition.

In the midst of Daryl's endless singing I am playing a game of my own: nod your head up and down, up and down, fast. Now shake it back and forth, back and forth. If you go fast enough, the truncated marble of the Earth blurs to white. Now blink rapidly and the white clears into high-contrast white and blue splotches and blotches. The splotches and blotches seem to get bigger every day, although we aren't approaching rapidly enough to see a daily difference. Now hold a fixed stare without blinking, until your eyes dry out. At some point in all of this, the marble loses its familiarity, an alien thumbnail without a thumb, brighter than reality and approaching like the end of a dream.

I blink and shake and nod while Daryl assembles four eggs from stasis storage, a pat of butter, and a pan. We should eject everything in stasis storage and shut it down. It burns two units per hour. But I don't say anything. He swoops into the kitchen-area he's rigged—one hundred units worth of materials—and pulls the switch. A hiss and a suck and his feet hit the ground. A simultaneous tiny skittering sound from the entire floor in a perfect radius of two feet around him. He threw dry semolina into the air an hour ago to punctuate the Semolina Song. It ricocheted off the walls for several minutes before becoming inert all over the quarters. Some if it will be in my covers when I get in tonight. Something my mother used to say about attractive young men when I was very small that I never understood back then: "He can eat crackers in my bed anytime!" Even in the golden past, was there always some small price to pay for the kind of thing we did last night?

Fifteen units cooking semolina. Should leave the semolina in dry storage. Should really eject the semolina. Should never have brought semolina in the first place. But I don't say anything. I keep expecting to see semolina sticking to Daryl's broad moon face and clustering around his opaque eyes. I expect that he generates his own small gravity field out here and that he will inevitably draw the results of his mistakes and his scattering of spirits back to himself.

He wastes gas turning on the gravity, heating the skillet, reconstituting the water, boiling it. Fifteen units per minute on his jury-rigged range. Should at least use the cooker. Five units per minute in the cooker. He says it doesn't taste the same in the cooker, live a little. Should eject the cooker when he's not looking, along with the pan and the range. He uses butter from stasis storage to cook with. Should eject everything in stasis storage when he's not looking.

Barring any further accidents—I've done and redone the figures every week for ninety weeks now—barring accidents, these once-a-week skillet fests will deliver us back to the company's door when the two-year cycle is through with our pigs nearly dead, our tanks empty, and our fuel drained to the last drop. Without batting an eyelash, the manager will say "good job" tonelessly, hand us credit scrip and a document of our cancelled indenture, and we'll be free to sign up for another round or kiss our futures goodbye. It's a game, an experiment for them, but not a game that they play against us. They play the game against chance and their own skill in choosing crew members. We're just the players, with no players in reserve. If we fuck ourselves up, they'll retrieve the data and the cattle and put the information toward the next cycle. They'll inform our families and hand over the bodies, or in my case, cremate and recycle. If we fuck ourselves up, we're fucked.

I put that at the bottom of every fuel inventory I've written for the past nine months, which Daryl never reads. It says, "Please God, no more or we're fucked." It's intended as a reminder to myself. I whisper to myself on the long week's approach to Saturday when I do the fuel inventory, "No more or we're fucked." I tell myself to just try, for one week, to make up some units. And every Saturday night, when I hear him coming to me I tell myself to tell him no. Even once a week is too much; he takes too much for granted; I have to think for us both. No more or we're fucked. And every Sunday, he wakes up singing and I say nothing.

Eggs don't smell like anything, but when they hit the butter with that fractured smack, the browning-butter smell changes and slicks the air. My mouth doesn't water, my eyes do. The dry gold dust of the air we make out here becomes morning all at once, the morning of our week: wet, moist, greasy, and full of things that still need to be done. The smell of things comes close for a moment on plastic plates and cold forks. I walk into Daryl's circle of gravity and am sucked down. The smack on the soles of my feet is better than coffee. We eat standing in a two-foot radius, warmed by each other's bodies.

Less than a half hour later, I'm suited up and in the pigpen. The molded interior is a nonreflective white that glares off our masks but doesn't blind us. Near the entrance is what I call the pigfirmary, a small room with a transparent door so that Daryl can isolate a sick pig but I can still see in. Inside are two pig-sized stasis chambers, one containing the body of Liz, our first herd mother, or rather, containing what remained of Liz's body by the time Daryl reached her that morning. As well as being all-around stupid, the herd is vicious to other sick pigs. Daryl hoped to study Liz's physiology when back on ground to discover what exactly had caused her sudden incapacitating colic when she'd been so consistently healthy before. This colic is a major killer of higher-bred pigs and the constant threat hanging over herd mothers' otherwise proverbially healthy heads. Bred to produce gas, sometimes it gets trapped in their abdomens and no one knows how, what triggers it, or how to prevent it. Daryl's answer is his new feed, but it's experimental. He was feeding it to Liz, too. Another major waste of units, that stasis chamber. But sick and dead pigs are not things you argue about with Daryl.

Whenever I come in here, I check in with Liz first. It's my way of paying respects and my little fuck you to Porkbella, the second herd mother who replaced Liz. Unlike Liz, who was installed by the company, Porkbella is one of Daryl's own. He designed her and sequenced her DNA himself at the last laboratory he worked at before he was fired. He grew her and birthed her and trained her up from a piglet through adolescence. He made sure she was in top condition when he put her in stasis. He had a stable of six adolescents and seventeen fetuses when he signed up for this cycle. He picked Bella, his favorite, to bring. When Liz burst from colic, it only took Bella a week to recover from stasis, and four days to whip the herd into shape. We only lost eleven days of fuel production and she made it up within three months. She significantly improved efficiency, no doubt about it, and significantly encouraged Daryl's profligacy.

Anyone would treat such a pig well, but Daryl loves her with a passion that enclave boys usually reserve for their pet raptors. Not that Bella isn't a predator. He brought his own feed for her, cases full of flat, hand-sized green pellets, using the storage reserved for his extra clothing and books. He insists that if the company had given him storage room enough to bring feed for both pigs, we'd never have lost the first one. He insists that if we could feed it to all the pigs, they'd produce almost as high a yield as the cattle. He insists that efficient feed and care could make up for ineffi-ciency in absolutely everything else. I insist to myself that if he'd used his space as it was meant to be used, we'd never have run out of books, or clothes, and I wouldn't be letting him distract me from saving up units. But I don't say anything.

After paying my respects to Liz, my recent habit is to locate Bella and greet her with a kick. She hates me. She's jealous. I have to watch out for her. She's stopped going for my lifeline; I've foiled her at that too many times. But once, six months ago, she caught me in an explosion in the mint which lost us three hundred units, destroyed my second-to-last suit, and gave me third-degree burns over half my body. Daryl wasted another thou-sand units regenerating my skin tissue while I was unconscious. An utter waste of units, something he did for himself, not for me, although I'm sure he convinced himself otherwise. He still believes that it was an accident. But I saw the look on her face.

The moment I leave the pigfirmary, she makes a beeline for me, moan-ing with pig joy as she trots over, the way she does with Daryl. She starts rubbing herself against my legs and I can feel a vague sort of roughness from her bristle through the soft legs of my suit. I am immediately suspicious. Normally, she ignores me, and when the shit starts hitting the fan, some-times literally, she's as far away as she can get. I still don't know how she can tell me from Daryl, unless it's the height difference. With our masks and gloves and suits on, with the anti-odor seals and the shuffle we use to get around in the pens, with glare making our masks opaque from their point of view, we look like the same faceless creature. Daryl says they just know, just the sort of faith-based-belief mumbo-jumbo with which he approaches everything from shoveling pig shit to genetic sequencing.

He spoils Bella to the breaking point. She does her job well and it's a job even Daryl can't do. The herd pigs fight him, even when he's in the pen scratching their backs to a chorus of piggy moans. They've become unmanageable with breeding. He tells me pigs used to be among the smartest of domestic mammals, but no more. Herd pigs are unimaginably stupid. Bred for only one thing, with "unnecessary" characteristics bred out without forethought, they won't work for anyone or anything but a bred, trained herd mother. I know all the stories about the early days of the company, when they sent harvesters out for five years with only one herd mother and the installation would be towed in at the end of the cycle with the depressurized quarters haunted by dessicated human bodies. The herd pigs, minus the herd mother, whose bones would often be found in the rig, would be mostly alive and nearly buried in their own shit.

Bred for intelligence and aggression, a good herd mother like Bella can keep a herd of over three hundred in line. They won't shit without her permission and they eat what and when she orders them to. She lines them up at the food dispenser, cutting out the ones that have displeased her. They eat by her leave, then she trots them in groups of ten to the manure trough exactly forty-five minutes later. They shit by her grace. The herd is like her hive-cum-harem, with her queen bee and sultan. Without her, they're almost too stupid to eat, shit, or even go to sleep. With her, they're a well-oiled, fuel-producing machine. If Daryl butters her up enough, she'll even hit the switch that washes the slurry into the tank. She dances to the beat of the Porkbella Song.

I don't know enough about pig farming to understand the intricacies of Bella management, but she's thriving. I've never seen that pig whole. She's so enormous she can't get far enough away from me in the pen to fit her entire body into the view within the flat front plate of my mask. Her long snout or her hindquarters always end up bending around the peripheral plates. I think of her as permanently bent. As she plays at affection for me this morning, I wonder if she knows our lives depend on her ability to make pigs shit.

I kick her away and enter the tank, holding my breath for a second even though the gas can't penetrate and I know this. Bella actually tries to climb in after me and I have to kick her away again. That's twice now, I think with satisfaction. I close and seal the hatch behind me, and immediately the pressure reasserts itself, making it difficult to move through the air. Probably three units lost opening the tank. Bella, strangely, starts bumping the outside of the tank, calling to me. It's a petulant, demanding squeal I know from the times I've been in the pen with Daryl to work and he was ignoring her. I ignore it, too. The slurry, a simple mixture of pig manure and reconstituted water, is a sludge today, not a soup, which means that either the pumps are clogged, or the mixers are. Probably the mixers. I just fixed them last week, though. They warned me of this in the training. Wear and tear on machinery is simply higher in space and near the end of the cycle, breakage accelerates and maintenance begins to become a constant issue.

As I clean and scrape, clean and scrape, my mind wanders away. Out here, where away from night and day your senses grow sharp from deprivation and lights, every sound, new smell, or uncommon phrase strikes you with pungency, like oleander in the first summer rain after a long, dry spring. In the thick silence of the tank, my mind's ear returns to what Daryl smiled ruefully and said before he went off to the pens. I pull my mind back, and clean and scrape. But it escapes again, circling the sound of my name, toying with what "Yayoi" sounds like spoken with an accent, spoken for the first time in months. In his voice "Yayoi" sounds over and over again. Clean and scrape, Yayoi, Yayoi. My mind dances with me, offering this rhythm, like an errant child wanting to distract me with song so it can go examine the forbidden treasure box. I pull it back. It reaches again.

Then I'm standing in the first summer monsoon on ground and I'm thirteen and the rain is purifying me and I look up for the first time into weather realizing that there's nothing up there but water and pressure. I should be alarmed that I've left the ship in my imagination and returned to ground. I do not permit this, ever. I should be alarmed by Bella's squealing, or by my distance from the fact that I'm knee-deep in disease-ridden slurry and surrounded by toxic, explosive gas. But all I can see is the gray-white sky above me letting fall rain and, out of the corner of my unwary eye, the long-haired boys standing under the eaves of a rare, abandoned house, waiting for me as I raise my arms to the rain and celebrate my freedom from everything. They stand there in a line, five of them, two more than I can handle by myself, slightly bigger than I am now, as will happen when boys start to grow. I can see now, they are not animated by the devil, they are just boys. But, unfortunately, I am a girl.

* * *

When the bells sounds for lunch, I am still in the tank. Normally I keep time better. With ten minutes from the bell until the food is dispensed, and only another ten minutes until the food is recycled—I set the limits myself—I can feel lunch coming on by the lurch of my stomach and I'm usually half out of my suit by the time the bell goes off. But today I'm full of omelette and there's something wrong with my mind and with my body. I feel like I've failed in some essential way and I can hardly move at all.

I rush out of the pen into the airlock and try not to hurry cleaning my suit. It doesn't do to rush, ever. That's how accidents happen. Daryl isn't in the quarters when I get there, but I assume that he's at prayer in a corridor somewhere. He's extraordinarily sensitive about some things. He decided it would be better not to force me out of the quarters five times a day so he finds a spot—a different one each time—to lay his prayer rug and mostly manages to avoid me doing it.

Our food is turning to slush in the dispenser as I leave the corridor, which is weighted during work hours (ten units per hour), and push off into the atmosphere of the weightless quarters. I palm myself forward faster and faster. I can see the two ration cakes disintegrating and I have one minute at most before the sieve opens and the food gets sucked out. I arrive with one hand on the pole, just in time. The blue one, with Daryl's meds, is nearest, but I grab my pink one just before both would've been sucked out. Daryl's cake goes. Two units. My cake is just together enough to hold. It's cold and the gelatinous consistency is breaking down rapidly into liquid. I slurp it fast to get it down before it melts.

I palm over to my porthole seat to digest and strap in to wait for him. I feel like I owe him an explanation for missing his food, although in reality, I don't owe him a damn thing. He owes me for getting his food for him most days. Owes me period. You can tell what kind of family he's from, on ground, someone who thinks prayer is more important than eating because he's never had to choose between the two. Someone who can take for granted that his food will be there when he's finished communing with his god. A long-haired boy, his eaves following him wherever he goes. I never thought that I would stand shelter over someone like him, not willingly. He doesn't understand the game. No, that's not true, he understands the game as a *game,* something to be played, something with no stakes. He thinks we're the players, not the playing pieces. He thinks he has a right to lose. He bounces around out here breathing air wrung out of space dust, air he's hardly earned, playing pig like the god of some pork-eating race.

My mind slips again and I'm ten years old and my mother is standing in a doorway, the doorway to our house and a man is trying to come in. She says no to him and closes the door. She walks around, barring the windows one by one and rechecking them, finishing by checking the door again. "We'll go now," she says to me. "I've had enough." And I'm afraid, in spite of everything she has said about a better life and about safer neighborhoods and food, food all the time. I go to the window to see if the man is gone and I lean into it to see out into the darkening yard. It's empty, the yard, but I know he's out there and the fear grows in me, knowing this, and grows and grows until I have to shriek from sheer pressure. Instead, I open my eyes.

The distant marble is half cut off in the porthole, just like this morning, but less vivid. Not much time has passed. Daryl is still missing, probably decided to skip lunch. I unstrap and palm over to his locker and pick the lock. I haven't done this in months, but suddenly I need it. I open the cheap, rattling door and the smell of him comes out. He keeps all his torn and worn clothing in here, meaning to sew it back together, but never getting around to it. It's so much easier for us to be naked in the installation and save the fuel it would require to clean our clothes and the energy to mend them. I am so used to the sight of him naked now that it almost doesn't turn me on anymore. I grab a pile of cloth and press it to my face. I could easily go and find him and press him to my face. In fact I *should* go find him. It's protocol. We're supposed to check in with each other at lunchtime and again at dinner. But after what he said this morning before escaping to his pigs, I can't. If I go to him now, in this bizarre mood, I don't know what I'll say, what I'll do. I'm going to have to let him go, permanently. Thank god we're only here for three more months. I put one of his shirts on, or what used to be a shirt. It hangs off me in rags. Cheap material. I can almost imagine that I'm him, I suddenly smell so much like him.

Thus armed, I go through his locker. I have a ritual here. First I find the family pictures and go through them one by one, counting off his store of family members, so many, all alive and well-fed and cared-for: his father and mother, his two older brothers and three sisters, his wife, his first son, his second son, his daughter. They are all married now, his children, married in adolescence, like he was. He is now a grandfather—he found out right before we launched—a grandfather at thirty-one. It is so strange to me, I still get a delight from it.

There is nothing about his life that is familiar to me, nothing about his background. We didn't move to a traditional enclave like the one he grew up in. We moved to one of the few "open" enclaves that accepted Christian families—or didn't exactly accept them, but didn't ask for proof of religious affiliation with one's application. So we never came into contact with any traditional, wealthy old families like Daryl's. It's hard to understand someone who doesn't know what wealth a family is. And I must close the locker on that.

I am startled awake by the dinner bell and struggle against an incomprehensible restraint to get up. It's a moment before I realize that I'm still strapped to the seat. I unstrap myself. I float over to the dispenser and grasp the pole lightly with one hand. If I inflate my stomach and then blow a puff gently downward, I can rise slowly, a few inches per minute. My hand dragging on the pole slows my progress and stops me after an inch. Inflate. Blow. Rise. Inflate. Blow. Rise.

The dispenser whirrs and spits out two double rations. It's detected the food recycled at lunch and is making up for it. It doesn't always—I just fixed it last week. Thirty units spent testing. Four units each for double rations. It's another endless arrhythmic beat out here—when the food dispenser's sensors go out. I take the food out immediately—Daryl's in my right hand, my own in my left. Daryl would never eat anything I'd touched with my left hand, and for some reason I am unwilling, or unable, to lie to him about such things.

The cakes are firm and oaty and I eat them slowly, in nips, pretending that I'm a pig. A neat pig. They're still warm and if I hold my breath I can almost imagine myself eating a real oatcake, or, almost, an oatmeal cookie. Little bits crumble onto my lips and then cool and turn to droplets there, that are just beginning to run when I lick them off. Daryl doesn't come. Finally, I put his cakes in a baggie and seal it to the wall over his bunk. He's definitely not coming. Suddenly it occurs to me that there must be an animal down if he's missing two meals. Shit.

I go for the cattle pens, quickly now. My feet smack the weighted floor of the hallway. It hurts. I curse my feet. I curse the gravity. I curse my stupidity in not going after him right after lunch. We've already lost more than our quota of units today. Knowing Daryl, he's probably sitting in a pen mourning a lost cow with the slurry going cold in the tub behind him and a thousand capital units dissipating into the pen air. He has no sense at all.

The whole installation is arranged so that the harvest from the cattle pens—the capital units—never comes under our control at all. We can't convert any capital units into fuel for our own use. They go directly into hull-exterior holding tanks, which explode if tampered with. Only the units from the tanks in the pigpens are for our use. But there'd be nothing to keep us from collecting slurry from the cattle pens before it goes into the tank and taking it out to the pig pens and running it through the tank there. So they set the moderator to calculate the number and weight of the cows and amount of their feed, and then estimate a weight and volume of slurry per day. If the slurry falls more than 5 percent below the estimate, the moderator begins to replace it with the harvest from our pigpens, i.e., our fuel. That runs life support, the food dispensers, our own gravity and light. Daryl's lost us up to fifty units at least twice through sheer stupidity. We're already down I don't know how many units today.

The weight warning sounds, dammit. Five seconds later the weight lets go and I lift into the air on a long stride and bump my head against the ceiling. I have to pole all the way to the cattle pens. I'm so certain it's a burst calf that I actually put my cattle gear on without checking the com to see if he's there. He's not in the first pen, nor in the second, though, like an idiot I run around both calling to him through my mask. Do I have to search through all hundred? I finally calm down and hit the com. He doesn't answer. I hit it again. No answer. It must be a pig down this time.

I don't know why I have to get there. There's nothing I can do. I know what comes next. But in my eagerness I almost forget safety and have to remind myself—I hurry out of my suit—never rush, ever—and pole like a maniac toward the pig pen. I should've gone there first. We can afford to lose a calf. Down into the weighted room, into my suit, boots, gloves, mask, check, calm down, check again. Adjust.

The pen is much as I left it for lunch. I can't distinguish most pigs. Bella is obvious but not the others. Daryl knows every one by name, weight, feeding patterns, and trenchant personality points. I turn into to the pigfirmary and there they are, Bella lying on her side, not squealing but breathing heavily, her abdomen distended, Daryl holding her head on his lap and a scalpel in his hand, his right hand. It's Bella. I almost smile.

I can only hear a low murmuring sound through his mask and mine, but I can tell by the rhythm and the relaxed set of his shoulders and the slight rocking of his upper body that he's praying. By the rhythm of his rocking I can pick up the place—I never learned Arabic but the sounds of the words, so familiar from my school days, the five times a day, the intervention of the word "Allah" every so many syllables—the sounds I can remake with the mouth in my mind, never forming with my lips, ever. I'm struck, with an irony more bitter than usual, by what stereotypes we make: the Christian mechanic, the Muslim shepherd. Only the Muslim is butchering a pig, and the Christian is standing while someone prays, mouthing "Allah" in her mind, eyes wide in the white light with eagerness for what comes next.

Daryl lowers the scalpel and cuts an incision into her abdomen. She is awake but numbed. His hand returns to the incision and cuts another one, this one deeper, just as the blood starts. Her blood is darker than black and runs down to the floor, whitening the room around it, clinging to what gravity there is. It is now the only thing in the room. The third incision breaches the wall of her stomach and the gas is released, deflating her. I move forward to help but Daryl has all his implements within reach. He adds a clotting agent, waits two minutes, then cleans the wound and clamps its lips together and sprays a disinfectant over the whole. Shifting sideways, he lays her head on the floor and moves to mop up the mess.

Daryl turns and sees me then, as I see that his mask is fogged. He must not be able to see too well. I take the gauze from him and finish mopping up. The gauze is made alive by the color. I wipe some of the blood onto my sleeve, then push it into my arm. I almost wish it would penetrate the seal and the blood and gas could reach my skin. The blood is a tear in the pressure of this room, releasing it, leaving emptiness. He returns the scalpel, clamper and chemicals to the disinfecting bins. Then he goes back to Bella and tries to sit down. I throw the gauze into biowaste and grab him. I gesture eating. He lets me lead him out.

I have to wash him and take his suit off and then pole us both back to the cabin, dragging him with my right hand while I pole with my left. His dinner is a liquid in its baggie. The sight of it animates him again. He rips it off the wall as I pull the weight in the whole cabin. Ten units. He hits the floor with a thud, dropping the food as he hits. I go to pick it up but he gets there first, tearing the bag open in one corner and sucking it down in one long slurp. The baggie is ruined but tonight seems a night reserved for waste. I let him rest for a while.

"What are her chances?" I ask finally.

"About 20 percent for recovery. She probably can't rejoin the herd."

"Why not?"

He looks at me in surprise. "You saw what they did to Liz before I got to her."

"Can't you grow another?"

"In three months?"

"Can't you herd them yourself?"

He doesn't answer. Stupid question. Stupid. Wake up.

I immediately stand up and check the gauge. Stupid. I know what it says. I sit back down and pull the nearest monitor to me and call up the fuel inventory. We're just where we should be at this point in the cycle without interruption. But we've just been interrupted, permanently. If we turn off the weight everywhere, turn off the lights in the quarters and reduce its air volume, turn off our dispenser and live off of Bella's rations, this three months' loss will still deliver us to the company one and a half months dead. I crunch numbers again, close the quarters, put Daryl and me into the hallway at night. We still fall one month short. I close the hall-ways, restrict us to a small area near dry storage. It still leaves one week. I put us in suits, attached to the air valve—put us in restraints, buckled to the wall for the next three months. It still leaves three days. Reduce the amount of air. Two days. Reduce again, to the point we might die anyway. One day. I check, I recheck. One day. One day. It's the two pairs of lungs. That puts us over.

Daryl begins to pray. I am shocked. I've never heard prayer before, right in front of me, with no walls or mask to muffle it. I think that he should damned well pray before I realize that it's a prayer of mourning. He's griev-ing for that pig.

Then the fear grabs me down like into a weighted room. I've never felt such a desire to live before—not since I've been out here. Not since I left the enclave. Never. Going on this cycle always seemed like a step toward death or forgetting. Now the humiliation of what we do, the littleness of Daryl's loves and comforts, my free rein to my paranoia, and the terrible distance from safety, it all suddenly appears as the hair shirt it is. I don't want to die. I don't want to forget. I don't want to wait to live. I want to live now.

I am staring at what remains of the Earth as it sets over the prideful horizon of the ship's hull. I'm naked but I'm not cold yet, even though the tempera-ture of the quarters has dropped since I cut life support down. My body is still warm. Every irony comes to me from a distance, cobwebbed.

I've restricted life support to a small area and programmed it to turn off permanently in twelve hours. By then I'll have rigged a small tank to my suit and will only have to create atmosphere inside it, and I'll still be mobile. I'll liquefy Bella's rations, put them in another tank, and run a tube to my mouth. Food and drink. I've cut gravity entirely—in fact, smashed the gravity controls in the quarters to protect myself from myself, and my learned habit of luxury. I've reprogrammed every control, set every gauge on conserve mode. I've counted and recounted every unit I have. It should be enough. I have a little leeway now. Just enough. I'll have to be careful with that. I need to consider mixing some sedatives in with my food-slurry. It will be a long three months.

Just the thought of it makes me drowsy, but I can't doze off yet. Daryl's body is still floating in the main section of the quarters, the part I've cut out of the atmosphere. There was relatively little blood, but every few minutes I hear a dull, mild pop from a droplet that floats into my little circle of air and explodes from the pressure. My skin is covered with tiny pinpoints of black blood. I'll have to find something absorbent to remove it with. Or maybe I'll just leave it there to be absorbed by my underclothes. I'm concerned about the energy I'll waste collecting and removing the blood but I'm more worried about how its constant presence will affect my mental state over the next few months. I need to get up now and clean up, remove his body. I'll put it in the pigs' tank, with Bella and Liz. The human body isn't much good for gas, but every little bit helps. I wonder how many units he's good for? Surely no more than thirty.

I made sure there was a second scalpel near to his hand, one the same size as mine. He saw it, but didn't reach for it. I wanted him to leave some scars on me—proof that I had acted in self-defense. I wanted the opportunity to die fighting, too. But he came to me full of grief and looked up at me and let me decide for both of us.

His blood entering the room was no different than any other blood, no darker, no brighter, no more real. The release of pressure, the dissipating of blood throughout the room he had inhabited and dominated for so many months, lasted only a moment. It did exhaust me. I wish he had earned this exhaustion with me. I wish he could understand that there are no mistakes in writing such stories except that when you write in blood you have to conserve enough ink later to underline and re-underline the word *life.*

THE PEOPLE

by LINDSAY CARLETON

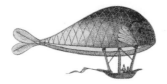

THERE IS SOMETHING I want to say. Something for us, for the small group of small people here tonight. Something for the folding-chair circle gathering bare in this room. Something for those of us without addiction, without its purchased power. For those of us taking small heavy steps anyway. I want to make our spines straight; we deserve to live without this familiar scurvy. We can walk public and healthy and tall. We can be proud and blend in. I want us to be approached by salesmen wearing patent leather in shoe stores. They will talk to us while their hands are clasped behind their backs. I want us to have a scotch on the rocks in a bar with windows while it snows outside. I want us to feel warm while sitting on stools high enough that our feet don't touch the ground. I want someone with expensive suspenders to offer us a cigar and slap us on the back. I want us to be casually invited to some Saturday party. I want us to go. We can't even imagine it. I can imagine it.

They are on some triple-digit floor. Some building very high and made of glass and silver. They can talk on speakerphone and see tornadoes drop. They can watch as the rolling wind destroys our homes, the things we hide beneath. They think that is amazing; then they go play squash. The entrance to this silver building is pink and marble, some cold womb. There are paintings of people with no clothes on and there are lights that run like days, straight along the ceiling. They call them tracks. There are dark men wearing stiff navy blue sitting by the elevators. They have guns. There is no other way to get in. Everything they press lights up. They have red wine and seafood for lunch. We know this only because they like to have big windows, let in lots of light. They do not want everything tinted and so, sometimes, sneaking up to some low pane, we can look inside. I saw crystal at a Christmas party once; I can imagine what that would feel like in my palm, in our palms.

I can imagine walking inside. We are wearing nice belts and we have umbrellas. The guards say hello and tell us to proceed upstairs. Merry Christmas, they say. And to you as well. The elevator has velvet walls, it must have velvet walls. A solid color, gold. We can fit inside easily, all of us. We can turn around and talk to each other on the way up. We are laughing when the doors open. I can smell it. Roasting meat and candle wax. Clinking glasses and soft voices. It is very warm, and someone takes our leather gloves, our coats. The bartender with the black bow-tie has our drinks ready when we get to the bar. He passes us those warm moist towels using a pair of tongs.

There are large chairs right by the tree. They are real chairs and it is a real tree. We can smell leather and pine. We sit side by side in them, discussing political party lines and voting trends. We can see by the reflected white and red lights, but we don't have to. There are men in this room whose faces we have seen on television. They wear large rings and shake our hands. Everyone has such soft skin; they touch our wrists and laugh. We enjoy the night. They have welcomed us, and before everyone leaves, we step up on the small stage. We look tall behind the podium. I put my hands up in the air, signaling for the crowd to quiet down. I say something like, *If I could just say a few words.* People tuck their hair behind their ears and look up at me, at us, to listen.

We have them quiet now, you see? We have them rapt and they are standing below us. We could do anything. We could do *anything.* This is what we do: We tuck our right hands inside our jackets. We stand up straight and I begin our speech by saying, *Thank you all for coming.* As if we owned the place. As if we owned the sky it invades. And then I tell them.

We are not like you. We are not with you. You do not know our names from graduating classes. You do not know our faces from Christmas cards. We do not have suited closets and platinum bed frames. These (I hold up my glass) are our first martinis. Lemon twisted. I pause and take a sip and watch them slip their hands inside their pockets, slip their elbows off the tables. They wonder what the punchline is and we look at each other as if we know and then I tell them. I tell them who we are. They have long faces now, they put down their crystal glasses of wine, but they do not leave. They do not move. No one wants to be the first one to move.

We continue: We are on your outside looking in. This is not a swagger, this is a limp. We walk irregular through well-lit streets only because we have squeezed through those cracks which, try as you might, you can never quite seal. We have squeezed in here tonight. You are not airtight.

You have pushed us out into the atmosphere, and there we survive. We are bound to our own strange hand by a Salem curse of what has become abnormal genetics. We are called the extreme and the wicked, we are the horses that draw and quarter status quo. Imagine: your rope burn versus our strong flank. We are those you avoid direct contact with, like the sun. But we are here now. We are tall now, and we are bright.

You do not recognize us, but we know each other. I have seen your concrete on the corner. Your clean black boots in the city snow. You throw quarters and threats at our bowed heads in the winter. But this is not always fashionable. Sometimes, for decades at a time, you show us into your curtained parties for selfish entertainment. You call it charity. You welcome us in your dry-ice way and walk down a large hall several feet in front. We are supervised from behind expensive and bent glass, white wine and whispering. We are checked for cleanliness so as not to soil the bone-colored carpet, and you never let us eat your dip.

You know we are not like you; sometimes you discuss it from underneath your fresh breath. You use words like *odious* and *unique,* but these words do not seem to describe us, you are missing something. You know. You smell us with a gland you will not admit you have, you use too much deodorant, and you push from your center. We exist just to the left.

Now we take our jackets off and hang them neatly over a chair. The only sound comes from the bartender. He is cleaning up while watching us; he might be proud—he is certainly amused. We smile at him; we clear our throats and proceed.

We say something like, *You see, ladies and gentlemen,* your center is a circle, a small, exclusive circle. You constructed it this way, a long, white time ago. And it is strong. Our ribs and skulls and fingertips know that it is strong. But in our isolation we have discovered that left of it can be anywhere, it can be everywhere. We might be all around you, in a ring. Perhaps we are the ring on your finger, your symbol of union. The bond of love. We could be the ring around your collar, brushing your business jugular every workday. We could be the ring around your hard-boiled egg, blackening your fat-free lunch. We could be the fence around your yard, the only thing between you and chaos. We could be your halo, your ticket to heaven. We could be the hoops you spend your life jumping through. We could be the innertube that keeps your blond child afloat while you work on your tan and your gossip. We could be the giant whales encircling a meal of thousands of tiny fish who are blinded by our underbellies. We could be in your home when you get there.

They look wide around the room now. They are trying to find someone they share a bank account with, someone they had left standing by the restroom. They think of the art in their houses. Originals and gold frames. They think we cannot possibly mean it, that we could be home when they get there. We could not beat them to the door, they think. We do not know their security codes, we cannot break their glass. They think that is the point, our breaking their glass. They think we want what is inside their walls. The things they have had appraised and insured.

They are afraid now, rubbing palm on silk on thigh. They want to leave, but someone has checked their coats. Someone has their coats. They are cold they fold their arms they feel tired and they finally know:

We could be anyone. We could be.

SOUL OF A WHORE

A PLAY IN THREE ACTS

by DENIS JOHNSON

ACT III

Act One, which appeared in Issue No. 9, took place in a bus station in Huntsville, Texas, where two convicts fresh from the Huntsville prison—Bill Jenks, former TV preacher, and John Cassandra, a reformed hellraiser—encountered Masha, a demon-possessed stripper. At John's urging, Bill Jenks reluctantly accomplished an exorcism, during which Masha's demon delivered three mystifying predictions concerning the future of Bill Jenks: "You will meet your mirror; you will raise the dead; and when you die, on that occasion an innocent will be killed."

Act Two, which appeared in Issue No. 11, took place a year later. Bill Jenks, now traveling with Masha and John Cassandra as his assistants, drove the very same demon from a comatose hospital patient, and in the process fulfilled the first prediction by meeting "his mirror," the patient's brother: state executioner Will Blaine. In a private talk with the demon, Bill Jenks revealed he'd gone bankrupt and offered to bargain with the demon for help; the demon refused and repeated the two as yet unfulfilled predictions. Meanwhile, in another part of the hospital, Will Blaine seduced Masha, and took her away with him.

Act Three begins the following year.

SCENE 1

Another year later.

Split scene: Left, peepshow talk-booth {BJ's hallucination} in BILL JENKS's living room. Right, front porch of BJ's rural home outside Dallas.

LIGHTS UP STAGE LEFT

{BILL JENKS loads quarters in a slot as a screen rises on a peepshow talk-booth, revealing MASHA in a silk robe and platform shoes.}

{Each holds a phone receiver.}

BILL JENKS: Slut... slut... slut... slut... slut.

MASHA: You realize, of course, you're nothing but a faggot,
      The balled-up, writhing, Adolf Hitler kind.

BILL JENKS: People eat you in their fantasy.

MASHA: You're sloppy drunk.

BILL JENKS: I'm paying for the call.
    ...You want to hear your story?

MASHA: All I hear
Is your brain sizzling like a T-bone.

BILL JENKS: Listen, child:
  I'll tell you the repeating saga of Masha.

MASHA: Preacher's comin', duck and cover, boys.

BILL JENKS: You like to blame us for yourself, then run away.
    You're always breaking free, breaking out,
    I'll show you the pattern. First, you busted free
    From Daddy; then a hotrod boyfriend, maybe,
    And then one of your teachers, and then some artist
    Who painted you nude, then some criminal

Made his living jackin' Coke machines,
Then Sylvester of the Purple Prairie—
Then you ditch your pimp and come to me,
So you can break my chains and fly away
Into the cage of your latest master and captor.

MASHA: What about your pattern, honey?
Jack 'em up like monkeys till they're jumpin'
High as Heaven on that down-home Bible jive—
Cleanse me save me change me fix me, preacher,
Use me, preacher, eat my wallet, suck
My sorry sap.

BILL JENKS: You slinky slut.

MASHA: Unbind 'em, heal 'em, fleece 'em, and forget 'em.
All God's chillun got a pattern, sugar.
All God's chillun got to walk a chalk line.

BILL JENKS: Slut slut slut slut slut!
—I'm sorry I'm sorry I'm sorry I'm sorry I'm sorry!
I deeply regret the misunderstanding that led to...
The misunderstanding.

MASHA: How long do we have to stay tangled together?

BILL JENKS: Until I fathom what that knot is knit of.

MASHA: Look... I got tired of *preaching* in my ears,
The mindless mechanical bark, bark, bark.
Okay? Don't make it into a work of art.
Don't make me a testimony to the lie
You're living.

BILL JENKS: Lie? What lie, you Jezebel?

MASHA: Everybody's selling a fantasy.
Your trouble comes from hating the glistening guts
Of that one gospel fact. You'll happily
Confess to dealing crap to your disciples,

But you won't witness to the simple truth
They're selling it all right back to you,
They're the closest thing to God you've got—
The audience is everyone and no one—
Anonymous mother you're suckled by and hate
And love. You want to see a whore? Go seek
Among the pews. They sell themselves to you.

BILL JENKS: Crawling on your belly like a Jezebel.

MASHA: At least I don't fall down to a phony God.
    You bow to them. You fear their punishment.
    You take the blame because they see a lie
    While looking in your direction.
    It ain't your lie. It's just their fantasy.
    You want to go to Hell because *they're* stupid.

BILL JENKS: Masha, Masha, what has become of you?

MASHA: I was a part of your pattern—thanks for the save.
    Thanks for the exorcism and the gray suit.

BILL JENKS: Heck, you ain't halfway exorcised. I'd give
    An estimate of twenty-five percent,
    If that. Hell, you're a carnival of demons.

MASHA: It's Satan's world. You buck the tide you get
    All waterlogged and wrinkled-up. And drowned.

BILL JENKS: You ride the flow and paradoxically
    You end up burning in a lake of fire.

MASHA: Tell me you've lived one day in fear of Hell.

BILL JENKS: I sure have lived in fear. Mostly in fear
    Of Heaven and its possibilities
    For boredom and monotony and Sunday
    Every day, and Jesus hanging around.
    …I can just about smell you through the glass.

MASHA: What are you talking about?

BILL JENKS: Is it bulletproof glass?

MASHA: Do you have a gun?

BILL JENKS: A lot of people do.
    How's the security here? Do they protect you?

MASHA: Who? Where? Why on earth would I need protection?

BILL JENKS: Who? The demons who employ you here.
    Every sex emporium needs security.

MASHA: What are you talking about, what are you *on*?
    I DON'T WORK IN A SEX EMPORIUM.

LIGHTS DOWN on MASHA. BJ alone in his living room with a phone in one hand,
bottle in the other.

MASHA'S VOICE: I've got a house, and I've got a minivan
    And twenty-three pairs of shoes. I'm legally married.
    I am the wife of the executioner
    For all of Texas, and I am the president
    Of the Texas Citizens for Victims' Rights.
    All you see of me is your fantasy.
    That's all any of you ever see.
    I should rob banks! —Nobody ever sees me.
    I'm like one of those Rorschach ink-blot messes
    Showing the twisted story in your head.
    ALL YOU'RE SEEING IS THE STORY IN YOUR HEAD!

[*BILL JENKS hangs up and crawls toward the door with his bottle.*]

BLACKOUT

LIGHTS UP STAGE RIGHT

BILL JENKS's front porch, next minute.

Off and on throughout scene, JOHN works on his cross (it rests against the rail), attaching tokens to it with contractor's glue. His hair grown shoulder-length, and sporting a beard, he still wears his prison whites.

JOHN [*sings*]: If I got paid a nickel
            Every time you told a lie
            I'd put those nickels in a sack
            And tie that sack around my neck
            And jump into the river
            And sink beneath the water
            If I got paid a nickel
            Every time you told a lie

            If I got paid a dollar
            Every time you made me cry
            I'd pile those dollars in a stack
            And climb that stack and grab the moon
            And hide the moon in Houston
            Where you could never find it
            If I got paid a dollar
            Every time you made me cry

            If I got paid a nickel
            Every time you told a lie

[*Meanwhile, BILL JENKS crawls out of the house and across the porch, lugging his bottle, and sits bracing himself against a post.*]

BILL JENKS: Woman claims to be the proud possessor
    Of forty-six shoes…

JOHN [*sings*]: I'd put those nickels in a sack
            And tie that sack around my neck
            And dive into the ocean
            And mingle with the fishes
            And tell 'em all my troubles
            'Bout a woman who deceived me
            Every time she told a lie

BILL JENKS: …Who's come for a little BJ?

Come get a little BJ!
Come on and get a quality BJ!
Where are my innumerable followers
To take me back in a tearful ceremony?
I got a zillion bucks, and I can't touch it.
My attorneys won't return my calls.
I held a press conference. Who was there?
Who was there, John? —Wasn't it a guy
From the *Neonazi Tribune*, something like that?
The Sword and the Blade. The Cross and the Ball, shoot,
I don't know. *You* get the sense of it.

JOHN: Would you shut up?

BILL JENKS: I might. It all depends.

JOHN: The suckers love you, Bill, so just shut up.
We'll always love you. That's what makes us suckers.

BILL JENKS [*sings*]: If I got paid a nickel
                Every time you kissed a pickle…
…If I don't pull somebody outta their grave,
I might as well get in it, too.

JOHN: You've gotta train your mind on Huntsville, Bill.
In twenty days they strap my mother down.
If you're gonna raise somebody from the dead,
It might as well be my mother, right?

BILL JENKS: Look here.
What was your mother in for, in the first place?

JOHN: You know what she was in for.

BILL JENKS: No. I don't.
Her current fame obscures her former fame.

JOHN: It wasn't nothing she was famous for.
Vehicular Homicide. To be exact
You'd say Vehicular Infanticide.

BILL JENKS: Vehicular *Infanticide?* Oh, God,
    Sometimes can't you feel the English tongue
    Kind of licking around inside your stomach?

JOHN: Is that enough to say?

BILL JENKS: Well... what'd she do?

JOHN: Ran over my baby sister with the Chevy.
    Pretty much on purpose. So she drew
    A twenty-five-year slide. She almost made it.
    But then they charged her with another murder,
    They claimed she killed that empty-minded girl—
    That nameless, brainless Jane Doe, may the Lord
    Have mercy—claim my mother perpetrated rape
    And murder with a broomstick. That is false.
    Even over a couple dozen years
    And twenty prison walls, her innocence
    Travels out to me like radiation.

BILL JENKS: Bathes us in its sacrificial light.

JOHN: Laying in the dirt, drunk and sarcastic.

[*BJ aims around with a Derringer, miming shots.*]

BILL JENKS: Bullseye. Bullseye. Bullseye.
    I just have one more thing to say about Masha:
    She used to say Mushmeller for Marshmallow
    And her name was Mar-sha, not Masha.
    And she had thighs like marshmallows, which
    I never touched one time, not even dreaming.
    Announcement! —I have never read the Bible.

JOHN: Is that thing loaded?

BILL JENKS: Always assume it's loaded.

JOHN: Well, then, unload it please. [*BANG*] Thank you, you hick.
    ...The way of a fool is right in his own eyes.

BILL JENKS: Proverbs, chillun.

JOHN: Proverbs, 12:15.

BILL JENKS: The proverbial Proverbs.
                              [*Lies back.*]
                                             Hey—ow! Watch the head!
   Man, that's black. That sky is solid velvet.

[*JOHN examines BJ—passed out—takes the gun, considers attaching it to the cross.
He points it at the dark. BANG.*]

HT'S VOICE: STOP. DON'T SHOOT.

JOHN: Who's out there? Come up here and get killed.

A space of silence.

HT [*sings*]: Wake up this morning
                  Blue dog called my name

                  If you ever get to Houston
                  Boy you better walk right
                  You better not gamble

[*He materializes from the dark.*]

   …You better never have no fun a-tall.
   …Wrap yourself around me! Gimme squeeze!
   I waited for you at the Huntsville Greyhound!
   Man, I broke parole to see you. Man—
   Baby baby baby—how you doing?
   I'm doing good, myself! I'm travelling!
   They call me Hostage-Taker cause I took
   Some hostages, and that's my Claim to Fame.
   Who is this guy? How come he don't talk?
   Brer Jenks has got hissef a Tar Baby.
   [*Sings*] "Mistah Blue-bird on mah shoul-dah!"
   OK OK OK let's settle down.
   I waited for you! First the Houston bus

And then the Dallas, and you never came!
That's the day things started going wrong.
Parole boss say be here, or I'll get mad.
You miss the meeting and he gets his sharpened
Fingers motorvating on that phonepad
Wop bop-a-lu-bop, a wop bam boom! —Like *that*
He violates your ass, and you got warrants.
That's what happens when the bus don't come!
—How long has Brer Jenks been like this?

JOHN: I saw you on TV.

HT: —Now, don't believe
   Just every single thing that TV shows you.

JOHN: I didn't say believe. I say I saw.
   I saw you on there.

HT [*with BJ's jug*]:   Want a snort?… To fame!
   Woo. Woo. That strangles up your vocal chords.

JOHN: How'd you get here, anyhow?

HT: I walked.
   I walked across the fields. Across, across.
   That's why I'm all red dirt up past my knees.
   …They let you wear your hair and beard in the joint?

JOHN: No. I been out a couple years.

HT: A couple?

JOHN: Yeah. Two years.

HT: Then what you wearing whites for?
   Been gambling? Gambling treats you mean as drinking.
   Either one, your wardrobe goes to hell.
   Now, look at me. I'm mussed, I know, but look—
   A brand-new suit. Use me as your example.

SIREN *in the distance*—

HT: —That's that blue dog calling me. That skinny
      Blue dog... [*Of the cross*] it's kinda Mexican, ain't it?

JOHN: Yeah, it's Mexican. And so's my mother.

HT: So's my mother? What'd you say about—

JOHN: No, *mine. My* mother's Mexican, not yours.

HT: How do you know my mom ain't Mexican?
      She could be an African Mexican.
      I could be an Afro-Hispanic American,
      So leave each other's mother out of it.
      Did you just see a worm crawl outta my brain?
      Some days I feel screwier'n Japanese jazz!
      Been starin' in the pit of hell so long
      But that's all right...
      Let me introduce myself.

JOHN: You introduced yourself.

HT: I introduced myself? Okay, okay,
      Then let *you* introduce *your*self to *me.*

JOHN: I'm John Cassandra.

HT: And this here's Preacher Jenks.
      Me and the preacher have a history.
      I'm charmed I'm sure. 'Cause I heard all about you,
      Uh-huh, the Cross-boy and the preacher-man.

JOHN: What's your purpose here?

HT: My purpose on this earth?

JOHN: No. On this porch.

HT: I'm just here long enough to cure my nerves.

BILL JENKS: My age, you get to feel this vernal weather
    Down in the gristle...

HT: Brother Bill!

BILL JENKS: Quite so!
    Is it autumn, or is it spring? I can't decide.
    We've got this barometric memory
    That kind of senses atmospheric change
    Based on what we've seen since childhood.

JOHN: Bill,
    Will you shut up?

HT: How long has he been like this?

BILL JENKS: It's a proper question.

JOHN: No, the question
    Is how long are you gonna *stay* like this?

BILL JENKS: Either until autumn or until spring.
    Old HT. I saw you on the TV.
    Let's us have a drink.

HT: Brer Jenks! I'm out!
    ...You're out! We're out! It's time! —We hit that number!
    Baby, don't you remember? I finally hit that number.
    I pulled some mischief, slick as babyshit—
    Guess where? Do you know where? In Canada!
    Been up there for a year. I got a car,
    I got a name, I got ID, the total package,
    I had it all up there, but I missed home.
    Not home in Willard. Home back at the Walls.
    I missed that smell. The voices echoing.
    The same day over and over and no way out.
    I kind of missed that feeling like you're trapped.

BILL JENKS: What I hear, you ain't gonna miss it long.

HT: I feel like I'm full of poison—emotional poison,
    Physical poison, and every kind of poison.
    My mind got fat. My dick won't make no juice.
    What are they *thinking* about in Canada?
    They make you feel ridiculous…

BILL JENKS: It wasn't Canada that made you famous.
    There ain't no show called *Canada's Most Wanted.*
    Nope, I believe they showed your photograph
    On one they call *America's Most Wanted,*
    Had it on now several Sairdy's running,
    Account of this thing you did in Ellersburg,
    And not the Canadian Ellersburg, no sir,
    This other Ellersburg down here in Texas,
    The Texas Ellersburg. A quite bad thing.

HT: *I* know. —Well, it looks like… well, it looks like…

BILL JENKS: *Well*, HT, it looks like a double killing.
    It looks like they think you did it, like they think
    You did this double killing up there. So they think.

SIREN in the distance—

HT: It was a desperate situation, Brother Jenks.

BILL JENKS: They're looking for you, Brother Hostage-Taker.

HT: Don't go believing everything you hear.

JOHN: Sirens? Sirens are hard not to believe.

HT: That's just a train. The good old KC Flyer.

BILL JENKS: They want you, they want you bad, the worst. "The most."

HT: I'm saying it was a desperate *situation.*

BILL JENKS: How could it be desperate? There's nothing *there,*
    It's *Ellersburg*—a crossroads with a store,

A gasoline pump, and a Coke machine.
It's like a scene from 1957.
Thing still dispenses Yoo-Hoo for a dime.

HT: Man, you don't get it, I'm *here*, I'm *here.*

BILL JENKS: And Mom and Pop slopped over on the floor—
Which one was Mom? Which one was Pop? We'll wait
On Ellersburg's most talented mortician
To figure that one out.

HT: He had a gun!

BILL JENKS: Hey, so do I. You gonna blow my head off?

HT: What are you saying? Man, we have a deal!
Twelve months in a prison cell together—

BILL JENKS: Hey now, what was that movie, what was that movie—
...*The Defiant Ones*, with Sidney Poitier.
"Charlie Potato, Charlie Potato!" ...Boys,
I'm going to Huntsville, Texas, boys,
To raise this bastard's mother from the dead.

JOHN: Thank God!

BILL JENKS: No. Get back. There's foodstuff caught in your beard.

JOHN: Thank God. Thank God!

HT: So—where do I come in?

BILL JENKS: Come in?

HT: Come in. Come in.

BILL JENKS: You don't come in.

HT: I don't?

BILL JENKS: You don't come in. Where would you fit?

HT: That's what I'm asking in this stupid place
   With sirens screaming awful bloody murder
   And blah blah blah—now where do I fit in?

BILL JENKS: Sidney... You've got no role in my movie,
   Sidney. My movie's got a cast of one.
   It's all about this preacher silhouetted
   Against a gory sunset outside Dallas
   Tyin' up a rope to lynch himself.
   That's the picture I'm trying to get across.
   Kind of a tragic silly mystery.

HT: Man, we have a deal, we have a deal!

BILL JENKS: What deal? When did I ever make a bargain
   With such as you?

HT: Man!—twelve months in a cell?
   A solid year? Me smelling your shit
   And listening to you playing with yourself,
   Coughing, farting, talking in your dreams,
   Crying all night long the first eight weeks?
   —And I remember the night you didn't cry,
   First night you slept the night entirely through.
   I didn't sleep all night that night, for joy.

BILL JENKS: Ah! Those were the days! And then they stopped.

HT: Brother, Brother. I waited at the Greyhound...
   Do you want to know why those people got killed?

BILL JENKS: There was this guy I knew, he was a—well, *you* know,
   I don't know what you'd call him, maybe a faggot?
   That what you are? A homosexual?

HT: Oh, God, oh, God, this ain't my people here!
   I got to get with my people, not these people!
   Gimme a *sign*!

...Do you know why that Mom and Pop got killed?
Can you ever guess why those two persons died?

BILL JENKS: 'Cause buckshot blew their brains up.

HT: Can you guess?
　　Or should I trace it back for you? Listen:
　　I'm all set up, I got a job, I'm in a suit,
　　I'm in the Houston public library.
　　Carpet. Silence. Air-conditioning.
　　Holding *Street Rod News* in my black fingers.
　　The time has come to buy a powerful new
　　Machine, because I'm free... White guy comes over.
　　Now, I'm just looking at my magazine—
　　I'm looking at pictures of engines, powerful engines—
　　Look up, 'cause now he's going hem-hem-hem
　　With his throat. I say to myself: white man
　　Coming up in the public library...
　　Light brown hair, blue eyes, the one
　　Explain your options on the life insurance,
　　Sell you a washer-dryer combination.
　　I'm thinking, First my beautiful suit, and now
　　This white man in the public library.
　　Not young, but not exactly middle-age,
　　Just nonchalant, you know, ain't nothing to him.
　　He says, "This is my name," and all like that,
　　White man in the public library.
　　"Don't get me wrong, I gotta show you something.
　　Come over here to this part of the library
　　For compact discs and videos and all,"
　　And I don't know is he a *cop*, some *Mormon*...
　　What am I gonna do but follow him there?
　　He leads me like we're on safari, man,
　　We're gonna capture something with our stealth,
　　White man in the public library.
　　Like we're stalking on a quiet field of birds
　　Or moving through a church,
　　And there, across the room,
　　White man in the public library
　　Shows me a beautiful young black woman.

She's standing by the racks, what can I say,
Looking like a lump of Lawd Have Mercy.
Short sleeveless dress of graphite gray,
Smooth black arms, incredible black face,
Had that sticky-outy posture like she tore
Herself from *Vogue* or *Ebony* or *Cosmo*;
The tiniest littlest dab of spit would melt her.
He showed her to me.
He looks at me with this face,
Like a bird-dog saying with his face, there
Master, I didn't leave
No marks of my teeth in her feathers.

JOHN: ...Then what? ...What then?

HT: Then we stood still. And then she moved. And then
She passed into the rest of things.
And him, he's gone like he weren't never there,
White man in the public library,
And I felt very confused. I said, I said,
"I *can*not stop being confused by this.
I stand here in my slick new suit, so clean...
A white man shows me a black, beautiful woman..."

JOHN: The same suit you have on.

HT: This very suit.

JOHN: There's not much left of it.

HT: Why, no, not much.
It's done been eat to bits in all the confusion,
The ongoing saga of my continuing
Confusion, which has not stopped, from then till now,
You see, because I continue to feel confused.
They'll never let me out, I don't suppose.

BILL JENKS: Nope. Calendars and clocks, my man.
And bars and walls and years et cetera.

HT: Do you understand a little better now?
   Now do you understand why I killed those people?

JOHN: I know who understands: God understands.

HT: God is just a little jumped up white man.
   That was God in the Houston library.
   White man in the public library.
   I can't stop the thoughts,
   I'm cookin' too hot!
   [*Leaving*]
   My suit? ...Take a look at yours!

BILL JENKS: Give you a sign? Here's a sign... He gone—
   Into the sea of Spam and Wonderbread...
   Sidney. Sidney. I ain't Tony Curtis.
   I'm strictly *Looney Tunes*! I'm Daffy Duck!
   Woo-woo! Woo-woo.

SIRENS; TRAIN WHISTLE.

JOHN: ...Give me something of yours.

BILL JENKS: Something? My what. My shoe? What something? What?

JOHN: Something that's lucky or important or that means
   Something.

BILL JENKS: Lucky.

JOHN: Like your Derringer.

BILL JENKS: I'm not sure I'm in favor of gun control.

JOHN: We glue it to the cross, and you'll be healed.

BILL JENKS: I'm not sure I'm in favor of being healed.

JOHN: This is how the Mexicans cure their troubles.

BILL JENKS: By gluing items on the cross. With Jesus.

JOHN: Trinkets, yeah, things that have touched them, tokens,
    Things to represent their scars and glories.
    To sacrifice. To crucify their sorrows.

TRAIN WHISTLE.

BILL JENKS: …It's always the most relentlessly simple things
    That tear at you and break your heart. Like trains.

SIRENS.

    SO LONG, SIDNEY!

JOHN: Maybe he can't be helped.
    But did you really have to be a shit?

[JOHN exits into the house.]

BILL JENKS: …Where on earth did you get that silly notion?
    Don't you know what the emblems are about?
    They don't stick pagan symbols on the cross.
    Them Catholics have the whole thing codified,
    Everything's got a meaning—all this stuff:
    These crossbones are the bones of Adam,
    Said to be buried at the foot of the true cross.
    These are the hammers and these the nails that banged
    The Savior to the tree in agony.
    These aren't lucky dice—except for the guy
    Who won his garments—they cast lots, remember?
    The Roman soldiers gambled for his clothes.
    They stripped Christ bare, and one went home a winner.
    Where do you get this stuff? Here is the sun
    Whose face the storm obscured when Christ was killed,
    And here is the moon that bled. Where do you get
    Your silly notions, John? …The moon that bled.

[BILL JENKS raises his Derringer, takes aim: CLICK.]

BLACKOUT

SCENE 2

Twenty days later.

Corner of 10th and J Streets in front of Walls Unit, Huntsville, TX.

[JOHN CASSANDRA, costumed as a clown, poses on his cross.]

HUBBUB, VOICES O.S. *[fading out]*:

> Shoot her full of poison,
> Throw her in a grave!
> Shoot her full of poison,
> Throw her in a grave!
>
> Two! Four! Six! Eight!
> There's no rhyme or reason
> To capital punishment!
> Two! Four! Six! Eight!
> There's no rhyme or reason
> To capital punishment!
>
> Justice for the innocent!
> Killing for the killers!
> Justice for the innocent!
> Killing for the killers!

LIGHTS UP

Public Information Office across the street from the Walls. JERRY and STEVIE. JERRY at the window.

JERRY: Stevie, has Texas gone and joined the circus?
>   Or is it the universe, or just my life
>   That's grown a populace of runts and freaks?

STEVIE: Jerry, should I toss this coffee out?

JERRY: I have a daughter, Stevie, you touch my daughter
>   I'm gonna jump straight up somebody's ass.

Is that a concept of too wide a girth
To fit inside our brains?

STEVIE: Well, I don't know.

JERRY: You *kill* someone, someone kills *you*. Come on.
    Has justice run away and joined the circus?

STEVIE: I couldn't say. I don't know. Maybe so.

JERRY: Do you call life in prison "punishment"?

STEVIE: I'd never actually touch your daughter, Jerry.

JERRY: You'd better kill 'em: send 'em all to hell,
    If hell awaits them, and be done with it.
    …Here come the preacher man. Oh looky here.
    I'd like to thump this guy. If I was bigger
    Man I'd grab his legs and bounce him on
    His head until his children's crying stopped me.
    Good afternoon, good— Huh-uh, man. No way
    I let you in with liquor on your breath.

BILL JENKS [*having entered*]: *You* have liquor on your breath, I think.

JERRY: A lunchtime margarita don't equate
    To waltzing in here zig-zag stinkin', partner.
    You'd like a little coffee.

STEVIE: I tossed the coffee.

JERRY: She tossed the coffee. Bubble us up some more.

STEVIE: Maybe for later, you mean? —Right now it's almost—

JERRY: —Haven't got the time. The hour is nigh.
    You've made the acquaintance of the son? —I think
    The word I'm looking for is "colorful."
    You'll pale beside him, pardner. Alley-oop.
    This way. We're at our maximum

Or we'd have half Ukiah, California,
Squooching their butts down in the seats. "Ukiah."
That'd be Indian for "cracker." Maybe "Okie."
My people generate from Tennessee,
Just like Elvis Presley and Davy Crockett.

BILL JENKS: Elvis generates from Mississippi.

JERRY: Elvis came from Memphis, Tennessee.

BILL JENKS: He was born in Tupelo, Mississippi.

JERRY: Jesus Christ was born in Israel,
    But that don't mean he ain't American.

STEVIE: I'm not sure we have the time for this.

JERRY: Stevie, how long is the woman going to be dead?
    ...Go on and round 'em up. We'll be along.
    [*STEVIE exits.*]
    —Enough. Will you at least concede that Elvis
    Presley was a *son* of Tennessee?

BILL JENKS: I so concede.

JERRY: All right, enough dispute,
    All right—my daughter gave me this, no sense
    Offending her bounty. Silver plated. Cheers!
    Go on, raise you a toast to Mississippi.

BILL JENKS: Mostly I've lived my life in California.

JERRY [*as they move*]: Oh, well, I've never been to California.
    Right this way—look down, these sonabitchin'
    Paparazzi will fill your eyes with moons—
    I mean, I might get out there, maybe for
    A ball game on the order of the Series
    Or a playoff, if Texas could field a decent team,
    But all we have is the Rangers and the Astros.

[They enter the Witness Room, joining JOHN (still costumed as a clown), and STEVIE.]

JERRY: What are you supposed to be? A clown?

JOHN: We're here to raise my mother from the dead.

JERRY: "Ukiah," that'd be Indian for "Him
    Who Picks His Nose and Eats It."

JOHN: Who's this guy?

JERRY: The PIO.

STEVIE: A son, here: this is John.

JOHN: The PIO?

STEVIE: You know the Reverend.

JOHN: The PIO?

JERRY: I think we need this man
    Struck from the list.

JOHN: The PI-EI-O?

STEVIE: The Texas Department of Criminal Justice's
    Public Information Officer.

JERRY [*to JOHN*]: You're the one who parked his big old cross
    Down there out front. I'm gonna have it towed.

[JERRY has pushed a buzzer.]

JOHN: This is gonna be strange.

JERRY: It's strange already.

The curtain opens on the death chamber: BESS tied down on the gurney, the head of which cranks up to make her visible; WILL BLAINE in attendance.

BESS: Who put me here? I didn't do anything!
     Jesus God! I didn't do anything!
          WHY DO I HAVE TO DIE? WHAT DID I DO?

JERRY: Will—now, haven't we got her tranked?

WILL: She's tranked.

BESS: They said I'd die, and then come back to life.

BILL JENKS: Who told you that? Who told you, Ms. Cassandra?

BESS: I don't know. I heard it in a dream.
     I don't know who was talking in that dream.

BILL JENKS: I'm Reverend—

BESS: Shit. I have no need of Jesus.
     I'm paying for my own goddamn sins.

BILL JENKS: Ms. Cassandra? May I call you Bess?

BESS: Sure, please do. Who else is in the room?

JOHN: Hi, Mom —Hi, Mom—remember me?

BESS: Oh, sure.
     You kind of look familiar. Is that John?

JOHN: Hi, Mom.

BESS: You got real big.

JOHN: I know.
     Mom, we're here to raise you from the dead.

JERRY: Cut the mike, please… Fellas, listen up:

Reverend, how did you get on the list?
This woman doesn't know you.

JOHN: She's my mom,
    And he's the family's spiritual counselor.

JERRY: Across that chamber in the other room
    I've got the Reuters, UPI, AP, the Huntsville
    Courier; down in that baking street
    I've got the TV news and video from France
    And Germany and every goddamn place,
    And I'm not gonna have an incident
    For these assholes to be reporting. Clear?
    …Go on now, give us back the audio.

BESS: Hello? Hello? That was a little scary.
    …John, are you the only of my children
    To make the trip?

JOHN: I guess I am.

BESS: Okay.
    I wasn't expecting trumpets and a crowd.

JOHN: I think they harbor some resentment due
    To certain things that ruined their childhood, Mom.

BESS: John, I always thought you were retarded.

JOHN: I'm not retarded. I just had big teeth.
    They made me talk real slow. But now I'm grown—
    Grown up—and so…

BESS: You've grown into your teeth.
    …Where'd the Reverend Preacher go?

JOHN: He's praying in the corner, Ma. We've come
    To raise you up when they pronounce you dead,
    Because we know you didn't hurt Jane Doe.
    We know you're innocent.

BESS: I'm not so sure.
    I know I'm guilty of Vehicular
    Infanticide, because I do remember
    Squashing little Amy with the car.
    …Amy. What do you think she'd look like now?

JOHN: Amy? Amy would resemble rotten bones.

JERRY: Folks, we're looking at just a couple minutes.

BESS: You children bothered me, I don't know why.
    I'd start off every morning with the notes
    Of music in my heart, and I was young,
    But minute by minute my mind would get all red,
    And photographs in magazines would make me cry,
    Until my life was squeezing all my blood—
    Now, isn't that peculiar don't you think?
    And here the little children all around.
    I should have killed you-all while you were sleeping.
    I guess I didn't really think things through.
    I don't know why I thought I had to use
    The car. Do you believe in demons? Well,
    Nothing in this world can take away
    The deeds I've done. They don't belong to demons.
    I won't give my crimes to Satan.
    I'm keeping my crimes for me.

JERRY: It's six p.m.

STEVIE: May God have mercy on you.

JERRY: I'll just read the order of execution.

BILL JENKS: The order? Isn't that the warden's function?

JERRY: The warden's waterskiing off Honduras.
    Or else he's scuba diving off Belize.
    Vacationing, in other words. It falls to me
    To read the order of execution. Steve,
    Will you please read the order of execution?

STEVIE: Isabel Cassandra, formerly
    Residing in Odessa, Texas:
    Having been convicted of the charge
    Of murder perpetrated in the course
    Of aggravated sexual assault
    Upon Jane Doe (name and address unknown),
    Be informed that the sovereign state of Texas
    Undertakes to execute the sentence
    Imposed July 19, 2001; to wit:
    That you shall be confined until this day,
    Maintained in health, granted communication
    With family, legal counsel, and the press,
    And then, upon this day, at such an hour
    As suits the warden, you shall be called forth
    And taken to a place prepared for such
    Administrations as shall have the swift
    Result of death to you; and therein put to death.

JERRY: May God have mercy on you, Bess Cassandra.

[*WILL lowers the head of the gurney; BESS lies prone.*]

JOHN: Mom, are you prepared?

BESS: What part of me
    Can be prepared? I can't talk to this part
    Or that part, I can't say, "Get ready, arms
    And legs, get ready, guts and lungs and liver—"
    Can't even cross my hands over my chest.
    …Well, thanks for coming by to say goodbye.

JOHN: Woman, if I could say goodbye to you
    I would've said it thirty years ago.

JERRY [*low, to BJ*]: The sodium thiopental's going in.

BESS: John?

JOHN: Mom, Mom…

BESS: Why are you dressed like a clown?

JOHN: There's reasons for it, Mom.

JERRY: She doesn't hear.

JOHN: It's something I've got going.

STEVIE: She can't hear you.

JERRY [*low, to BJ*]: Next pancurium bromide will collapse
    The lungs and diaphragm. And finally
    Potassium chloride stops the heart.

BILL JENKS: How long?

JERRY: Seven minutes from the start to finish.

JOHN: …Seems like seven minutes are almost up.

BESS: …Am I supposed to be dead? When do I die?
    …I still don't think I'm dead. I think— Oh, hey,
    My IV thing popped out. It did. It's out.
    Your poison's spilt all over.

WILL'S VOICE: IV Team!
    Get your unit reestablished, please.
    Never mind. Stand down. I'll reconnect.

BESS: Will it hurt—uh—will it hurt the mattress?

The curtain closes across the window.

BILL JENKS: Mr. PIO. What's going on?

JERRY: Will? We gonna have to clear the site?

WILL'S VOICE: Negative. Sixty seconds.

JERRY: All right. Stevie—go and see about the boys.

Who's over there?—it's Blake for UPI,
I think, and *damn* it, *damn* it all to hell—

STEVIE: I'll see if we can't close the lid.

JERRY: Oh, yeah.
Another perfect termination. Thanks.
I owe you, Steve.

STEVIE: You do. You'll pay me, too,
Tonight at Mursky's.

JERRY: Drinks are all on me.

[*STEVIE exits.*]

JOHN: Hello? Hello? What's going on in there?

JERRY: This thing's been a fiasco from the start.

JOHN: Why can't the guy at least say hi or something?

JERRY: I've never seen the like, and I was here
For Karla Faye. A healer and a clown.

BESS'S VOICE: Uh-oh. OH NO.

JOHN: Mom? Mom? —What's going on?

JERRY: I can't stand to hear you squawking
About it in my ears no more!

JOHN: You don't act like a government official!
You act like a baby!

JERRY: *I* act like a baby?
TORCH THE JAILS AND LET'S BE DONE WITH IT!

JOHN: There's something funny going on in there!
Did you just hear the mike switch off? HELLO!

[Bangs on the glass]
　　HELLO HELLO GODDAMNIT HEY HEY HEY—

*The curtains part abruptly to reveal HT with an arm locked around WILL
BLAINE's neck and a long crude stiletto shoved up under WILL's chin.*

HT: I AM THE NIGGER OF DEATH!
　　[To WILL] ...Let's let the public get a look at you!
　　You hiding back there like the Wizard of Oz.

[Sings]
　　　　　　　　　Let the Midnight Special
　　　　　　　　　Shine a light on you
　　　　　　　　　Let the Midnight Special
　　　　　　　　　Shine his ever-lovin' light on you

　　　　　　　　　Welcome! Welcome! Welcome to my show!

BESS: I hope you know this wasn't my idea.

JOHN: You're still alive!

BESS:　　　　　　　　　And really loving it.

BILL JENKS: Hello, HT. What are you playing at?

HT: A little game that I'm inventing called
　　"Let's Execute the Executioner."
　　If anybody interrupts the game
　　I'll blow up every motherfucker here
　　Including me.

JOHN:　　　　　You're gonna blow us up
　　With a knife?

HT:　　　　　　I didn't say I blow you up
　　With a knife. I blow you *up*, is all I said.

JOHN: Well, what's that in your hand?

HT: Don't get sarcastic.

JOHN: Hey, I'm not. I'm quite sincerely trying
    To form some sense of what you're threatening
    To blow us up with here today, and what
    I'm seeing in your hand looks like a knife.

HT: Quite true. But what's this in my other hand?
[*HT releases his chokehold on WILL and pulls a gun from his pocket, points it at
JERRY while keeping the point of his knife to WILL's chin.*]
    I want everybody in this room with me.

JERRY: We can't do that.

HT: You can't when you're dead!

JERRY: We can't sir, it's impossible. The chambers
    Don't communicate.

HT: What are we doing *now?*

JERRY: There's just no access. They're designed that way
    With just this kind of contingency in mind.

HT: How about this contingency!

[*HT shoots.*] *The glass doesn't break.*

JERRY: That one, too.

HT: But I still got this guy! His head ain't bulletproof!

JERRY: Of course. We're all cooperating here.

[*HT fires all his bullets uselessly at the glass.*]

HT: You think I'm outta bullets? Well, I am!
    But whatchoo think these honeys are? Big tits?

[*Having dropped both knife and gun, he finds in his pockets two hand grenades.*

He yanks the pin of each with his teeth and spits each one at WILL.}

> Nothin' clamps these levers down but me.
> Anything happens to me, —I get distracted,
> Maybe you bore me and I fall asleep,
> Sharpshooter shoots my *head* off—we *all* die.
> Now get around in here. Yes—you and you.
> [*To JOHN*] No—you, sir—no. Don't want no clowns in here.
> The Reverend Mister Billy Jenks. That's right.
> Go out that door, go down the hall, and come —
> You think I'm stupid? No. I'm just insane.
> Go out that door, and come around in here!
> You don't say boo to *no*body. Or else!

JERRY: You have my word.

HT: I have your what what what?

JERRY: Stay calm. We'll do as you request.
    You have my word as a Texan.

HT: Oh… OK…

JERRY: OK, Preach, let's get on under the Big Top.

[JERRY and BJ exit.}

HT: …Ma'am, I'm sorry to mess your execution up.

BESS: Oh, that's OK, I guess.

HT: Well, I'm just saying.
    I'm just improvising, so I hope
    You don't resent some wrinkles in the plan.

BESS: I'm not in a position to resent much of anything.

HT: Hey, if you want, I'll make these folks untie
    Your arms and legs and kiss your ass.

BESS: No, thanks—
   All in all, I'd rather be put to sleep
   Than blown to bits.

HT: Yeah… Ain't you the lady
   Flushed her little baby down the toilet?

BESS: No, that wasn't me.

HT: You put it in
   The trash incinerator.

BESS: Guess again.

HT: The grinder in the sink.

BESS: Not even close.

HT: Where *are* those guys?

WILL: It doesn't really matter.
   I'll have you on the gurney soon enough.

HT: The gurney? For probation violation?

WILL: I saw you on *America's Most Wanted.*

HT: Is there no person on this earth who ever
   Watches any other program? Try
   And hide! I'm like the president!

WILL: You're guilty of a double homicide.
   Today should be your execution day.

HT: The day's not over yet.

WILL: You goddamn right.

HT: You make my point. You see these things?
   I splay my fingers, on the count of five

We mount to glory on a hand grenade.

WILL: That's fine with me!

JOHN: Hold on, hold on!

WILL: I'll get blown up as long as you do, too.

HT: I think we're in agreement here. Let's die!

[*BJ and JERRY enter.*]

HT: Don't move, don't anybody move! I swear to God!
    …Hey, hey, Reverend Billy Jenks, did you
    Imagine the trajectories would bang
    Us face to face on execution day?

BILL JENKS: You get me believing in things like fate, HT.

HT: I know. It's just too marvelous for words,
    The crowning thing that sets it all aflame!
    Actually, I heard it on the news
    How you'd be here and all, that's why I came.

BILL JENKS: Will Blaine.

WILL: Excuse me, preacher, I've got business.

HT [*To WILL*]: Oh no you don't! You don't go back in there!
    You do not press that button. No you don't!
    Not as long as you live! Right here. Right here!
    Did I see your hand mashing on that button?

JOHN: Mom? Are you all right?

BESS: Who? Me?

JOHN: Talk to me. Don't just lay there.

BESS: Blah blah blah.

How's the weather? Blah blah blah your health.
How are they treating my Johnnie at the circus?

JOHN: When men go murdering murderers, they mock
God's saving work and make a clown of Christ.
That's the message. That's the statement.

BESS: Well,
I'm glad I lived to hear the explanation.

JERRY: What are your demands?

HT: Uh-huh... Demands?

JERRY: Have we surprised you with the question?

HT: Yes,
I'd have to say you kind of did.

Monitor sounds a flat reading: Beeeeeeeee.

You pressed the goddamn button, didn't you?

JOHN: Why'd you press it, fool?

WILL: It's what I do!

JOHN: ...NO! ...Don't cover up my mother's face!

JERRY: This woman is deceased.

JOHN: But—seven minutes!
Seven minutes! You said seven minutes!

JERRY: In general the process takes that long—
But often Phase One stops the heart, and then—

HT: And then they screw you out of five or six!
They gyp you! ...Bring this woman back—
Dose her up with speed or something! [*To WILL*] You!

JOHN: That's exactly what we came here for.
    …Hostage-Taker, this is the very thing
    That brought us here. The Reverend Jenks is powered
    To deal with demons and restore the sick,
    I've seen him do it with a word, a breath,
    Two years I've dogged his steps, I've watched him work—
    Deafness, stammering, cancer, withered limbs—
    I've seen him pinch their one last mustard seed
    Of faith and scatter it into blossoms—
    Blindness, palsy, lunatic torments—
    And I believe this man can raise the dead.

BILL JENKS: With your permission—

HT: Do it to it.

WILL: She's dead. This ain't a coma.

JERRY: LET HIM TRY.
    …Leave it alone, Will. Let this run its course
    And you and me go get a drink at Mursky's.
    Country-western, and Scotch in plastic cups.

WILL: I'm sick of cowboy music.

JERRY: Let him try.
    …We've done a bunch of these.

WILL: A couple hundred,
    Right around two hundred.

JERRY: Let him try.

BILL JENKS: No—leave the shroud.

HT: …Go on. Go on.

BILL JENKS: …One time, when Jesus healed, he said—"Who touched
    My garment? Something just went out of me—"
    He stood in a crowd pressing from all sides

But knew a particular touch had drawn his power,
Sensed a healing had gone out from him…
All I have is a knack for crossing paths
With people just about to heal themselves.
A gift for sticking in my head and smiling
Just when someone's gonna snap the picture.
I've never healed one person of one thing
In all my lying life.
If I had, I'd feel it, wouldn't I?
Wouldn't it jump a little in my blood?

WILL: This gets me in my guts. Get up from there.

JERRY: Two hundred? Is it really as many as that?
You ever walk the rows at Joe Byrd Hill?
How many rows have we ourselves laid out?
I bet you'd hike a half a mile of graves
Fed by our work, Will Blaine, yours and mine,
And then you'd come to a couple of plywood boards
Hiding the hungry place that waits for this one.

BILL JENKS: …Lord, it's all about that open mouth.
We don't want to die and go in there.
They claw down with a green and yellow John Deere
Backhoe and scoop a darkness under the grass,
Takes six or seven seconds to produce
The only thing on earth that lasts forever.
God in Heaven, we beg you to widen your eyes.
Look here at this woman put to death
By bureaucrats. See her. Remember her.
You made this woman's life—remember that.
Make her now, again. GOD, GIVE HER BREATH.

[*HT speaks in BESS's voice.*]

HT/BESS: …Don't raise me up! I want to stay in Hell!

JOHN: No! She's not in Hell!

HT/BESS: I always was.

I lived my life in Hell. But now it's simpler.

WILL: You're channeling through the black guy, Mom.

JOHN: There's no such thing as channeling. That's Satan
    Talking in my mother's voice.

HT: It always was.

JOHN: It's just a trick of demons.

WILL: We have demons?
    We don't have mediums, but we do have demons?

JOHN: I just take it as it comes.

WILL: You do?
    From where? You take it as it comes from where?

JOHN: From Genesis and Exodus. No channeling.
    No mediums. No ha'nts. No clanky chains.
    Just men and women; devils; angels; God.

HT/BESS: Hell is full of music. Lonely music.
    Hell is full of sadness. Full of truth,
    Full of clarity. Hell is beautiful.

BILL JENKS: I know this son of a bitch. It's *you.*

HT/DEMON: [*facing BJ*]: *C'est moi*! The one who really loves you!—

BILL JENKS: The blue dog of Huntsville.

HT/DEMON: The demon of Simon's coma.

BILL JENKS: The demon of money.

HT/DEMON: The demon of your fame.

BILL JENKS: You've run me all my silly goddamn life—

Why?

HT: I really can't quite say; it's just
There's something about your style that pisses me off.

BILL JENKS: All my silly life.

HT/DEMON: And now no more.
I'm all through pimping you, Jenks—you're on your own!

[*JOHN cries out, flings himself against the glass. All freeze.*]

[*HT speaks again as a demon.*]

HT/DEMON: Now my work of half a century
Culminates. Warden, blow the whistle!
Beloved William Jennings Bryan Jenks:
You've come to failure, and today you die.
Beloved, my most interesting project,
My signature, my sunny revelation:
Count your heartbeats. Today you die.
Your breath stops. Your sight blackens, then burns
With visions since your birth, and you'll be met
At every turning with the leering truth:
Not one prayer you've uttered ever prized
The slimmest chink in you, not one escaped
The maze. They suffocated in their coffins.
The start to finish of your life's design
Tributes nothingness. And now the dark.

[*HT opens his fingers. Grenades fall.*]

BILL JENKS: Liar! Liar! I never raised the dead!

[*BESS sits upright and the shroud falls away.*]

BESS: AMY? ...Where'd she go? She was right here—

SILENCE. BLINDING LIGHT.

BLACKOUT

EPILOGUE

Corner of 10th and J, later that night.

STEVIE stands behind a microphone, JOHN's cross nearby. LIGHT from video crews, flashbulbs.

STEVIE: Can't we get this monstrosity out of here?
    People are tripping over it left and right.
    This is blasphemy. This thing's a scandal.

[Voices ad lib…]

Quiet! —I'm sorry.—Goddamn you! —I'm sorry.
Here is the information we've got for you.
This evening, shortly after five p.m., an as yet unidentified prisoner overcame
    and stabbed to death a guard in the Walls Unit, who remains nameless
    until notification of family.
Thereafter this prisoner gained access to the execution chamber in this
    corner of the unit, right behind me, and…
You have the statement. You have the statement…

[VOICES ad lib…]

Now, Mrs. Blaine has asked to say a word, wife of William Blaine, who
    supervised our teams in the unit there— She's the wife of Will Blaine,
    a very special employee of, a very…
The wife of Will Blaine, the widow, the wife, the widow… president of the
    Texas Citizens for Victim's Rights, Marsha Hollings Blaine.

[MASHA comes up, well-dressed, with well-coiffed, abundant hair.]

[VOICES ad lib…]

MASHA: I say today and innocent has been killed!
    Today is a Day of Judgment on us all!
    [VOICES ad lib…]
    Look at you all!—like wasps on watermelon!
    [VOICES ad lib…]
    Rahr! Rahr! Rahr!—like *curs* on *carrion.*

I LOST MY HUSBAND IN THAT PLACE TODAY.
...Maybe he's in a better place. Who knows?
...Some people go around with this idea
The Milky Way is just some big machine,
And we're being eaten alive by this machine,
Trodden down and gutted out and gobbled
And scattered out along beside the road
To fertilize the ditch, and that's our fate:
And I say, God above, let it be so!
Let there be no Resurrection Day!
[*VOICES ad lib...*]
LET THERE BE NO RESURRECTION DAY!
If Bill Jenks thinks that he can raise the dead—
Let him raise himself! WE'RE WAITING, BILL.
Let him raise *someone*, and then I'd say
That he was onto something—wouldn't you?
[*Of the cross*] Look here, look where someone's set up the means
Of execution in the gory Bible days.
Here they hung them after they'd been scourged.
You know what scourging was? They whipped the skin
Until it ripped, and then they whipped the muscles
Underneath, until their whips licked bone.
And then they hammered what was left up here,
And broke the legs of what was left, so that,
Without support, it slowly suffocated.
And that's the boy the power of whose blood
You plead, an executed criminal...
[*VOICES ad lib...*]
LET MY HUSBAND ROT IN THE GROUND UNTIL HE'S MUSH,
Let him rot in the ground till he's gravy,
Until he clarifies like honey in the heat
And dribbles into dirt that doesn't feel
A thing or think a thought.
May the dirt I called my husband never wake,
May that dirt stay dead until the whole
Universe collapses into cinders,
May the weight of general emptiness
Strive and grind against itself and work
The cinders down to black, stupefied darkness,
May he be dead until the final thought of God,

As long as his assassins stay dead, too.
…When Texas trips the lever of the blade,
And that blade dives down through a killer's neck,
And that neck pumps that evil blood six feet,
And that head goes rollin' into the world,
What drives that blood is the beautiful heart of Texas,
And staring out of that head are the eyes of Texas.
The dead face of the killer we have killed—
This is the face of liberty and justice.
This is the beautiful face of liberty and justice!

[*Weeping, she makes a smile and strikes a pose.*]

BLACKOUT

END

CONTRIBUTORS

CHRIS ADRIAN is a pediatric resident in San Francisco.

JESSICA ANTHONY's stories have appeared in magazines like *Rattapallax*, *New American Writing*, and *Mid-American Review*, where she was nominated for a Pushcart Prize. She lives in Portland, Maine, at work on a novel.

CHRIS BACHELDER is from Christiansburg, Virginia. He teaches at Colorado College in Colorado Springs, where he lives with his wife Jenn.

JOSHUAH BEARMAN lives in Hollywood, where he is a contributor to the *LA Weekly* and other publications.

RYAN BOUDINOT's work has appeared in *The Best American Nonrequired Reading 2003*, *The Mississippi Review*, *Hobart*, and *McSweeney's 12*. He lives in Seattle.

T.C. BOYLE's new novel, *The Inner Circle*, will be published in September by Viking. The following fall Viking will publish *Tooth and Claw*, a collection of fifteen new stories, including "The Doubtfulness of Water" and "Blinded by the Light," both of which originally appeared in *McSweeney's*.

KATE BRAVERMAN has published numerous collections of short stories and four novels, and has won O. Henry and Best American awards. She divides her time between the Alleghenies and San Francisco.

ROBERT OLEN BUTLER won the Pulitzer Prize for fiction in 1993. His new book of short stories, *Had a Good Time*, based on his collection of antique picture postcards, will be published in August by Grove Press.

LINDSAY CARLETON currently resides in Iowa City, where she is enrolled at the Writers' Workshop. This is her first publication.

SILVIA DiPIERDOMINICO is writing a collection of essays about women and cancer. She is a teacher who currently lives in Los Angeles.

PIA Z. EHRHARDT lives in New Orleans with her husband and son. More of her can be found at www.piaze.com.

DENIS JOHNSON's *Soul of a Whore*, directed by Nancy Benjamin, was staged by the Campo Santo Theater Company at Intersection for the Arts in San Francisco, and received the Will Glickman Playwright Award for 2003. He is currently working on a novel and on another play for Campo Santo.

JESSICA LAMB-SHAPIRO has published fiction in *Open City* and *Index*, and non-fiction in *The Believer*. She lives all alone in New York City.

CLAIRE LIGHT lives in San Francisco.

MALINDA McCOLLUM's stories have appeared or are forthcoming in the

Paris Review, *Pushcart Prize 2004*, *Epoch*, and *Zyzzyva*. She lives in Missouri.

JIM SHEPARD is the author, most recently, of the novel *Project X* and the story collection *Love and Hydrogen*. In person he's oddly unaffecting.

SUSAN STRAIGHT lives in Riverside, California, where she was born. She has published five novels; this story is part of a new collection.

WELLS TOWER's writing has appeared in the *Paris Review*, the *Oxford American*, the *Believer*, the *Anchor Book of New American Short Stories* and elsewhere. He is currently at work on a novel.

LAWRENCE WESCHLER, author of *Mr. Wilson's Cabinet of Wonder* and *Vermeer in Bosnia*, directs the New York Institute for the Humanities at NYU, from whence he is trying, forlornly, to launch his own magazine, *Omnivore*.